**KENDRELL
PUBLISHING**

THE
BLANCHARD
WITCHES
MY SOUL TO KEEP

MICAH HOUSE

The Blanchard Witches: My Soul To Keep

First published 2025

Published by Kendrell Publishing, Birmingham, Alabama

Edited by Crystal Castle

Cover design by Paul Palmer-Edwards

ISBN: 979-8-9922157-0-0

Library of Congress Control Number: 2024926481

Dedicated to all the Blanchard fans
who have traveled this journey with me.
It has been quite a ride.
Thank you for loving this family as much as I do.
I hope I have given them the proper respect
as we say goodbye... for now.

CONTENTS

CHAPTER ONE

Absolution

The magnificent city sprawled out below Artemis the huntress as she soared overhead. The ever-burning lights of Manhattan cast their glow down over ledges at spectacular angles, stretching across the streets and avenues below, dotted with the white and red glowing eyes of cabs and cars dashing around the city in the dark of the early morning. The temporary steel covered framework protecting pedestrians from construction dangers were littered with creatures of the night at this hour. The plywood and steel mazes all over the city were perfect traps at night with their blind corners. The streets were virtually empty at this late hour, but some still housed a few groups of revelers making their way home or to the next club, being ridiculously loud and jovial either way.

Artemis zoomed overhead on the broom she rode as a hilarious but efficient irony. Gliding around the majestic crowns of skyscrapers, her eyes never losing focus, never taking notice of anyone below more than momentarily. Only the time it took Artemis to appraise their species. She had more important duties at hand than these lost souls wandering below. She'd located the scent. Seth's scent. Sniffing the air with her wolf's blood, it was quite strong. Pausing atop the Flatiron Building, her hawklike vision scoured the streets below with methodic precision as her canine senses homed in on her prey. Her gaze penetrated through the shadows of Madison Square Park, then up Broadway toward the distant glow of Times Square. Artemis soared over the park then perched on top of the massive gold edifice of the New York LIfe building. She was flooded in gold light, like a Greek statue atop the massive roof. The scent was stronger up here though. Suddenly the wind from the northwest turned her gaze up Broadway once more, certain they were close by. Taking flight once more, Artemis sailed through the night uptown, toward the pulsing, burst of light from Midtown.

Seth and Yasmine Blanchard were down there walking the silent streets towards home. But they would not get there. Yasmine rested her head upon her husband's shoulder as they went. On their way to their apartment on 30th Street, they were passing Bryant Park. The park was empty now. By morning it would be full of ice skaters, bocce ball players, ping pong matches, and holiday shoppers meandering through the park's annual Christmas village. But at night—late at night—the park belonged to Seth and Yasmine.

"A great many people are alone on holidays," Yasmine remarked as they found a seat on a bench. "I like feeding on holidays."

"Why is that my love?"

"The ones left alone taste like mistakes and regret."

Seth gripped her chin and turned her eyes to his, "I know no regrets when I am with you."

She leaned forward and took advantage of the proximity of his lips. After pulling away from a long, passionate kiss, she asked him, "We did have children, I believe. Yes, I know we did. Sometimes it is hard to remember. Everything that is not you and me seems to be fading."

"Our children will be fine back where we came from. I forget where that was now. Like you said, everything which isn't you and me is becoming harder to recall. But I only need you and me."

Yasmine straddled her husband and began making out with him passionately. She allowed her fangs to project so that she could playfully pierce into his bottom lips as she kissed him. He ejected his own and began to scrap them across the thick of her throat. Their eyes met, both glowing red as they stared into the other's flaming gaze. The passion was all consuming. Seth could feel himself growing aroused. He moved his hands to her waist and began hiking up her dress inch by inch.

Suddenly Yasmine was ripped away, propelled so forcefully that she sailed 30 yards down the alley of towering sycamores. Seth watched as her body rolled to a stop, then righted itself, looking onward towards him with sheer terror in her face. Seth turned quickly to see the woman he knew he should remember, standing beside him on the bench.

"I know you," he said. "I think I know you well. I turned you."

"You do know me well, Seth." Artemis said as her pupils transformed into an almost diamond shape, like a tigress. "At least you used to know me. We once loved each other."

"You were my mother, weren't you?"

"Practically."

By now Yasmine was rushing back to aid her husband, her hands outstretched to send her freezing blast Artemis' way. This time Artemis was prepared. Using her lightning-fast reflexes and canine agility, she dodged the blast and struck her palm into Yasmine's chest sending her reeling backward again, smashing painfully into the wrought iron railing of the park wall. But Yasmine was not one to be so easily dismissed. Standing back to her feet she grasped hold of the heavy black iron rail, tearing a section from its footings as if it were made of cardboard. She flung the fencing through the air directly at her adversary. As it cruised towards Artemis, Artemis simply jumped into the air, evading the blow, landing back on her feet effortlessly.

By now Seth was given time by the distraction to dart away towards his wife. Yasmine rushed to join him. The moment they clasped hands to make a retreat together, Artemis pounced, landing on all fours, cutting off their way out.

"It ends now for the two of you," she said. "I have loved you both too much to allow you to remain what you have become."

"You cannot overpower us both," Yasmine sneered, eyeing Seth to understand her meaning. Suddenly the two of them charged Artemis. Thinking there was no possibility the one woman could fight off them both at once, they were sorely mistaken. Artemis did not flinch, nor did she dodge their strike. She simply outstretched her two arms and grasped both Seth and Yasmine by the throats, extending them outward from her, dangling in the air. With hurricane force she brought her arms together, smashing Seth and Yasmine into one another sending them both to the ground stunned.

As Yasmine shook herself loose from the shock of the impact, Artemis acted quickly. She grabbed Yasmine by the neck and the thigh, lifting her overhead to bring her crashing down, back first, onto the stone half wall of the colonnade entrance. Seth could hear his wife's spine break from the impact. Yasmine lay crumpled on the ground, unable to move. She was not destroyed, only immobilized so that Artemis could attend to Seth without distraction.

Artemis grappled with an enraged Seth. His love for his wife momentarily supplied him with greater strength than before, but it was still no match for the Huntress. Artemis wrestled him down to the ground, pinning him in such a way that he was unable to move.

"I must end you now, my son." Artemis told him.

With her knees still pinning him to the ground, she moved her hands to his head. It was her intention to do as she always did with vampires she destroyed, to remove the head quickly and end the undead force. As her hands gripped under his ears, she found herself trembling. Artemis Blanchard was the strongest creature walking the earth, yet she was finding it difficult to muster strength to do this one simple thing. This one task she'd been trying to perform for almost a year. City after city, with this one moment in mind. Now it was here, and she did not know if she could do it. It was Seth. Her Seth. But it must be done and only she could do it. He was not the Seth she'd loved and raised. And there was something even more important she could not lose sight of. She had promised God.

Yasmine Blanchard, watching helplessly on the ground, could not move. For all the strength and nourishment human blood could give her, it could not so easily heal a broken back. As she lay on the cold cement walkway under the leafless canopy of trees in Bryant Park, she could only watch in horror as the terrible woman readied herself to kill Yasmine's husband Seth. The woman—a woman Yasmine recognized but could not place—gripped the sides of Seth's head in her powerful hands, about to tear it from his undead shoulders at any second. Yasmine screamed from her motionless position yards away.

Seth stared up into the ferocious eyes of the woman who had been hunting he and his wife for a year. They had evaded her, traveling halfway across the country and back, then nestling themselves into this metropolis. And though he knew he should be frightened, he wasn't. He was grateful. He'd been given a whole year with his Yasmine. It was a year he never expected to have after he was told she was dead. Then when he discovered the truth, that she was only dead in human terms, he'd searched her out, offered himself to her, and appealed to whatever within her might recall what they'd meant to each other once. Yasmine had not remembered. Not at first. She tore at his throat, feeding herself with his warm pulsating blood just as she had countless others before him. However, as his blood coursed through her body, so came his memories. Memories she shared. The life they had shared poured into whatever was left of her. She remembered him. She remembered she loved him. And she saved him from death with her vampire's gift. As Seth looked into the eyes of his aunt Artemis, knowing she was now going to end his existence, then end his wife's, Seth smiled. He had gotten an entire year to be with Yaz again. It was worth everything.

Yasmine pleaded with the woman to spare her husband. Trying to pull her limp body closer with her arms in hopes of stopping the huntress, but Yasmine was out of strength. Her spine was severed. She could feel it. It would heal eventually, her vampire power never left injuries lingering, but it would take time. Much more time than these passing seconds could muster.

Artemis was trembling, still unsure she could actually do what had to be done. Seth had been like a son to her. She had raised him from six years old. She'd raised Yasmine too. How could she send them now to hell? But she knew how. She knew the way to gather the will to complete her task, to keep her promise. *A promise to God.*

She swallowed hard and steadied herself for the heart wrenching task. As her hands began to twist, suddenly Artemis was blinded by an explosion of an all-encompassing white light. Bryant Park slowly fell out of focus, cloaked by the orb which swelled and swelled until there seemed to be nothing that existed anywhere but that transcendent light itself. As it began to dissipate, Artemis saw her. Beryl. Beryl Blanchard was standing over her as she lay on the ground still gripping Seth.

Beryl's eyes were golden and glistening with a love unlike Artemis could ever describe. Beryl kneeled to the ground behind Artemis, wrapping her arms around her, placing her hands atop the hands of Artemis. For a moment Artemis believed Beryl had come to help. Come to supply her with the Holy strength she needed to complete this agonizing task. But that wasn't what happened. Beryl gently lifted Artemis' hands from Seth's head.

Both Artemis and Seth stared in mutual bewilderment at the glowing god before them. Yasmine was equally entranced at the sight of her. Then Beryl spoke.

"You are absolved of this task, Artemis. You have served God well, destroying the monsters who seek to upend His world. He excuses you from this one."

Artemis did not understand. "Why?"

Beryl smiled and stroked Artemis' cheek. "God understands the pain caused when you must commit your own child to death. He will not ask that of you. You are absolved of these two kills."

Artemis looked at Seth, then to Yasmine. A relief swept over her but also did a panic. They were evil and they would continue to kill if left to their devices. "But what of their victims? If I do not end them now, there is no stopping them."

"There has been a shift," Beryl said mysteriously. "A new course has only tonight been set. He wants to wait and see. These two may seek redemption."

She was gone. Another flash of light so bright no one could stand its burn, and Beryl Blanchard was gone. Artemis rose from the ground as Seth backed cautiously away from her reach. The three of them said not a word to one another. Artemis watched as Seth scurried to his wife, lifted her crippled body into his arms and walked out of Bryant Park. Artemis looked up to the overhead moon and was suddenly struck with the notion that whatever was happening now to the world, she was merely a chess piece on a great universal board. She was as lost as everyone else. But she would continue forth. Her promise remained. Seth and Yasmine were not the only monsters roaming the world. And she was, after all, The Sword of God.

CHAPTER TWO

So Much to Be Thankful For

It came as very little surprise to Demitra Blanchard when she found the nationally renowned news correspondent, Daphanie Channing, at her door that morning. She half expected Daphanie would return after the events of last night. Ushering her in from the cold November wind, she settled her guest into the living room where they could talk. "Please forgive the house being a little chilly," Demitra smiled. "The heat is on, but I just cannot bring myself to light the fireplace today."

Daphanie let out a little laugh, "I cannot say that I blame you. I don't believe I will be sitting in front of any roaring fires myself this winter."

Though they were making light of it, both were still rather traumatized by the events at Blanchard House the day before. What began as a peaceful family Thanksgiving turned into an atrocious series of events nobody could expect. A time-travelling assassin with a mission to destroy the entire Blanchard family had set fire to the house, engulfing it, and its inhabitants, in an inescapable blaze. Daphanie had been present for it. Initially dropping in on the Blanchards to confront them with her proof of their magnificent powers, she soon was as much a victim of the deranged killer as the rest of them. But that was yesterday. Thanks to the reality-altering powers of young Titan Blanchard, the fire was erased leaving the ancestral home of the Blanchards unmarred. As for the time jumping killer, Demitra took care of her.

Hearing they had a guest, Miranda Blanchard entered with a tray of coffee. "I wondered if you'd come by again before you return to New York." Miranda said, pouring Daphanie a cup.

Nodding gratefully, Daphanie accepted the freshly brewed coffee and admitted, "I had to. I feel we all went through a lot together yesterday. Maybe I am silly, but I feel a little bonded to you now. And if I am completely honest, I wanted to know how the wolf is doing. Did he make it? I thought about him all night."

Demitra reached out to pat the reporter's arm in thanks and replied, "He is going to make it." Daphanie sighed with relief, which Demitra could tell was genuine. "My daughter, his mother, is an extraordinary animal doctor. She pulled him through, and now his natural...or should I say...unnatural healing abilities are kicking in."

"I have so many questions." Daphanie said, feeling free now to ask everything she'd wondered about for so long during her investigation into the family. After the events of last night, and the familiarity which was born between them in their shared trauma, Daphanie felt she could ask now, and nothing was going to surprise her anymore. "You said the wolf's mother is...your daughter?"

Nodding Demitra did her best to explain, "Some years ago my daughter was seeing a man who turned out to be a werewolf." Raising a brow to her guest to signify the mutually understood absurdity of the sentence, Demitra was glad to see Daphanie did not react in complete surprise. "Fable's pregnancy resulted in twins. A human boy and a canine one."

"I cannot believe I am saying this," Daphanie chuckled. "But that sort of makes sense."

Miranda entered the conversation now, feeling a little protective over the family. "Miss Channing, I hope you meant what you said last night about being willing to keep this family's secrets. I have two small children who are witches and I do not want their lives upended by a reporter who thinks she may have a juicy story."

Sitting her coffee aside, Daphanie faced both her hostesses and revealed something she herself could not believe she was revealing. "I meant every word yesterday," she took a breath and added her caveat. "However, your secrets are not in my hands anymore. Last night I was approached by one of your own," she turned to Demitra. "Your niece Salem. She asked me to stay in Daihmler to work with her. She wants to bring the supernatural world out of the closet. She wants me to do a story on your world, and promised she could deliver all the proof my viewers would need."

"Salem is determined to put me in an early grave!" Demitra huffed, rising from the sofa to pace the room. "I cannot believe she is serious about doing this! This will place everyone in our society in danger."

Curious as to what the ambitious reporter's response to the request had been, Miranda, with a tinge of suspicion in her tone, asked Daphanie, "What did you tell her, Miss Channing?"

It was a fair question, as was the tone behind it. Daphanie couldn't be insulted.

Only yesterday she'd planned to expose the Blanchards to the world herself. "I am here, aren't I?" Daphanie said, joining Demitra mid-pace across the room. Putting her hand on the witch's shoulder, she gave it a gentle squeeze. "Whether you believe it or not, I am an honorable woman. I keep my word. This could be the story of all lifetimes. Nothing can ever come close. But I will not place your family at risk without your full approval, Ms. Blanchard. I will not be the cause of a rift in your family"

Demitra appreciated the support, patting the hand still on her shoulder. "I know you are an honorable woman. And apparently, a loyal friend. And my name is Demitra...Daphanie." Her guest smiled at the release of formality. "I am grateful you have come to me. I will of course do my utmost to change Salem's mind. I do not think this is a good idea. It is dangerous. Much too dangerous for her to arrive at such a monumental decision which will alter the lives of every member of our society."

Nodding in agreement, Daphanie replied, "I will wait a few days before I return to New York. Once you and Salem have spoken, let me know the final decision."

"It sounds as if you are willing to take the risk if the answer is yes?" Miranda remarked.

"I'm not sure," Daphanie answered honestly. "That is what I will be spending the next few days deciding."

As Demitra shivered on the porch, waving goodbye to Daphanie Channing, she could feel herself growing angrier with Salem over this egregious betrayal of not only the family, but all witching kind. Closing the cold out on the other side of the door, Demitra walked directly to the kitchen where her phone was charging. She was about to press Salem's name when another call came through. It was Sydney. Demitra waved the face of the phone in Fable's direction as she was stirring up warm broth with beef chunks to take up to Romulus. "Maybe now we will find out where Syd ran out to so fast last night." Fable remarked. Demitra answered but was immediately cut off by Sydney's urgent recounting of what had developed. Demitra motioned to Fable to stay downstairs, while she urged Hera from her place at the table where she was working a puzzle. Covering the phone with her hand she whispered to her little niece, "Take that soup up to Rom and stay with him while he eats it."

Hera did not enjoy being distracted from her nearly completed puzzle, but she wasn't the type to argue with her Aunt Demitra. As she went upstairs to feed her recovering cousin, Fable took her seat at the kitchen table, curious as to what was going on.

"This is so unbelievable, and yet it makes sense in every way," Demitra said in response to whatever Sydney had told her. "What happens now?" There was a dense pause of a few seconds while Sydney responded, then Demitra added, "Whatever they need. You let Vanessa know. We are here for whatever they need." Another pause, then Demitra said, "Oh, I was about to call her on another matter. It can wait. Salem should be there with them."

The mysteriousness of the call captured Fable's full attention. As Demitra was wrapping up the call, Arielle came down the kitchen stairs. She was dressed rather professionally in a pant suit and carrying a leather satchel. Fable mouthed, "Where are you going?"

In a low voice so as to not disrupt Demitra's call, Arielle answered, "Birmingham. My mother's house has a potential buyer after all these months on the market." Fable nodded in understanding while holding two crossed fingers in the air for luck. Arielle started for the door until Demitra reached out, grabbing her arm, signaling for her to stay a minute. Arielle exchanged confused looks with Fable, who shrugged.

It was only a minute before Demitra ended the call and waved to the girls to join her at the table. "We have had a shocking development," Demitra told them. "We now know who Theda was…is…you know what I mean."

"Hadn't we already figured that out yesterday?" Arielle asked. "Considering her hatred for the Blanchards, she surely was a child of Nacaria and my father none of us ever knew about."

"No," Demitra replied. "She isn't. I am afraid it is even more complicated than that." She glanced around the kitchen, empty except for the three of them. "We must keep this private for now. I do not want the children to know. Not yet. There are too many variables to figure out…Vanessa's wishes primarily."

"Mother, you are making zero sense." Fable sighed.

"Sydney just told me the reason she rushed out of here last night and why she hasn't come home yet. She's been with Vanessa. And Salem is with them now." Demitra explained. "Last night Sydney drove Vanessa to her father's house in Gordo, whereupon they met a little girl named Theda."

"What?" Arielle exclaimed. "Our stalker, Theda?"

"Yes." Demitra answered. "The woman we killed last night."

Always the petulant one, Fable interjected, "*You killed.*"

Shooting her daughter a dirty look, Demitra corrected her statement, "Yes, the woman I killed. She was the adult version of the same little girl. The girl lives in our present time. The version I killed last night was from the future. She's been traveling through time trying to wipe out our entire family line."

Arielle did not understand. "I don't see how Vanessa's father fits into any of this. Isn't he a minister? I've never really heard anything about him."

Fable turned to her friend and filled her in. "Before you became part of this family, Seth and Vanessa dated. Her father hated us. He is one of those crazy fringe religious zealot nutjobs." Suddenly Fable's mouth dropped as her eyes lit up with the dawn of truth hitting her. "Holy Shit! Theda! She can't be? Mom, seriously? Is she?"

Demitra nodded, "Theda is Vanessa's child. And she is Seth's daughter."

Arielle threw her hand at her mouth in utter disbelief. "Seth's daughter? That woman who nearly burned us all alive was Seth's daughter!"

Demitra cautioned her to lower her voice. "We don't want Hera or Con or Rom or even little Titan to know this. Not yet."

"Everything fits," Fable gasped. "It was right in our faces. Theda shot Vanessa yesterday, not because she thought she was Yaz, but because she knew exactly who she was. Her own mother."

"A mother she had been raised to despise all of her life by her vicious and manipulative grandfather." Demitra added.

CHAPTER THREE

God's Gifted Grace

Jerry shook his head with a crooked smile from his recliner when his wife shared the secret news. "This family."

"I know," Demitra replied. "I must say I did not see that coming. I thought for sure Theda was Nacaria's daughter."

Tossing his newspaper to the floor, he righted his reclined position back upright and leaned closer to his wife. "This will be a shock to Hera more than anyone. She is no longer Seth's eldest child or only daughter."

"Which is why I do not want the children to find out until I have spoken to Vanessa, and we figure out how to go about this. Hera has been through enough. Her mother supposedly dying. Then her father ran out on her. Then she not only discovers her mother isn't dead, but that both her parents are vampires now!"

"And don't forget her dreams," Jerry reminded her. "She dreams of their kills. I don't want Hera hurt anymore. No little girl should have to go through all she has."

Demitra walked to the window of their bedroom, peering out into the black night. "She is walking the same path Salem walked. The irony is not lost on me. I watched Salem shut herself off when she was little. Oh, she laughs. She loves. If you didn't know her before Nacaria left, you wouldn't know there is a difference. But I was here. I saw. Salem changed. She grew harder. She does not allow herself to break. I don't believe she has ever truly allowed herself to feel all the grief she has from losing David and Michael. She stores it and forgets it. And I see Hera learning to do the same."

"Yes, but Hera has Miranda," Jerry pointed out. "She loves Miranda."

"Salem had Artemis, and me."

Still hoping to convince his wife that the outlook wasn't so bleak, Jerry said, "And...Hera has you and me. Grandparents who love and adore her. And she has her brother and her cousins."

Almost laughing at the parallels Demitra turned from the window. "Salem had Mother and Sinclair. She had her own brother too. And her cousins. Oh, I'm not saying we aren't important. We are here for Hera, and it matters. But nothing fixes a heart that has been broken from a parent's absence. Especially if the absence was by choice. Hera will never put herself first or allow anyone else to, because Seth and Yasmine put themselves before her."

Jerry walked to his wife, opening his arms to comfort her. Giving in to the urge to let him soothe her, she rested her cheek on his shoulder for a while allowing his strength to seep into her. When she pulled away, she brought up the other dilemma. "I also must talk to Salem tomorrow. I must convince her to drop this *going public* idea. It could spell ruin to all our lives." She let out an amused chuckle, "Do you think I have enough problems on my plate, Jerry? Maybe I should ask Charlie for a case, just add something else to handle."

"We already have something else to handle," Jerry reminded her. "You are forgetting, my darling, the little matter of who Ocean is? When Pastoria traveled here from the past to be healed from her deadly wound, Sage and Sydney started fading from existence while she was nearing death. Pastoria nearly dying here at the age prior to having children almost wiped them out of history. But Ocean was not affected in any way whatsoever."

"I almost forgot," Demitra said softly. "With everything else today, it popped completely out of my brain."

Jerry eyed her with all seriousness. "I like Ocean. I think he's a good man. But he's not a Blanchard. I have been in this family long enough to know there are people out there who will go to great lengths to harm this family. Hopefully, Ocean is oblivious to his not being a real Blanchard. But I think we'd be remiss to just assume that."

"Are you implying he might be a mole? An enemy planted into this family?" Demitra was aghast at the thought. "That would be extremely hard to believe. I remember when he was born. He grew up with my children. Christmases, Easters, Thanksgivings, and summer break. I have known Ocean his entire life. I find it difficult to believe he has infiltrated our family on purpose. That is a really long time to be under cover."

"Are you saying no one out there would go to such lengths? No one would play the long game and wait patiently for the exact moment to present itself?"

"Who would have that kind of patience or time? They would probably be dead by now or so old they no longer..."

"Or," her husband interrupted. "Maybe they lived life after life without anyone ever even knowing about it. A person who has the power to live forever, has the kind of time and patience to implement a long-range plan for an endgame."

Her eyes swelled with terror at his implication. "You mean, the D'Angelo's. Thaddeuss or Atheidrelle. One or both of them could have orchestrated something so unspeakable. Do you really think Ocean might be one of them?"

"I am only saying, I have seen enough to know that I don't know the limits of what is possible. In this world, I trust you. I trust Fable. I trust Salem. I trust Howard. Everybody else...I like, or I love, but I never stop watching."

Salem had slept very little the night before, dozing here and there on Vanessa Collins' couch, only allowing herself to doze when the child, Theda, would drift off to sleep. But Theda did not sleep in long intervals, awaking in fright at the strangeness of her surroundings and the unfamiliarity of the people around her. Salem, Vanessa, and Sydney had taken shifts—two at a time—being with and guarding, Theda. Though Salem was not there for the initial showdown between Vanessa and her father Thanksgiving night when Sydney had figured out the secret. She drove Vanessa to confront Reverend Collins, she knew it had been traumatic on the girl. Within the time span of an hour, young Theda Collins, only a couple years older than Hera, had her world upended. Had cooler heads prevailed, it might not have had to have been so dramatic. But Vanessa was overwhelmed with the revelation her father had hidden her daughter from her for eleven years. Then her anger over the situation took over, heightening the intensity. The young girl witnessed this strange woman assail her grandfather with vicious accusations. Sydney, a social worker, did her best to calm the severity, but there was little she could do under the circumstances. Chief of Police, Charlie Bennet, arrested the reverend under a litany of charges including kidnapping, child abuse, forgery, fraud, child endangerment, and even attempted murder for denying Vanessa medical care during her delivery all those years ago. How many charges would stick remained to be seen, but it allowed for Reverend Collins to be taken into custody while Sydney assumed temporary responsibility for the child. It would all have to go before a judge in the coming days.

"I honestly don't know what is going to happen," Salem explained to the girl during the night. "Your grandfather did a very bad thing. He may go to jail for a long time."

"But what will happen to me?" Theda begged to understand. "That woman says she is my mother. But my mother ran away when I was born to be with bad people. She didn't want me. Grandfather says she ran off to be with witches and if she ever knew where I was, she would steal me and give me to them, and they would sacrifice me to the devil."

There was a terror in Theda's eyes Salem knew would take time to disarm. She made a few attempts using logic. It appeared to at least help the child to begin thinking for herself. "Now that sounds a little silly to me," Salem responded with a smile. "Sounds like maybe he was just trying to scare you so that if you ever met her, you would run away from her. Besides, if your mother did run away because she did not want you, then why would it be necessary for you and your grandfather to move away and keep your existence secret?"

She could tell by the look in the child's eye this was the first time she'd really thought about it rationally. "If it were the truth that she abandoned you because she did not want you, there would have been no need to move away and keep you a secret from her. She wouldn't have cared or come to see you anyway." Salem let that sit in a moment with Theda before she continued. "But if your grandfather took you to live out of town the way he did, that sounds more like he was trying to keep her from knowing about you. If Vanessa, your mom, well...she would want you to be with her because she loves you."

"But she's evil and dangerous," Theda insisted, glaring across the room at Vanessa who was tearfully listening in a chair by the window looking out at the night.

Salem stroked the child's hair gently and shook her head. "I have known Vanessa a long time. I have never even seen her yell at another person. I think she is a very nice woman. Did you know she is a schoolteacher?" Theda shook her head. "That's right. In fact, she teaches some children I know very well. They love her. She is kind to them and there for them when they need her. Now that doesn't sound like a woman who sacrifices babies to the devil now does it?"

The rest of the night was more of the same. Both Sydney and Salem attempted to soothe the child's fears regarding her mother, and Vanessa tried to show Theda how much she cared about her. "I am sad too," Vanessa admitted. "I am sad because I thought my baby died. But now I know you didn't and that makes me so happy. But then I get sad again because we have missed so much time together when we could have been loving each other and making memories together. Your grandfather did a terrible thing when he lied to you about me. He taught you to be afraid of me. That was not right, good, or fair to us. And he is my father. My own father. Doesn't that seem hard to believe? A father would do that. He made me think my baby died and kept you away from me all these years. We have both been hurt by the same man Theda. Please allow you and me some time together so that we can learn about one another and start to know each other."

When Salem left early that morning, Theda was asleep in Vanessa's bed and had allowed her mother to sit in the chair beside the bed with her. It was progress. Now Salem had other issues to handle. Her Aunt Demitra being the main one. She'd dodged her calls all night after Daphanie Channing forewarned Salem that she had spoken to Demitra about their plan. Daphanie was ambivalent about doing the story without Salem's entire family's permission. She was also waffling on whether the infamy such a story could give her name in history was worth the risk of them not successfully convincing the world and ruining her reputation. Salem already understood Demitra's fears because she shared them. However, Salem knew one thing the two of them didn't, and once she could explain it to both of them, their reservations would disappear. Driving home from Vanessa's house, she sent a text to both her aunt and the reporter to meet her at Blanchard House in an hour, giving her time to shower and change. Morning traffic was light, being Thanksgiving weekend. Few people were at work or headed there. Of course, she knew one man who would be, and she knew she needed to check in with him.

"I was wondering if I would hear from you today," Miles said, answering her call. "I barely got a sentence with you last night. You just showed up, said everything at home was fine and picked up Olympus."

"I know, Miles. I am sorry about that. Things were hectic."

"You said you would explain this morning."

"And I plan to," Salem promised. "Just not right now. It'll take longer than I have to truly fill you in. I've been up all night on a completely separate family matter, and I am headed home to negotiate yet another. But then I swear, I will come to you, and I will share everything with you. If you haven't rethought starting a life with me after the events of yesterday?"

He paused a little longer than she was comfortable. She had been joking but now wondered. But when she heard the shuffling of papers in the background, she knew he was preoccupied with ad work and his slowness to respond had nothing to do with her. With a distance in his tone that told her he was simultaneously reading something while speaking to her, he said, "No, no. We are good. Just call me or come by my place later when you can."

Releasing him back to his work, she continued weaving in and out of traffic trying to avoid the slow-paced motorists sharing the road with her. They may not have things to do, but she did. It was turning out to be a lovely morning, she noticed. The golden morning light crested over the tops of houses and shopping centers; Salem was struck with a sense of something wondrous happening. She made the turn onto the stretch of road running past Yerby Park. This was not the most direct way home, but it saved time by avoiding stop lights and lackadaisical holiday drivers slowing her pace. As she drove along the outer perimeter of the park the unfamiliar feeling grew. Then it became audible.

See me.

Salem felt faint. Immediately she recognized the voice ringing in her head. *Where is she?* Salem searched all directions between the cars zipping by. It only took moments to locate her. Beryl was standing under the white pavilion on the hill by Yerby Park's entrance. The entire structure appeared to be glowing with her very presence. Salem checked her mirrors to see if she had room to switch over two lanes to the park gates, but there was too much traffic. She wheeled over to the right-hand shoulder of the road where she parked the car and got out. She could still see the luminous figure watching from the pavilion several hundred yards away.

Salem lifted her hands, flexing her fingers outward towards the roadway. Everything stopped. Each vehicle in motion paused in time, still as a mountain. The occupants of each automobile were still themselves, frozen mid-sip of coffee, mid lyric of a song, or mid conversation on a cell. No one was aware time had stopped. Only Salem and Beryl were alive in that moment. Salem zig-zagged around the vehicles until she reached the other side of the street to the park. Passing one final car, she observed a tiny bird suspended in the air only inches from a car's windshield. The moment everything would resume motion, that bird was going to be obliterated. Carefully Salem lifted the bird from its breast between her thumb and forefinger and nudged the creature over a few feet into collision free air space.

Salem continued her mission, traversing the dewy hill to the white pavilion where the figure of Beryl Blanchard emanated even brighter. A warmth emitted from her presence which comforted Salem as she approached. Every emotion she might ever feel about anything at all somehow felt inconsequential the closer she came to Beryl. This magical being had once been her cousin. She'd once been her best friend and greatest confidante. Now Beryl was something else altogether. Salem felt woefully undeserving to stand in her presence.

"Salem," Beryl smiled magnificently.

"I cannot begin to explain to you---"

"How much you've missed me?" Beryl said, finishing the thought. "I know. I know it all. We have no real need for an exchange of sentiment. I know everything you feel. And you should know my deep love for you as well."

"Why—"

Beryl did not wait for the finish of the question. She presented Salem with a bottle. It was smallish, fitting in the palm of her hand. It had a white cork but the contents inside the clear bottle was bluish purple. Salem took the bottle. As her fingers touched it, it seemed to pulse.

"What is this?"

Beryl placed her hands on the pavilion banister as she turned her back to Salem to face the paused traffic. The cars sprang into motion once again, this time by Beryl's hand, to resume their morning routes. "We know of your plan," Beryl said. "Your idea to come out into the open. To alert the world of not only your kind, but the darker and dangerous creatures of the world."

"If everyone knew the truth," Salem explained. "Witches could protect The Natural Order out in the open. We could stop the monsters...or perhaps even..."

Beryl finished the thought for her, "Unite them with the fold." She smiled, caressing her cousin's cheek with her delicate holy hand. A flicker of sentimentality flashed in her crystal eyes which gave Salem a sense of the old feeling, back when they were confidantes and best friends. Behind those holy eyes, Beryl seemed to remember how well she knew the way Salem's mind ticked. "You believe bringing everything out into the open will force the darker beings to acquiesce. Perhaps forge an understanding. A treaty. A system of laws providing a peaceful coexistence with humans and witches."

"Something like that."

"If successful, you could be known throughout history as the one who saved the world. No more monsters. No more unnatural death. The Natural Order would be fully restored. Your plan Salem, has caught His attention."

"Do you mean I am right?" Salem asked. "Will it really work?"

Facing Salem again, Beryl let out a disconcerting sigh. "Free Will, Cousin. None of us can answer your question. However, you are presenting an opportunity. A chance."

"And this liquid?" Salem asked. "What's in it?"

"My blood." Beryl answered. "In essence, the Blood of God. With this blood you can achieve your goal. One drop sipped by a creature who once was human, will be restored to their humanity again."

Salem's eyes widened.

"Yes," Beryl answered. "Even vampires. Seth and Yasmine can be cured. Their souls restored, their sins wiped, and they can return to God's Grace."

"I can save Seth and Yasmine!"

"You can save everyone who fell into darkness...if they are willing. It must be their choice Salem. No tricks. No forced compliance. Free Will returned to the lost. A last chance for them to become God's children again. It will not be pleasant. They will relive the agony they caused as every affront to God is wiped away. But they will be redeemed."

With that Beryl vanished. Had it not been for the bottle in Salem's hand and her car parked across the highway, she might have believed the whole encounter was a hallucination. Salem made her way across the street, this time waiting for breaks in traffic rather than refreezing everyone. She walked in a daze-like condition. Her mind swirling with the possibilities this vile of Holy blood now brought. She could restore her brother's soul. Make him something like the way he used to be. Yaz too. Everyone really. If the evils of the world could have their consciences and their goodness restored to them, the world could become such a less dangerous place overnight. Beryl's gift could literally save the world.

And Beryl had given her something else besides this miracle bottle. She provided Salem with even more reason to convince Demitra to go public.

CHAPTER FOUR

A Deal With the Devil

Gripping the long wooden handle with the ax blade atop it, Echo shook his head at Knoxville Daihmler and said, "I don't have much—or really any—experience at this kind of thing, but isn't this a really weird date?"

Knox threw up his hands and replied, "Hey, not a whole lot to do in this town during the day, especially Thanksgiving weekend, unless you are into Black Friday sales. We've already done a lunch date. Then a drinks date. I thought I'd throw you a curve ball and see how you hit it back."

Echo grinned and grabbed his other two axes from the basket. All around them rang the sounds of axes being tossed at large round targets from several walled slews. The axe throwing craze had hit Daihmler and from the large and gregarious crowd at the bar waiting their turn, Echo was convinced it was rather popular.

"Great way to work out frustration or hostility." Knox commented as they found an empty channel to use. There were deep gash marks along the wooden boards of the back wall behind the red, white, yellow, blue, and green target. Some gouges even on the sides of the walls along the lane--proving some people are terrible tossers.

"Do you come here much?" Echo asked. "Got a lot of frustration?"

Knox laughed and said, "Not inordinately. But I am here a lot. I own the place."

Echo had not expected to hear that. "You own this place?"

"This and the rock-climbing center at the edge of town, and one trampoline park in Tuscaloosa. I'm trying to buy the smash room place, but they want too much for it." Knox shrugged and added, "What can I say? When I was a kid, I liked to climb things, smash things, and jump off the roof of the house into the pool. Broke a lot of bones growing up."

"You aren't the average gay guy," Echo remarked.

"These days, what is average?" Knox asked. "I had brothers and a tomboy sister.

If you didn't hold your own or join in the ruckus, you didn't fare well." Knox lifted his first ax, placing his feet into a well weighted stance. Eyeing the target with an eagle eye, he reared back his arm, exposing his round exaggerated bicep perfectly, then tossed the ax with impressive force. It turned a couple of flips through the air before landing on the yellow line, just below the white which encircled the red center. "Your turn," he told his companion. "Let's see what you got."

Echo did not position himself into any particular posture. He didn't balance his body like a golfer about to swing. He simply picked up an ax and threw it forward. The ax spun several times at a speed twice what Knox had managed. The ax blade planted itself tip-only directly in the center of the red circle.

"Shit!" Knox gulped. "Man, that was impressive."

"Beginner's luck."

Knox took another turn, hurling his second ax harder this time–a competitor's toss. His ax stuck just under Echo's, straddling the red and white line. He looked pleased with himself as he protracted his shoulder a couple of times, relieving the strain.

Saying nothing, Echo took his next ax and shot it with the same ease as his first. Knoxville's eyes barely believed what they saw as Echo's ax landed in the exact same place as his first, knocking his original ax off the board to fall to the ground.

"Are you a professional archer or something?" Knox asked, wiping his forehead.

Coyly, Echo grinned and teased, "Let's just say I've had to handle my fair share of weapons in my day."

After another few rounds of humiliating loss, Knox escorted his date to the lounge where they ordered drinks and a couple of burgers. With much of the awkwardness of the first few dates broken now, the two men used the remaining time to learn more about each other. Knox filled Echo in on what it was like to grow up in the town of Daihmler as a Daihmler. The once wealthy family now reduced to running restaurants like The Cobblestone, in Rosamund's case; or trying to build their own brand with a landscape design business, like Nash was doing; or cashing in on the high impact activity craze the way Knox was doing with ax throwing, trampolines, and rock repelling.

"Have you dated many people?" Echo asked, unsure whether it was appropriate.

"Some. A few relationships here and there, but nothing that lasted. You?"

Echo blushed. "One. And that didn't end well at all."

"Was he unfaithful?" Knox frowned.

"No. He just tried to kill me and my entire family."

Knox spit his beer back into the glass. "Damn. Bad relationship."

"Well," Echo remarked. "Things like that happen sometimes."

Incredulously Knox raised his brows and widened his shocked eyes, "No, man, I don't think they do. People don't usually try to kill other people."

"Oh," Echo said, shrugging his shoulders. "Happens to me a lot. A lot."

For a moment, Knoxville Daihmler did not know what to say. Then he remembered. Nodding his head up and down without saying anything, he winked at his companion. *He's a Blanchard.* Knox had grown up his entire life hearing the tales. And the rumors had been extra active lately with everything which had happened in Daihmler the last few months. Though his Aunt Rosamund never divulged whatever she might be privy to being such good friends with Mrs. Blanchard; Echo's comment lined up with the legends.

He raised his beer mug to Echo and toasted, "Here's to me never trying to kill you."

Across town, Howard Caldwell waited for his last appointment to arrive. He did not often meet clients after business hours, however when a representative of Sinclair Industries phoned to request an after-hours meeting, he naturally agreed. Though Howard's small firm oversaw the wealth management of many clients, none were as important than the holdings of the Sinclair family. Of course, there were no Sinclair's left. Olympia's third husband died many years ago leaving everything to Olympia and Yasmine. With their demise—or absence, in Yasmine's case—the Blanchard family controlled the company technically now owned by Hera and Titan. Howard was responsible for the signing off on all major Sinclair Industry decisions and left the day-to-day operations to the company's Board. He knew Roger Callahan vaguely from past company dealings, but when Roger Callahan came into the office at 6pm for their meeting, Howard knew at once this man was not Roger Callahan. He'd seen Roger Callahan before. He'd also seen Taub D'Angelo before.

"Oh my God." Howard gasped as Taub entered the office.

"Sit down, Mr. Caldwell. We have much to discuss."

Howard did not sit down. Instead, he charged forward defensively. Taub lifted his hand and propelled Howard gently back to his chair. "I am not here to harm you. Please do not force me to that. As we both know you have no active powers of protection. I, on the other hand, have a great many powers at my disposal."

"I thought you were long gone," Howard stated. "You ran like a coward. We thought you would be hiding the rest of your life."

"Thoughts can be misleading things. I could enlighten you, however, I do not have the time nor the inclination to prolong this visit. I require something from you, and you will deliver it to me."

Howard was adamant, "I will do nothing for you."

"I think you will." Taub said confidentially as he took a seat across from Howard. "You see I happen to know you are greatly fond of Yasmine Blanchard. As it happens, I know where she is."

"She isn't the same Yasmine I loved. I am not interested in her current whereabouts."

"What would you say if she could be the Yasmine you loved?" Taub asked with a raised brow and greedy smile.

Howard balked. "She is a vampire. Her soul is lost to us."

"Is it?"

Howard could not hide the fact that this conversation piqued his interest. Or perhaps it was piquing his emotion. Was this man intimating that Yasmine could be restored? He had to know. With a subtle nod, Howard signaled for Taub to continue.

"You are naturally aware you possess a great power." Taub said. "A power of the gods in fact."

Howard scoffed. "All I can do is bring back a dead person for a few minutes to talk to. Not that glorious of a power in the big scheme of things."

Taub laughed. It was a startling laugh. "You do not even know the depths of the power you possess. Of course, why should you. It is an old power, and no one was around to train you in its uses. You have not yet begun to tap into its full potential."

"I have no idea what you are talking about." Howard answered.

"Of course, you don't. But I do. I know far more than you on the subject. More than the Blanchards for that matter." Taub edged closer in his seat. "Mr. Caldwell, you cannot only speak with the dead. You can resurrect it."

Howard leaned back in his chair, not realizing until he did that he'd also edged closer in anticipation to what was going to be divulged. Now he felt deflated. "I already know that. I can bring someone back to life in the few moments after their point of death. But only if I am there right when it happens."

Taub grinned and shook his head. "No, my boy, the ability you speak of is the immediate resurrection without consequence. I speak of something greater. You can bring back the dead, any dead, no matter how long ago they departed."

"What?"

Taub was enjoying this. Enjoying the fact that he knew more than Demitra Blanchard. He explained the depths of the God Strain's intensity. Howard carried the Power of God Himself—at least a fraction of it. And if God can do the undoable, so could Howard. Within reason.

"There are prices to pay. You, after all, are only God-gifted by sheer accident of birth. It is diluted. It has consequences. However, you can indeed restore the dead."

"Are you saying I can restore Yasmine to what she was?" Howard exclaimed. "I can even bring my daughter back to life?"

"I cannot comment upon your daughter. Tess is not the reason for my visit. Only Yasmine concerns me. I have with me this vial," Taub said, withdrawing a glass cylinder from his coat pocket. "I recently saw Yasmine and spoke with her myself. In this vial is enough DNA matter to perform the ritual."

Howard was not buying it. "Why? Why would you even care if Yasmine became human again?"

"I have reasons. They need not concern you. The important question is, do you want Yasmine back?"

"What about Seth?"

"That is your affair." Taub said dismissively. "I mention Yasmine because of your deep affection for her. I can show you how to restore her. Afterward, if Seth is important to you, or your daughter, you will know what you need to know to do what you wish. So again, the question is, does the notion of having your Yasmine back appeal to you?"

"Of course, it does!"

"Excellent," Taub said, with tapping fingers not unlike a B-movie villain.

Howard paused and looked at him sternly. "You said something about consequences. A price to pay."

"Sadly, yes. There is always a price. As I explained, you have only a fraction of The God Strain's power. There will be something you must lose."

"Lose?"

"The balance, Mr. Caldwell. As you would call it, The Natural Order of things.

To receive a life, you must give a life. An even exchange to the balance."

"So...someone would have to die?"

"Yes, but think more about who gets to live! Your precious Yasmine! Imagine the delight of your family when she returns. She has children, I understand. Children who have lost both their parents. And here you sit, with the power to give one back to them. Can you really deny them that favor?"

"But someone else will die."

"People die every day, Mr. Caldwell. It's a natural balance. You would not be upsetting it."

"I can't do it." Howard said. "I will not be responsible for a person's death."

"Aren't you already?" Taub sneered. "Your own children's natural father. Haven't you already done this very thing? A life for a life. He went away, you got to live. You've already exchanged lives to the balance of the Natural Order. What's one more time? You can restore the heart of the Blanchard family to them. Your Yasmine."

Howard didn't know what to say. It was far too much to weigh. Every instinct inside him said to run out. To not make this deal with the devil. But it was Yaz. Yaz. How could he not at least consider the possibility? Yet, he had to have more information.

"Who takes her place in death?"

Taub shrugged. "That would be up to you."

"Me?"

"Of course! It would be your spell. Obviously, there are limitations to your choices. You couldn't, for instance, choose a death row inmate. Nor can you choose a total stranger. The bargain must be equal. The balance, you understand. If you bring someone back who will provide joy, then you must remove someone whose death would bring pain. It must be equal."

"I will not do it then," Howard asserted. "I have children. Grandchildren. Family. I will not risk one of their lives."

"No one is asking you to sacrifice a Blanchard, Mr. Caldwell. You couldn't if you wanted to. It would not be an equal exchange if you did. Yasmine is not technically one of your family members. She is Blanchard by association. Exchanging her with a real Blanchard would tip the balance too far. Your choices are limited to secondary Blanchards. Those whom a Blanchard loves."

"I don't understand."

Taub was enjoying the exchange—being the possessor of the facts in the presence of such a novice. "I recognize you do not understand. I will elaborate for you. I have researched your family's dynamics very well indeed before I came here. It appears to me the only candidates of equal value to Yasmine Sinclair would be your grandmother's husband Jerry, Seth's second wife Miranda, or perhaps...Salem Blanchard is engaged as I understand. He would be a sufficient sacrifice."

"Miles!" Howard gasped. "I couldn't do that to Salem."

"Fine. Pick Seth's mortal wife then. She isn't important."

"No, not Miranda either. The kids love her. All the kids love her. She's lost so much and been through so much. I couldn't live with myself. And my children are her friends. Their only link to their past is Miranda."

"Jerry then."

"No, not Jerry. I would never hurt Demitra like that. She waited far too long for love again. That is not an option!"

Taub smiled evilly. "It seems you are making my case for me. Miles. Salem's fiancé. He seems the least likely to cause the most pain."

Howard shook his head vigorously. "No! It would cause pain to Salem. She has been hurt too much in her life."

"The way I see it, she has a child she loves. A career she loves. This relationship appears new. Surely it would not be a life altering loss for her. Was she not far more devastated by the death of her husband and son years ago? Miles would pale in comparison."

Howard didn't want to think about it. But his mind could not stop. Miles. Even Salem herself was on the fence about Miles not long ago. Howard even had to bring the ghost of David back to her to help her decide to move on with Miles. And Salem herself admitted she didn't love Miles the way she'd loved David. Yes, Miles dying would be awful, but not devastating, as Taub put it. Still, this would be the most terrible thing Howard ever did in his life if he allowed Miles to die, but it wouldn't be the most horrible thing that ever happened to Salem. She'd already experienced those losses. Miles would hurt, but it would not ruin her.

Can I do this? Can I trade Miles for Yaz? Certainly, more people would be greatly affected for the good with Yaz back, but still. Miles' life held value. Maybe only really to Salem, but it held value. Could he do this? He knew he couldn't. Yet deep down inside, all he could hear was his heart screaming, *Yasmine.*

CHAPTER FIVE

The Safety Net

When Salem came downstairs and into Demitra's study, Demitra and Daphanie were already seated and waiting. Sliding the door closed behind her, Salem took the empty chair beside Daphanie, observing Demitra's position behind the desk, wondering if her aunt believed it might lend her more authority in this meeting.

"I have told Daphanie," Demitra began. "That this whole concept of yours that the world is ready to embrace and encourage our kind is a fool hearty venture. You know as well as I do, mankind cannot handle knowing all the secrets of the universe, so to speak."

"I do not know that to be the case at all," Salem contradicted. "Take for example here in our own lovely town, when that man tried to hold up Doreen McGillis' store and Romulus stopped him, the town declared Rom a hero. Likewise, when Sydney and Sage saved all those shoppers at Clayborn's from that mass shooter—"

"No one knows it was Sage and Sydney." Demitra countered.

Salem gave her the fisheye and laughed, "Oh Aunt Demitra, yes, they do. Everyone knows. Sage even had a couple come up to them and thank them one day in public. And those in town who do not know it was Sage and Syd specifically, know it was Blanchards."

"Gossip. Rumors. The same ones that have been around all our lives. No one takes it seriously."

Gesturing to Daphanie, Salem let out a condescending laugh and cried, "Aunt Demitra! The stories have spread all the way to New York. Daphanie Channing of all people showed up to our house with proof about us! This toothpaste is not only out of the tube, it has squirted all over the wall and floor."

Taking the mention of her presence as the opportunity to chime in about her own concerns, Daphanie was emphatic in her declaration. "The mystery surrounding the destruction of Duquesne House put you guys on my radar. However, I think if I return to New York without any new information, it will all die down and be forgotten. But what happens the next time something occurs, and the Blanchard name is involved? I agree with Salem, Demitra. You have reached the threshold of plausible deniability."

"Thank you!" Salem said slapping her knee. "Daphanie agrees and is ready to help us tell our story to the world before someone else tells it in a frightening light."

Waving her hands Daphanie denied the assumption. "Wait now. I never said I had agreed to be the one to tell this story. True, I am interested. I wanted desperately to uncover some unknown angle or sinister plot about the D'Angelo family or your own, which might garner me higher ratings. But that was before I learned the true story. When you add in the existence of witches and wolf boys and vampires, well that now becomes fantastical journalism. It borders on Q-Anon crazy. Space lasers and lizard people stuff. Unless we can absolutely ensure I will have enough physical and historical evidence to prove beyond doubt to the average person all this exists, then I am not willing to destroy my credibility in media."

"Proof will not be a problem." Salem assured her.

Having had enough of the deliberations, Demitra placed her hands authoritatively on the desk and declared her final statement on the matter. "We are not getting anywhere. The ultimate decision as the head of this Coven and the head of this family rests with me and we are not going to expose our world publicly. No more need be said on the matter."

Inflamed by Demitra's indignance, Salem stood from her chair and shouted, "This was never a situation wherein I was asking your permission, Demitra. Any deference I have given you by discussing it with you has solely been out of my deep respect for you. But let's be clear. I am not asking."

Standing now herself, Demitra was shaking in outrage at Salem's insolence. "I am your Hecate Salem!"

"And I, Demitra, am your Queen. I answer to no one. I have informed the Witches Council in both the Northwestern and Southeastern regions of my decision, and my safety net. The majority vote was in my favor. The final choice is mine. And we are going public."

Never in her life had Demitra been more furious with one of the children. She felt like slapping Salem, or even worse, spanking her. But Salem was no longer a child, even though sometimes it was difficult for Demitra to remember that. Salem was a grown woman nearing forty. She was not an inexperienced witch nor a novice to societal balance. Demitra realized, like it or not, she was no longer Salem's elder. She was Salem's subject.

The tension was palpable between the two witches making Daphanie incredibly uncomfortable. However, something was said that she wanted further elaboration on. "You mentioned a safety net."

Smiling, Salem's demeanor reverted to her more pleasant self as she told the ladies, "Yes. And now if you will follow me upstairs, I will show you both what that net entails. Aunt Demitra, I believe you will not be as terrified once you know the rest."

Salem led them upstairs to the third floor. Along the way, they passed Sage and Trix, both extremely curious as to why Daphanie Channing was back in their home and what Salem was going upstairs to do with them. But they let it go and went back to what they were doing. Opening the door to Titan's bedroom, Salem led them inside where they found Miranda putting away his clothes in a drawer. Titan was on the floor, as he usually was, with his toys.

Kneeling down to her nephew, Salem asked him, "Titan, will you do that thing again for me? You know. Like you did when the house was on fire the day before yesterday."

Titan walked to a shelf and removed a bucket of Lincoln Logs. He carried it to an empty place on the floor and one by one, began placing them in a horizontal line across the floor. Demitra wasn't sure what was going on or how Titan's quirky little tic was relevant to Salem's agenda. But she waited quietly to observe. Daphanie really didn't know what to think. Had she been called upstairs simply to watch a child play with his toys? Salem allowed him to get his line started with several pieces before she walked over to his dresser, gently ushering Miranda out of the way. Miranda gave her a hint of a grin because she knew what Salem had in mind. "Titan, look what I'm doing." Salem said to the boy, drawing his attention to the drawer. She lifted out his freshly folded clean clothes his mother had just placed there, and she tossed them down on the floor. Demitra and Daphanie stared at each other, shrugging. Salem spoke to her nephew once more. "Hey Titan, will you fix my mess please?"

The four women watched as the boy reached behind him where he'd laid the most recent Lincoln Logs and picked one up from its place in line. Everyone's attention being on Titan and not what had just happened in their presence, Salem directed their attention to the clothes. There were none. Salem went back to the drawer, reopening it, showing Daphanie and Demitra his clothes still folded neatly inside the drawer.

"What?" Daphanie said with squinted, almost perturbed eyes. "You brought us in here to show us how you can put clothes back in a drawer?"

Salem laughed and said, "I didn't do anything. Titan did."

Daphanie still looked unconvinced. Demitra, on the other hand, understood perfectly. She wore a look of amazement on her face as she crossed over to the child and stroked his blonde hair. "This is what happened when the fire disappeared, right?" she asked Salem. "And how the house miraculously went back to the way it was before the fire. Titan did that?"

Miranda, proud of her son's ability, nodded. "When he is putting his blocks, or cereal, or those logs, or anything in lines, he is making a physical representation of the passage of time. Salem and I figured it out the day of the fire."

Fascinated with this information, Demitra went down on one knee almost inspecting the boy, psychically. "All the while whenever we thought he was simply busying himself, or fixated on order, it wasn't that at all. All the times I walked down the hall and tripped over everyone's shoes he had lined up...he was marking time."

Unconvinced, Daphanie remarked, "Look ladies, I am not saying I don't believe you. But you must show me something besides some clothes in a drawer. Those could have already been there, or Salem shoved them back in while we were focused on the kid. I need another demonstration. A trick proof one."

"Then do anything you like." Miranda suggested. "My son will undo it." She asked Titan to start another line, which he obligingly did. Daphanie looked around the room, studying it for something she could not argue could be a trick. After careful consideration, she walked over to the rocking chair, lifting the angled floor lamp hovering over it. She carried it to the window and with the base of the lamp aimed at the windowpane, she smashed the glass and tossed the long lamp outside, watching it smack into the roof of the porch two stories below and roll off onto the lawn. "Undo that," she requested triumphantly.

When Titan withdrew his block from the line, Daphanie was not watching him, she was looking at the broken window and the lamp that used to sit in front of it. Somewhere between her wide-eyed focus and the urge to blink the lamp was back in place and the wind no longer rushed through a broken pane. The glass was there, exactly where it had been before. She went to it, feeling it with her fingertips. She reached down to the carpet below, pressing her palm into the fibers. There was no sign of glass shards. No trace of it ever happening. Astounded by it all she conceded to her new friends. "I am a believer."

Excitedly Salem bragged to Daphanie, "His power lives up to his heritage. My father possessed the ability to teleport. He could get to anywhere he thought of in a second's time. The man never took a plane in his life. Had no need. I myself have the power to stop time in place. I know it looks as if I am freezing people, but it's really that I am stopping the passage of their time. My niece Hera can do the same. As could my grandmother Olympia. My maternal line possesses a strong mastery over Time. Add to that my father's ability to materialize and dematerialize at will, traveling great distances, and the result seems to be that the next generation spawned from either myself or Seth, has some kind of accelerated time power. My son Olympus has the power to teleport into different times and dimensions. Much like Theda did when she was trying to kill us. Olympus caused a lot of trouble for the family while I was pregnant, until we figured out his power. We have temporarily bound him, meaning he cannot access it until he's old enough to understand it. And it seems Titan has inherited the ability to erase any little fragment of time or specific event he wants to erase."

"Though this is mind-blowingly interesting," Daphanie admitted. "How does this relate to your cause? I agree it is spectacular, but how does it pertain?"

Demitra gave the explanation. As she spoke Salem could feel the change in her. It felt as if she might now be less adamant against Salem's plans. "The safety net, of which Salem speaks, is Titan."

"Exactly," Salem said. "Miranda will make sure Titan is marking every minute of time while we go on the air and tell the world the truth. We will preserve his record—I already figured out how—and then we wait. We let it all play out until we know for sure if the public can handle what we must show them. If the world benefits from us stepping out of the shadows, we let it ride. However, if anything of monumental catastrophic proportion results from our going public, we just have Titan go back to his time record and remove the moment from history."

"This changes everything." Demitra admitted. "I am not saying I feel differently, but I will say I am now open to strategic discussion."

Daphanie touched her brow and said, "I have never heard of anything more extraordinary."

"Oh, I have!" Salem quipped, suddenly remembering what was in her pocket. Lifting out the small glass tube she exclaimed, "I have a bottle of God's Blood. Wait till I tell you what it can do!"

CHAPTER SIX

Reconnaissance

The drive down to Mobile Bay on the coastline of Alabama took a few hours, but necessity dictated it. Not wanting to make the drive alone, Demitra asked Trix for company. Jerry would have naturally agreed to accompany her, but he'd taken several days off from work recently due to the family crisis and she did not think his boss would be amenable to another. Likewise, Howard was much too busy to ask, having to once again go out of town to fight with the Sinclair Industries Board of Directors who did not enjoy answering to a Blanchard representative. Trix, however, had the day off and was someone Demitra could trust to keep a secret.

Trix sat silently in the passenger seat, taking in all she'd just been told in confidence. "I know I should not be surprised," she eventually said. "This family has more twists and turns than a miniature golf course. Still...Ocean not actually being a Blanchard, that's a biggie."

"You mustn't say anything to your sister yet," cautioned Demitra. "Until I can discover who his father really is, I see no need in upsetting Arielle or Ocean."

Winding a strand of her dark curly hair around a finger, Trix translated the meaning. "What you really mean is that until you can determine whether or not Ocean is an enemy, you'd rather not tip him off about what you know."

Shooting her great granddaughter a side eye as she steered along the causeway, Demitra replied, "This is another reason why I asked you to come along. You have the keenest sense for bullshit of anyone I know. If Stella Blanchard lies, you'll know it. And while you distract her with your suspicion, I'll read her mind."

"Do you think he's a D'Angelo?"

"I don't know. We really know very little about that family other than what your mother told us. But even then, Blackie revealed what was necessary for us to go into The House of Duquesne. I have little doubts there is much more to that family she left unsaid. For all we know, Thaddeuss, Atheidrelle, and Blackie may not have been the only siblings. If a D'Angelo rebirthed into Ocean…"

"Then my sister is marrying a monster." Trix finished. "And giving birth to one."

They arrived at The Bluegill restaurant on the Battleship Parkway right on time. In the distance Trix could see the great battleship in the harbor, now a historic museum. Upon walking in Demitra realized she hadn't seen Stella Blanchard in years. Maybe a couple of decades. However, she was recognizable the moment she saw her seated at a table by the window. Still slender, except for the 10-15 pounds age naturally adds to hips and torso. She was still an attractive woman, despite the lines spreading at the eyes and sides of the mouth. Demitra had the same lines, so she was not going to even think the words, she looks old. Stella rose from her chair with a polite greeting and forced smile, which Trix knew right away was out of southern magnolia manners and not because she was pleased to see her dead husband's cousin. Demitra introduced Trix, stumbling as to what to call her, she settled on granddaughter and hoped Stella did not do the math.

Of course, Stella must have known who Trix was and how she was related, Stella had been married to Seneca Blanchard after all, and presumably spoke to Ocean on occasion. However, if she did know the story, she wasn't interested enough to mention it. "So, Demitra, not to sound as if it isn't nice to see you again—after all these years—but surely this isn't a social visit. We were never close, and I haven't been a part of Blanchard goings on for a long time."

"I know." Demitra smiled politely. "But it was imperative I speak with you. Especially before the wedding."

Stella's face turned slightly sour. She took a sip from her glass which was clearly not iced tea. "The wedding," she sighed. "My son doesn't call me very often, but he did unfortunately reach out to invite me to his upcoming nuptials."

Trix leaned in, "Unfortunately, is an interesting word choice. You do not approve of your son marrying my sister?"

Unabashed to elaborate, Stella looked directly at Trix and answered, "No, I do not. Arielle Obreiggon is the reason my Forest is dead. How Ocean could fall for the girl who killed his brother is beyond me."

"Oh, I get it," Trix remarked. "You're a bitch. That's why I've never heard of you."

Demitra grasped Trix's arm, signaling restraint, as she took on Stella's challenging statement herself. "Arielle is a lovely girl," Demitra responded. "Kind, gentle, and loyal. She was not responsible for Forest's death. I was there. Arielle was as much a victim of Atheidrelle Obreiggon as Forest was."

"Then why is my Forest the only one who is dead?"

"Must I remind you, Stella, my mother died that day also. She died to save Arielle's life, but you do not see me holding that child responsible. What happened to Forest was horrific, but it was not Ariell's fault."

"You have your opinion, I have mine. But as mothers-in-law have done for ages, I will be at the wedding, and I will smile and make nice. Ocean will never know I despise his choice of a bride. And now that you and your family have practically indoctrinated him into your clan, chances are I won't have to see her all that often. I almost never hear from my son as it is now."

"Shocking." Trix offered. "And you seem like such the nurturing type."

The waiter came, allowing the tension to settle down. Once he left with everyone's lunch order, Stella pushed the conversation along. "What do you want, Demitra? Why have you come all this way?"

Holding nothing back, Demitra said it bluntly. "I want to know who Ocean's father is?"

People with secrets often have tells in their reactions which let one know, despite the denials, they've been caught in their lie. Stella Blanchard displayed no such tell. She genuinely appeared shocked by the accusation. "What the hell do you mean? Seneca was Ocean's father!"

Trix mindspoke to Demitra, *GG, she believes it.*

Demitra, getting the same impression, softened her tone somewhat before she went on. "Stella, I am afraid he isn't Seneca's son. And only you know who Ocean's father truly is. It is important that I know."

"This is absolutely ridiculous." Stella cried, "Who are you to tell me my son isn't who I say he is? How dare you infer---look, I know Seneca and I were estranged all those years at the end, but when my children were born—" she stopped. Both Demitra and Trix took notice.

"What did you just remember?" Trix asked in her interrogating voice.

"Nothing," Stella said. "I am offended, is all."

Shaking her head, Demitra said, "No, Stella, I saw it in your eyes and your mind. There was someone else, once. Who was it?"

Stella caught herself about to lie, but she knew it was no use. Her mind could not think that fast, especially when she had only just now remembered the one indiscretion she ever had. It had been so utterly shut from her mind for so many years, she never once considered it might be necessary to recall one day. But before she was going to give them what they wanted to know, she wanted information herself. "How are you so positive Ocean is not Seneca's son?"

Demitra told her the story. Or at least part of it. Halfway through Stella threw up her hands and called an end to the tale. "I have done my utmost to avoid your world and its dangers. I do not want to hear any more than I must."

"The important thing," Demitra noted. "Is that when Pastoria began to fade from history, so did her offspring. Had Seneca been alive, he would have begun to fade away as well. Yet Ocean didn't."

"Your inference is that Ocean was not related to Pastoria?"

"That's right."

"Then explain how he is a witch?" Stella asked. "He must be Seneca's son."

"How many others were there?" Trix asked.

Stella's glare conveyed better than she could that she did not appreciate the insult. "I am not a loose woman. I did not sleep around on my husband. Except...once."

"We need to know." Demitra urged, placing a hand of reassurance on Stella's arm.

"Why is it important?" Stella asked. "He must be Seneca's son. The other man was just a normal guy. He was not a witch."

"How do you know?" Trix asked. "Did you date long or was it only one night?"

"Once, only."

"Then you can't possibly know."

"I am telling you he was an average normal everyday businessman. He was in town for one day. I don't even remember his name, that's how inconsequential he was. I was young, newly married. Seneca and his brother Drake and Pastoria were their own little club. I was always excluded. Everything was always too complicated for my little brain to handle. Their witch stuff took precedence over everything, even my marriage. I went out one night while they were at a Consort. I met a man. I was already a little drunk. He bought me a couple more. He was in town for the weekend, handling something for a client. I felt so alone."

"I do understand." Demitra said empathetically. "I am not judging you, Stella. I can imagine how difficult it was for you back then. It is not easy being married to one of us. But if Ocean isn't Seneca's son, and if that man was the only other one—"

"He was! I swear on my sweet Forest's grave."

"Then that man was not simply a normal businessman. He was a witch—or perhaps even something else altogether. And he might, he just might, have been a D'Angelo. If that is the case, Ocean may not be Ocean at all. He could be one of them."

"You're talking crazy! I know my son. He may be...different, like the rest of you... but he is a good man."

Showing a rare softer side, Trix agreed with Stella, "I believe so too, Stella. I like Ocean a lot. He is a good person. I don't believe he knows he is not a Blanchard. Which means if he is a D'Angelo; he is in danger if they come for him. And if he is not, then what is he? What creature has powers like his?"

The drive back to Daihmler was no more illuminating than the drive down. Both Demitra and Trix believed Stella Blanchard had told the truth, but the truth provided no answers. They weighed possibilities between them, both understanding that Stella had been just as in the dark as they were over the man's true identity, and nature. "So, what do we do now, GG?"

"I don't know."

"Do I let my sister marry this man if there is even the slightest possibility, he is playing us?"

"I don't see much choice," Demitra admitted. "I must believe Ocean is as clueless as we are about this. Maybe his father was a witch. Just a simple harmless witch. Maybe he was a water creature—even one of The Rain People. I have no idea. But Arielle loves him. I believe he loves her. For now, we tuck this in our back pocket and wait it out. Maybe nothing ever comes of this. If it does, we are at least informed."

CHAPTER SEVEN

The Devil Keeps Dealing

Nights now were spent in the little apartment on the third floor of the Brownstone on 30th Street. Seth only went to his nightclub, Nightshade, to check on things. Any blood he collected was whatever he managed to secure on the street from a homeless vagabond. Yasmine could not walk. She lay in bed now paralyzed from the waist down from the injuries Artemis inflicted to her spine. She and Seth sat up every night in the bedroom, him holding her hand, one of the only remaining limbs she could feel. Where once they danced away the evenings in their nightclub, now they listened to the howl of winter winds hustling along the avenue outside their window. Sometimes an occasional rattling garbage truck would come by, offering its melodic beeping as it backed up to hoist the heavy clunky dumpster into the air. The sound of its contents tumbling into the truck sometimes reminded Seth of the bass beat of Nightshade. Yasmine had not improved. Seth worried now she may never heal. Her vampire self-healing abilities may apply to cuts or bullets, but a severed spine was proving to be out of its capabilities.

And then, like the answer to a devilish prayer, old friends dropped by for a visit. Seth was astounded when a knock came at the door so late in the night. Opening it he was even more taken by surprise at who was standing on the other side.

"Bianca Duquesne!" Seth gasped, as she entered the small living room. She was as stunning as ever with shoulder length straight black hair curving in under her chin line. Behind her walked Taub D'Angelo.

"He isn't Taub," Bianca alerted Seth the moment he parted his lips to speak. "Thaddeuss survived the battle by assuming his son's body."

Closing the door behind his guests, Seth exclaimed, "You are Thaddeuss?"

Smiling maniacally, Thaddeuss answered, "Yes, my boy. And still possessing all my amassed powers. And where is that lovely creature of a wife you have? I have greatly missed my Yasmine."

With a look of hopelessness in his eyes, Seth showed them into the adjoining room where his wife lay immobile and deflated. Bianca rushed to her bedside, lifting her hand into her own and stroking her arm gently. Thaddeuss looked disheartened and not just because he liked Seth's wife. He looked as if he himself had lost something precious. "What happened to her?"

"That creature," Seth said bitterly. "Whatever Artemis Blanchard has become. She severed Yasmine's spinal cord. She isn't healing, no matter how much blood I bring to her."

"She will not heal," Bianca informed him. "Not that way."

The loss of hope Seth had been carrying lifted slightly. "But there is a way?"

Laughing, Bianca said, "Of course! Newbies. You think you are all so powerful, until you aren't. New Vampires have such a low success rate because you all venture off on your own, believing you know everything. I can tell you there is much to be learned from those who came before you. We who have lived centuries have done so not from luck, but from experience."

"What can you do for Yasmine?"

Thaddeuss interceded now. From the look on his face, he was reinvigorated from whatever loss he presumed before. "Bianca, my dear cousin. Before you offer any of your ancient knowledge, I think now would be a good time to enlist our friends into our cause."

Bianca grinned viciously. "You are a hard and cruel man Thaddeuss D'Angelo. However, I agree. Whereas we came here only hoping we might persuade Seth and Yasmine to help us, now it seems it will be an equal exchange of favors."

"Favors?" Yasmine repeated softly from the bed.

Thaddeuss took a seat on the edge of the mattress as he explained in detail his plans to wage attack once more on the Blanchards, but this time on their home turf. Taking them by complete surprise.

"Thaddeuss wants to steal Tess Blanchard's baby."

"Reclaim," Thaddeuss corrected. "You see, her child is also my child. And it has unfathomable power. I want that baby. And you want Yasmine to be restored to vitality."

"How?"

Bianca answered. "To heal a vampire from something as severe as this, only the blood of another vampire will suffice."

"You mean she could have simply drunk from me this whole time?"

"Not unless you are ready to die. You see, it will require the killing of a vampire. She must drain one of her own kind completely dry. A healing of this magnitude requires much."

"Where can I find—"

"I will supply one for you," Bianca smiled. "I have done this before. Only a few times, but I know how to go about it. Leave it to me."

"Only," Thaddeuss warned. "If you agree to join us. And I will require vows for this bargain."

Though Seth was a vampire, he was still nonetheless a witch. And vows for a witch meant staking your witchcraft on it. A vow was a self-spell of sorts. If you broke your word and reneged on the promise, your powers as a witch would disappear. Seth would honor his promise if he wanted to ensure the ability to keep he and his beloved shielded by clouds from sunlight ever again.

Seth made the vow. He was not afraid of Thaddeuss going back on his word, because in truth, the Vow was an even greater loss for Thaddeuss. He had amassed dozens of other witches' powers through his unnatural lifetime, and he was not about to post them against a loan we did not plan to repay.

CHAPTER EIGHT

The Miracle of Christmas

When did I become my mother? Demitra asked herself as she sipped hot cocoa quietly in Olympia's wingback chair watching the younger people decorate the house for Christmas. There was a time when Demitra would have been leading the chaos of Christmas decorating with the children and her sister while Olympia observed from her chair. Now Demitra was the one sitting down while Echo and Sage hauled everything out from the 3rd floor tower room. They were now assembling the tree while Fable opened the crates of ornaments and Sydney hung the stockings along the fireplace mantle. Miranda took charge of the foyer, wrapping the stair banister with magnolia leaf garlands she'd bought at Paxton's Garden and Pond. Demitra was impressed by the impact it made. It certainly looked more refined than the red and gold tinsel garland she used to put there. Miranda bought matching magnolia wreaths for all the exterior doors and enough garland for the entrance to the porch and front door. Jerry was already outside hanging those while Howard and Trix were on ladders stringing colored lights across the top of the porch and the railings.

This was a first for Blanchard House. No one had ever strung lights on the outside before, but Trix insisted. Last year had been her first Christmas, and when she noticed other houses around town with lights lining the outside of their homes, she had become almost giddy. And Trix Blanchard was never giddy about anything. While she and Echo were growing up, their world had forgotten about Christmas. That tends to happen when you are too busy trying to stay alive in a land overrun by vampires. But last Christmas the family was still in deep mourning for their departed loved ones lost that Thanksgiving. No one felt much like yuletide. The holiday had been perfunctory, for the children. This year was altogether different. The Christmas spirit had returned and Trix was insistent there be lights outside as well.

"With my bad back," Howard complained, reaching his hands high above him to nail his end of the light strand into the facia board. "Can someone explain to me why we are the ones assigned to this task?"

From the front door where Jerry was affixing the garland, he shouted, "Because your daughter, my granddaughter, wants it."

Trix grinned and called back, "Think of it as my Christmas present. Although I will still be wanting actual Christmas presents."

"Just seems like a waste of time to me," Howard grumbled. "Nobody from town ever drives out here. Who's going to see it?"

"Half the town lives here!" Jerry chuckled. "It'll be pretty to look at even if it is only us who see it."

Back inside the house, the lights were finally on the tree and the ornaments were being hung. Demitra was still observing from her chair, stroking Romulus' fur as he sat at her feet. He still seemed weak from his injuries and probably would be for a while, but there was a sadness to him as well. She could sense it with her psychic abilities. He wished he could participate. Rom had never decorated a tree in his life, only watched while the two-legged family members did so. The ache for all he was missing was growing as he was getting older. Once, not long ago, she wouldn't have been able to pick up on his emotions. Now they were so palpable she couldn't help not to. Demitra twitched in her chair as if she'd just been jolted by a frayed wire. It startled Rom who peered up at her to make sure she was alright. Her mind was racing. Without considering the senselessness of it, Demitra began voicing her thoughts. "It wouldn't make a difference whether his emotions were stronger now or not," she said to the air as her family looked at her as if she were crazy. "I don't tap into animal thoughts. My power is human centric."

"Uh, GG, are you okay?" Echo asked, stepping off the step ladder where he'd just hung the star.

As if she had not even heard his remark, and she was so lost in her revelation that she probably hadn't, Demitra continued her soliloquy. "There should be no reason for me to be able to feel Rom's inner feelings. But I do."

"Mother," Fable asked, coming closer. "Are you having a vision or are you lapsing into senility? What are you talking about? What does Rom feel?"

Demitra knelt on the floor, rubbing her hands through Romulus' coat. He licked her cheek once as if saying thanks. "I can feel Rom's melancholy in having to, yet again, miss out on something everyone else is doing because he is a wolf." She gripped her grandson's face into her palms and, looking him straight in the eyes, she said, "But all that is over now my darling. Take your human form." His shiny azure eyes widened. In them she could read all his confusion, yet the burgeoning of understanding. "You can do it, Romulus. Try. Try for GG. Try for Christmas."

"Mom!" Fable shouted. "What are you doing? It is not the full moon cycle, and it is also the middle of the day. He can't transform."

Smiling at her daughter, her own lavender eyes brightening, Demitra said, "Oh, but I think he can."

Sydney, Sage, Echo, and Miranda watched in stunned fascination as Romulus closed his eyes and began to shiver. Within seconds his body was trembling violently, he howled a blood curdling cry. Jerry, Howard, and Trix rushed indoors to see what was happening. Demitra shook her hand at them to not interfere as she gripped her daughter's elbow, stopping her from the same. Romulus' back section raised, shifting him onto two legs with his front paws clawing at the air before him. Though his fur hid much of what was transpiring, the way it was shifting and rolling let the others know the bones beneath were reshaping, restructuring themselves while his skin began to adhere to the new design like shrink wrap closing in over something. He was transforming into a boy. As if it were a full moon, Romulus Blanchard was shapeshifting into the human form he had only recently begun possessing as he was growing up. Within the span of minutes, the bright-eyed boy they'd come to know once a month was standing before them. Demitra acted fast, grabbing a blanket from the chair to cover his naked body.

"Momma!" Rom exclaimed, running to Fable. "Momma! And it's not nighttime."

Tears streamed from Fable's eyes, and she embraced her son. "Romulus, I don't understand." She looked to her mother for answers. "Mom? What just happened?"

"You happened, Fable," she said. "I cannot believe the answer was right in our face all these years. When you operated on Rom, he'd lost so much blood, you used Con's blood for a transfusion. The curse of the werewolf which split itself when they were born, was diluted again when you put Con's blood into Rom's system. Romulus is more human now than he was before. And because of that, he has the power to change into whichever form he wishes and at any time."

"You can be a boy now!" Echo shouted, lifting the child up into the air. "My cousin the real-life boy! I can take you to my friend's new trampoline park when it opens!"

Divided in her feelings when she ought to be thrilled, Fable's face struggled to appear pleased. But she loved her wolf son. Yes, she was thrilled when Rom began to change into a human boy at full moons because she got to do so many things with him, he had never been able to do before. But in her mind and heart, her son Rom came with four legs and a beautiful coat of chestnut fur. She didn't want to say goodbye to him. Pulling him into her arms she wept, "This is exciting isn't it, son? Just don't forget who you are. Remember it is also a lot of fun being a wolf."

"But now I can do lots of new things!" Rom's eyes grew large and glistening as he turned to his cousins and said, "Can I help decorate the tree?"

Everyone laughed and excitedly welcomed him to the Blanchard tradition. Rom dashed upstairs to put on clothes, and to tell his brother and cousin the news. When he returned downstairs, Miranda had discreetly removed most of the already placed ornaments, putting them back in the boxes so that Rom could have the pleasure of doing most of the decorating.

"This changes everything," Miranda remarked to Fable as they stood together watching the younger children hang the family decorations on the tree. "This means he can attend school now. It also means we need to come up with a proper explanation of how you suddenly developed a second nine-year-old son."

Fable tensed. "None of those things occurred to me. But it won't matter. He is just excited now. When the newness wears off, he will go back to himself again."

Miranda patted Fable's back. She kept the rest of her thoughts to herself. She knew this would not be the end of Rom's wishes to be like the other children permanently. But Fable, it seemed, was not yet ready to accept the change. Fable stepped into the kitchen where her mother and Jerry had begun making cookies for the children. She'd hoped to seek their counsel on the school issue, but from the moment she passed into the kitchen she knew she was interrupting something. "What's happened now?"

Jerry shook his head smiling, "No, relax. Nothing like that." He motioned her closer where he could lower his voice to not be overheard in the living room. "Vanessa wants to come over tomorrow and chat about Theda. We think she's decided about whether to tell her who she is concerning the family. Just be ready to explain to the boys about her if she wants Theda to know."

"I think it is important she knows. She is Seth's daughter. Her place is here in this family."

Demitra nodded, "I agree. But ultimately that is for Theda's mother and Hera's mother to decide."

CHAPTER NINE

Family Trees Do Branch Out

Echo didn't get out to Northport very often. It was a good half-hour drive from Daihmler despite it not technically being very far away. When he finally arrived at the building which had once been a restaurant supply wholesaler, he was excited and pleased at its appearance. Newly painted in oranges and grays, it looked very modern. He walked in and found Knoxville bent over a folding table reviewing construction plans with the contractor. He gave Echo a wave to let him know he saw him as he wrapped up his meeting. The construction appeared to be progressing at a rapid pace. The foam block pit was finished, including the long balance beam over it where future patrons would battle with padded staffs to see who got knocked in. The crew was also stringing some of the trampoline pads across the large square cutouts in the floor. It looked as if there were going to be a couple dozen different ones. Knox came over, looking proud, and gave Echo a welcoming kiss. "It's coming together as planned," he beamed.

"Looks like it," Echo grinned. "You are taking the recreation biz by storm. Ax throwing. Shooting range. And now a second trampoline park."

"We need it," Knox replied. "This facility is going to be strictly kid oriented. Too many kids are sitting around getting fat playing video games. And those who might like doing something active only have sports options. But what about the kid who isn't good at baseball, or soccer? Or ballet or cheer? Where can they go to exercise, make friends, and have fun? Now they can come here."

"I love that idea."

"I'm going to have afternoon day camps and weekend clubs. In time I hope to be able to supply a couple of buses to pick up the kids who don't have a way to get here."

Echo gripped his shoulder and said, "I had no idea the man I'm dating has such an altruistic heart."

Blushing, Knox answered, "I do. But don't get me wrong, they're gonna pay for it. It takes a lot of money to run and staff this kind of place. But for the parents who are willing to pay, they'll know their kids are in good hands and getting safe, clean exercise."

"I will enroll Lucky when he's older."

Knox made a face. "I sometimes forget you have a kid."

"Funny thing," Echo laughed. "I do too. Way more often than I think I should admit. For example, where is she right now? I haven't even thought about it. I guess Miranda is watching him. I really should know these things."

Knox made a joke about echo's supersized family and how luxurious it must be to have built in babysitters around the clock. He showed echo around so he could see the other rooms in the facility, all with varying trampoline activities. Basketball, volleyball, rope swinging—all with trampolines beneath them.

"When do you open?"

Knox rubbed his face and said, "I am hoping in a month. Waiting on a few inspections. And the new sign for outside."

"What are you calling the place?"

"Tramp Club." Echo didn't say anything. He simply stared at Knox with questioning eyes. "What?" Knox finally asked. "You know like Fight Club but with trampolines. Tramp Club."

"And the connotations of the name still haven't registered with you?"

Suddenly Knox's face reddened. "Shit! But I already ordered the sign! Maybe I can stop them?"

"I would."

Knox ran off with his cell phone in hand quickly alerting the sign company to pause work until he came up with a better name. Echo was laughing fully now when he returned. "You are ridiculous Knoxville Daihmler. How could you possibly—"

"I don't know. I was thinking Fight Club. Not Whore Town."

"And Jump Club never occurred to you," Echo suggested. "Or Bounce Club. Or simply...Air."

"Man, those are actually not bad."

Vanessa arrived at Blanchard House at lunchtime with Theda. Though the winds were kicking up in their November chill, it was nice enough for the children to play outside after everyone had lunch. Hera appeared to like having another girl to play with and Vanessa held hope they two might become friends. Thankfully, having never met Con or Rom before, no explanations were required as to why Romulus Blanchard was now a boy. Theda would only know him as one. Once the children were outdoors, running off to the creek, Vanessa addressed Miranda, Demitra and Fable. "I spoke with Salem about this last night," she began. "I wanted her to join us, but she was flying to Charleston to see her sister." She reached out to take Miranda's hand, "You are so important to me, like a sister. I think I want our daughters to know they are sisters. Unless you do not feel Hera can handle it yet. I will honor your wishes if now isn't the time."

Miranda gave her hand a gentle squeeze before releasing it. She needed her own hands free to work out her anxiety, wringing them together as she stood from the table to pace a few feet around them. "I've thought of nothing else since we found out. Hera has been through so much already. I hate the idea of giving her one more thing to handle. However, this secret cannot remain quiet forever. Eventually, the truth will come out. I don't want it to be such a shock that it damages her. Harboring it any longer would do that. She would know we kept it from her, and that is the same as lying. I promised her I would never abandon her and I would never lie to her. Who Theda is can't stay hidden long, so if it must come out it should be now, while Hera can see it is news to all of us."

"Do you think Hera will accept her?" Vanessa asked. "Right now, I am all my daughter has and she doesn't even know me or fully trust me yet. She needs family she can always rely on. For that to happen, I need a family too. I need all of you."

"You've got us." Fable said, now being the one to squeeze her hand. "We are your family now."

"Yes, we are," Demitra proclaimed. "And if Hera should be told the truth about Theda, logic dictates Theda should be told the truth about herself."

"No, I'm not ready for that." Vanessa wavered.

"Then you must get ready," Demitra stated. "Your daughter is a Blanchard. Your daughter is a witch—one with great powers she must learn to control. I will need to train her and educate her on its proper use."

Miranda stood behind her friend and put her hands on Vanessa's shoulders. "It is unavoidable, Vanessa. Theda has been kept in the dark for too many years already. It is time for the truth. She deserves that from us if we are to truly call ourselves her family."

It was decided it would be done that day. The children were called inside and gathered in the upstairs den for privacy. Vanessa sat with Theda on one of the sofas facing the children who were seated on the floor. Fable, Demitra and Jerry took seats on the second couch. Vanessa did not know what to say. She began twice but then stopped. She looked to Demitra for guidance or perhaps to take over, but Demitra gently shook her head and let her know it should be she who began the conversation.

Taking a deep breath, Vanessa tried once more. "Kids, I have something to tell you which we adults only recently found out. Hera, you and Con know me as your teacher, and I hope you consider me your friend as well."

"Of course we do!" Hera chimed in.

Vanessa smiled at the children, feeling a tiny wave of relief before sharing the rest with them. "Theda is my daughter. I didn't know about her until Thanksgiving night."

The children looked at Theda strangely, then back to Vanessa. It was Hera who spoke up first with a question. "Miss Collins, you are so nice. You and I have had so many talks at school when I felt bad about my parents leaving. Did you leave your daughter too?"

Vanessa moved forward on the couch so she could grasp Hera's hands. "No, Hera. I would never do that. I did not know anything about Theda until a few days ago."

Con's face was perplexed. "How can you not know you have a kid?"

Fable was about to say something, but Vanessa waved her off, choosing to handle it herself with honesty. "My father was not a nice man. He told me my daughter died when she was born. But really, he had been keeping her hidden from me all her life."

"What a terrible man!" Con shouted in outrage.

"Yes, he is." Vanessa smiled.

"My father was a terrible man too!" Con commented, sympathetically. "My momma told me about him. I'm sorry your father was bad too, Miss Collins."

Vanessa reached forward to stroke Con's soft brown hair. "Thank you, Con, we share that in common now, don't we? Well, you can understand how hard this is for Theda and myself. We are just beginning to learn about each other. And because of this, we need to know everything about each other, don't you agree?"

The kids nodded their heads. Vanessa again looked to Demitra to take over but was again denied. "You are doing just fine," Demitra stated.

Vanessa placed her hand lovingly on her daughter's knee and said, "My darling little girl, you are having to understand so much already which you are too young to have to deal with, but there are two more things you need to know about yourself." Theda said nothing, only stared at Vanessa, fearful of what other shocks might be about to spring out at her. Vanessa directed herself to Hera when she spoke again. "Hera, you remember me once telling you that your father and I were boyfriend and girlfriend a very long time ago before he married your mother."

"Uh-huh."

"I loved your father back then, but I knew he loved your mother, so I moved away. I did not know it then, but I was going to have a baby. When it was born, I was told she died. But she didn't."

Looking at the blank faces the children were displaying, Demitra finally stepped in. She hoped they would come to understand without the need for a *birds and the bees* discussion. She moved to the couch, taking the seat beside Theda while pulling Hera up to sit beside them and lifting Titan into her lap. "Theda," Demitra began. "Hera and Titan are your brother and sister. You all share the same father."

The girls looked upon the other curiously. Much older in mind than their years, they both understood what this meant. Hera reached her hand out to Theda. Quivering with uneasiness, Theda extended her own hand until their fingers touched lightly. Titan watched at full attention, but what his little mind retained was anyone's guess.

"We are sisters?" Hera said as their fingers at last clasped lightly. "I never had a sister before."

"I never had a sister or a brother," Theda replied.

Wiping a tear he didn't know he had shed, Jerry leaned over toward the girls. "And Theda, you have cousins, aunts, uncles, and a grandfather and grandmother now. You will be safe and loved in this family."

Demitra echoed her husband's sentiment. "You are a part of our family now, Theda. Not only because we love you and your mother, but because you are one of us. And we are very special."

"How?"

Demitra thought carefully as to how to say it considering the way Reverend Collins must have raised her. "You've seen witches in storybooks and movies, right?"

"I have never seen a movie. And I only know witches are evil. They try to kill people. My grandfather told me."

Sighing, Vanessa interjected, "Your grandfather was wrong about witches. My father was wrong about nearly everything."

Making direct eye contact with the child, hoping it would calm her. Demitra told Theda, "We are witches, Theda. I am a witch. Your sister Hera is a witch. Your baby brother Titan is also a witch. And your cousins Con and Rom."

"But witches are evil," the child gasped, visibly becoming frightened. Vanessa stroked her hair slowly, terrified this was all too much to have thrown at her.

Romulus moved closer to his new cousin. "Witches aren't bad. We help people."

"You do?"

Demitra took over again, "We do. And one day when you grow up, you will help people too. I will teach you all about the amazing things you'll be able to do."

"I can blow things up!" bragged Hera. "I blew up this mean lady the other day who—"

"Now is not the time, Princess," Jerry warned.

Fable, afraid Hera's exuberance may have derailed the argument about witches not being evil, walked over, leading Theda from the sofa to the window. "Let me show you something neat," Fable told her. "All of us have different things we can do. My mother will help you figure out what you can do. But can I show you what I can do? I think you will like it."

Theda didn't say anything, but she did nod timidly. Fable pulled the curtain sheers back and positioned Theda at the glass. Closing her eyes in concentration, Fable sent out a call. "I really love animals, don't you?" she asked the girl. Theda gave another nod. "Well, I can talk to animals, and they can talk to me."

"You can?" Theda asked with eyes widening.

"Watch the yard," Fable advised. "I just asked some nearby deer to come into the yard to say hello to you."

Fable had no sooner gotten the words out of her mouth than an adult buck with proud heavy antlers emerged from the woods with two does and three little fawns. Theda's mouth hung open as she waved to the deer outside below. The male deer tipped his head towards the window. "Look, Theda!" Fable exclaimed. "He is saying hello to you."

Theda was amazed by what she saw, "Do something else? I like panda bears!"

Fable grinned, "I am afraid we don't have any panda bears in Alabama. But do you like birds?"

"They scare me."

"Oh, birds aren't scary at all," assured Fable. "Birds are friendly, beautiful creatures. It's cold out now but I bet somewhere nearby is still a red bird or a bluebird that hasn't flown away for Winter. Let's see shall we?"

Theda nodded excitedly as Fable sent out another request. Within a minute a vivid red cardinal fluttered towards the house. Fable lifted the window allowing him to enter. He perched delicately on her finger as she spoke to him out loud. "Thank you for visiting us. Would you be willing to let my little niece hold you for a moment if she promises to be gentle?"

Theda never did hear the bird answer, but she knew he must have because when she turned the palm of her hand over, he hopped into it. She held him very carefully even though his feet tickled her hand a little. The bird twisted his head in funny angles as he examined Theda's face. "I think he likes me," she whispered proudly.

"Of course he does," Fable smiled. "Birds are very intelligent. They do not allow bad people to hold them. He knows you are good, or he would not be sitting in your hand right now. You see, Theda. Witches are not evil. Nature understands we all share the world together."

The bird turned slowly in the child's hand and flew off again into the afternoon sky. When Theda turned back around to the rest of the den, her demeanor was notably changed. She was no longer afraid. On the contrary, she seemed almost excited to be part of the family now. Vanessa mouthed a thank you to Fable, who returned a wink, as they all sat back down.

Demitra went on to explain to Theda how from then on, Saturdays she would come to Blanchard house for witch lessons, but she was to never speak about their secret abilities to anyone outside of the family. She also told her that she was welcome at the house anytime she ever wished to visit, not just Saturdays. As she wrapped up the chat, she reiterated Jerry's sentiments in how she should consider Demitra and Jerry her grandparents.

"And can Theda spend the night sometimes?" Hera asked eagerly.

"Of course, she will!" Jerry exclaimed. "Children stay over with their grandparents lots and lots. The two of you can have sleepovers any time you want, as long as it is okay with Theda's mom."

Later that afternoon, after Vanessa had taken Theda home, Demitra popped into Hera's room to make certain she was as settled with this new information as she made them all believe. Taking a seat on the edge of the child's bed, she asked, "Do you have any questions or anything you'd like to say about what we discussed today?"

"I don't think so."

Not necessarily believing there could be no concerns, Demitra elaborated. "Do you have any fears or worries about having a sister?"

"Not really," Hera answered. "Maybe she will be my best friend."

Relieved of the optimism, Demitra smiled. "My sister was."

"Should I tell her about Daddy? You all spoke of him like he is dead. But he isn't you know. Do I need to tell my new sister he's a vampire?"

"No, my dear, I do not think Theda needs to have any of that in her mind. This is all new to her. Let's allow her time to process what she learned today before we give her anything else to think about. And Hera, your father is not coming back here. Please don't let yourself worry about that possibility. Your father knows if he returns here, we will destroy him. This is the last place he would ever come back to."

Far from the still, peaceful landscape of Daihmler, Hera's vampire father sat by his wife's bedside in their little New York apartment. He was holding Yasmine's icy hand as something began to pulsate beneath her flesh. He could not call it life so much as a kind of force returning. Watching from the doorway, Bianca was impressed by her own handiwork. "She is healing," Bianca told Seth. "The vampire blood I procured for her is working. By tomorrow I believe Yasmine will be fully herself again."

"How can I repay you for what you've done?"

Laughing heartily in the corner, observing the scene, Thaddeuss gave Seth a reminder. "By keeping your part of the bargain. Just as we have kept ours. Yasmine is returning to strength and once she is at full power again, you will accompany us to your former home. You will help us retrieve the baby which rightfully belongs to me."

"Of course," Seth stammered. "I said I would if you saved her. But you also said we would have backup. You assured there would be more than merely the four of us."

"And there will be my boy. I have already taken care of that. I can promise you and your lovely wife quite a reunion once we reach Daihmler, Alabama."

CHAPTER TEN

Flies in the Kitchen

Demitra was desperately tearing through the pantry looking for any box, can, or jar left open, but she found none. She moved to the bottom cabinets under the kitchen counter, searching for any pot or pan left unwashed. It was absurd to think anyone with a reasonable brain would have put a dirty pan back in a cabinet without washing, but there were a lot of children in the house, and a fair amount of lazy adults. Of course, just as she found in the pantry, nothing was out of order. Despite not yet finding the reason, something was rotting or unclean because the dozens of tiny fruit flies fluttering around the kitchen and perched on every doorframe or windowsill told the story. Fable came down the back stairs, yelling over her shoulder to Con and Hera to hurry up. As she reached the bottom, pounding feet resounded behind her as Rom, in his human form, bounded down to catch her. "Momma! Why can't I go to school with them? I can go now! Look, I'm normal!"

Snapping angrily as she whirled to face him, Fable said, "There was nothing abnormal about you before! You are just wearing a human shell. But you were normal already!"

"Whatever," he answered flippantly. "You know what I mean. I want to go to school with Con and Hera."

Ignoring his pleading heart, Fable swatted at her face and exclaimed, "What are all these gnats doing in here? It's early December!"

Almost as frustrated with the flying insects as Fable was with her children, Demitra replied, "They are not gnats, they are fruit flies. Someone has left something out that has spoiled, but for the life of me I can't find it."

Fable walked to the back door and opened it, a rush of cold air infiltrated the warm kitchen. Closing her eyes for a moment, Fable reached whatever intellect the flying nuisances had and asked them to flutter away outside. Demitra watched in fascination as all the little flies, even more than she originally thought existed, swarmed together in one mighty black cloud and exited the house.

"Why do I always forget that you can do that?" Demitra sighed. "Thank you. But I'm afraid there will be more if I can't find what's attracting them."

"Momma, why can't I go to school!"

"Shut up about school Romulus!"

Hearing the shouting in the room as she came down the stairs, Sydney tried to lend her cousin some support. "Rom, it isn't as simple as your mother just taking you into school. You have to be enrolled. You must have all your medical vaccines and shots up to date. You must have an education in all the prior grades. You can't just join the 4th grade! There is a great deal we need to take care of before you could possibly consider school. You don't even have a birth certificate."

"It's not fair."

"Bananas." Fable said out of the blue.

"What?" her mother asked.

Fable walked to the refrigerator and reached up. Her hand finding nothing, she dragged a chair from the kitchen table and stood on it. "Bananas," she repeated, pulling out a rotten black squishy cluster of what was once yellow and ripe. "Somebody put bananas up here. They must have gotten pushed back pretty far, that's why no one has seen them."

Taking the putrid, rotting mess from her daughter's pinched fingers, Demitra dropped it into the trash and tied up the bag to throw out. "How did you—"

"The flies told me."

"Of course."

"Momma, what about me going to school!" Romulus whined again.

"Maybe after Christmas break when the second semester starts," Fable answered. "It just depends on what documents Howard can doctor up."

"Speaking of Christmas," Demitra remembered. "Did everyone see Arielle's text about New Year's? She and Ocean are getting married on New Year's Eve at Oleander. We will all be going to Charleston right after Christmas."

Appearing in the doorway with a broad smile on his face, Jerry exclaimed, "Our anniversary, my darling!" He gave his wife a morning kiss as he grabbed his phone off the charger on the counter. "I wish I remembered our wedding, but still I know it was the best day of my life!" Demitra wrapped her arms around her husband and kissed him properly to send him off to work. Over his shoulder she exchanged telling glances with Fable. *What he doesn't know won't hurt him.*

The children came downstairs for school whereupon Sydney offered to drive them, since her office was nearby. Fable took her up on the offer gladly since she had surgery on a terrier's leg first thing that morning.

The kitchen was quiet for a while after the first shift of Blanchards left to begin their day. Demitra had peace for a few minutes except for Romulus pouting at the table. Miranda popped down to warm bottles for the babies before returning upstairs to feed the twins. Echo rushed out of the door wordlessly, only stopping to kiss his great grandmother on the cheek. She'd been ready for him, but he was too quick for her. Waving an envelope in the air as he dashed off, Demitra yelled out after him, "Kisses are nice, but I still know you got a speeding ticket in the mail!"

Trix was right behind him, grabbing a pop tart from the cabinet before she ran off to the Police Academy. "Fix this for your brother," Demitra said, handing her the ticket. "And did you talk to Arielle?"

"Yep, Trix shouted over her shoulder. "Wedding. Charleston. December 31st. Flights are all booked."

Boasting a prideful smile as he came downstairs, Sage announced, "And as best man...yours truly."

"Good," Demitra smiled. "Everyone knows. Will your mother and Ocean's mother be there?"

"I assume," Sage replied. "I didn't ask. Where are my bananas?"

"It was you!" Demitra cried.

CHAPTER ELEVEN

Pink Oleander

The city of Charleston was even more charming than its usual self. Salem drove through its narrow streets past the ancient colorful homes dripping with both history and porches. Storefronts were decorated for Christmas. Magnolia leaves have never been used as eloquently as they are in Charleston at Christmas. Thick wreaths of glossy green and bronze magnolia hung on almost every door. Large swaths of green garlands stretched along the streetlamps and over intersections, crowned with wreaths at every swoop. Ocean was looking out at it all lost in his thoughts. She did not require her aunt Demitra's psychic ability to know what he was thinking.

"It's a little terrifying, isn't it?" she asked her cousin.

"Huh?"

Salem patted his thigh and admitted, "I have spent some time myself on the other side of that blank face. When Michael was almost due, I think both David and I started panicking." That damned dominant masculine inability to admit emotional insecurity flared up as Ocean pretended not to know what she meant. "Don't ever try to hide your fear behind a steel wall from another person who lives behind their own. I get it. We are driving along all innocently and then we turn into this picturesque town with all its Christmas splendor up. Then you start thinking about how next Christmas your child will be almost one year old. You get excited about next year. Then wham! The white panic!"

"Panic?"

"You know what I mean," Salem laughed. "Oh, Dear God, how am I going to do this? Who on earth would allow me to be a parent? I can't handle my own life and now I am supposed to become fully responsible for someone else's."

Ocean let out a slight sigh as he squirmed in the passenger seat. "Yeah, maybe something like that."

"It happens to every parent. And it continues to happen well after the baby comes. You are a good guy Ocean. I've known you all your life as my cousin and I can't think of anyone I'd be happier with as a brother-in-law."

He gave a nod of thanks, but his worries weren't going away. He was making peace with the fact that Arielle was ungodly rich, and he wasn't. Though that still kicked him in the gut sometimes. His job as a cop would in no way supply the kind of lifestyle Arielle was accustomed to so he would never ask her to live off only what he provided. However, for the first time in adulthood, Ocean wished he'd chosen a different career path. He liked being on the force, and Charleston was going to be great. But only now, when a child was soon to enter the world, did he stop and assess how dangerous his job was. Could he put his wife and baby through that daily stress? Yet he knew he could not quit. Even his tiny bit of income helped keep him feeling like a man. He was certainly not the type to live off her money.

By the time she and Ocean reached Wadmalaw Island things grew even cooler—it felt like the beginning of winter. Ocean reached over to turn the temperature dial up a bit. He mumbled something, but she didn't catch it. A few seconds later she realized he'd made a remark about the odor outside. She'd long grown accustomed to the swampy marsh. Its putrid smell was not what was bothering her now. It was filled with memories. Salem had not been back to her father's ancestral home since last Winter's Consort. The Winter Consort came on the heels of the battle at The House of Duquesne. Arielle had arranged for Oleander to be the hosting site primarily because of convenience. Deceased witches had to be cremated at Consort meetings, it was a generations' old custom. The sheer number of witches who died in The House of Duquesne facilitated the need to hold the next Consort nearby. It seemed simpler than shipping all the bodies elsewhere.

Salem would never manage to untwine her memories of Oleander with the memories of the two terrible Consorts she'd attended there. The first when she cremated her son, and the second when she stood watch as her parents, sister, and cousins were laid upon the pyre. One look at Ocean, still quietly staring ahead, told her he too was remembering the same bitter memories.

"It's hard, isn't it?" she said, placing her hand over his. "This place isn't pleasant for us."

He gave a nod and wiped his eyes. "I think about it every time I come out here to see Arielle. Dad and Uncle Drake. The way they died. Then the cremations. Bodies so sliced up they had to be bound together with wrappings. Sticks forever in the mind." He stopped talking for a moment, switching from his traumatic memories to what she must be thinking. "What I feel is nothing compared to what you must go through."

Salem squeezed his hand. She had seen so much death in her time. Too much death. It had changed her. Hardened her. But it also made her stronger—more in control of her emotions and her determination. Sometimes Death is the strongest teacher.

"Loss is loss," she replied. "No one's is greater than anyone else's."

Ocean tilted his head back and forced a brief unexpected chuckle. "You and I have had a lot of similar experiences, Salem. We've lost parents. Grandparents. A sibling. Why do we not talk more?"

Salem found the statement ridiculously poignant. "You know, you're right. I guess we cling to the ones we are used to clinging to. I go to Fable or Demitra, because they are all I have left. You go to Sage or Sydney. We really should be closer, you and I."

He nudged her arm with his own and said, "Well, I am about to be your brother-in-law somewhere in the not-too-distant future."

As they continued the drive across the island, nearing their destination, they both grew quiet again, attention drawn to the majesty of the landscape. Centuries old oaks reaching their crooked fingers across the lane as if trying to clasp hands with their neighbor. Long tendrils of Spanish Moss dripped down from every limb, tickling the top of her car as they passed beneath. Wrought iron gates met the road every quarter mile or so marking the entrance to one of the many ancestral homes hiding behind the thick walls of trees, shrubs and overgrown vines. With Winter leaves shed, the vines resembled ancient ropes, twisting and climbing and choking out whatever they encased. Old families dwelled here, living in a world of their own somewhere down their winding driveways. The gates of Oleander loomed ahead, brighter, more vivid than the others they'd passed, proving Arielle had indeed been busy bringing youthful luster back to a very old homestead. Salem suddenly became animated with excitement to see her baby sister again. Her very pregnant baby sister. Ocean was sharing the excitement. He stirred upright from his slump, as if unconsciously shifting his body closer to the dashboard...closer to Arielle.

Arielle met them outside the moment they pulled up. With open arms she rushed the car. Quickly Salem turned off the ignition and jumped out to meet her, her own arms now open to the embrace. She stopped short, feeling rather foolish, when she saw that Arielle's waiting embrace was meant for Ocean first. Ocean swept Arielle up from the ground, kissing her passionately. Salem smiled. Her sister looked happy. Arielle had waited a long time for happiness. Breaking free of Ocean's hold, she ran around the front of the car to hug her sister. It was almost as passionate, but only almost.

Salem marveled at the exterior changes to the house. The newly painted pink façade really gave the place a more genteel feeling. The last time she'd seen Oleander, it was still the stark white wood, columns, and cornices with black plantation shutters encasing every window and door for contrast. Now the pale pink and dusty green adornments gave the estate a breath of innocence, as if none of the bad things had ever happened there. Arielle gave Salem a summary on the changes she'd made, as if seeking her approval. She explained the shade of pink was called Creole pink. The green, which she called verdigris, was meant to emulate the foliage the island was famous for. When Salem praised the choices, Arielle beamed like a kid with an all A's report card.

As the three of them walked inside the great house, Salem found herself pleasantly surprised to see Arielle kept everything as it had been when their parents lived there. Nacaria and Xander dedicated months of their lives restoring the interior of Oleander to the showplace it had once been before his first wife Atheidrelle changed it all to reflect her gothic ancestral home, The House of Duquesne. Salem recalled how excited her mother had been changing the decor during the short time she'd lived there. Salem half expected to see Nacaria sweeping down the stairs in her light blue sundress.

"It is good to see this place again," Salem smiled. "I'm glad you have kept it the way Mom and Dad changed it, except the pink. I really like the pink."

Arielle looked relieved. "I was worried about it at first, but when I called to ask you and you said you thought it sounded lovely, I went with it. I love the way it turned out."

"I didn't understand why you wanted my input in the first place," Salem said. "You should do whatever you like with it."

Arielle twisted her lips as if confused by the statement. "I wouldn't change anything without consulting you first. It's just as much yours as mine."

Salem had once again forgotten that trivial detail. In her mind Oleander was Arielle's now. It was Arielle's childhood home and the Obreiggon family's birthright.

It continually slipped Salem's mind that she was just as much an Obreiggon as Arielle. Xander left Oleander to all four of his children. With Cassandra dead and Seth now what Seth was, Oleander belonged equally to Salem and Arielle. No wonder Arielle kept calling Salem with every tiny decision regarding restarting the tea plantation.

By now Ocean was rubbing Arielle's stomach, making her blush as he talked to his child inside her. Salem liked to see them being playful. She and David had been very playful together. Miles wasn't very playful, but then again, she and Miles were not as young now as she was when she and David married. Arielle and Ocean were young, or at least young enough to still find love entertaining.

"Where is your Christmas tree?" Salem asked, seeing no signs of the holiday at all. "All of Charleston has decked the halls left, right, and sideways and Oleander looks like its May 18th."

Frowning at her sister's disappointment, Arielle confessed, "I really didn't see the need. We will all be going home to Blanchard House for Christmas. I'm all alone here when Ocean isn't here. A tree would only make me feel sadder. Besides, the decorators will be coming in here the day after Christmas to stage the house for the wedding."

"Oh, yeah, that makes sense."

Salem wanted to respect the couple's need for privacy, so she excused herself outside to the grounds. She wanted to walk out to the grave of her son. Michael was only a baby when he died with David in that terrible car crash. He'd been laid to rest here at Oleander. It was probably not the wisest decision on Salem's part, made mostly to antagonize wicked Atheidrelle years ago. But now, with Arielle at the helm of the Obreiggon heritage, she was glad her son was connected to this place. His grandfather's ancestral home. Michael had been an Obreiggon too after all. Besides, it no longer seemed so much like the enemy's house as it had the first time Salem ever came here. She'd built a wonderful relationship with her father. Her mother eventually married her father, and they lived a happy life together here. Michael's grave being at Oleander was logical now. It all worked out despite itself.

"Hi, baby boy." Salem said, lowering herself to sit on the grass around his grave. Around the headstone sat lavish pots brimming over with colorful mums in oranges, reds, and golds. His aunt Arielle certainly kept his grave up splendidly. Salem stroked his name Michael Lane Blanchard with her fingertips, the way she once used to stroke his hair. The name was not completely accurate on the stone. Michael was never known as Blanchard. That was added for Consort recognition—Blanchard being the witching family. Salem allowed the inaccuracy when the stone was laid in part to stamp her family name in stone for Atheidrelle and all of her vile friends to see every time they passed. Another youthful, petty decision Salem sometimes regretted. But only sometimes.

"I can't believe how long it's been since I last held you, my darling." Salem smiled sweetly at the stone. "To me you will always be my baby boy. But I guess now you'd be ten years old." She paused, looking towards the trees overhead. "Wow. I can't believe that." She laid her cheek to the grass over his grave and curled her knees inward to her chest, the way she did when she would lay on the bed with him. "You have a brother now, Michael. His name is Olympus. Oh, Michael, that brother of yours sure put us through some trouble a year ago. I remember thinking I was in for it when you developed telekinesis and would move toys around at your daycare. But your brother! He almost upended the world. We had to bind his powers till he's older."

For a moment Salem felt guilty. Why was she laying on her dead child's grave speaking about her living child as though he were something special? Both boys were special, in their own ways. She wondered if this was how siblings are made to feel when a parent raves over one of their accomplishments to the other. She felt so strange. Michael had been her world once. Now he wasn't. Olympus consumed her thoughts and hours. It felt disloyal somehow now at Michael's grave. Would Olympus ever feel a connection to his dead brother? Or was Michael Lane now only a footnote in Blanchard history? The idea brought her to tears. Michael was her first. Did that also mean he would always be her favorite? How could he be when now there seemed to be days where he slipped her mind completely as she lived with and raised Olympus. Oh, it was never more than a day, but sometimes she did forget to remember him.

It always filled her with shame. Michael had been her son. She had to strive harder to keep him in her thoughts and not relegate him to merely a headstone in a patch of lawn on an island in Charleston. Salem sat up. She kissed the tips of her fingers and traced his name once more. This visit did not help her. In fact, she felt all the worse for it. She got up from the lawn and went back to the house.

The next morning, after a large plantation style breakfast, Arielle and Salem set out for the city while Ocean went into town to meet with the police captain. It took about 45 minutes to reach Mara's house in the historic district of Charleston. Mara greeted them at the door and showed them inside. Arielle made polite introductions, although Salem and Mara had met before rather briefly. They settled down on a plump sofa while her cousin and her sister began to speak upon the subject which brought Salem to South Carolina.

"Now that I am Queen of the Consort, it is up to me to bring our society into a new age." Salem began.

"Yes, I remember your speech touched on that idea the night you were voted in." Mara replied. "I found myself becoming excited by your enthusiasm."

Salem smiled appreciatively. "I have a plan I am putting into motion at the first of the year. However, I need to test the waters, so to speak. I was hoping you might know the whereabouts of your mother and Gideon Duquesne."

Mara was more than a little surprised by this statement. "You plan to destroy them, I take it? Finish what was started last year?"

Salem looked down uncomfortably, "I am afraid I cannot yet divulge my reasons. But it is not to kill them. I simply wish to speak to them."

Mara did not press the issue, replying simply, "I know where they are. I feel certain I can arrange a meeting, if you wish."

Arielle, having a better understanding of Salem's plan, but still honoring the secrecy, was not in favor of this clandestine meeting. "Personally, I think it is simpler and safer for all concerned if you end their miserable existence once and for all."

Salem gave her sister a disapproving look. "I am hoping it will not come to that."

"What makes you think it won't?" Arielle challenged. "I fully understand your idea, but what is the point? These people tried to kill us, Salem. They have killed hundreds of people over their unholy life."

Mara made a beleaguered face, "Well, we've all killed people. At least when necessary."

Salem didn't exactly like the way Mara phrased that but decided it best to assume she meant in the line of duty and "people" being her term for monsters. Salem continued her argument, "I am not saying it is an idea that will work, Ari. All I am saying is that The House of Duquesne taught me the world is not as idyllic as we grew up believing. All the creatures we thought Constantinople Blanchard's generation and Olympia, Pastoria, and Zelda's generation rid the world of, still exist. Maybe they are more cleverly hidden now, fearful of what witches would do if we discovered them, but they do remain. I don't want our children spending their lives in battle to save a world from something that is never going to go away. I have a proposition to make to the Duquesne vampires and if they accept it could pave the way with more of their kind."

Mara nodded, "I can convince Gideon and my mother to meet with you. If they refuse, I only need to threaten to stop bankrolling their lifestyle. But you will have to go to Denver."

CHAPTER TWELVE

Denver Sunrise

Salem Blanchard arrived at Denver International Airport a little after 5pm. The Denver Rail train took her from the airport directly to Union Station in the center of town. Salem happily found this part of the city bustling with commerce. The train station had been beautifully restored some years ago and was quite the hub of activity now, full of shops and restaurants. There was even an enormous Christmas tree lit with twinkling white lights which danced off the gold and silver ornaments. Denver was charming. She found herself wishing she might stay over a day or two, but she wasn't there for sightseeing. Her trip was to be short and strictly business. She also overheard someone say the big snowstorm would be rolling in by the end of the week. Salem had not packed for snow.

While there were a couple of daylight hours remaining, she grabbed a bite to eat at a nearby restaurant called Stoic and Genuine. Feeling a little self-conscious about dining alone when so clearly this was a date destination, she wished Miles were with her. She felt like people were staring, wondering if she'd been stood up or why a woman like she would be alone. Fable used to say *pretty people never eat alone*. Salem smiled to herself now remembering how adamant her cousin used to be about everything and so concrete in her positions. Fable had eaten many meals alone over the years. Salem wondered if she should point that out when she got home. Still, Salem wished Miles was with her now as she watched the hand-holding couples staring lovingly over candlelight. Then again, Miles was still registering how Salem being a witch made her a far different kind of woman than he'd ever known before. She couldn't have brought him on this trip. It was much too soon to introduce him to vampires. Besides, there was quite a real danger involved in what she was about to do.

Once the sun set, she walked through the outdoor 16th Street Mall to Commons

Park. Though there was a chill in the air, her long plum colored tweed coat kept her toasty. For Colorado the weather was considerably mild, especially with a snowstorm headed their direction. She followed the walkway along the Platte River until she came to the Millennium Bridge. The white cable-stayed bridge looked very much like a sailboat to her. Perhaps that was the intention. She did not have time to stop and read the plaque as she walked to the highest wood decking of the bridge and waited. It did not take long for her guests to arrive. As the moon was rising over the horizon of mountains in the distance, Salem could hear the steps of two people approaching, then stopping behind her. She turned slowly around to face them.

"I have immobilizing abilities, if necessary," she warned.

"You are in no immediate danger from us," the man informed her. "I recall you are a formidable adversary." His sleek facial features and dark hair gave him a sinister appearance even though a handsome one. His female companion was rather lovely. Long black hair and flawless skin. She looked very much like an older version of Mara, only lacking some of Mara's magnetism. The woman looked to be in her late forties or early fifties. He looked to be the same age although Salem knew he was much, much older.

"My daughter explained the circumstances when she contacted me," the woman informed Salem.

"You are Alexandrea D'Angelo," Salem said. It was not a question although the woman corrected her.

"Alexandrea Duquense, if you please."

"Alexandrea is my bride," the man clarified. "I am Gideon Duquesne. Of course, we have met before. Briefly."

Salem remembered it all too well. "Yes, in the battle at The House of Duquesne. You fled for your life."

Gideon did not appreciate the hint at cowardice in her tone. He, too, made a correction. "I fled to save my beloved from destruction. Alexandrea is very new. Freshly undead, if you will. I've no doubt that battle might have gone quite a different way had Bianca and I not made our retreat. You see Miss Blanchard; my Alexandrea means more to me than my family home—or its descendants."

"Mara assured me you meant no harm to us with this meeting," Alexandrea said. "But may we know why you requested it?"

Salem raised a brow and rubbed the bridge of her nose between her thumb and forefinger before replying, "Absolutely. But curiosity has the better of me. May I ask you a question first?"

"Proceed," Gideon allowed.

"Why are you in Denver of all places?" Salem asked. "I expected to find you nearer to Charleston since it is the only land you've known for centuries. Why here?"

Gideon smiled devilishly and gave a mild attempt at a laugh. "You would appreciate my reasoning for relocating here. You see, I grew very fond of one of your relatives. Yasmine endeared herself to me during her stay in my ancestral home. And she has great power—not at all unlike your own. My wife and I came here in hopes of finding Yasmine."

"In Denver?"

"Do not act so surprised," Gideon chuckled. "It is a marvelous city. And she was here, in fact. It seems we just missed her by a few months. I still get hints of her essence in many locations around this city, even as far as Breckenridge. Oh, she and her husband did a lot of damage in Breckenridge. Yet alas, they have gone. I suppose we will have to keep looking for her."

Salem had not expected to learn any of that information. It seemed curious to her how the man—inhuman as he was—could feel such fondness for her sister-in-law. And something else he said intrigued her. "Pardon me for expressing surprise at your affection for Yasmine. I did not think..."

"Vampires have emotions?" Gideon grinned. "My dear, we have the same feelings as when we were human, only far more enhanced. Yes, I came to care for your brother's wife. I felt very paternal regarding her. Everything was so new for Yasmine. I guided her as best I could."

"And her power?" Salem questioned. "Her power to stop time. I was not aware vampires had powers such as witches do. Frankly, seeing her with powers last year was quite a shock to me."

Gideon squinted his piercing eyes as he replied, "Did you not know? Yasmine was with child when her attackers infused their immortal blood into her veins. Yasmine's embryo, though it will never be born, has the power of the witch. It now forever resides within her womb, and she is quite adept at harnessing its capabilities. She is quite a remarkable vampire because of this. You can see why she was a priceless find to Thaddeuss."

Salem understood so much more clearly now. This was why Yasmine was so valuable to the Duquesne vampires. And Thaddeuss. It all made sense now. Steering their chat back to her purposes, Salem announced, "It may not be anything you are particularly impressed by, but I am the Queen of the Witches' Consort."

"Which district?" Alexandrea asked. Salem forgot momentarily Alexandrea had been married to a witch herself—although Salem was not certain whether Alexandrea was a witch herself. But as Taub D'Angelo's wife she would have surely been well-heeled in Consort matters.

"There is only one Consort now. It seems my election sparked a unification of the four corners. All Consorts merged into one, and I am their Queen."

"Congratulations my dear," Gideon bowed. "To hold such prestige among your kind is an impressive feat. However, what could the Queen of Witches need from the two of us? Is this a sporting warning that my kind will be under attack now? Because my dear, we have always been under threat by your kind."

Salem shook her head in response while she took a bold step closer to them. She wanted them to see she did not fear them. "I want you to join us." The statement took the vampire by surprise. Never would he have expected such a declaration from the mouth of the Queen of Witches. Gideon was unresponsive for a moment. In all his hundreds of years, this left him speechless. Salem continued, "Our world is changing. Cell phones, social media, YouTube, TikTok, Instagram. It is not as easy for your kind or mine to remain hidden in this world anymore. I have decided it is time to step out of the shadows and reveal our world to the rest."

Gideon was fascinated. "My dear, the repercussions of such a decision would unleash chaos and havoc onto the entire world. Not to mention this would place my people in far greater danger than yours. Or is that part of your plan? To push vampires into the open would make it much easier to find and destroy us."

"It will." Salem admitted. "Forgive me if I don't give a damn about that part of it. Wiping out blood sucking fiends who kill and destroy will not cause me sleepless nights."

"You are forgetting your brother is a blood sucking fiend, as you call us."

Salem's eyes narrowed in resentment, "I never forget that. Nor do I ever forget the reason he became what he is now is the fault of your kind."

"Why are you here Miss Blanchard?" Gideon asked frankly. "Surely not to warn us that you plan to out us to the world?"

"No," Salem said, removing a small bottle from her purse. "I hope to reunite you with the world. With this."

He eyed the strange bottle with its deep blue fluid. It seemed to pulsate under the streetlight, as if it was alive. "I am intrigued." Gideon said.

"Do either of you know anything about my cousin Beryl Blanchard?"

"I confess I know very little about your people," Gideon admitted. "Other than you destroyed our family home and the protections it provided."

For a moment Salem felt a slight sense of shame until she reminded herself these people were insatiable killers. "My cousin is no longer a part of our realm of existence. She has transcended to a higher being. Have you by chance heard of The God Strain?"

This statement caught Gideon's immediate attention. His wife shook her head. She did not recognize the reference. Gideon, on the other hand, was astounded. "Your cousin has become a part of The Almighty?"

"She has." Salem answered. "And she has provided me with this."

With piqued interest, Gideon moved closer to the bottle, inspecting its glistening aura through his ancient eyes. He'd lived a long time, longer than most, and he'd seen Holy artifacts once or twice, but nothing emitting such pulsating power. "The Blood of God."

It caught her by surprise how even the vampire held the contents of the bottle in such esteemed respect. "God, it seems," she continued. "Has not lost hope in the lost souls of His world. He is presenting…a second chance."

"A cure?" Alexandrea gasped.

"An absolution."

Gideon pulled his attention away from the bottle itself and returned it to the witch whose hand it rested within. "Explain."

"Your soul, Mr. Duquesne." Salem said with a tilt to her head. "The restoration of your soul."

Walking to the edge of the bridge rail, Gideon looked out into the night. His first instinct was to laugh, for what did he care about a soul after so many centuries? Yet, he didn't laugh. He contemplated. He'd lived without it so long he struggled to remember what it had been like to have. Sensing the risk in his being so far removed from his soul that her offer would be meaningless, Salem appealed to his wife. "Mrs. Duquesne, you were human not long ago. Don't you miss it? Don't you miss compassion? Goodness? Being a human being?"

"My humanity was consumed by other humans only out to use me, imprison me. Gideon has been the only person to ever show me love."

Well, that was a terrible idea, Salem told herself. Hoping to salvage the moment, she replied, "Not all humans are as corrupt as the D'Angelo family."

Gideon gave Salem his answer, "I see no compelling reason to regress the advantages my current situation provides."

"I find that hard to believe," Salem remarked. "It seems to me your kind lives in perpetual fear of discovery. Of vanquishment. And after vanquishment...damnation. I can release you from that damnation. There is also the possibility of restitution. Centuries ago, the name Duquesne carried importance. It is a dead name now. No one carries your lineage. With your humanity restored, Gideon, you will exist again. The Duquesne name can come back into greatness." She looked at Alexandrea, then back to Gideon. "You could have children."

If nothing else garnered a reaction of hope, this statement did. "Children?"

"You left your human life at what? Age 40? 45? You'd still be 45 Mr. Duquesne. Time to replenish the family line. Time to make the name Duquesne into what it once was before the D'Angelo's erased it from history." She took a chance. Removing the cork stopper from the bottle, Salem signaled for the vampires to step forward if they were willing. Alexandrea looked to her immortal husband for a sign. His nod was barely perceivable, but it was enough. She took his hand, and they stepped forward towards Salem's outstretched hand, together. With their heads tilted back and mouths open, Salem dispensed one tiny drop from the vial into each of their throats, then she stepped back from them. Gideon's face looked frightened—an experience he had not felt in centuries. He felt the foreign substance coursing through his system. He felt sick. He felt physical pain. Yet pride was strong within him. He grasped his wife's hand and fled through the park. Salem understood it would be rude to follow. Redemption, for some, is a very private moment. Gideon did not wish to have she or anyone witness his journey back to the light.

Stumbling through the streets of the RiNo Arts District, Gideon and Alexandrea Duquesne felt clumsy and unsure in their footing. Not drunk, but not at all stable. They'd departed Salem on the bridge without a word. Unable to form any words as the sudden rush of heated electricity swarmed beneath their flesh. It could only be described in their minds as long dead wiring coming to life again although neither had the ability to vocalize anything to one another. Passersby assumed they were drunk. Turning a corner into a small alley, Gideon grasped the side of a trash receptacle to steady himself before steadying his wife. Alexandrea stared into her husband's face to see elation. Life. An almost rebirthing of something long dead and discarded. His soul was returning. As was her own. She, being less removed from her soul, acquired it more quickly than he. She recognized the sensation. A sensation in her living life she was so accustomed to that she never found herself aware of its existence until now when it was returning. But in Gideon's eyes, she could see the magical swelling of remembrance as his light pushed through every second of darkness from the last few hundred years. When it was over, he stood tall and proud, almost younger. She was about to speak when a sudden burst of the brightest light either ever witnessed appeared and swelled into a figure.

The woman was brilliant. Golden. The most glorious vision they could have ever imagined.

"Welcome back to God's arms," the woman said, her voice almost echoing through the alley. "I am Beryl. And you have accepted Salvation. Do not squander the greatest gift ever bestowed."

They fell to their knees. They did not know why except that it felt right to do so in such a presence. Beryl lifted them gently by the hands back to standing positions.

"Do not bow for me. I am not worthy. I am not the one who saved you. I am only a miniscule fragment of Him. Use your redemption well. Do not dishonor His forgiveness."

The woman faded away as quickly as she'd appeared. Gideon looked upon his wife with a splendorous smile—a joy she'd never seen in him before.

"Alexandrea my love! I feel...clean. I feel...."

"Saved."

Gideon Duquesne had not seen a sunrise in nearly 300 years. Sitting perched upon his two legs, arms wrapped around his knees, watching the sunrise spill forth over the mountain tops of Silver Thorne, he was overwhelmed by the breathtaking beauty. A beauty his memory did not do justice to. Whereas Alexandrea was too new to the world of darkness to have forgotten light, Gideon felt like a newborn seeing something exhilarating for the very first time. Nothing compared. He clasped his wife's hand and squeezed.

"I had forgotten the majesty humans take for granted."

She smiled his way and laid her head upon his shoulder. "I feel alive again."

"Is that what this feeling is, my love?" he asked. "This is what it feels like to be alive."

CHAPTER THIRTEEN

Keep the Home Fires Burning

Mara Rappaport did not like the way her neighbor Jennifer stared at Brandon every day as he came home from work. Jennifer was a college student renting the garage apartment of the historic home across the street. She was very pretty. Blonde, bubbly, and the type who only felt seen when through a man's eyes. Sometimes Mara hid herself behind the curtains to see what ploys young miss bouncy breasts would put into motion to attract his attention when he'd come home from work. She always managed to be outside when Brandon came home as if she'd memorized his schedule. Wearing her overly snug clothing, the girl would toss her hand up and wave, shouting a cheery hello across the road. Brandon would return the greeting but hurry inside. On occasion she'd get desperate and ask him to bring in a heavy package from her porch or check to see why her engine light was on. Brandon always obliged politely yet kept a respectable distance of unfamiliarity which Mara appreciated. Mara never brought up her disdain for their neighbor to Brandon for worry he might feel she distrusted him. She didn't want that. She knew he was faithful. He'd never dare not be. And mentioning little things like this always seemed to make him nervous and ill at ease at home. The problem was Jennifer, not Brandon. But Mara Rappaport knew how to handle situations like slutty Jennifer.

As the fire trucks were spraying their last remaining droplets onto the smoldering embers of the garage structure, and likewise the apartment Jennifer rented, the crowd on the sidewalks were finally dispersing. The show was over. The structure was nothing but a charred outline of a building now. The blanket of smoke which had covered the street earlier was lifting now. Mara watched from her porch as an unfamiliar car rolled through the thinning haze to park along the sidewalk a block away, clear of the fire trucks. Mara noticed at once from the driver's long auburn hair that it was Salem Blanchard again. *My, two visits in one week*, Mara thought.

Mara met Salem at the bottom steps leading up to Mara's house. "Well, hello again."

Salem looked back to the smoke circling into the air from the smoldering timbers and stone. "Seems like you just had quite the excitement on the street. I hope no one was hurt."

"The girl who lives there died; I heard one of the firemen say." Mara replied with a disturbing lack of emotion. "Must have been horrible for her. Care to come inside where the scent of burned wood isn't so jarring?"

Mara led Salem into the parlor where they took a seat on the ornate period sofa befitting the old Charlestonian house. Salem greeted Ashby who was sitting in the window, still watching the show outside.

"Terrible to have that happen." Salem said to the child.

"Fires are very common in old houses. Wiring. Although that wasn't the cause here." Ashby said with even less emotion than her sister had displayed.

"What brings you back to see me?" Mara asked her unexpected guest. "Did my mother and her new husband give you trouble?"

"Not at all." Salem informed her. "They were rather amenable to my plan. I am grateful for your help with the matter." Salem paused to reconsider her decision to share more with Mara, but decided to do it, thinking it would be alright. "I wanted to let you know, in case you see your mother again, Alexandrea and Gideon are human once more."

Standing from the sofa in disbelief, Mara looked astonishingly at her guest. "How is that possible?"

Smiling apologetically, Salem answered. "Unfortunately, that is the only part of the story I am not yet at liberty to share. However, trust me when I tell you they are no longer vampires. They are no longer a danger to you or your sister."

"This is astounding," Mara gasped. "I am completely bewildered."

Nodding in agreement, Salem said, "It is a great deal to acclimate to. But I felt you deserved to know. But I am also here for another reason."

"I'm listening," Mara said, still processing Salem's last bit of information.

Salem explained how, as Queen, she plans to transition the Consort towards the future with more logical and modern infrastructure. One of the ways to achieve this was going to be the disbanding of the antiquated Council and the creation of a brand new one with more liberal and forward-thinking Council members.

Mara's face widened in surprise, "Are you asking me to sit on this new board?"

Salem blushed slightly, "No, not you. I'm sorry. Not that you aren't perfectly capable." Salem's eyes turned to the window. To Ashby. "I want your sister."

Mara was beyond surprised. "Ashby! But she's only 15 years old."

Ashby withdrew herself from the goings on outside and directed her attention to the conversation happening a few yards away. "I will be 16 soon."

"Why would you possibly want such a young witch?" Mara gasped. "And...she's my sister so I love her, but Ashby isn't like other people."

Salem folded her hands together as she leaned back in the chair. "That is the very reason I believe we need her. Your sister, although young, speaks only the truth. From everything I have heard about her from Arielle and Echo, she is incapable of lying. Also, Ashby has the keenest intuition I have ever run across. I've looked at Council reports on her abilities and her school records. The notations from teachers..."

"Which is why we had to pull her out of traditional school," Mara pointed out. "She did not win much popularity with peers."

"Because she speaks what she sees," Salem said. "She speaks from a deep sense of realism. Ashby's omniscient abilities and lack of filter in her comments will be invaluable to me in this new Consort."

Ashby took a seat on the sofa, nearest Salem's chair. With her own hands delicately folded in her lap, the young witch said, "You want me to be a detector of lies for you. You want me to use the knowledge in my brain to scan other people's motivations, and if any exist, their true intentions."

"I do," Salem told her. "I need someone I can trust who is capable of seeing through..." she couldn't find the right word.

Ashby did. "The bullshit."

Laughing at her candor, Salem replied. "Yes. The bullshit. Deceit, selfish intent, subterfuge. All of it."

"And what of the occasions where I believe you are incorrect in your thinking? If I suspect you of having less than altruistic intentions?"

Looking the girl directly in the eyes, Salem admitted, "Then I want you to tell me so. Ashby, power corrupts. It always has. I believe I am above that. But if for some reason even I stray from the greater good, I need you, Ashby, to tell me when I am wrong."

Mara, being very protective of her sister, wasn't sold on the idea of allowing Ashby to hold such a responsibility. She explained her hesitancy to Salem, citing the need to think it over a while.

Ashby, requiring no time to consider the matter, displayed a sign of her growing adulthood by telling Queen Salem, "I accept the post. I will serve on your new Council."

Brandon Rappaport heard the news of the fire at his office. A sudden panic swept him—a panic which both frightened and bewildered him. He found himself dashing out the office door to his car to get home as fast as he could. While he dipped in and out of slow-moving lanes, speeding home as swiftly as possible amid the heavy traffic, he found himself questioning his motivations. He was rushing home to see if it was his house that had burned down, but why? What was the outcome he secretly hoped for? The reporters on the news were kept at a distance while the fire department worked to control the blaze. No one was one hundred percent certain which house on the block perished. Brandon asked himself the terrible question, *Am I hoping Mara is dead? Am I hoping to be free?*

He brought his car to a stop a block away, fleeing the vehicle without even closing his door. His footfalls along the sidewalk were hard and powerful, increasing speed as he drew closer and closer. Then he saw his house. It was still standing. Suddenly he felt his heart flutter with a sensation surprising to even him. Relief. Happiness. Mara was not dead, and Brandon was glad. He raced to his front door, calling her name as he pulled it open. Mara was coming down the stairs as he entered. She saw his flushed face and frantic expression. He didn't give her time to come the rest of the way down the stairs. He lifted her into his arms and accosted her neck, face and lips with his kisses.

"You're okay! You're okay!"

She was dumbfounded. Ecstatically so. This man thought she might be dead, and the thought had elicited fear within him. As he gripped her tightly in his arms, she began to cry. Mara had dreamed of this day all the while fearing it may never come. Brandon did love her. He truly did love her. She wrapped her arms around his neck and pushed her body into his as if trying to merge into him.

"Mara, I was so scared. Thank God you are okay."

He half carried her downstairs to the parlor and fell onto the sofa with her whereupon he pulled her as close to himself as possible. He could not stop kissing her face. "If I lost you…"

"I'm fine my darling," she smiled. "I am fine. Ashby is fine. Oh, my love, thank you for being concerned. Thank you for loving me."

"I do love you, Mara. So much. I guess I didn't know how much till I got out of the car."

Brandon regained his composure and eventually let Mara have some breathing room. He walked outside to the porch and looked over to the charred garage across the street. It was then it hit him, *that was where that flirty girl lived*. Mara joined him, placing his evening cocktail in his hand. He took the drink and felt her lean her head onto the side of his shoulder.

"How did it happen?"

Mara shrugged. "Things just happen sometimes I suppose."

Brandon realized there was not an ounce of empathy for the poor girl who died in that roaring blaze. She didn't care at all. Mara's indifference told him all he needed to know that she caused the fire. Mara had caused that poor girl's tragic death. The realization sent shivers down his spine. Yet somehow it changed nothing for him. Still, he loved her. He was beginning to understand her. Mara was like a child. Needy. Territorial. No sense of right and wrong. Brandon Rapport fully grasped at that moment he was in love with a psychopath, and he was growing used to it. She was a wonderfully loving wife, but she was terribly damaged. Perhaps it stemmed from her childhood. Perhaps she was born this way. Maybe being as powerful as she was, she held no sense of right or wrong because she could do almost anything. He didn't know what had made her this way. He only knew he was becoming used to it—maybe even drawn to it. This woman, who could manifest anything she wanted either through her enormous wealth or her witchcraft, couldn't acquire a conscience. But maybe that was what Brandon provided. And being able to supply that missing component in her life made him feel connected to her—and protective of her. Whatever she did was no more her fault than if a child broke a vase trying to reach a toy beside it. Mara was only a child.

CHAPTER FOURTEEN

Christmas Eve, North and South

The flickering firelight in the background was a nice addition to the festive and cozy feel of the room. One never knows what Alabama weather will supply for Christmas Eve. The early cold front which would normally be something to complain about was giving the holiday an authentic feel. The Christmas tree in the window was glowing with colorful lights and the tinsel dangling from the branches reflected the orange tones from the fireplace. Everyone was home and the house was at capacity. The children were upstairs in the den watching a Christmas movie while the adults were gathered downstairs listening to the traditional melodies of Bing Crosby, Andy Williams, and Nat King Cole drift over crackling fire.

"This eggnog is delicious," Arielle said complimenting Miranda's bartending skills.

"Give me that!" Salem snapped, snatching the mug away. "You are pregnant! No alcohol."

Lifting it from Salem's hand into her own, Fable quipped, "Yes, leave the drinking to the professionals. You are a messy drunk anyway, Arielle. Remember Yazzy's wedding shower?"

It went unnoticed to all but perhaps Demitra, that this was the first time anyone had reflected on the past without mourning for it. Yasmine was lost to them now, but it was nice to remember the good times and not have to associate it with the present. Miles, unaware he was helping to direct thoughts away from lost loved ones, said, "This time next year, I will have Salem and Olympus with me in New York for my family's Christmas."

"You will?" Salem remarked from her resting place on his shoulder.

"Yes," he went on. "It is only fair. One year we will do Thanksgiving here and Christmas there, and the next year we will do Thanksgiving there and Christmas here."

"If I were you, I'd skip Thanksgiving here altogether." Trix cajoled. "Those never work out too well around here."

Ignoring the remark, Salem said, "I must admit, I would love to see the Thanksgiving Day parade in New York."

"Spoken by a person who has never been to it," Miles laughed. "It is awful. Crowds everywhere, streets blocked so that you are trapped for hours, unable to leave. No, trust me. It is far more enjoyable on television. But Christmas Eve in New York is magic. Hundreds gather in Washington Square Park to carol together by the arch. Skating in Bryant Park. 5th Avenue all lit up. The Rockettes at Radio City. And the tree at Rockefeller Center is something. But I prefer to see it Christmas morning. There aren't as many people around but everyone who is there is filled with spirit and friendliness."

"It sounds great." Salem smiled.

Ocean gripped Arielle tightly in his lap from the corner chair by the fire. "We will have our two rugrats this time next year. I can't wait. I want to do just what my dad did every year." Jerry, Demitra, and Trix exchanged knowing eyes as Ocean explained. "Every Christmas Eve Dad would put on his Santa suit and walk past our bedrooms dragging a big black sack." Ocean's eyes lit up as he recalled his childhood. "Forest and I both waited on it every year. We didn't know it wasn't the real Santa of course, but he always made so much noise coming down the hall headed towards the living room. We'd crack our doors open and spy on him going by. Now neither of us ever questioned why he came down the hall when the fireplace was already in the living room. We were teens before that obvious revelation occurred to us."

Sage grinned, sitting up and tapping his sister's shoulder. "Sis, you remember. Our dad did that too."

Sydney giggled, "You still don't know, do you? Don't you remember that time we saw Dad talking with Santa in the driveway? That wasn't our father in the suit. Uncle Seneca came to our house after Ocean and Forest went to sleep."

"That was Uncle Seneca!" Sage cried. "I never knew that."

Jerry stood up from the sofa and stretched his arms out. "Speaking of Santa Claus, I have a doll house to finish assembling, two bikes to wrap bows on, and an electric Jeep to plug in to charge."

"Who is the Jeep for?" Miranda asked. "Not Titan?"

"Of course, Titan!" Jerry exclaimed. "Who else? Con and Rom are too big for that."

"Do you think Titan will ride in it?"

"He rides on Romulus," Jerry replied. "Or used to, before Rom stopped using his wolf form. So why not a vehicle of his own." Jerry disappeared to the kitchen, popping his head back in to shout, "Come on Echo! You said you'd help."

Compliantly, Echo stood up with exaggerated reluctance. "Why do I always have to help Granddad?"

"Because you're the boy," Trix smiled.

"Yeah, but I'm the gay boy. I don't want to put bikes together."

"Maybe he'll let you paint the doll house," Salem laughed, giving her cousin a playful wink.

Within moments they heard the creak of the kitchen stairs rising from the mechanical hinge system which opened the secret room down below.

"Are they going into the vault?" Trix asked.

Demitra nodded, having another sip of eggnog. "That's where Jerry stashed the kids' Christmas presents."

"Does Hera ever play with dolls?" Fable commented. "She's a little too old for that."

Her mother waved her hand in the air, "Lord, don't tell him that. He bought the biggest doll house you've ever seen complete with dolls and furniture."

"You know she's just going to blow it up." Trix said.

"Either way, she'll love it." Miranda smiled. "I got her a boomerang, archery kit and ten 3D puzzles to keep her busy while you are all in Charleston."

"What do you mean?" Arielle asked. "Isn't she coming to the wedding? And more to the point, aren't you?"

Miranda shook her head apologetically. "Arielle, I don't think you need a bunch of children running around your house in the middle of wedding events. I'll stay here with the children."

Disappointed at the news, Arielle frowned, "But Miranda, I want you to be there. You are my sister-in-law after all."

"I know, Ari, I'm sorry. But think about it. Lucky and Jinx are far too young to make the trip. I doubt any of us would feel very safe 10,000 feet in the air with Jinx on the plane. Trix and Echo are your siblings. They must be there. I will stay home with the kids, and you go have a beautiful wedding. You know I love you. But really, I am better here with the children than us all there with them."

Demitra let out a sigh. "You know, I never even considered all of that. It is generous of you Miranda. Thank you."

"Still, we are talking about a lot of children." Salem said. "Miranda, even you shouldn't have to deal with all these kids on your own. I'm taking Olympus with us, but that still leaves you with two babies and four kids."

"It's fine." Miranda assured them. "Vanessa is planning to stay here while you are all gone, and she will help. Also, Skillet said he would be over some to help keep the children entertained and Rosamund can't leave the restaurant on New Year's Eve so she said she would stay over at night and help out. I have it all covered."

"Howard is giving me away," Arielle reminded them. "He's still coming, isn't he?"

"Yes," Demitra said, calming the nervous bride to be. "Howard wouldn't miss your wedding for the world. You can ask him yourself in the morning. Now, I am going to bed. You parents need to hang some stockings and put your presents out."

"You aren't helping?" Fable asked.

"My darling daughter," I am now nearing 60 years old. I have done my tour of duty. I pass the torch to the younger generation."

Christmas morning was a frenzy of activity from the moment the sun came up over the house, sending its light into the children's windows like a pesky alarm clock. Con was the first out of bed, stampeding down the hall to wake his brother and cousin. Hera dashed into her brother's room, dragging Titan from his slumber and down the stairs with her. Behind the hurricane of squealing children shuffled the sleep deprived adults, messy haired, and slovenly dressed, mustering their faux bliss as they stumbled down the three flights of stairs to the living room. By the time they entered, each was successfully wearing their holiday face of smiles and forced joy at watching the little ones as they tore through wrapping paper. By the time coffee was ready and the muffins premade the day before were reheated in the oven, the kids had uncovered the fully bounty of their loot and hauled their treasures to their rooms, except for the dollhouse which Jerry and Echo carried up for Hera.

Howard and Rosamund timed their arrival well, just missing the chaos and the cleanup. As they sat down to visit the family and exchange adult gifts, the older Blanchards were on their third cups of energy. Howard made sure Arielle knew he was not missing her wedding, which pleased her to hear. Sage and Sydney each received phone calls from their mother, however brief, to wish them a Merry Christmas. Celia Blanchard informed her children she would see them in Charleston at the wedding, as she would be accompanying their aunt Stella. Perhaps being Christmas, their immediate dread of knowing they would have to be around their mother in person in a few days was doused with a little bit of hopefulness that they may enjoy seeing her again after almost two years.

Vanessa and Theda arrived midafternoon to join the family for Christmas dinner. Vanessa had overdone herself on presents for her newfound daughter and what she did not splurge on, Demitra had. Theda was very well represented by Santa's generosity this year. The children had their dinner upstairs in the den while the adults gathered around the dining room table, all ignoring the shared tension in the air, still not completely cleared of the memory of Thanksgiving. However, by the time dessert was passed around, everyone had relaxed with the knowledge that no time traveling assassins, or house-engulfing flames were coming to tarnish this holiday.

As the guests went home and the Blanchards were readying themselves to retire for the evening, Arielle got a text which seemed to please her. When she read it to the family, more than a few were surprised. "You invited, Daphanie Channing to the wedding?" Trix questioned.

Arielle's cheerily bright face gave an excited nod as she answered. "Yes, and she has agreed to come!"

"Why would you invite her of all people?" Sage asked.

"Why not?" Arielle replied. "I think we all sort of bonded after Thanksgiving. Besides, if Salem and she are going to out all witching kind to the public in a month, then she should see what we are about in good times and bad. Why not have her to Oleander and see two witches get married?"

None of the others appeared to share Arielle's elation, except for Salem and Demitra. Salem thought it was a spectacular idea and Demitra took the last word on the matter by saying, "I like Daphanie. I believe she might become a cherished friend to this family. I for one, am happy to see her again."

The ice skaters at Rockefeller Center had begun dwindling out as the night chill of the city blew down the avenues sending the natives angling for the streets while the tourists shivered in place. New Yorkers knew the buildings lining the streets, held back the winds blowing from the river while the avenues offered them a channel to gain speed. Seth, Yasmine and Bianca were immune to such temperament. They stood below the iconic dazzling tree, blending in with the others around, only they were not captivated by the lights. They were biding time to feed.

"It's thinning out a little more," Bianca observed. "In a few minutes I think we will be safe to have dinner."

Yasmine smiled devilishly, "I'm starving. I haven't fed in weeks. I think the vampire blood you fed me has increased my appetite."

"Who was the vampire you killed and drained for us, Bianca?" Seth asked, wondering why he hadn't thought to before.

"He was no one of importance," Bianca revealed. "Someone I passed on the street not long ago and recognized by scent was one of us. He was too new to do the same, so when I found him again, he was unprepared for my attack."

"Oh," Seth replied. "I guess I assumed you turned someone, then drained them."

Shaking her head Bianca explained, "Had Yasmine not been as bad off as she was, that might have been sufficient. However, I am afraid her injuries required more seasoned blood than a freshly made subject could provide."

"I am in your debt, my friend." Yasmine said thankfully.

Laughing a little as she turned back to notice the crowd decreasing even more, Bianca answered, "I am afraid you are in Thaddeuss' debt, not mine. And he will collect in a big fashion."

"When do we start for Alabama?" Seth asked.

"Thaddeuss says tomorrow. He has acquired something he called a motorhome to transport us. He has even hired a driver. He says we will be quite safe inside."

Seth gripped the railing of the rink. The fluttering flags mounted on poles surrounding them flapped loudly overhead. "I don't see why we must go so soon. Yaz needs more time to gain her strength."

"Yasmine is fine," Bianca stated. "After she feeds tonight, she should be back to normal. Besides, it must be now. Thaddeuss says the family are all leaving for Wadmalaw Island back home in Charleston. The house will be vulnerable, and the baby will be unguarded."

"How can he possibly know that?"

"Thaddeuss D'Angelo is still well connected in many ways. Nothing happens on Wadmalaw without his knowledge, even still. It seems your sister Arielle is getting married at her home on Wadmalaw. The family are all attending. Flights have been scheduled for everyone, except the children. No doubt they will be left behind with a governess I presume. It is the perfect time to strike and collect Thaddeuss' child."

"I still do not understand his obsession with a little baby. He isn't the paternal type."

Bianca laughed loudly, drawing attention from the few people left standing around. "You don't know. I had not realized that." Bianca leaned her back against the railing and looked up to the stars above. "That baby is very special indeed. It has the God Strain flowing in its veins. If Thaddeuss can possess that child, he will grow up to not only still remain Thaddeuss, and retain all of his amassed powers, he will also have a little of the Power of God. Imagine what he can do with that! None of us ever need fear anything ever again. We will have a god on our side."

Yasmine joined them at the railing where she stood overlooking the small skating rink. Four skaters remained, possibly completing their last rotations before going home. "I am so hungry," she said. "I think it's safe now. I'm going to try."

Yasmine stepped away from the rail, positioning herself more center of the plaza, thrusting her hands high above her head, she blasted out her power. The few dozen people still meandering around enjoying the final hours of Christmas night, stopped in their tracks. The passing cars on the street stopped in place as if they were merely snapshots of traffic. Everything and everyone within range had been paused in time. Of course, her range was not widespread, its perimeters only reaching a block or more, but it was enough.

Before Seth had finished looking out at the frozen public before him, Bianca had already pounced below and eviscerated the skaters. The soft whitish blue of the ice was now streaked with whatever blood she'd left in their bodies which was now flowing out onto the ice. Seth grabbed the woman nearest him and fed from her arm, draining her completely dry before dropping her to the cold, dirty, gum scarred concrete below. Yasmine had viciously gone after the youngest prey. Six bodies of children lay at the feet of their immobilized parents, their brightly colored scarves stained with dark seeping blood. Returning to the plaza from the skating rink, Bianca saw the carnage of children. "Wouldn't two adults have provided the same nourishment?"

Smiling with her blood-stained lips, Yasmine's black eyes danced as she explained, "I felt their joy from this morning when they opened their presents! It was jubilant!"

In a murmured voice, Bianca nudged Seth and said, "She is a little more vicious than any of our kind I have ever known."

"I am aware." Seth responded somewhat apologetically. He was very aware of his wife's tendencies. Although humans were only a source of life for them, Seth did not take as much pleasure in their demise. His wife, however, often tortured and tormented her prey. He had determined not long ago this must be due to her having damaged her soul well before she had become a vampire. It wasn't easy for him to recall much about their life before, but he seemed to remember her having somehow been propelled back in time once where she had been in close proximity to herself at a younger age. Their souls each vying for dominance as two of the same souls cannot survive in the same place and time. He'd managed to rescue her before Yasmine perished, but the event had compromised her somehow. It was the only explanation he had for why her vampire nature was so much more unstable than his.

CHAPTER FIFTEEN

A Change of Plans

The house was a bustle of packing and preparing for their flight out in the morning. Demitra stood contemplating which of her three new choices should be the dress she wore to the wedding. Rosamund sat on the bed inspecting each garment with almost the same intensity. "I like the soft yellow best," she offered her friend. "It is subdued but elegant. Your hair will look stunning with it."

"Really?" Demitra questioned. "I never really liked how I looked in yellow, but the dress was too gorgeous not to buy. And where else will I ever wear it if not to this? But I still like the plum colored one. I like the cut of it and it'll bring out my eyes."

"Your lavender eyes are out no matter what you wear," Roz teased. "I say yellow."

"I still think plum."

"Okay," Rosamund said, tossing the green one over to the chair in the corner. "The green is definitely out then."

A knock at the door interrupted the deliberations, Echo poked his head inside. "GG, are you still not packed?"

"I don't know which dress I should wear for the wedding. For all intents and purposes, I am the closest thing to mother-of-the bride Arielle has."

"Well, decide there. Just pack them all. But I hate the yellow one. That green over there is beautiful. I say green."

Rosamund got up from the bed and started towards the door, "You are not helping Echo. What do you want?"

"Oh, yeah," he said absentmindedly. "Granddad and Fable need you downstairs."

Demitra made her way downstairs, leaving Rosamund alone in her room. Rosmund took the opportunity to finish the packing, leaving out the green dress entirely. As Demitra came into the living room she found grim faces. "What?" she said, dreading the answer.

"We can't go to Charleston." Fable announced.

"We who?" her mother asked. "We all of us?"

"No," Fable clarified, pointing toward herself and Jerry. "We, us."

Demitra caught her husband's eye and exasperatingly asked for an explanation. "I don't know why it never occurred to any of us to check," he began. "But New Year's Eve has a full moon."

"What?" Demitra gasped, the gravity now dawning on her.

"Mom, there is no way I can leave Miranda here to handle Con. I have to stay behind to make sure he, and everyone else are safe."

"And I can't let Fable do this alone," Jerry added. "This is all still new to the boy and Con is accustomed to me staying outside his enclosure all night with him. He needs me here. And Fable needs me here too, even though she keeps saying she doesn't."

"You shouldn't miss the wedding because of Con."

"Con is my grandson," Jerry said aggravatedly. "And you are my daughter. I love Arielle and would be there if I could, but my place is here. Demitra, I am sorry, but I won't leave them on a full moon."

Demitra walked to her husband and placed both arms around his neck. "Have I told you lately how immensely proud I am that you are my husband?"

Blushing, Jerry replied, "Not since this morning."

"I love you very much, Jerry Miller. Thank you."

Although it was meant to be a goodbye lunch to end the old year before they saw one another again in the new one, Nash was very pleased to hear from Fable that she was not planning on leaving town after all. "Kid has the flu," she lied. "What can you do but wait it out? So I will be home with my son New Year's Eve."

"Well, I have had my flu vaccination so maybe I can join you?"

From her face he could tell she wasn't keen on the idea. "Probably not a good idea." She replied. "It's the gross vomit kind of flu. Besides, I'll be helping with the other kids since I'm staying home. I'd rather you keep thinking of me as a sexy goddess for a while before you see me as exhausted, spit up wiping Mom."

"I never said I thought of you as a goddess."

"I believe it was implied," she retorted, tossing her hair jokingly. "But maybe New Year's Day we can get together at your house and watch football?"

"Somehow I don't think we'd be watching much football if you came over to my house."

"Good." Fable said. "I hate football."

CHAPTER SIXTEEN

Sins of the Mother

Despite the Winter weather, every part of Oleander was robust with florals from the front gate to the circular drive. The entire lane was lined with mounds of potted pink and white poinsettias, arranged so densely they appeared to be wild. Protruding from these tender pink and white petals at an even pace were tall rose topiaries, each with a lollipop shaped head covered in alternating green, yellow, and light orange toned roses that appeared to be fresh and dewy. As the Blanchard caravan arrived from the airport everyone was breathtaken by the splendor. The front balcony on the second floor was strewn column to column with garland of Carolina Sapphire and Magnolia, thick as a ship's rope. These garlands were carefully dotted with bursts of colorful flowers sticking out in every direction, looking wild and natural. Arielle and Ocean met the family at the door, helping them in with their luggage which was passed off to staff to place in their appointed bedrooms. The banister of the staircase was draped in a cascading waterfall of pale colored roses of yellow, tangerine, and soft green mixed with giant heads of antique green hydrangeas, silver bell Eucalyptus, and Carolina Sapphire. The fragrance was overwhelming in the most pleasing way. The stately home had never looked so beautiful and welcoming as it did on this day. It was a perfect analogy for the life and light Arielle had brought back to this once great home, after too many years of darkness in its hallways.

Salem and Echo stood in amazement at the transformation the wedding designers had created, both being the only two who'd been to Oleander multiple times. Echo noticed someone moving around in the parlor off the main foyer. The muscular build of the man was what initially caught his eye. Involuntarily moving into the room, he saw the man bent over putting last minute touches into an arrangement on the coffee table. Echo hadn't realized he was leaning in now arm above his head against the doorframe, admiring the man's craft...and posterior. Arielle broke him from his stare with a tap on the shoulder.

"Echo, I'd like you to meet Clarke, my floral designer. Clarke this is my brother."

As the man turned around to see he had an audience, Echo was blushing while his sister was suppressing a laugh. "Hi," Clarke smiled, his deep brown eyes caught the light coming in from the window making him appear even more mysterious and sexy. Arielle stepped back into the foyer to her other arrivals, leaving Echo struggling for words.

"You're Arielle's brother?" Clarke said, reaching out to shake his hand.

"Yeah," Echo stammered. "Yeah, just got in." Searching for anything to say to this complete stranger, Echo said, "Beautiful. I mean your work. This place looks incredible."

"Thank you, I appreciate that."

"You work alone?" Echo asked. "Single? I mean, are you alone? Meaning, did you do this all by yourself?"

Trying not to laugh at the fumbling idiot, the designer replied, "No, I have helpers for the installation. Tomorrow, before the guests arrive for the wedding, I'll be back with my husband to touch up anything that may need sprucing."

Echo's chest, which he realized he'd been holding high and out, relaxed a little as he replied, "Husband. Oh. You are together. Work together, I mean."

Collecting his bucket of floral trimmings from the floor, Clarke, the floral designer, made his exit, pausing in the doorway to offer Echo a friendly pat on the shoulder before saying, "Yes. We are together. Though I appreciate the interest."

Echo was not even sure why he was talking at all to this man or continuing to keep it going when he asked, "So this husband of yours?"

Clarke grinned again and answered the unasked question, "For years. Fully satisfied. And he'd kill you if you tried."

Left alone still hugging the doorway, Echo felt like kicking himself for making such a fool of himself. He had Knox at home and Knox was a dream! Still, there had been no talk of commitment yet, so Echo wasn't in the wrong to seek other entertainments. But still, he felt a little slimy about it.

The mild weather in Charleston kept the necessity for heavy coats at bay. Salem was able to dress Olympus in a light onesie before taking him outside onto the grounds. Miles wasn't certain at first where they were going but once he saw the headstone with the fresh flowers atop the grave, he understood.

"I never bring flowers." Salem said, looking down at the small grave. "Never any need. Arielle has never failed to keep his grave up."

Miles placed his steady hand on her back and caressed it gently. "This is your son?"

"Yes," Salem answered. "This is Michael." As if only now remembering Olympus in her arms, she diverted her attention to him and with it, a change in her tone as she spoke to her living child. "Olympus Blanchard, this is where your big brother sleeps. His name was Michael Lane. Or does it make you the big brother now? You are older than Michael ever got to be."

Miles' hand moved quickly to her shoulder, gripping tightly as if to supply her with his own strength. Salem passed Olympus off to him and kneeled on the grave. "Michael, I just wanted to say hello, as I always do when I am here. And I really wanted you to meet your brother. I promise I will be back again before I return home. I love you baby boy."

Miles continued holding Olympus with one arm and took hold of his fiancée's hand with the other. "The things you have suffered, Salem. No one else could withstand it all. I admire you very much. I love you very much."

For it to be the day before her wedding, Arielle was not nervous in the least. She seemed to be enjoying playing hostess to her loved ones so much that the wedding seemed secondary. She'd planned an enormous dinner for everyone that evening and the caterers were preparing it as the Blanchards came down for pre-dinner drinks. The mood was no different from any other night they'd spent together at Blanchard House despite the more opulent surroundings. "I really hated Fable and Jerry couldn't make it," Ocean was telling Demitra. "Arielle wanted to switch the wedding to Blanchard House so they could be there, but I told her I doubted sounds of a caged howling wolf would make for a proper wedding backdrop."

"I agree," Demitra said. "But you know they send their love."

"Well while we are all here together," Howard said, rising and clearing his throat, "As the acting father-of-the bride I feel like making a toast."

Arielle was delighted at the idea, quickly pouring herself a glass of wine, which Trix swiftly swiped from her, replacing it with a bottle of water from the bar. "No alcohol!"

Howard chuckled at his daughter's quickness and went on with his speech. "Arielle, you have been in this family ever since that fateful day when Salem sprung you on all of us." The few who had been there laughed. "You were such an innocent naive little thing." Arielle blushed. "Seems like such a long time ago. But from the moment you came into our lives, we all fell in love with your kindness, your understanding, and your ceaseless ability to see the positivity in nearly everything. No man could ever be good enough for you in my opinion," he glanced to Ocean. "But you have chosen the closest thing to good enough you possibly could have. We Blanchards welcomed you into the family a long time ago, but tomorrow you officially become one in name as well. And we all celebrate Arielle and Ocean tonight."

Voices rang out from the entry hall as the sound of heels clicking against the tile floor echoed against the high walls. Arielle's housekeeper escorted two women into the room as their luggage could be seen being hauled up the staircase in the background. "Mom!" Sage cried out, moving to greet her. "You finally made it."

"Yes, Stella and I took a wrong turn and had to backtrack a little, but we are finally here." Sage offered her an embrace, which she appeared to return earnestly. Over his shoulder Celia Blanchard spied her daughter Sydney across the room. "Sydney, dear, aren't you going to come say hello to me?"

"Just waiting my turn," Sydney replied, offering her own gesture of an embrace. Behind them, Stella Blanchard approached.

"Sorry, I was overwhelmed by this house. I got caught up looking around." Stella wedged past her niece and nephew with their mom and found Ocean coming to meet her. She gave him a warm smile and kiss on the cheek. Pulling Arielle towards him, Ocean smiled proudly making the introduction. "My new daughter-in-law," Stella smiled with some strain. "You are a lovely little thing, aren't you?"

Arielle, so happy to be aware of tone and inflection, took no notice of Stella's disdain for her. Perhaps no one did, except for Trix and Demitra...and most likely Ocean. Of course, no one had any idea Demitra, Trix, and Stella had met clandestinely recently. And they weren't about to tell anyone. "We were just toasting the happy couple," Demitra informed the late arrivals. Dinner is almost ready but perhaps you two would like a drink?"

"Allow me!" Howard said convivially, pouring two glasses of wine into crystal goblets which he delivered to their hands. "I am Howard," he told Celia as she took the glass from him. He likewise offered Stella a glass.

"Howard?" Stella repeated after he'd returned to his seat. "Yes. I am sure you are both confused by me. I know we have all met before somewhere through the years. I handled so much business for Olympia and Pastoria. But if you have any confusion as to how I suddenly became a Blanchard, it's probably too complicated to explain. But I am."

Howard talked nearly an hour on the phone with Rosamund as he readied himself for bed. The conversation was of nothing important. She went through her day, he went through his, they talked about a few news stories they'd heard, and she got his advice on advocating for a lower price from the restaurant's linen distributor. All the mundane back and forth between a settled and comfortable couple. She teased him for brushing his teeth while she was talking, and he let her know he knew she was applying a toning mask to her face while he talked. "How did you know that?" she laughed.

"Because your voice changes after it hardens. Your lips move slower, and your words are more pressed together because you can't flex your mouth. You forget I've been with you before when you put one on."

"Just trying to stay alluring to you."

"Well, stop it, because I can't possibly be more lured."

A knock came to his door. It was late and took him by surprise. He said goodnight to Rosamund and answered the door. Of all the people in the house it might have been, it was the least expected. "I must speak with you?"

Howard allowed her into his room and closed the door behind them. "Is there something I can do for you?"

She seemed upset, almost frantic. She quite informally took a seat on the edge of his bed, and she pressed her hands together and asked, "Are you Arielle's father?"

Again, another unexpected turn. "No, of course not! You misunderstood the situation. Arielle's father is dead. She used to work for me in my office as my assistant. We grew very close. I guess you could say she is *like a daughter* to me."

"But from what I understand, your children are her brother and sister."

Nodding his head, Howard admitted, "True. My daughter Trix and my son Echo are her half siblings. They shared the same mother. But Arielle is no relation to me other than by choice."

"So, there is no blood connection between you and this girl? She isn't a Blanchard, I mean."

Howard did not understand the line of questioning, nor why any of this was her business. "Mrs. Blanchard...Stella, what are you trying to ask me? How is Arielle's lineage so imperative for you to understand? She is a nice girl. A wonderful girl. Your son is lucky to have her."

"I need to make sure that *our son* is not marrying his sister."

CHAPTER SEVENTEEN

A Father's Pride

His bed sheets twisted, depicting the restless night's sleep. Howard awoke earlier than his alarm thanks to a call from Rosamund. "Hello," he answered groggily.

"Good, I woke you up!" Rosamund cried. "You haven't told anyone about Ocean yet, have you?"

Rubbing his eyes with his free hand, squinting at the wall clock to see the time, Howard answered. "No, not yet. It was so late last night when Stella and I finished our talk. I think it was 2am when I called you back. You are the only one I've told."

"Great," Rosamund replied. "I changed my mind about my advice last night. Don't tell anyone right now."

Now sitting on the edge of the bed with his feet planted on the floor, he was becoming more awake, and more aware. "Really?" Howard replied. "Not even Demitra?"

"Not anyone. Honey, it is their wedding day. If Ocean isn't even aware his father wasn't Seneca, don't spring that on him now. Not today."

Staring ahead at his suit hanging neatly on the back of the door, he argued. "But he is my son, Roz! Don't you think on a wedding day, of all days, a boy should know his father is with him?"

"His father is with him, in his heart." Rosamund insisted. "To Ocean, his father is looking down on him today with pride. Let him have that. Once they are settled into married life, then you can tell him who you are."

Howard much preferred her almost total support of his wishes the night before over this more logical, levelheaded Rosamund this morning. "I have missed almost everything with every child I have. All their childhoods. Everything. Now I have a son who is getting married today and I can't even tell him how proud I am."

The moment she clicked her tongue Howard understood he was wrong. He didn't yet know how he was wrong, but he was always wrong when that tongue clicked, and it didn't take long for her to explain why. "You are being selfish, Howard. I understand why and I don't think you are terrible at wanting it, but putting your children first is the main rule of parenting. Your son is happy today. And I fully expect him to accept you as his father when the proper time comes to tell him. But this isn't the day to rock his world. Be as proud as you want. Just keep it to yourself. Then after it's all over, call me back and gush ad nauseum over your eldest son's wedding!"

"You are right," he admitted. "As right as always. But I am bursting to tell someone. Can't I at least tell Demitra?"

Another click with the tongue. "Howard Caldwell, I am going to make a deal with you. If you keep your mouth shut and not divulge this secret to anyone until you get home, I will not interrogate you on how it is that you managed to have sex with a woman 30 years ago and not even be able to see her face now and recognize it. Or how you didn't even get her name back then. And I will also not ask you how many other women you have forgotten over the years. Do you accept these terms, or should I start writing all of my questions down on a notepad, so I do not forget any of them?"

"I accept your deal."

"Good. I love you. Enjoy the wedding."

Before last night Howard had already felt proud to be the man escorting Arielle down the aisle on her special day. She meant so much to him. But now...now everything was magnified. As the music carried from downstairs up to the floor above, Howard waited outside Arielle's door with butterflies in his stomach. He tapped lightly at one of the heavy oak panels. She opened the door looking more beautiful than he could remember her. Her full-length white gown fanned out along the sides, helping to distract from her baby bump. She wore no veil, simply a few white daisies meandering down her side swept braid. The flowers, against the crimson of her hair, gave her an ethereal look as if fairies had dressed her for the occasion.

"You ready?" he asked, smiling with pure happiness.

"I am," she smiled.

Howard helped Arielle down the stairs where the wedding planner fanned her dress out again, readying her for the walk. Howard led Arielle from the house, walking her slowly down the white carpeted path to the pavilion in the side garden, her arm entwined with his. Howard was not only overjoyed to be sharing this milestone moment in her life, but he was also getting the privilege of handing this magnificent woman over into marriage with his son. His son.

He saw Ocean up ahead, waiting, hands folded into the other, beaming from ear to ear as he witnessed his bride approaching on Howard's arm. The guests all stared at Arielle, and some went back and forth between her and Ocean, observing the shared joy between them as they looked upon each other. But Howard could look no other way but at his son, as if seeing Ocean Blanchard for the first time. He was such a handsome guy. High cheekbones, chiseled jawline. That hair Howard could have done without. Chin length, much too long for a guy his age, but at least he still had his hair, and it hadn't receded on him the way Howard's had. *And it is the same color as mine. Or the black mine used to be.* From the corner of his eye, Howard caught sight of Echo seated near the aisle. Same dark hair. *Like your brother,* Howard thought. *That is your brother down there about to get married.* Howard wished everyone knew what he knew. He wished they could share in this spectacular and wondrous craziness that so far only he knew.

Reaching the end of the procession, Howard placed Arielle's small hand into Ocean's, squeezing both with his own before letting go. He perhaps held them a moment longer than necessary, both bride and groom giving him a puzzled look before he released them. *I just held my son's hand on his wedding day. I held his and his wife's hands in my own.* Howard took a seat next to Demitra and looked stalwartly forward at the ceremony.

As Queen of the Consort, and the bride's sister, it was no surprise to anyone that Salem was performing the ceremony. She welcomed the guests and thanked them all for being there on this special day. From that point forward, Salem's attention was focused primarily on her sister.

"And this is a very special day, especially for me." Salem smiled with teary eyes at her sister. "Arielle and I did not grow up together. I met my little sister right after she finished high school. At the absolute worst point of my life, this bubbly, ridiculous, red-haired girl showed up on my doorstep and lifted me back into life. Arielle, you have been not merely a sister, you've been my best friend." Arielle wiped tears from her eyes listening to the beautiful words. "You came to me, a lonely, isolated girl. You made a place not only in my heart, but in the hearts of every member of my family...and quite interestingly, ended up related to several of them in your own right." Echo and Trix shared a little laugh as Arielle turned around, sending them a demure wave from the front. Salem continued, "You became one of us from the very start. All you've ever been missing is the name. And today, as you marry my cousin Ocean—who is truly the only man I could ever love and respect enough to hand my sister to—you will officially be a Blanchard, beginning your own little branch of the family tree. Arielle, my radiant, confident sister, I love you very much."

Salem began the exchanging of vows. As Arielle and Ocean made their promises to one another, Salem looked out over the guests, finding Miles smiling lovingly at her. They would be next, and she was looking forward to becoming his wife. Howard saw the exchange between them and the joy he was experiencing from seeing Arielle marry his son, sank into shame. He had almost let himself forget his entanglement with Taub D'Angelo. A life for a life. But Miles was still here. Still alive. Perhaps Taub decided not to go through with it. However, it had not been Taub's spell in which to renege. Howard had cast it. Taub's only role was delivering Yasmine's DNA sample, and the spell itself. Howard suddenly thought about the possibility that maybe he had read the words in the spell wrong. It was all Latin. Howard didn't know Latin any more than he could speak Russian. He could have mispronounced something, rendering the spell incomplete. It was possible. Part of him rejoiced at the idea, finally ridding his guilt over what he'd chosen of his own volition to do to Salem. But if the spell were somehow voided, that also meant Yasmine would not be restored to her human self. She would not come home to her children and the family who loved her. He was so deep into thought, he wasn't paying attention when Demitra rose to her feet, with everyone else, clapping and cheering for the married couple. Howard jumped to his feet, joining in as everyone looked onto the new Mr. and Mrs. Blanchard.

CHAPTER EIGHTEEN

The Attack on Blanchard House

The door was bolted tightly in multiple locations. Though she could not hear her son's sobs, Fable knew he was crying inside the steel reinforced cinder block fortress. Constructed months ago, to house Con Blanchard during the full moon cycle, the prison which kept him safe from harming people, still filled his mother with dread. Jerry patted her shoulder and reminded her they'd been through this several times before and everything was always perfectly all right. He had his chair and side table set up on the lawn beside the enclosure and his newest western novel for company to pass the night. When she mentioned it would be cold as the sun went down, he pointed to his electric heater plugged into the outlet on the exterior of the building. "And I have a cooler with sandwiches and cola. I am all set. You go back to the house and try to relax. I'm sure Miranda needs your help with the children anyway. I've got this. And I've got Con."

"You are the best you know."

"I've heard rumors," he smiled, opening the door to her Jeep and reissuing his demand for her to go back to the house.

As Fable walked into Blanchard House, Miranda was ready with a glass of wine for her. "And dinner is ready in the kitchen. The children are eating in the den watching a movie and the babies are asleep for the time being. So, it's just the three of us."

Fable took the wine, following Miranda to the kitchen where Vanessa was portioning out dinner onto plates. The ladies took their food to the table and proposed how to pass the evening. "We could watch our own movie?" Vanessa suggested. "Or watch the new year roll in and see who is performing."

"Or we could make margaritas and homemade fudge," Miranda said.

"Oh, I like that idea!" Fable exclaimed.

"Oh, Sydney sent pics of the wedding!" Vanessa told them. "The party is still going on and everything looks so beautiful."

"Now if we can only get you and Sage together," Miranda teased. "You might have your own wedding down the road."

"You and Sydney have got to stop with that." Vanessa scorned. "I like Sage. But right now, I have my hands full exploring a new relationship with my daughter. I don't have time for romance right now."

"Speaking of romance," Miranda said. "Fable you should have no problem keeping your date with Nash tomorrow because Skillet called to say he is coming out tomorrow to teach the children how to use their archery sets."

"Does Skillet know archery?" Fable asked with a smirk.

"You know him," Miranda grinned. "I am sure he thinks he does. But it will keep the children occupied for a few hours for you to see Nash."

"If I go," Fable frowned. "Depends on how depressed con is tomorrow."

Outside the walls of Blanchard House, the full moon had risen into the black skyline. It's cascading light illuminating through twisted empty limbs which reached up like boney fingers in search of something. Had anyone been on the porch of Blanchard House they might have taken notice of the stillness in the air. Birds were not chirping. Squirrels were not pouncing across the brown dormant grass collecting discarded acorns. And any animals in the woods were silently backing up giving a wide berth to what was stalking across the meadow.

Thaddeuss D'Angelo stood at the white rail fence smiling proudly at what was about to commence. He'd been there long enough to observe only three women were at home. Easy to overpower considering only one of them had power. Behind Thaddeuss stood his three allies. Seth and Yasmine Blanchard looked forward with inquisitive eyes, understanding they'd been here before. Bianca Duquesne stepped forward placing her cold white hand to Thaddeuss' shoulder. "Ready?"

"Not yet," he answered, turning around to look at Yasmine. "Thanks to Howard Blanchard falling for my little trick of resurrecting the dead, I am waiting for our fourth partner. Once we get the signal, we will advance onto the house."

"From what little my head can recall about Howard," Seth commented. "I find it difficult to believe he'd do as you asked."

Thaddeuss gave a hearty maniacal laugh. "My dear boy, I used his love for your wife against him. He believed he was restoring Yasmine to human life again when he cast the spell I provided him. He has no idea what was really in that vial I supplied. But they are all about to find out." He now addressed Yasmine, "Are you ready for your reunion, my dear?"

"I think I am," she replied. "Although I do not remember very much about that life—or him, I am excited to see him again."

Seth remembered him better than she. He remembered hating him for things he'd done. But somehow now he didn't. He understood a little better their fourth partner's reasons for what he did back then. Now, they were on the same side. Seth gripped Yasmine's hand and steered her eyes towards a section of land beside the great white house. "I believe we were married in that field, my love."

She returned a smile, "I remember. In my mind I can see pumpkins lining a path with flowers floating beside me in the aisle."

"Our wedding day."

Bianca gave them a playful wink, "You two love birds can reminisce after we've killed this family and taken what belongs to us."

Thaddeuss flashed a look of satisfaction towards his undead relation. "You seem eager for the fight now my dear Bianca. Has your prior reluctance to participate diminished?"

Bianca stared ahead at the house, her angry eyes blazing red. "I am remembering how it felt the night the Blanchards invaded our ancestral home and destroyed it. And with it, many we both cared for. It is time we unleashed a reckoning upon them."

Fable heard the microwave ding, signaling the popcorn was ready. She went to the kitchen to get it out and put it in a large bowl. Vanessa was pouring the melted cheese from the stove top onto the platter of nachos, while Miranda finished blending the margaritas. There was a loud bang at the front door. It was more than a knock—louder than a typical caller should make. Ruder perhaps. Startled by the noise, Fable set aside the popcorn bowl and went to the foyer to see who it might be. As she pulled the door open, her face turned from one of natural irritation to sheer horror. Never in her life did she expect to see what was standing before her now.

"Hello, honey," Patric sneered with a sadistic glee shining through his eyes. "I'm home!"

Patric, Fable's ex-lover. Patric, Yasmine's brother. Patric, father of Rom and Con. Patric, the werewolf. Patric, the fiend the Blanchards barely survived eight years ago...was back!

Her survivalist instinct kicked in, allowing no time for her to question how this was happening, but simply reacting to the fact it was happening. Releasing an involuntary scream, she bolted down the glass hallway leading to the second wing of the house. She could hear the maniacal laughter erupting from Patric's throat echo from the front door. She'd forgotten the depth and terror his laugh could instill. Slowly his footfalls traced after her as she backed her way down the hall. Built by her grandmother years ago as a way to add-on to the house without disturbing the trees on that part of the property, the hall meandered at uneven angles among the oak trees. The glass walls meant to allow light to pass so as not to cast the tree in darkness, was proving to be a short-sighted mistake. Fable's eyes peered out into the illuminated night to see dozens of wolves lining up around Blanchard House, sealing them inside, unable to escape.

Hearing her shriek, Miranda and Vanessa darted to the foyer. There was no sign of Fable or any visitor, only the door standing open. Vanessa stepped toward it to close, only to retreat a few steps back as the shock set in. "What is it?" Miranda called from behind here.

Vanessa could not find the words. Staring ahead at Seth and Yasmine ascending the porch steps, all she could do was wave her hands behind her hoping to convey to Miranda to run. Seth stepped to the door, looking at Vanessa but not recognizing her. She looked into his blazing eyes, the eyes of the devil. The horror of seeing the monster he'd become twisted with the unforeseen surprise that he did not even know her. "Seth." He ignored her, looking past her to Miranda. Regarding her as no threat to him, Seth gave a lazy push aside into Vanessa's sternum. Though he used little force on her, it was enough to send her slamming into the side wall.

His eyes never leaving their position on Miranda, Seth smiled at her, his protruding fangs glistening under the overhead light fixture. "Wifey, dear," he smirked, drawing nearer. "I think I remember you!"

Unsure of his intentions and not quite in control of her own reaction, Miranda must have smiled slightly because Seth then added, "Do not flatter yourself over it. It isn't an affection I am recalling. More of a relief of responsibility I handed off to you before I could find my sweet Yasmine."

Yasmine was through the door now, looking around at her surroundings as if she had never seen any of it before. Her eyes took notice of something behind Miranda, a child. Miranda felt something cold nudge her in the back. Turning around she saw

Hera there, clutching the family rifle. The child handed it to her. Miranda pushed Hera back up the stairs, ordering her to hide. Whirling around to face the invaders, Miranda cocked the gun, aiming it at Seth. "Leave us alone. Just live your new life and leave us alone."

Her words were useless as Seth drew closer. Miranda fired the gun directly into his chest! Seth recoiled back, stumbling over his feet. Though he did not bleed, his shirt was scorched and shredded from the shrapnel and chunks of his stomach had been blown away. Still, he remained steady, even amused. "Emptying you of your blood will fix that right up." Miranda flinched as he lunged for her, but suddenly some mysterious burst of energy pushed by her like a speeding car rushing by a pedestrian. Seth tumbled backwards, landing on his back across the room. Miranda turned to see Hera still standing halfway up the staircase, her hand outstretched.

"Stay away from my mother!" Hera roared. She stood steady and unafraid. Miranda almost didn't recognize her. Whatever hidden rage Hera had been tapping down for the last few months had somehow forged itself into a warrior.

"Baby," Miranda said cautiously, "Go back upstairs. I need you to guard the others."

"Hera!" Vanessa shouted from the floor, recovered from the daze of her fall and scrambled to her feet to the safety of the living room. "Meet me upstairs!" Vanessa ran off to the kitchen to use the back stairs, assuming the child would meet her on the second floor. But Hera was defiant. She moved, but it was down, not up, as she now stood on the tread in front of Miranda. Guarding her from harm.

CHAPTER NINETEEN

Under Siege

There was no exit from this side of the house, Fable realized for the first time. Yet another dawning realization about Olympia's added wing of the house. Glass hallway and no back doors. She shut herself into Sydney's bedroom, locking the door behind her although she knew that would not stop Patric. He was already at the door the moment she locked it and he used no effort punching through it as if it were made of paper. Wood splintered out and dropped to the floor as he used his feet to kick the rest in. She really saw him now. Their initial encounter at the door had lasted only seconds. Now as he loomed in the doorway, she could see he was half transformed into his wolf form and still half a man. The combination presented a hulking figure. His bare chest was covered in hair and heaving in and out with adrenaline or maybe just raw evil power. His hands were claws, razor sharp and lethal. His face still closely resembled the unnaturally captivating man she once knew, only exaggerated now by a nose that looked more like a black snout, and ears which had moved higher on the head, hair covered, and pointed. His eyes glowed with a ravenous hunger or intentional menace. She wasn't sure. She heard a crash from behind her at the window. Her initial thought was one of Patric's wolves had gotten in, but when she turned to see, it was Jerry! His own shotgun in hand, smashing through the glass, taking aim at the monster stalking his stepdaughter.

"Fable, move to the side please," Jerry said calmly, his forefinger squeezing into the trigger.

"Jerry," she said slowly, not taking her eye off Patric. "That gun isn't going to work on him."

Sneering at him from only a few yards away, Patric growled, "No. It's not."

Fable did not even see him pass; he was that quick. She only noticed he'd moved when she saw Jerry being snatched through the window and thrown across the room into Sydney's dressing table. The gun fired into the ceiling. "Jerry!" she screamed. But Patric had already seized him by the shoulder, his serrated claws dug into his left shoulder. He lifted Jerry into the air by the same shoulder, as if he were merely a lightweight stuffed animal in an arcade being lifted by the mechanical claw. Jerry's body weight fought against the suspension, inching down from gravity, forcing Patric's talons to slice their way up with every inch he slid.

"Please don't hurt him,"

Another woosh went by too quickly to anticipate. Fable felt it graze her hip. Suddenly a medium-sized wolf lunged into Patric's torso. The wolf snapped and bit at him, the impact forcing Patric's arm to drop, allowing Jerry's shoulder to slide free, landing him to the floor. Fable grabbed his legs, pulling him to her. It was only now as she helped Jerry to his feet that they both recognized the wolf. It was Romulus!

Still gnashing at the intruder, Rom was ferocious. But he was no match for Patric. Grasping Rom at the sides, Patric tore him from his hold and threw him into the corner of the room behind Fable and Jerry. Rom whimpered as he landed, but immediately sprung back to all fours. Looking forward at the crazy monster who'd broken into their home, Rom felt something unfamiliar inside himself. He could not quite determine what it was.

"You are mine," Patric said, directing the observation to Rom. "I too, feel that surge." Patric addressed Fable now. "We had offspring. I sired a son."

"He is not your son!" she yelled. "He is nothing like you!"

He laughed. Genuinely laughed at her absurd remark. "Fable my darling, I am looking right at the boy. I would say he is very much like his father."

Romulus began to growl. It was a succession of short pulses. Fable had never heard him do that before. Then, without warning, he leapt out of the window into the night. Fable was equally worried and relieved by his departure. Patric's eyes were narrowing. Fable feared he may be completing his metamorphosis into full wolf form. She tried to play for time with questions.

"What do you want, Patric? How are you even here? How are you alive?"

"It is a mystery to me as well, Fable." His teeth were elongating and his arms lengthening. His chest was gaining mass, and his legs were slowly bending into haunches.

"We killed you!" she yelled. Fists clenching, ready for a fight. Jerry stepped beside her, readying himself to shield her if the beast were to pounce. Fable kept talking.

"We ripped you to shreds!"

Patric stalked closer, grinning in an almost playful hostility, "And don't think it hasn't been difficult to forgive you for that little aggression." He was almost fully formed now. The largest black wolf Jerry had ever seen. It was monolithic. But then Patric's concentration was interrupted when Romulus jumped back through the window again, but he wasn't alone. There was another. Another wolf accompanied him—roughly the same size and statue. Where the first one had been a chestnut brown, this wolf was a dark gray. Patric's face reverted to nearly human, as he looked at Fable and asked, "Did we sire a pack? How many are there?"

"Just these two," Fable answered.

Con was not as restrained as his brother. Whereas Rom's brain operated at a mostly human level, Con was nothing but a wild animal in his current form. Con growled viciously at not only Patric, but his mother and grandfather as well. His bared teeth dripped with saliva, and it was clear he was contemplating whether to kill the competition for his meal or go for the meal itself.

"Now this one!" Patric exclaimed with a hint of revelry. "This one is definitely mine. He has the hunger. The instinct. He is readying himself even as we speak for the kill."

Romulus slid into position in front of his mother and Jerry, sending another succession of growls, again in a specific rotation, as if conversing with his brother he would fight back if he charged at them.

"My boys," Patric said proudly. "I came here for other reasons, but now I shall leave with my offspring beside me."

"You are not taking my boys anywhere Patric!"

"Who is here to stop me?"

"I will stop you," Jerry shouted, grabbing a table lamp from the bedside table and twirling by the cord as some sort of makeshift mace.

Patric growled, his features once again transitioning into total wolf formation. But before his mouth had completely altered itself, he cautioned, "My sons' mother is now under my protection. You, however, I will devour in sections."

"NO!!" Romulus screamed. His cry distracted Patric from striking Jerry. Patric stared at the naked boy who now stood where his offspring cub had been. "I love him! He's my grandfather."

The unadulterated amazement seared into Patric's canine eyes was palpable.

Once again, he released some of his wolfness so he could speak to the boy. "You can manifest at will. And at so young an age. Remarkable my son."

Stepping forward in front of both Fable and Jerry, Rom repeated his plea. "He is my grandfather. He loves me. Don't hurt him."

Fable was astounded when she heard Patric's reply. "For you my son, I amend my earlier declaration. Both your mother, and this man you care for...and who I can reliably suppose must care greatly for you, are under my protection. Neither I nor any of my pack will harm either of you."

"Thank you," Rom said, almost smiling. He shifted forward a little, the movement startled Fable who instinctively grabbed him by the arm, pulling him back. "But he's my father," Rom told her. "I never had a father before."

"Now you do," Patric said, extending his arm towards the child. "Come with me, my son. I will show you the ways of the wolf. Embrace your true nature."

"You are not taking him. Either of them!"

"Again, Fable. Who here can stop me?"

The question was answered on its own, taking everyone by surprise as a massive white wolf came crashing through the glass ceiling in the hallway. It was enormous, almost mythical. Its mighty hand grabbed the door frame, ripping half of the wall away from the room. Patric instantly formed his full beastly brown form, leaping at the great white beast!

Upstairs Vanessa had given up on Hera joining her and ran to the den to get her daughter. Theda was understandably frightened, asking Vanessa over and over what was going on. They'd heard the commotion below and Hera had run out to go investigate. Theda had followed only to hear some of what was happening downstairs and retreated to the den, unsure what she should do other than stay with her little brother until someone came back. She told Vanessa that Romulus had turned into a monster. How he'd disappeared before her eyes and turned into a big dog, jumping through the glass window. She ran to see what happened and relayed how we had landed three stories below on the ground and ran off on four legs through the field behind the house.

Vanessa didn't have time to calm her child, nor explain anything she'd witnessed. She only told Theda to stay with Titan in the den while she went to get the babies from the nursery. Then they would make an escape down the backstairs and back door. Vanessa dashed to the nursery at the end of the hall. When she opened the door, she found a strange man and woman inside, each with one of the babies in their arms. "I do not know who you are, my dear woman," the man said rather politely. "However, if you will stand aside to let us pass, I will not be forced to kill you. But please do understand, it is no bother for me at all to do so."

"What are you doing with Trix and Echo's babies?" Vanessa asked.

"Thank you for clearing my little mystery up for me," the man smiled. "I had no idea there were two of them. This whole time I believed there to be only one child. Tess' child. Now, I understand completely. Tess died before her baby was able to reach maturity. I should have guessed with my nephew's special powers Echo would have mimicked his sister's body and brought her baby to fruition. I suppose he transformed Trix as well. Imagine my delight to discover I have two children with the power of God within them. Why I will be even stronger than I dared dream."

"Your children?" Vanessa repeated.

"Yes, my dear. Allow me to introduce myself. I am Thaddeuss D'Angelo, father of these two delightful vessels. Now you will excuse me while my companion and I take our leave. Bianca, let's make haste."

Yasmine crept closer to the daring little girl guarding the plain looking woman on the stairs. Yasmine paused by her husband, helping him to his feet before she continued her way forward. She eyed the girl strangely before saying, "I believe I am your mother."

With unblinking focus, Hera stared down at the vampire coming nearer. With defiance in her young voice, Hera asserted, "You are not my mother."

"I suppose we will see," Yasmine grinned, flashing her razor-sharp incisors.

With deft agility, Hera spun herself around, thrusting her hand towards Miranda, using her levitation powers to raise Miranda high into the air, sailing her overhead and into the living room out of harm's way. Yasmine was midair before she realized the child had been quicker than she. The vampire landed herself behind Hera, grabbing the girl by the arms, making it impossible for her to expel another blast of her great power. The child struggled beneath Yasmine's grip, but she was too weak in comparison. Seth looked at his ferocious wife with satisfaction at her mighty reclamation of the situation. They shared a moment of triumph between them as they both readied themselves to kill their victims.

Hera watched in horror as Seth jumped into the air, grabbing Miranda by the leg, dragging her back down to the ground, breaking Hera's spell. Miranda, equally terrified as she saw Yasmine inch closer to Hera's neck, the child struggling uselessly against her hold. "Let go of my daughter!" Miranda bellowed. But her cries only further amused Yasmine, whose response was to nick Hera's shoulder with her teeth, twisting the child to show Miranda the flow of blood now trickling down her arm. "I am going to drain this little bitch dry while you watch!" Yasmine boasted. "And only after you watch her die will my husband end your miserable existence."

Not knowing what she should do, Vanessa froze in place staring at the dastardly looking man and the eerily pale woman holding babies Jinx and Lucky. The babies were stirring now in their arms, becoming agitated. Vanessa wasn't like the Blanchards, she was just a woman—no supernatural gifts to fight these kidnappers with. But she couldn't just stand and do nothing. She also couldn't risk them killing her. She had a child of her own hiding in a room down the hall. Relying on the only superpower she had, Vanessa took a step forward in hopes of reasoning with the man. She knew it wouldn't work. He was not a parent at school in a conference over little Jimmy's behavior in class. Still, it was all she had in her arsenal. "Sir, is there any way we can talk about this? If you are the father of these babies, maybe some sort of arrangement can be made with the Blanchards over visitation. I could talk to them on your behalf if you will allow me to."

Thaddeuss seemed almost entertained by the frightened woman's suggestion. "I don't believe I require your assistance in the matter; however, it was a delightful suggestion." He was holding baby Jinx, and she was becoming rather fussy. She did not like the stranger gripping her so tightly. Thaddeuss offered Vanessa one final warning, "Now please, step away while we pass, or my next action will be to sever your torso from your legs."

Vanessa stepped backwards involuntarily, feeling almost as if she were being pulled. Suddenly baby Jinx let out a sharp cry and Vanessa felt something break away beneath her feet! Before she'd had time to comprehend what happened, she found herself smashing into the floor below. Above her was a small hole in the ceiling. She'd fallen through the floor. Except for a few scrapes and possibly some splinters lodged in her thighs, she was unharmed. She heard a loud clang nearby and diverted her attention its direction. The sword...Olympia Blanchard's father's sword which always hung mounted just above the open doorway to the second-floor staircase landing, had fallen. Instinctively, Vanessa scuttled to it. Now positioned at the head of the stairs, she could hear and see what was happening in the foyer. Yasmine had Hera in her clutches, the child's arms pinned behind her unable to move. Yasmine was moving in to bite her!

Miranda screamed over Seth's back as she saw Yasmine moving in for the kill. Seth held Miranda down, keeping her from moving. But to Miranda's amazement, Vanessa jumped from the upper landing towards Yasmine, in her hands flashed the family heirloom sword. As Vanessa came down onto the staircase, the sword stabbed into Yasmine's side, sending her staggering backward over the rail. As Yasmine crashed to the floor, she snatched the sword from her side and hurled it like a javelin straight for Vaneesa. Hera was fast with her reaction, now that her hands were free. She waved the approaching missile to the side with her telekinesis, sending the sword stabbing into the wall several feet from Vanessa.

"Kill that little bitch's mother!" Yasmine roared to her husband, in full fury now.

Seth pulled Miranda up from the floor, slamming her against the wall. Pinning her arms to the wall, he protracted his deadly fangs and moved towards her with a gleam in his eye which she knew would be the last image she ever saw.

CHAPTER TWENTY

Battle at Blanchard House

Arielle, now dressed in a light blue suit of tweed waved excitedly from the back seat of the antique Bentley as her new husband smiled to his happy bride. As the driver started the engine, she tossed her bouquet towards the crowd. Guests parted to the side to reveal it was Salem who caught it. Arielle blew her sister a kiss as the car drove away. Miles put his arm around Salem's waist and enjoyed the unspoken moment between them as their own impending marriage approached. Sage slapped his hand down firmly onto Miles' shoulder and said, "I would say this is a clear sign that the two of you need to set the date!"

After another hour of winding down, the band was packing up, the caterers were cleaning up, and the wedding guests who had driven in from the other islands or downtown Charleston made their departures, leaving only family remaining. The Blanchards gathered in the parlor for one last glass of Champagne before retiring to bed. They would all have to be at the airport in the morning to return home.

"Well, the happy couple is off to the warmer beaches of Miami. Hard to believe our little Arielle is a married lady now." Demitra said. "And you'll be next, Salem."

Salem raised her glass and commented, "Looking forward to it." Miles patted her leg and mirrored the sentiment. Salem was about to announce she was ready to go to bed when she leaned over to place her glass on the coffee table, but the moment she placed it down, something stole her attention. Right beside her, between she and the table, a miniscule orb materialized and the moment she saw it expanding rapidly as it burst open—revealing young Theda in the room.

The Blanchards jumped startlingly at the sudden entrance. Salem grabbed Theda's shoulders and exclaimed, "Theda! How on earth? What are you doing here? How did you know how to get here?"

Theda was as shaken as her aunt. It was soon obvious to everyone the child knew little more than they. "I don't know! I don't know!" she cried. "I was scared. I didn't know what to do. There were so many screams and scary noises. And Hera never came back. And my...my mother..." it was the first time she'd spoken those words regarding Vanessa, "My mother didn't come back for us."

"Slow down, Theda," Demitra urged, moving to her knees on the floor beside the trembling child. "Tell us what happened?"

"I don't know what is happening," Theda shouted. "What is happening to me? How did I get here?"

Salem stroked her blonde hair gently and answered, "I don't know honey. You tell me. What were you thinking the moment before you appeared here?"

Theda was shaking fully now, riddled with confusion and fear. "I-I...there were these screams. And my mother didn't come back. Hera ran off. Rom changed. It sounds like a lie, but I swear it's not. Rom turned into a big dog and jumped out the window. And I was alone with the little boy. My brother. And I was so scared. Then I thought of you."

Salem smiled, pleased that she had. "And you remembered how I told you that you had a family now and we will always take care of you?"

"Yeah."

"That is your power as a witch, darling." Demitra explained. "You have the ability to do something we call *blinking*. Your father's father had the same gift. You can move yourself instantly to wherever place you want to go. Obviously, you wanted to come to your aunt Salem because you were afraid. It is a good thing. We are glad you did. But tell us, darling, what is going on at home which made you so frightened."

Theda could provide no more information than she had already imparted. Understanding the severity of whatever situation was going on at Blanchard House, Salem asked Theda if she believed she could repeat what she did and hold Salem's hand while thinking of Blanchard House.

"You mean, can I take you there with me?"

"Yes," Salem said. "You are the only way we can get there fast. Do you think you can do it again, this time with me? Then once I am there, you must do it one last time and come back here where you will be safe."

"How?"

"Think of Aunt Demitra," Salem told her. "You should pop right back here to her."

"I'm going with you!" Demitra argued.

"No, you aren't." Salem said. "Whatever is happening sounds like it needs active powers."

"I'll go." Echo volunteered.

"Us too," Sydney said motioning to Sage.

Trix also agreed to accompany them.

Salem shook her head. "We cannot expect Theda to be powerful enough to take us all. And I need her still strong enough to get back here. Echo, let's see if she can transport you and me. That'll be difficult enough."

Moments later, Salem, Echo, and Theda were standing in the third-floor den of Blanchard House. "You did it, Theda!" Salem congratulated. She saw Titan safe on the floor playing with his blocks. Salem rushed to him, lifting him from the floor and placing him beside Theda. Placing his hand in his new sister's, she instructed the girl. "Take Titan back with you. Think of Demitra. Go, now!" Theda evaporated into the tiny orb right before their eyes. Salem hoped she was collected enough to zap back to the right place. "Okay, Echo. Let's see what the hell is going on here."

Seth had Miranda firmly in his clutches. He pushed her head to the side and moved down into her throat. "No!!!" Hera shrieked, running at them. Vanessa tried to grab the child before she bolted down the stairs, but Hera was too quick. Yasmine, sneering wickedly, made her move towards Hera, but before she could catch her it had already happened. Yasmine felt something splatter in her face, momentarily obscuring her vision. She wiped the vicus substance from her eyes to reveal the agonizing sight. Seth was gone. Only Miranda remained, her own face and body dripping with a reddish, pinkish substance. That corner of the room was covered in it. Dripping from the walls, the ceiling, and splattered in an outward pattern along the floorboards. Yasmine looked back at the little girl. Hera still had her hands outstretched, aimed directly to where Seth had been standing. Etched across the child's face was a smirk of accomplishment. Hera's eyes glowed with satisfaction.

"Hera?" Vanessa said softly, stepping down towards her. Slowly she lowered Hera's arms back to her sides and looked out to Miranda's shell-shocked face. Hera had just combusted her father into oblivion. Miranda looked around, now realizing the slimy liquid spattered across her face and body was the remnants of Seth. Blood, sinew, muscle tissue, and flecks of shattered bone covered Miranda, and the room.

Salem was at the top of the stairs when she felt the shockwave course through her bloodline. Looking down to the carnage dripping across the foyer, she knew at once—what she'd felt was her brother's eradication. Yasmine stood motionless, rendered almost comatose by what she'd seen. She did not move. She did not blink. Her red eyes widened, the pupils receding to almost nothing as something in her inhuman vampire mind snapped. Vanessa, standing center of the room with Hera, saw it as it happened. She saw the precise moment when Yasmine Blanchard, a creature of the night, fell into complete madness. The stillness of the moment broke as Yasmine lurched forward, almost flying to Hera. Ripping the child from Vanessa's hold, she gripped the child by the back of the head and swept her towards the wall. The child had no time to react or to defend herself. Hera saw the white plank boards of the foyer wall coming closer and closer to her until she felt her nose reach its surface and crack against it. Stunned into senselessness, Hera's sight grew dimmer with each repetition into the wall. She felt her cheekbones shatter just before losing consciousness. Salem and Vanessa looked on in horror. Yasmine's shrill banshee cry reverberated through the room as she continued to smash Hera's face into the wall. Over and over, too many times to process, Yasmine pounded the little girl's head into the hard pine boards of Blanchard House. Miranda scrambled to them, tossing herself onto Yasmine's back in a futile effort to save her child. Yasmine was undeterred. With Miranda hanging onto her from behind, clawing and scratching and trying to pry the monster's hands away, Yasmine continued her assault. Salem tossed her hands forward, releasing her power to freeze time towards the deranged vampire. It didn't work. In that terrifying moment Salem remembered, Yasmine now had the same power. She was immune. Blood was spurting now from Hera's head as it continued to pound into the cracking, breaking boards of the wall.

In one blinding swing, the herculean white wolf made impact with Patric's skull, knocking him six feet into the side wall of the bedroom. Dazed, but not debilitated, Patric rose on his powerful haunches and roared a horrendous guttural bellow. Fable and Jerry looked at each other in paralyzed confusion.

"Who is that?" Jerry asked.

"And is it helping us or about to slaughter us?" Fable added, unsure of which.

Whatever or whoever the massive beast was, it was clearly not one of Patric's minions. Patric sprang through the air, connecting with the white wolf, both rolling together through the opposite wall. Patric, in his brown wolf form, and the newly arrived white wolf tussled viciously, biting and snapping at each other, rolling down the hallway. They were obscured from sight for a moment until the brown wolf was sent sailing back into the bedroom by the white. Patric's face shifted back to a halfway point somewhere in the middle of wolf and human. The alteration provided him with the capability to speak again. "This is my family!" he growled to the attacking beast. "I have come to reclaim them. They are coming with me."

"No, we aren't!" cried Fable.

The giant white wolf stalked back into the bedroom. Mimicking Patric, he too released part of his wolf physique, acquiring speech himself. His face was still too distorted with fur and exaggerated canine bone structure to be recognized, but when he spoke, Fable thought she heard a ring of familiarity. "This family is under my protection. You will take no one when you go." Then, within an eye's blink, the larger wolf resumed his full form and stomped his muscled leg hard into the floor. Patric, much to Fable's surprise, backed down.

Withdrawing into the doorway to leave, Patric spoke one final time. "I will go. But I will be back." He looked at Fable, then his wolf offspring, "I will come back for my boys."

The white wolf released another earth-shaking roar, and after, he began to shake, quiver to be exact. His giant form began to shrink, to shift into whatever human form he normally possessed. As the final bits of hair fell from his skin, and his legs and arms resumed human form, Fable stood open mouthed, unable to fully understand what was taking place before her eyes. An escaping gasp from Jerry, beside her, let her know he was equally flummoxed.

Patric recognized him at once, "Teague."

Fable exchanged quizzical glances with Jerry as the old man, now standing naked before them, reached down to pull the sheetrock and debris covered bedspread up to cover himself. Rom moved closer to the old man he knew so well. "Skillet?"

Skillet reached out to tousle Rom's hair. Con growled and lowered himself, assuming a stance ready for attack. Skillet turned his head sharply to see the small wolf. "Con!" he said, raising his cracking voice. "Stay in place." Con, seeming to understand, obeyed. Skillet faced Patric in the doorway. "I sired you, son. You ain't never gone match me in our animal form. I suggest you get outta here or I'm gonna have to rip you apart. And that ain't something I look forward to havin' to do."

Patric, signaling an understanding that the words were true, backed out into the hallway and in an eye's blink, transformed back to his animal form and sprinted back the way he came, towards the foyer. Jerry had retrieved the shotgun, regardless of its uselessness in the situation. Fable waved him back, "It's all right, Jerry. I think he means us no harm." She stepped closer to Skillet, extending a hand of friendship which he took in his own.

"Course, I don't mean you no harm, Miss Fable," the kindly old man smiled. "I been a'lookin out for you and your boys ever since they was born. You may not a'seen me doin' it. But I been here all these years, keeping my distance, but makin' sure if these boys needed me, I'd be around."

Skillet. The old man who had worked at the family-owned restaurant for a decade or more. The man who always seemed to be around in the background through the various milestones of the Blanchard's lives. He'd befriended the children over the years, even taken them fishing on his off days. This genteel unassuming man no one had given much thought to, was a werewolf himself!

"He called you something?" Jerry questioned.

"He called me Teague." Skillet answered. "Was the name I went by when he was a boy. Couldn't go by it here when your aunt Artemis was my boss. She'd a'known right off. Besides, I always been pretty good with a skillet. Practically the only belonging I ever had livin' out in forests and caves, trying to steer clear of folks so I never hurt anyone. Thought the name suited me."

Everything made perfect sense now. This kindly old gentleman, with no family of his own had practically forced himself into the Blanchard family's circle without ever seeming threatening or obtrusive. He'd helped out at parties, worked night and day at the restaurant, and spent his rare free time with the children. Teague, the wolf who'd dragged Oliver Sinclair to safety after the car wreck which killed his and Yasmine's parents. Teague, who accidentally bit Oliver in the process and spent the child's early years raising him and teaching him the ways of the wolf. Teague had sired Oliver and Oliver had come to Daihmler under the name Patric once he'd grown into manhood—seeking out his sister Yasmine and impregnating Fable in the process. And Skillet had followed him. And Skillet had stayed in Daihmler all these years, looking out for Fable's boys.

Fable touched the old man's face gently with her fingertips. "You are the wolf who started it all. And you've been here all this time...looking after us?"

Skillet nodded. "Tryin' to make sure your children never turned out like their daddy. Never thought I'd have to be protecting them from him though. But when I felt his presence tonight, I came right over. Ain't nobody hurting this family on my watch."

"We need to see where he went and if the others are okay?" Jerry reminded Fable.

Fable had completely forgotten about the other children in the house, as well as Miranda and Vanessa. She had to make sure they were all unharmed. "Skillet, will you stay with the boys?" She knew she hadn't even had to ask. Leaving Rom and Con with the old man, Fable and Jerry made their way back to the main part of the house.

When they came into the foyer, they were not prepared for what they saw.

Echo stood defiantly in the third-floor hallway, staring straight into the faces of Taub D'Angelo and Bianca Duquesne as they stood holding the babies. None of them had spoken for several minutes, each mentally calculating what to do next. Echo had caught them coming out of the nursery with the babies and was prepared to fight to the death for them, but when Vanessa's frantic hand came from behind clutching his elbow, Echo did not know what to do once she said, "They need you downstairs, fast. It's Hera." In the silent moments which followed, Echo weighed every possibility of how he might save his son and niece and still make it downstairs in time to save Hera.

Vanessa knew it was imperative that Echo get down there to heal Hera before she died in Miranda's arms. She tried one final time to plead with the intruders. "Please, Mr. Thaddeuss..."

"Thaddeuss!" Echo exclaimed.

Confused by the reaction, assuming Echo knew who the man was, Vanessa replied, "Yes. His name is Thaddeuss."

"His name is Taub."

"Oh," Vanessa said. "He told me it was Thaddeuss."

A cunning smile emerged on Echo's face as the newly imparted information set in. "Alright, Uncle Thaddeuss, let's do this!" Echo pushed Vanessa hard to the ground before he sprinted forward, charging Thaddeuss head on. Thaddeuss D'Angelo let out a raucous laugh at the boy's hubris and released a blast of his fatal propulsion. From her vantage point flat on the hallway floor, chin resting on the rug, Vanessa saw a searing red-light surge from Thaddeuss' hand. The light behaved like some kind of laser sailing down the corridor in three irregular lines. The light made contact with Echo, passing through him and overhead past Vanessa. To her horror she realized what the blast had done as Echo's body began to shift upon itself, sliced in three parts—three pieces, sliding off of themselves. Her eyes were glued to the slaughter a few feet from her. She did not shift her gaze to the other end of the hall. Had she, she may not have felt so hopeless.

Thaddeuss D'Angelo did not understand what he was seeing at first. Looking at Echo as the blast cut threw him, his evil grin of vengeance was replaced with astonishment when he saw his own face staring back at him. As Echo's body began to fall to the ground, Thaddeuss felt strange inside his own. Queasy. Sick.

"Thaddeuss!" Bianca shouted, stepping backwards away from him.

Thaddeuss looked down to see his own body severed in the exact same way as what he believed he'd done to Echo. In a kind of ridiculous denial, Thaddeuss grasped frantically at his sides, as if attempting to hold himself together. It was useless. His torso slid off his legs, hitting the floor with a thud. With nothing to support it, his upper body from chest up, plopped down beside them as his legs and arms fell like matchsticks onto each other. His eyes were still open in the moments before death—just long enough to see his nephew, Echo Blanchard, walking towards him in full living formation, uninjured in any way. Bianca had not even been aware of how she'd grabbed the girl baby from Thaddeuss as the began to crumble. Echo marched directly to her and looked her in the eyes. "I am needed downstairs. Why don't you just hand me the babies and take your sorry ass as far away from this house as you possibly can."

Saying nothing in return, Bianca smiled, handed him the babies and made her escape into the night through the window at the end of the hall. Vanessa met Echo at the stairs, taking the babies from him so he might help Hera...if it wasn't too late.

The chaos had died down and now all eyes were watching Echo as he was summoning the inner healing light from within him, hoping it was not too late. If Hera was breathing it was far too shallow to detect. There was not much remaining to her head and skull, but the brain, though distorted, was still there. The others in the room stood together in a huddle, holding each other with bated breath—powerless to do anything more than watch. Though it was hard to conceive, things could have gone worse. Had Patric not dragged Yasmine out with him when he fled, they could have all been too occupied fighting her to focus on Hera.

Miranda couldn't speak. Paralyzed by the real possibility she had lost her child. Vanessa kept her reassuring arms wrapped around her friend's waist, watching from over her shoulder as Echo was doing his best. Salem was on Vanessa's left, their arms entwined with Fable on the other side squeezing Miranda's hand while she leaned back into Jerry for her own support. A short inhalation of air was heard in the deafening silence. A gasp followed. Then the sound of coughing. Echo's tear-stained face looked up at the others, "She's back. She's okay." Hera sat up, held steady by Echo until her lungs were filled again with oxygen. She was covered in blood. Her own. Though the wounds were now healed, vanished as if having never been inflicted, the memories still covered her clothes and skin. She looked over to the tearful members of her family.

"Mama?"

Miranda rushed to her, falling onto the floor and pulling Hera into her arms.

CHAPTER TWENTY-ONE

A Debt of Gratitude

It had been three days since the New Year turned but the night of horror that hit Blanchard House still lingered heavily in their minds. Demitra came home to more than one ripple to calm. Though Hera appeared to be emotionally unscarred by the night, Demitra wasn't so sure it was true. Resilient as the child may be, it was illogical to believe she could be unaffected. She had killed her father with her own hands—not merely killed him—obliterated him. The stains of his bodily fluids still marred the foyer walls. As if killing her father was not traumatic enough, Hera's own mother's assault upon her nearly smashed her into nothing. How does a child come back from that? Yet Hera gave every appearance she was fine.

And then there was Patric to consider. How did he return? Nothing Demitra knew from witchcraft made something like that possible. Further worrying her, this monster was out there somewhere with Yasmine. Both cruel. Both murderous. How many innocent citizens had they already killed? When would they come back seeking revenge on the family? Rounding out those major dilemmas were a few minor ones. Theda was still shaken by the things she witnessed on New Year's Eve. It hadn't been the best preview of what it was like to be a witch. Still, she'd shown impressive skill with her power. With Demitra's help, it could be cultivated into something wondrous. Demitra then remembered the matter of Skillet. She had not spoken with him yet but had made plans to see him that very afternoon. Topping it all off was the unforeseen turn of events that Howard was, Ocean's natural father. Demitra could not overlook the irony. Before the wedding the biggest concern on her mind was whether Ocean was an enemy plant with ties to the D'Angelo's. Now his paternity was the least significant stress on her plate. He had not been a D'Angelo after all, and the real D'Angelo threat she never saw coming! Ocean would have to be told the truth about himself once he and Arielle returned from their honeymoon. It could wait a while. Demitra found it amusing how she had worried how Ocean may react upon finding out he wasn't really a Blanchard. As it ended up, he was not only truly a Blanchard, but one of Olympia's Blanchards. Demitra's own great-grandson. Not only that, Ocean had a brother and a sister now. She wondered how Trix and Echo would take the news. She'd told no one, except Jerry. After Howard revealed the news to her New Year's Day, they decided to keep it between themselves a little longer.

The Cobblestone restaurant was not yet open for lunch when Demitra and Fable walked into the bustle of waitstaff setting the tables and preparing for the lunch crowd. Old Skillet caught sight of them from across the room where he was placing silverware in crisp linen rolled napkins at each chair.

Demitra waved him over. He had a look of nervousness on his face as he shuffled forward, placing the tray of linens on a nearby table. "Yes Miss Dee?"

Fable let out an accidental chuckle. "You look like a guilty child, Skillet. You aren't being fired or anything."

The old man looked relieved to hear it. "Then what can I do for you ladies?"

Demitra placed her hand on his shoulder. "Skillet, I think it's we who want to know what we can do for you. You saved my grandsons, my daughter, and my husband the other night. I am indebted to you."

"Naw," he blushed. "I been waiting years to see if I was gonna be needed. Was happy to do it."

Demitra pulled a chair out and sat down, directing him and Fable to do the same. Lowering her voice as a couple of waiters passed by, she said, "That is exactly what I mean. You have quietly lingered in the background of our lives looking out for my family. That has been a remarkable showing of compassion and loyalty."

Skillet placed his hand to his mouth to conceal his grin. He did not like it when people fussed over him, although he was touched by her kindness. "I care about this family, Miss Dee. Seen for myself all these years what good folks you all are. And truth be told, this whole mess started with me. If I'd been more careful. If I'd not pierced that little boy's neck that night I dragged him away from that crash, he'd never turned into what he became. And none of this would be happening to you people."

Fable placed her hands in his and gently squeezed. "Skillet, I would not have my boys if you hadn't. Yes, Patric is dangerous, but I wouldn't choose any other path if it would have kept me from having Con and Rom."

"You're a real good momma, Miss Fable. Them boys are lucky."

"But what I don't understand, Skillet," Demitra broke in. "Is how you have managed to remain a kind, and seemingly gentle person. How is it Patric is such a monster, yet you have kept your humanity. You both have the curse of the werewolf inside you?"

To answer that question, Skillet said he needed to take them somewhere. Following his directions, Demitra drove a few miles away to Herron Street. She'd passed along this road all her life. It was nothing out of the ordinary. A few fast-food places. A post office. A couple of gas stations and a strip mall. Behind the mall was one of those oversized self-storage facilities which spring up like ragweed in less desirable parts of town. Skillet told Demitra to drive to the last row of units. The back row abutted a line of trees and dense thickets, but behind that the rumble of the interstate could be heard. Skillet withdrew a key, opening the lock on #875. Rolling the garage-style door open, Demitra and Fable saw where he lived.

A reclining chair, which looked to have possibly come from the outlet mall, sat next to a small round table. A single lamp sat on the table plugged into a wall outlet, with another cord running to a mini refrigerator. On the opposite wall stretched a long metal rod fastened to the top of a chest of drawers on one end and to the wall of the storage unit at the other. A few wire hangers of clothes dangled between. However, the most curious thing in the unit was a tall storage safe in the middle of the room. The black iron housing of the safe was visible beneath worn sections of peeling green paint. Whatever lettering was once written on the front had long since been scratched off. It looked like an antique bank safe from days gone by. Skillet lifted the heavy arm of the door and opened it. The safe was empty inside except for what looked like a thin spattering of shed animal hair.

"I can unhitch the lock from the inside with my little finger through this little hole," Skillet showed them. "Only thing that'll get in that hole is my little finger. In my wolf form ain't no way I can get to that lock. I stay in here on full moon nights."

Demitra and Fable were flabbergasted. Fable inspected the small shell of the vault and knew it must be torturous to be confined inside there for hours on end. "You put yourself inside here every time? Just to keep yourself from hurting anyone?"

The old man nodded. He walked around the tall box as if seeing it's tiny circumference from their perspective. Placing a hand on the side wall of the safe, he hung his head and admitted, "I hurt a lot of folks in my younger days." Feeling some sort of anger within himself, he smacked the safe with the flat of his hand and said, "I say hurt. I mean killed. Don't sting so bad when I put it the other way. But I killed them people. Can't ever shed that sin. Worked in a bank way back when. Bought this safe when it closed. Rigged it to keep myself in. Ain't killed nobody since. Sure am glad of that."

Fable touched his arm. She could feel him trembling at his awful memories. "How are you so kind, Skillet? That's something Patric certainly isn't."

"Well, Miss Fable, way I figure it is him getting turned so young sorta warped his mind. Grown men, if they got much of a conscience, hate this curse. We grieve from it. It ain't fun. It's painful and messy and we don't even get everlasting life. We keep growin' old and havin' to make a living like everybody else. But we got this curse to deal with on top of it."

"And then, of course, "Demitra added solemnly. "There are people who enjoy the kill. I think Patric would have been that kind of man despite his werewolf condition."

"Hard to say," Skillet pondered. "I am a pretty nice feller, I think. But when that change comes over you, you just become this beast. Can't help it. I'll admit I was rightly scared the other night when I felt Patric's presence in town. I knew I had to keep myself out of that safe that night so I could hunt him if he went after Miss Fable and her boys. I'm pretty sure I went straight to y'all's house without attacking anybody, but I was sure scared I would."

Fable snatched the car keys from her mother's hand and with a look of exhilarated excitement, cried, "Skillet! I think we can absolutely guarantee you'll never have to worry about that again!"

Salem left work and drove home the minute Fable called her. She reached the house at almost the same time Fable and Skillet did. They went straight up to Salem's bedroom. Skillet did not know what to expect, only trusting Fable's word when she said she had the answer for his troubles. Salem removed a glass vial from her drawer and showed it under the light to the elderly man.

"What's that in there?"

Fable wrapped her loving arm around the old man's shoulder and said, "Skillet, this is your restoration. One drop of this and you will never have another night where you need to fear your condition."

His eyes flickered with a hopefulness he had not remembered feeling in ages.

"Do you mean you gotta cure for this curse, Miss Salem?"

"I do." Salem replied. "You will never again have to suffer the torment of worrying if you have killed. And you will never have to feel the bodily agony transformation causes you. You can be free Skillet."

The old man bore an expression of relief unlike any they'd witnessed before. As if every burden he had ever endured was lifted. Then, his eyes went dark again, whatever joy he had been overcome by, left. "I can't, Miss Fable." Skillet scowled, with a shake of his head. "I can't drink that stuff."

Fable didn't understand. Salem seemed as confused as she. "Why not?" Fable asked. "Skillet, what in the world would keep you from ending your torment?"

The old man gazed tearfully at the kind witches. With a scratch to his whiskery chin he replied, "You and your boys."

She understood now. Placing her caring hand upon his shoulder, Fable urged him to reconsider. "Skillet, thank you. I cannot tell you how much your friendship and loyalty mean to me. But not at the sacrifice of your wellbeing. Of your soul. Me and my boys will be fine. Please take Salem's cure."

Still shaking his ornery head, Skillet declared, "Not till I know one' hundred percent, Patric ain't a threat to ya'll. Till then, I need to be able to fight him. I'm his maker. He can't beat me and he knows it."

They spent another ten minutes trying to dissuade Skillet from his stance, but he wouldn't budge. As long as Patric was alive again, Skillet would remain a werewolf. He left them alone to go downstairs to see the boys before Fable drove him home. Once Fable and Salem were alone, Fable told her cousin, "Well, I guess he won't be your first test case. I was kind of hoping to see that elixir in action. I suppose you will have to wait a while longer before you restore your first soul."

Fable's statement was incorrect, though she had not known. Salem's first test run with the Holy Blood had been Gideon and Alexandrea. And there had been one more since, one no one would have imagined. Salem knew something no one else knew, one additional event which took place on New Year's Eve.

CHAPTER TWENTY-TWO

My Brother's Keeper

A great deal more had gone on New Year's Eve than anyone other than Salem was aware. The trauma of the evening wrecked everyone's nerves at Blanchard House. They had all retired to bed to sleep or perhaps to process. Salem called Oleander before bed to make sure Theda and Titan had made it there safely, and to let Theda know she and Titan could return if they wanted. Theda zapped herself and her little brother back, where Vanessa swept her into her arms and took her home. As the house became quiet and still, Salem could not settle her restlessness. Standing in the foyer staring at Seth's remains still clinging to the walls, she was not quite prepared to say goodbye. Though Miranda had long put him to bed, Titan was not yet asleep when Salem crept into his bedroom. The boy looked out from his covers to see his aunt approaching. Sitting at the edge of his bed, Salem asked him the question of all questions. The one which would tell her if it was time to mourn her brother once and for all...or if there was still a chance.

"Did you mark it?" Blinking with drowsiness, Titan gave the appearance of a nod, though she wasn't exactly sure. "Can you show me?"

She lifted back his blankets, allowing him to slide down from the bed to the floor. She watched his little feet stagger sleepily along to his long row of blocks on the floor. He stood eight blocks down from the last one he'd placed, looking at her for instruction.

"Yes," Salem told him.

"Downstairs." It was the only word the boy uttered, but it was all she needed to hear to know what she was expected to do. As his hand reached for the yellow block, Salem raced down the hallway, throwing up her hands to freeze everyone in their sleep to keep them unaware. She took the stairs two at a time until she reached the foyer again.

Seth was staring at her in a state of confusion. Though his bodily remains still hung on the wall where he had exploded only hours ago, he had been restored to the present. Titan's bewildering power had once again removed one element from history, returning it to what it had been before.

Her first instinct was to run to embrace him, but it took only seconds to remember the monster he still was. Seth bared his glistening fangs which looked even whiter against his searing red eyes. He hissed at her. It should have been frightening. Standing before her was a murderous rampaging vampire...but the hiss was so over the top she found herself laughing.

"Really?" Salem said, stepping closer to the fiend who had once been her brother. "Did you really just hiss at me, Seth? It's a little precious, don't you think."

"I will rip you to shreds, witch!" he growled. "Where is my wife!"

Flicking her wrist at him, Salem immobilized him with her power, keeping his head free to hear, think, and speak even though the rest of his body could not move a muscle. "You and I are going to have a chat, little brother."

"Where is my Yasmine?" he snarled, snapping his teeth at her but unable to reach.

"Seth," she began. "I need you to listen to me. I need you to try and remember who I am to you. I can help you if you will only reach inward to that hidden place where you *know* me. More importantly, where you know *you*."

She lifted his motionless hand into her own and squeezed. The fury in his eyes intensified. With her other hand she caressed his cheek. Checking his eyes again she saw something waver. The redness lightened. Something flashed. It was gone as soon as it appeared, but it told her there was a chance.

"You and me, Seth. Remember. Remember the night they took our mother away? Remember how we held each other all night, afraid and alone? We had only each other. I am your sister. I am the one person who will never give up on you. Find me Seth. Find me in what's left of your heart. I can heal you."

His eyes were almost his own again, but the war raging beneath them was one she was not winning. She had to rely on something more. "And Yasmine, Seth. Remember our beautiful, sweet Yasmine? Remember how innocent she was when we were growing up. She was the heart of this family, Seth. *That* Yasmine, not the one you have now. You loved her Seth. And she's out there now, alone and frightened and raving mad because she thinks she's lost you. But you can find her. *We* can find her. And we can restore her to what she once was. But first you must go back to who you were."

She withdrew the vial of blood from her pocket. "Allow me to give you a drop of this blood Seth. It's the way back. You will return to who you used to be. And you and I will find Yaz together. She needs you, Seth. And I need you. Be my brother again." He was staring at her now. His look was one of confusion, not rage. She dared think it might also be a look of hope. She couldn't be sure. But it was her only chance. "Seth, I am going to release you now. When I do, you will have two choices. You can strike me down and kill me. Or you can allow me to give you this cure. By taking it, you will be absolved of your sins. God will wash away your kills. You will have your soul returned to you. But it must be a choice you make." She waved her hands, freeing him of her hold. Mentally she readied herself for defense but was careful not to make any sudden movements to incite him.

When she saw her brother opening his mouth, she thought it was all over. He was going to sink those fangs into her throat and end her forever. But as his mouth opened, his head tilted backwards. Seth was opening for her to give him the cure.

Tears streamed from her eyes as she removed the cork from the vial and lifted its contents over his awaiting mouth. Allowing one single drop to fall before recorking the bottle, the blood hit his tongue. As he lowered his head, his body began to quake. Seth fell to his knees as he began to convulse. He bellowed from the pain. Salem fell beside him, pulling him into her arms.

"It's the evil dying, Seth. With its death you must feel all the agony you caused. You are reliving the terror of your victims. But it will end. And when it does, you will feel your soul growing back inside you."

Never had a more tortured expression crossed any face she'd ever seen in her lifetime. She watched her brother experience every kill he'd made, every drop of terror he'd caused, every stab of pain he'd inflicted, but from the other side of it. He was feeling what his victims had felt. Salem cradled him as his convulsions lightened to more of a tremor, and then only sorrow. His devilish eyes grew soft and tender again, and as the last vestige of evil melted away, he lay on the floor, clutched in his sister's arms, sobbing uncontrollably for all he'd done. Seth Blanchard had come home.

Sneaking Seth out of the house without anyone noticing him was the easy part. Everyone tucked away upstairs in bed made their getaway seamless. Where to hide her brother was the problem. For now, Salem decided the best place to stash Seth would be at Miles' house. He was still in Charleston and his flight wouldn't arrive until late afternoon, and it being New Year's Day, the flight would probably be delayed a few hours. It would give her time to think about her next step.

As she drove through the empty streets of Daihmler, her brother was strangely quiet for a man newly restored to his humanity. His silence worried her a little. Was it the shock of everything he'd experienced? Was he still suffering residual anguish from reliving the pain he caused his victims? Was this simply quiet introspection? She needed some clarity to know for certain he had indeed changed and was no longer the monster he'd been. As Salem navigated the deserted roadways, the faint glow of streetlights cast eerie shadows inside the car. Deafening silence filled the spaces between them over the hum of the engine.

"I am not going to hurt you," he said, breaking the tension. "I can tell you are thinking it."

"Can you blame me?"

"Salem, I feel really weird. Removed. I remember all the things I have done. I'm so ashamed. I can't shut it out."

"Perhaps, you shouldn't try. It is all part of you now. It changed you. But that doesn't mean you can't find your way back to the real you again."

"All I care about right now if finding Yazzy." He gave her a suspicious look and said, "And you don't really think things can go back to normal again, otherwise you wouldn't be stashing me someplace away from Blanchard House."

Blowing a strand of hair out of her eyes, she raised her hands from the wheel to gesture a *who knows*. "I don't know what to expect. The normal you remember isn't the normal that exists today. Only a few hours ago your daughter killed you and she was almost killed by her own mother right afterward. I don't think waking everyone up to announce Seth is alive and human again is the greatest idea right now. I need to think. I'll figure out how to reintroduce you back into the family."

"Don't tell anyone about me until we find Yasmine." She did not like hearing him say that. It carried an ominous tone. Then he continued, striking fear back into her heart. "If Yasmine refuses to take your little cure, then I will have her turn me back."

"Seth! No! That's crazy."

With all frankness and sincerity, her brother turned to her and stated, "I left everyone and everything behind to be with Yasmine—whatever way that meant. My love has not changed. If necessary, I will make the same choice again."

Salem could not believe her ears. It was perhaps the most horrible thing she'd ever heard her brother say. Outraged, she chastised him, "Seth Blanchard, you have children. You have sisters. You have a family who loves you. Are you really saying you will throw us all away to become a vampire again?"

"No," Seth replied. "I will throw you all away to be with Yasmine again. I will not live without her."

"And what if she kills you when you find her?"

"Then I get the beauty of dying in the arms of the person I have loved most in the world."

Once they'd arrived at Miles' house, Salem slipped Seth inside without any neighbors noticing.

"The couch is comfortable. I've napped there several times and there is a blanket on the top shelf in the closet. The bathroom is through the other door. There's probably food in the fridge..."

"I'm not hungry. I just want to find my wife."

Without warning the front door opened. "Salem? What is going on here?"

"Oh my God, Miles!" she exclaimed. Her reaction caused Miles to have a reaction of his own, tossing his suitcase into the room but turning around to leave again. "Miles! Wait!" she cried, chasing after him. He was almost back to what was clearly a rental car, when she grabbed him by the arm.

"Salem don't!" he said. "Go back to your little tryst."

She laughed, realizing this was the second time tonight she'd laughed at a wholly inappropriate time. "Honey, seriously, it's not like that. He is my brother."

"You don't have a brother," Miles snapped. "Except..." He started to open the car door then stopped. With a look of incredulousness across his face he turned back to Salem, "Salem Blanchard, is that...Seth? Seth the vampire!"

Her hands on his shoulders, doing her best to calm him down, she gave Miles a brief rundown of everything. When she was finished talking, he was staring at her blankly. Salem wasn't sure what it signaled but then it was he who surprised her with a laugh. "Salem Blanchard—soon to be Thorsby, you are the damnedest woman I have ever known. Is this part of being Queen of the Witches? Trying to tame monsters?"

Resting her forehead on his chest in relief that he wasn't furious, she smiled. "No, it's more a big sister thing. I had to try. And it worked, Miles. He isn't a monster anymore."

"Why is he here?"

"I thought you'd be back later today. I didn't expect you to drive all the way back in the dark of night."

"Sounded like you needed me."

She kissed him for the gesture. "Okay, well let me get him out of here. I'll take him to my office. I can't let the family know about him yet. Things need to die down and I need to know when we find Yasmine that she too, will take the cure. If she won't I may have to kill Seth all over again."

Miles told her to leave him there. She tried arguing the point, insisting she would not risk his safety for her little experiment. He countered that anywhere else would risk Seth being discovered. Miles said that if Salem felt he was safe to be around, that was good enough for him. She took Miles inside and made introductions. Seth was standoffish but polite, and Miles was arm's-length welcoming. Salem decided to stay the night herself and phone Blanchard House in the morning to tell them Miles got in late, and she was with him.

The light was shining through the window of Miles' bedroom casting across Salem's closed eyes. She opened them and rolled over to say good morning. He wasn't there. A wave of apprehension swept over her. Jumping from the bed she rushed to the living room to see if Seth was still on the couch. He wasn't. Frantically, she began to check the other rooms, until she went into the kitchen. Miles was standing at the window, watching something. He saw her come in and motioned her to join him. With relief filling her body, she wrapped her arm around his waist and looked out to the yard. Seth was out there, standing completely still in a little patch of lawn where rays of light shone down over the roof with its first tendrils of the morning sun.

"He's been standing there since I got up a few minutes ago."

Salem walked outside and stood beside her brother.

"It tingles my skin without burning."

"It has been a long time for you," she smiled. "You've forgotten its warmth. But you don't ever have to live in darkness and shadows again."

"We will see," he replied cryptically.

"Stop talking like that Seth! There is no way I am going to let you go back to being a vampire again."

"Then help me find Yaz."

CHAPTER TWENTY-THREE

A New Set of Troubles

Charlie Bennet, Chief of Daihmler police summoned Trix Blanchard to his office. She'd been called away from training at the Academy, which meant it was serious. Entering his cluttered office, he motioned from his desk for her to shut the door behind her. He did not offer her a seat and she did not take one herself. He was her superior now and she knew not to take any unnecessary liberties.

"What the hell is going on?" he demanded. "You have any ideas?"

Regardless of his standing as her boss, Trix still hadn't learned to suppress her moxie. "What is going on?" she repeated. "In reference to what? The weather? The current tensions in The Middle East? Do I expect the groundhog to see his shadow next month? What do you mean?"

"What I mean, Cadet Blanchard, is murder."

"Clarify."

"Do the Blanchards know anything about these murders?"

Forgetting formalities, Trix sat down in the chair opposite his desk and replied, "Chief Bennet, I have no idea what you are referring to."

Slamming the newspaper down on his desk, it was turned so that she could read it, he snapped, "These murders!"

Scanning the caption to the article, Trix saw a story about a couple of mauled bodies being found on the outskirts of town. She read from there a little further, "The reporter describes this as an encounter with a bobcat."

"I know it does," Charlie said. "No one but me knows this for what it is. About a decade ago we had a string of mountain lion deaths. Turns out it was a serial killer. But I know it was a werewolf. Now that wasn't something I ever wanted to know, but thanks to your family, I knew it. Now, all these years later, the same thing looks like it is starting up again. Is this the same as last time? That's what I need you to tell me."

Trix leaned forward, resting her hands on his desk as she answered, "Yes. It is the same. We are aware of the situation, and we are on it."

"On it, in what way?"

Trix leaned back again in her seat. "We know who it is. We are searching for him, and when we find him, we will kill him. Do you have any further questions for me Sir?"

A little distracted from her bluntness, but pleased she was the first Blanchard to not try to give him the runaround, Charlie replied, "I guess that is all Cadet. You may return to your training. Thank you for telling me the truth. I hope you will keep me posted on your family's progress."

"Certainly," she smiled.

"Good. I would like this matter to end before the public starts asking questions we do not want to answer."

Demitra was standing on the porch when the rental car pulled up and parked. Almost as if they were lifelong friends having a reunion, Demitra ran down to meet her as she got out of the car. Daphanie Channing had a bright smile on her face as she embraced Demitra. "It is so good to see you, even under these questionable circumstances," Demitra told her friend. "Come on in the house, I'll get Jerry to grab your bags."

"Oh, I'll take them to the hotel later," Daphanie remarked.

"Hotel?" Demitra cried. "No, you'll stay here with us. Won't that be easier anyway while you and Salem work on your interview?"

Once inside, Daphanie was welcomed by Miranda, Jerry, and Sage. It was a far cry from the first time they'd met the famous network personality only this past thanksgiving. Of course, then she was merely an irksome reporter investigating the Blanchards and their secrets. One time traveling assassin and a roaring house fire later, and they were all close friends. The story Daphanie was so eager to tell a few months ago was still in the works, only this time it was at behest of none other than Salem Blanchard, who practically begged Daphanie to assist her in bringing the supernatural world to light on national news. Demitra informed Daphanie that Salem had texted to say she was running late, but would be home soon, commenting afterward, "That girl has scarcely been home since New Year. I suppose she's planning her wedding."

Having a light lunch in the kitchen, Daphanie was thrilled to see Romulus well and healthy with her own eyes after being shot on Thanksgiving, but what really astounded her was his being a human.

"Do you mean the transfusion of his brother's blood turned him into a human being?"

"Isn't it neat!" Rom grinned. "I can be a boy all the time—except...the other day I had to go back to my other body when my Dad showed up. I was scared he was going to hurt us."

"What is this?" Daphanie questioned. "Your Dad? But I thought—"

"As did we," Demitra remarked. "I will explain later. There is a great deal to fill you in on, especially regarding Thaddeuss D'Angelo."

Across town, Fable had not seen the empty parking slot due to the oversized pickup truck sticking so far out into the street that it obscured her view until she had passed it. Pulling into a café parking lot to turn around and go back for it, she was dismayed to see another car moving in on it before she could get there. To her benefit however, another spot a few cars down was backing out of their old space, allowing Fable to slide in. Much to her surprise as she was walking towards Howard's office, she saw it was Vanessa who'd won the coveted parking space.

"Fable?" Vanessa waved, smiling at her friend. "Are you here to see Howard too?"

"Hey, girl. Yeah, he told me to drop by this morning around 11 o'clock."

"Me too," Vanessa replied as they both went in together.

Echo was deeply concentrated on whatever it was he was working on at his desk. He barely acknowledged the ladies as they went past him to Howard's office. He directed them to sit down and passed each of them an envelope full of documents. "Since you both basically require the same things, I thought I'd kill two birds with one stone."

Opening her envelope, Vanessa found all the necessary medical records and official documents needed to act as Theda's legal guardian. Fable's packet contained virtually the same, only hers had been professionally and quite convincingly falsified.

"Does this mean I can enroll Rom in school?" Fable asked with a tinge of disappointment in her voice.

Howard took both mothers by surprise when he announced, "I have already enrolled both Romulus and Theda at Daihmler Elementary acting in my official capacity as your attorney."

"You are an attorney?" Vanessa replied. "I didn't know that."

Howard chuckled. "I am a man who wears many hats. Olympia sent me to law school while my father taught me the business end of estate management. Olympia Blanchard wanted all-in-one service from me. She used to say, "I know I can trust you so why take a chance on a stranger for my legal needs." He looked over to Fable whose face was still grimacing over losing Rom to school. "This is absolutely ridiculous, but there is also a phony news clipping in your papers telling the heartwarming story of how Daihmler's own patron mascot, Romulus the wolf, once saved the toddler of his owner's college friend, Felicia, from drowning in the Blanchard pool."

"Felicia?" Fable grinned.

Pleased she got the inside joke, stemming from the time she pretended to be her own college pal using the name Felicia to gather information to help her mother. "Thought you'd enjoy that," Howard chuckled. "Long story short, Felicia—out of extreme thankfulness—changed her son's middle name to Romulus, in tribute to the Blanchard pet who saved his life."

"So, now Romulus can use his real name in school?"

Nodding, Howard answered, "It is an absurd tale, but if anyone should question why your newly orphaned friend's child, now adopted by you, shares the same name… you can show them the article."

Vanessa looked over all the papers Howard had so carefully procured and smiled, "School starts back in a few days. I guess Theda and Rom can join Con and Hera now."

"Yes," Howard said. "Although Theda will be in the 5th grade and Romulus still needs rapid tutoring to catch up to those fake records from his *previous school*."

Salem rushed through the door of Blanchard House, shouting apologies to the famous reporter she'd kept waiting. Daphanie assured her no offense was taken. With so many people in the house, Salem asked her new comrade to take a walk with her. The winter air was mild enough that it was not an unpleasant walk. Their conversation was awkwardly light, of the chit-chat style, until Salem led her to the iron gate of the family cemetery. The rusty hinges creaked as she opened it, nodding to Daphanie to enter. Daphanie walked along beside Salem through the various aged headstones until they came to one where she stopped.

"This was my husband. His name was David Lane."

"Yes, I know about the tragic accident. It must still haunt you."

"Every day," Salem admitted. "And this little grave is where people believe my son is buried. But he isn't. Witches are traditionally cremated. My son's few remains are buried in Charleston where his cremation took place." Looking up at the reporter, she added, "We witches hold so many secrets it becomes hard to keep track. Secrets which have been necessary to shield us from the rest of the world. You and I are about to end all that with your televised interview at the end of the month."

"Hopefully, it will be regarded as historic. The day the world finds out all the hidden things they never knew. If we are believed. That is the one concern."

"We will be. I am going to supply you with all the proof we need." Salem walked over a few yards to another grave. The headstone upon it was broken, left littering the grave in chunks or smashed marble. Daphanie could not make out the name. "This grave belongs to my sister-in-law, Yasmine Blanchard. But it is as empty as my son's."

"Yasmine isn't dead," Daphanie remarked, surprising Salem with her awareness. "I am pretty sure I have met her, and your brother, in New York. They own a nightclub of all things. A club where several people disappeared without a trace. They use the name Buchanan now."

"They aren't in New York." Salem revealed. "Not now. They attacked the house on New Year's Eve. My niece, Hera, destroyed Seth...her father. Afterward, Yaz... her own mother, smashed her nearly to death into that cracked section of the foyer wall. Echo saved Hera but Yasmine got away. She is deadly and she is now insane, because she believes Seth is gone."

"Believes?"

Salem's phone suddenly rang from her pocket. Withdrawing it, she glanced at Daphanie. "Speak of the devil. This is Miles calling. He has Seth with him."

Daphanie did not understand, but the mystery of how Seth was alive became less important as she watched Salem's face answering the call. "Miles?...Seth?...what do you mean! What did you do? Seth! If you didn't, then how? Are you sure? He can't be...he just can't be."

Daphanie kept silent on the car ride to Miles' house. It had been instinct which caused her to follow Salem when she ran from the graveyard to her car in a panic. Whatever it was to cause this reaction, Daphanie waited for Salem to tell her unprompted. A few minutes into the drive, she did.

"I told you Seth is alive again," Salem suddenly blurted out. "No one at home is aware of that. Do you remember what my nephew did the night of the fire?"

Daphanie gulped dramatically. "How can I ever forget. He erased the entire event. Restored the house and everything."

"He did it again on New Year's Eve. Hera did kill her father. She blew him into a million pieces. Then her brother undid it, bringing Seth back."

"But why?" Daphanie asked. "If Seth Blanchard is a murderous animal—"

"He isn't." Salem stated, then sighed. "At least I hope not. I'm not sure."

Clutching the dashboard in reaction to Salem blowing through a traffic light, Daphanie asked her to slow down, then added, "I am trying to keep up Salem, but you aren't making much sense."

"Part of our story was going to be the redemption I can offer the evil beings of the world. An elixir said to restore lost souls. I used it on my brother. It gave every appearance to have been successful. Although we are about to find out for sure. You see, Daphanie...that was my brother Seth who called. He called to tell me that my fiancé Miles is dead."

CHAPTER TWENTY-FOUR

Only Curses Never Die

Daphanie was more than a little fearful of what was about to happen as she followed Salem into Miles Thorsby's house. Rushing in she swept through the front rooms looking for him. It was dark inside the house. Daphanie found a wall switch, filling the living room with light while Salem disappeared to the kitchen. Coming back in after not finding Miles, Salem and Daphanie both now saw Seth standing at the window. They had not seen him there in the dark.

"I placed him on his bed." Seth told them, still facing the window looking out into the night.

Salem rushed to the bedroom. Daphanie heard the sobs and followed, not wanting to be alone with Seth. Salem was holding Miles in her arms, crying while she cradled him against her. Daphanie went to her and placed her hand onto Salem's shoulder to let her know she was not alone. As if the touch triggered a more collected side of her, Salem released Miles back down to the bed and turned his head back and forth, searching for something. She then lifted his arms, rolling his sleeves while she inspected the body.

"What are you doing?"

"Checking for puncture wounds." Salem answered methodically. Daphanie watched in wonder as Salem continued looking the body over. The woman who'd only seconds ago been distraught now seemed somehow steely, removed. Daphanie then remembered how she'd been a half hour ago at the cemetery. She was rather matter of fact then as well. *I guess this is what happens when one woman suffers so many losses.*

She followed Salem back to the living room where her brother was still standing at the window. "He hasn't been bitten."

"I didn't kill him, Salem," Seth said abruptly. "And I've been watching through every window tonight to see if Yaz might be out there, like maybe if she can sense me. But she hasn't been here either."

"Then who?"

Seth turned around, the light hitting his face somehow provided Daphanie with relief. He did not appear menacing. In a sympathetic tone, he said, "I think he just died, Sis. I'm sorry. He was a nice guy. We talked a lot today. He really cared about you."

"He did." Salem agreed. Her coolness caused Daphanie to bristle. "I'll call the paramedics."

Salem disappeared into the kitchen to make the call. Daphanie wasn't quite sure what to do in the situation. She glanced at Seth, "I could have made the call for her."

"She prefers to handle things herself," Seth shared. "My sister does not like to be coddled or fussed over."

"Her fiancé *just died*," Daphanie emphasized. "She is allowed to cry." Daphanie did not expect Seth to react the way he did to her statement. With a low chuckle and two widened eyes he folded his arms and said, "My sister does not cry. Not where anyone else can see it. Comes with the territory." He went back to the window, presumably still hoping his wife would show up. "We've had a lot of death."

The family was waiting on them when Daphanie pulled Salem's car into the drive. Demitra met them on the porch, taking her niece into her loving arms. "I am so sorry, Salem," she offered. "Are you positively sure it was—"

"It was." Salem said. "Heart attack. The medic confirmed it."

She went into the house where Trix, Echo, Jerry, Miranda, and Sydney stood with sorrowful eyes. Salem wanted those eyes to stop looking at her. She did not want to hear "I'm sorry," she did not want pity or attention. She only wanted to get to her room and close the door. Pushing through the others, Fable approached offering no hug and no condolences. She simply took Salem's hand and led her upstairs. Opening the door to Salem's room, Fable went to the bed and turned down the covers. Salem sat on its edge where Fable lifted her feet, pulling off her shoes and covering her up. Salem clasped her cousin's hand, "It's my fault."

"How could this possibly be your fault?" Fable said dismissively.

Salem laughed. It was a grim sort of laugh. Fatalistic. An acceptance of a truth she had made herself forget. "The curse. Atheidrelle's curse."

"Don't start with that," Fable warned. "Don't even go there."

Salem looked incredulously at her cousin, "You know. You were there when my mother told us why she tried to undo Atheidrelle's birth. Atheidrelle cursed me to never have love. Love will always be ripped away. David. Michael. Now Miles. Atheidrelle's curse on Nacaria's children is still working its evil. Miles is dead because I loved him."

It was a somber night at Blanchard House. No one knew what to say. As close as the family could be, in truth no one living in the house except Demitra and Fable had a relationship lengthy enough with Salem to know how to help. Jerry, Trix, Echo, Sydney, Sage, and Miranda cared deeply for Salem, but they hadn't yet learned enough about the complexities of her inner workings to have any idea what to do for her. Only Fable and Demitra had been there when this happened before. This death was different, however. David and Michael had been family. Well-loved and greatly mourned. The Blanchards did not know Miles. Not well enough for any real devastating mourning. The grief they felt in their hearts was solely for Salem and the pain she must be going through.

"I wish we could do something," Echo told Sage in the kitchen as they cleaned up the pot and mugs from the coffee they'd made no one wanted.

"It's rough, man." Sage replied. "She's been through so many losses. It is not right."

Echo put the last coffee cup back on the shelf and closed the cabinet door. "I called my dad and told him. I really thought he'd have been here by now."

"I called Ocean so he can tell Arielle." Sage announced. "They were in the airport about to catch a flight home."

Salem was not asleep as the clock struck 2 a.m. beside her bed. The open window brought in a cool breeze. It shook the lacy curtain sheers, bumping into the tiny wind chime she'd made as a child which always hung on the end of the curtain rod. She could not feel anything. She wanted to, but it would not come. She wondered how she'd become so callous. Then she remembered the events of her life and understood. Although her eyes could not present tears, she knew they wanted to. Miles was gone. He'd been the only man since David, and it had taken years to be able to open up enough to allow him in. Now that too was gone.

She'd been lost in thought when the door slowly creaked open. Facing the wall, she did not turn her head to see who it was. Only when she felt the depression in the mattress did she know. Neither said a word as Arielle slid into bed against

Salem, wrapping her arms around her sister's waist. Salem settled back against her and finally drifted off to sleep while Arielle gently ran her fingers through Salem's hair. Arielle laid there with her until morning.

The night air felt thick with danger. The group of friends tugged their coolers of beer out of their trunks and dragged them up the narrow rocky walkway to the top of the cliff. Three guys and their girlfriends had foregone studying in favor of a late-night drunken cliff dive. It was much too cold for such things, but for the young, nothing seems impossible. If the Polar Bear clubs in Alaska can plunge into arctic waters, why can't a group of University of Alabama students? Besides, they made a fire on the cliff top to warm themselves after the dive.

The leader of the group, a sandy blonde guy named Scotty decided to start the adventure. Telling his friends to clear the way as he made a short run from the side of the rockface towards the edge of the cliff's ledge, he began his sprint forward. Each footfall hit the ground harder as he reached the end and lurched himself forward to clear the rocks below and dive clearly to the water below. His girlfriend cheered him on as his buddies roared in support. Scotty sprang upward, bent his body over and sailed straight down to the dark water below. His friends heard the splash as he plunged into Lake Tuscaloosa. Scotty touched bottom and sprang back to the top, expecting much fanfare. He heard the screams. He'd really impressed them. Now it would be their turn. As he made the long trek back up the rocky path, the screams were growing shriller and more frantic.

"Hey guys I made it! I'm okay. I told ya'll it was not a big deal. It's your turn now."

But as he came closer to the top again, he began to realize the cries were not about his descent. Something was wrong—and the cries were sounding now like fewer voices making them.

Scotty raced to the top and as he reached the small overhang on the side of the cliff his eyes bulged in terror.

A woman had his best friend Mac clutched by the throat. Terror shined through Mac's eyes. Mac was a big guy. Scotty could not understand why he wasn't fighting off the petite woman. He could hear his girlfriend screaming near a bush almost out of sight. Scotty's eyes found her. Some kind of wild animal had her by the arm, shaking and dragging her across the jagged shards of the ledge. Her left leg was covered in blood and her right leg...was gone. Gone. Scotty couldn't believe his eyes. The leg lay by itself a few feet away. Also screaming nearby lay Mac's girlfriend Debbie, bleeding profusely from the neck while holding her own severed arm in her other hand, shockingly attempting to put it back where it once belonged. The other girl was dead. Her neck ripped open, and her body was not moving at all. Their other male friend, Jessie was simply crying like a child against the embankment. He was unharmed but almost waiting his turn, knowing it was futile to run. Scotty dashed towards Mac, still under the woman's grasp. She was screeching at the top of her lungs like an insane person.

"You aren't my Seth! You aren't my Seth!"

Scotty watched as she began smashing Mac's face into the stone rock beside her, pausing every so often to lick the blood from the stone. In seconds Mac's face was obliterated. Scotty grabbed a loose rock from the ground and attempted to strike the woman. She whirled around, grabbing him between the legs by the crotch. Scotty screamed in agony as she stared at him with disturbingly sick satisfaction.

"You are not my Seth either."

He felt it when it happened. As his swim trunks tore from his legs in her clutches, so was his manhood, ripped from between his legs. In the moments before he lost consciousness, he saw his trunks and his penis tossed over the cliff as she pounced on top of him, fangs protruding from her lips.

"Well, that was a lot of fun Yasmine," Patric grinned, wiping his mouth and surveying the carnage at their feet.

"None of them were Seth, Olley. None of them were Seth."

Patric reached his arms out and took his sister into his chest. She sobbed uncontrollably. "I know my dear. I know. No man will be your beloved Seth. But you will find satisfaction in punishing them for that."

"I have to find him!" she cried frantically. "I have to find Seth!"

Patric was growing afraid now. His sister's mind was broken. She could not accept Seth's demise. He hoped a kind of sanity might return to her eventually. Until then, he would wait it out. He'd need her to attack the Blanchards again and retrieve his boys and their mother.

CHAPTER TWENTY-FIVE

The Mourning After

Sydney and Sage made breakfast that morning, although no one was eating much, except the children who loaded their plates and disappeared upstairs. Echo leaned on his forearms over his plate on the kitchen island, his head hanging just staring at the food he had no appetite for. "I can't stop thinking about how Salem must be feeling up there in her room." Echo continued his thought. "I came from a world full of death. It was everywhere. When I came here, I thought things would be different. Peaceful. But look at how much death we've had in the last year. Is this just what life is? A series of lulls until you lose something new?"

Sage leaned against the sink; his hand clenched into fists he was beating slowly together. Nodding towards the table where Sydney now sat with Ocean, he said, "Syd, Ocean, and I have lost practically our whole family. You lost Tess and your mom. We've all acquired scars that won't heal. I think life is *loss*. But you have to shore up those losses with gains. It makes you more prepared when the next loss comes. You have Lucky and Jinx. Ocean's about to have his own. Salem has Olympus. It makes a difference."

"Did Arielle say how Salem was doing last night?" Sydney asked her cousin.

"No," Ocean answered. "I haven't seen her. I think she slept with Salem all night."

Fable came downstairs. She wasn't quite in the mood for food, nor was she in the mood to hear her cousins prattling on about life and loss, so she ducked out to the front porch to have her morning coffee. She was surprised to see Howard there at the railing, staring out into the clear blue light of the early day. "She's still upstairs in her room if you came by to see her."

He turned around, "How is she?"

Fable thought something felt off with him. Howard seemed stiff. Anxious. "She's still sleeping. We didn't talk last night. But I know she's heartbroken. She finally had her chance at love again. Now this."

"They say everything happens for a reason. Maybe there's a reason for this."

"I'd like to meet this *they*," Fable scoffed. "She has had enough suffering for 3 lifetimes. I hope this isn't one too many. How much can one woman be expected to take?"

Howard looked grim, almost sick. "Salem is strong. Unbreakable."

"No one is unbreakable, Howard." Fable snapped. "We all have to be there for her now, on top of everything else we're facing. Patric is still out there somewhere, and he has Yasmine with him. Both must be found and destroyed."

Yasmine. Howard thought. She did come home. He'd been waiting ever since his deal was struck with Thaddeuss. Every day he half expected her to call or show up, all normal and back to her old self. It had not happened. However, she was in Daihmler now. And Miles died last night. A life for a life. An even trade. That was the deal. Wherever she was, maybe, just maybe she had turned into her old self again. If it were true, then Howard might be able to shut out some of his guilt over what he'd done to Salem. Today might just be the day Yasmine came home...the real Yasmine.

Back in the kitchen, Trix came downstairs with Arielle following behind her. She had the appearance of not having slept very much. As she passed, Echo patted her large baby bump, bloating his face in that pesky brother way to intimate she was fat. Trix smacked Echo on the back of the head while Arielle stuck her tongue out at him on her way to give her husband a kiss. "I was with her all night. Sorry."

"Don't be," Ocean replied. "How is she?"

Sighing, Arielle remarked, "I honestly don't know. She woke up a little while ago and told me she wants me to go somewhere with her, but she's being very mysterious about it."

"Is it true your mother—sorry—your aunt Atheidrelle put a curse on Salem?" Trix inquired as she crunched a piece of bacon.

Arielle raised her left eye and replied, "Do you mean *our aunt Atheidrelle*?"

"Shit!" Trix gasped. "You know after all this time I never really connected that. She was both our aunt, wasn't she?"

Arielle grabbed a plate and tossed a few pieces of country ham on it topping it with eggs, tomato gravy, garnished on top with a dollop of grape jelly. Trix made a face until she recalled that when she was pregnant, she ate celery dipped in cheese and rolled in crushed Froot Loops.

"Atheidrelle cursed Salem and Seth when they were little. If Atheidrelle could not have Xander's love, then no child of Xander and Nacaria would know love either."

"And you believe in it?"

Arielle pointed her loaded fork in her sister's direction and said, "Seth's first love died. Salem's husband and their baby died. Then look at what happened to Yaz. Now Miles. I'd say so. Atheidrelle's hate was the kind that followed you to the grave."

"What can we do for Salem?"

"Nothing," Arielle said. "I have been through this with her before. Give her space. Let her feel what she wants when she wants or feel nothing at all if that's what she needs. Just be here, quietly, supportively. She'll come to you when she needs to lean, and when she doesn't, let her be rigid. As for me, I'm going to eat, shower, and then go with her wherever it is she wants to take me."

Though Arielle had never seen where Miles lived before, when Salem turned into the driveway, she understood this was where they were. It made sense now. Arielle could see how Salem might need support when going back. They were there for Salem to grieve or possibly even to collect some of her things. Whichever the case, Arielle was glad she'd come with her sister. But when Salem paused before unlocking the door, she had a strange expression on her face. Staring into Arielle's eyes, Salem told her, "He isn't dangerous now. He will not try to harm us."

As the door swung open, Arielle saw Seth. With a gasp, her first instinct was to protect herself by blasting him with her telekinesis. But as he came towards them, she recognized the sparkle in his eyes that she had almost forgotten used to be there. The same blue tinge their father had. The moment she saw those eyes, she recognized her brother was himself again. She ran into his arms. Seth spun her around, kissing the top of his little sister's head. He pushed back from her to investigate the bump he felt between them. "You are pregnant!"

"And you're human!"

"Not that I'm not happy to see Arielle," Seth said to Salem, "But I thought we agreed to tell no one about this."

"I'm not no one," Arielle snapped, punching his arm. "I am your sister."

Back at Blanchard House, Howard was at the window of the living room, staring out in thought. Demitra was curious. "What are you looking at so intently?"

Snapping from his thoughts, he replied, "Just looking out. Anything wrong with that?"

"I am not sure," she said. "You've been looking out of that window or standing on the porch as if you are waiting for a delivery or something."

He left the window and sat down in the chair facing her, "I thought Salem and Arielle would be back by now. I hoped to tell Salem how sorry I am for her. I know it must be hard. But at least this isn't like the others. David was a whole other thing. And Michael. Nothing could be worse than Michael. And Nacaria and Xander were her parents. This isn't as damaging as those, surely."

Demitra was a little surprised by the statement. "Howard, she lost her fiancé. I don't believe ranking deaths in order of importance really does much to lessen the pain she is feeling."

"I didn't mean it the way it sounds. It's just surely there have been worse losses she managed to get over. She'll get through this one too."

"I don't think it's a question of which death hurts more. It's cumulative. It's more a matter of how much suffering can one person be expected to bear."

Howard half whispered to himself, "I didn't think of it that way."

Demitra stared at him suspiciously. Something was off. Howard was very tense. Howard was never tense. "Are you okay, Howard?"

"Me?" he replied. "What would be the matter with me? I'm just worried for Salem, that's all."

Ocean came in from the kitchen, asking if Arielle was back yet. Demitra told him she wasn't but asked him to join her and Howard in the study for a chat. It was an odd request, but Ocean went to the study. Demitra and Howard followed behind with Howard giving her a quizzical look. "Now is as good a time as any," Demitra said to him softly. "He and Arielle are going back to Charleston tomorrow."

With his hands clasped together behind his neck, his head swirling in disbelief, Ocean Blanchard...son of Seneca Blanchard...grandson of Pastoria Blanchard ceased to exist at 1:57pm that day in the Blanchard House study. In his place, doing his utmost to understand and accept, sat Ocean Blanchard...son of Howard Caldwell...grandson of Beryl Blanchard...great grandson of Demitra. "Are you two being serious right now?"

"I am afraid so." Demitra nodded. "I knew you were not Seneca's son on Thanksgiving when Olympia brought a dying Pastoria here from the past for us to heal her. She was at an age she had been before she ever had children. As she lay dying, before Echo healed her, Sage and Sydney began to disappear. If Pastoria died without ever having had children, her grandchildren would no longer exist in our present. But Ocean, you did not fade. This proves you are not, nor have you ever been, Pastoria's grandson."

"My Dad wasn't—"

"No," Demitra said. "I hope it helps to know Seneca loved you immensely. He never knew you were not his son."

Ocean looked at Howard, "But how are you—"

"I couldn't understand how if you were not a Blanchard, you were still a witch." Demitra continued. "I met with your mother secretly, and she admitted to one indiscretion, long ago, but she told me he was a routine normal business man. I will tell you now, for a while I feared you were a D'Angelo trying to pull something on us."

"What?"

Howard picked up from there. "The night before your wedding your mother recognized me. I was the man she spent that night with. The night you were conceived. I'd been in Mobile on Blanchard business concerning Pastoria. I met a woman at a bar. She was nice. She seemed to need someone that night. I did not know who she was at the time. But I am your father Ocean. You are still a Blanchard...through me."

Ocean was trying to put it all together in his mind. This revelation carried so many connotations to it he couldn't quite put them all together. Almost as if sparring against an electric tennis ball machine, thoughts and new facts came at him in a succession of hits. "You're my grandmother?" he asked Demitra.

"Basically," she smiled. "Great grandmother to be accurate. Beryl would have been your grandmother. Just like Trix and Echo."

"Oh my God! Echo and I are brothers! And Trix is my sister."

"As was Tess," Howard added. "You are my son Ocean."

"And you knew this at the wedding? And neither you nor my mother said anything to me?"

Howard took his hand and held it as he said, "I didn't want to upset your big day. But son, walking down that aisle with your bride, and placing her hand into the hand I knew then to be my own son...it was the proudest moment I have ever experienced in my life."

The entire family was taken by complete surprise at dinner to learn the truth about Ocean. Trix and Echo sat with stunned faces staring first at Ocean, then at each other. Similarly, Sydney and Sage looked at one another almost as if they'd lost someone. Of course, it was Fable to be the person who found humor in it. "Well, looking at you now, Ocean," she said. "With this new information, I don't know how we missed it.

You, Echo, and Trix all have the same black hair, similar cheekbones. I never could figure out how Forest, Syd, and Sage all had brown hair and you had jet black. You got it from Howard! Hopefully, you will keep yours longer than he has kept his."

"Do you know what this means!" Arielle squealed excitedly, leaving her chair to wrap her arms around Howard's neck. "You are my father-in-law! This baby will be your grandchild, and Lucky and Jinx's cousins!"

Trix placed her palm on her forehead, sorting it all out in her mind. "I have said it before, and I will say it one more time, we have the most fucked up family tree!"

Echo gave a half-hearted snicker, equally blown away by the news. "So, Ocean is my big brother? This is going to take some adjusting."

"What?" Ocean exclaimed with a grin. "You don't like me or something?"

Shaking his head Echo recovered from his implication, "No, no. Not that. I think it's cool I'll have a real actual brother—if only to pass Trix off too when she is impossible." Trix swiped his leg under the table. "I only mean this is mind blowing."

Arielle crossed to Echo, giving him the same neck hug she'd given Howard. "Oh, little brother, it's not any more different than when I learned about you and Trix." She stood up suddenly with another revelation. "Oh, do you guys know what this means? Echo is my brother...and my brother-in-law! Now that is funny! I guess everyone gets a surprise brother these days."

Her remark sparked a stroke of fear in Salem, as she recognized Arielle's slip. Luckily, no one else at the table applied her statement as meaning she meant Seth. Arielle glimpsed Salem's eyes and realized her mistake. She knew Salem did not want the family to know yet. Salem offered a change of subject, alerting the family she'd arranged for Miles' body to be shipped back to his family, but she would not be attending his funeral.

"Are you sure that is a good idea, Salem?" Demitra asked.

Solemnly, Salem replied, "I do not know the Thorsby's and they do not know me. Had we been married; things might have been different. But we weren't. They should mourn their son as such, and his part of my life is a separate thing. Besides, Daphanie and I have a lot of work to do to prepare for my interview."

Daphanie looked up from her plate somewhat surprised. "Salem, I assumed we would postpone—"

"Not at all," Salem asserted. "You have convinced the network to allot you two hours of prime-time air in less than two weeks. You and I must be ready. We will begin tomorrow."

CHAPTER TWENTY-SIX

The Trail She Leaves Behind

The reports on the murders at the lake consumed the local television channels and Seth had seen every one of them while confined to the hotel room Salem had stashed him in. He was certain Yasmine was responsible and pleaded for Salem to drive him out to the lake.

"Hold on," Salem said, grabbing his arm as he made his way to the door. "I agree the killing at Lake Tuscaloosa has to be the work of Yaz and Patric, but we cannot just rush over there."

"Why not?"

"Because she isn't still there, Seth!" Salem explained. "Those bodies may have been discovered yesterday but they were killed days ago. Aunt Demitra has been called in to check out the crime scene today. Let's wait and see what she picks up psychically. She may see Yasmine's current location, but if you go there, it will be your psychic trace she will pick up. If Demitra figures out where Yaz is, I promise you and I will get to her first."

He knew she was correct in her thinking. They would have to wait. In the meantime, he had questions about his time away from the family. When he first became human again, Seth had not considered anything else but his wife. Now, as he'd been in hiding for a few days, with nothing but time to think, he realized a great many things had changed during his absence. My time without my soul," he began. "Seems like a hazy dream you can't fully recall after waking. Salem, did our mother die?"

"Yes," Salem told him with a sorrowful frown. "At the House of Duquesne. She and our father." She clutched her brother's hand while they sat on the hotel bed, adding sweetly, "They died in each other's arms."

He was silent now although she could see in his eyes he wanted to know more.

"Seth, what else do you want to know? Would you like me to tell you about everything that has happened while you were gone?"

"How are the kids?" He asked. "I haven't seen them in…"

"Years," Salem added. "Two years." He looked down at his feet. He hadn't realized it had been that long. "Miranda has been an excellent mother to them. Hera had a very hard time, and Miranda was there for her every step of the way. And Titan… Titan is the reason you are even alive. He has amazing power, your son."

"He wouldn't know me if he saw me."

"No, he wouldn't." Salem admitted. "But that doesn't mean it's too late." She stopped a moment, unsure if she should tell him, but decided she should. "You have another child, Seth."

"I know." Seth told her, taking Salem by surprise. How could he have known? But as he continued talking, she realized he was not referring to Theda. "Yaz was pregnant when she got bitten. She was going to have another baby. It's still in her, which is why she has her powers."

"I am not talking about Yasmine," Salem revealed, grabbing Seth's full attention. "Vanessa Collins was pregnant when the two of you broke up."

Seth jumped to his feet, "What! That was ten years ago!"

"Twelve," Salem corrected. "Vanessa had a terrible time. Her father cruelly made her believe the baby died. She has only recently been reunited with her… your daughter." Seth could do little more than stare dumbfoundedly. "So, you see brother, though I understand how much you love Yasmine, and I hope we find and cure her, but there are other people you owe a responsibility to. Hera, Titan, and Theda above all."

"All I can think about for now is Yaz. We must find her."

Salem smiled at her brother and squeezed his leg. "She is going to find us. I have a plan." Looking at his sister quizzically, Seth recognized the gleam of daring in her eye. Giving his leg another squeeze, Salem told him, "You and I are going to go on national television in a few days. I am going to tell the entire world everything they have never known. And you are going to let Yaz know how to find you."

The air was chilly when they stepped out of the warm car. Though it was not yet Winter, the temperature change sent a shiver down Jerry Miller's spine. Or perhaps it was because of the task before them. Demitra joined her husband while she buttoned up her black wool coat. As the wind blew across them Jerry couldn't help but marvel at his wife's classic beauty. Her raven shoulder length hair was almost the same shade as her coat, only the beginnings of the silver strands here and there breaking the blur between them. He almost commented aloud on her loveliness but stopped himself. It wasn't the time or place, not with the gruesome task before them.

Jerry let Demitra take the lead up the steep trail to the top of the cliff ledge, his hands outstretched behind her ready to catch or steady his wife if her foot were to slide along the rocky path. Halfway up the path yellow police tape stretched across, tied to two pine trees, blocking the entrance to the crime scene. Of course, the police had long come and gone, collecting anything pertinent to the investigation. No one was there now. Reaching the top, Demitra and Jerry saw only the blood-stained rocks and earth demarcating where the bodies were dropped by whoever or whatever killed them. Ordinarily the putrid smell would have nauseated Demitra but after the explosive body parts which had sprayed all over the Blanchard House walls Thanksgiving, this crime scene was nothing.

"This is terrible." Jerry commented. This was his first time joining his wife on a case. It was much different than an episode of NCIS.

"It is always terrible." Demitra replied. "However, I fear this one hit much closer to home for us."

"Do you really think this was Yasmine and Patric?"

"Who else?" she answered. "From the description of the bodies, it must have been."

Deciding to stop hypothesizing and start proving, Demitra closed her eyes to summon her powers. She opened her eyes again and scanned the area, moving slowly from one rock facing to another, allowing her fingers to trace the stains of blood. She shuddered a few times as her visions blazed through her mind. Jerry stood back, allowing her to do her thing without his interference. A few minutes passed until Demitra sighed, released her concentration and turned to her husband with teary eyes.

"Jerry, they died in such agony. Without dignity. They were cruelly killed for the sheer sake of cruelty."

"Was it them, darling?"

She nodded. "Yes. It was Patric and Yasmine. Mostly Yasmine." Demitra stared out over the grayish green lake below. She was standing where Yasmine had been standing when she gripped the frightened man by the throat. "She's insane. Patric is killing because it is his nature. Yasmine is killing because she is furious. She's trying to find Seth and she is taking her anguish out on her victims because they are not him. Those men died horrific deaths. She isn't simply feeding herself. She is punishing men because she cannot have her own."

"Can you find her? Can you stop her?"

Demitra appeared to be listening to the wind even though Jerry knew she wasn't. It was more like she was trying to connect psychically somehow to some great distance perhaps only the wind could travel. "She is here. Somewhere at this lake."

Jerry ran his hand through his hair and rested it on the back of his head as he scanned the landscape. "Lake Tuscaloosa is huge, Honey. That doesn't narrow it down too much."

"The last time Patric was holed up in an abandoned loft. This time he is hiding out here. Maybe a cave. Maybe a summer house or cabin left vacant by the owners until Summer. But they are here. Out there."

CHAPTER TWENTY-SEVEN

Welcome News

Somehow being married to Mara had become a little easier the more Brandon lived with it, but it was an isolated life. Socializing with others carried far too great a risk. If for any reason, most irrational, Mara grew to believe another female had her sights set on Brandon, the "rival" often would die quite suddenly within the next few days. Or if Mara felt any flash of jealousy towards one of Brandon's friends for having memories or life experience with him which she either did not approve or felt sadness of having not been a part of, that friend might meet a sudden end as well. For this reason, the Rappaports had become recluses among Charleston society. Brandon missed company. Missed parties. Missed having friends. This was why when Mara's cousin Arielle introduced them to her fiancé, Ocean, it was a welcomed event in Brandon's secluded existence. By the time Arielle and Ocean married, Brandon and Mara had spent several entertaining evenings with the other couple. Brandon now considered Ocean Blanchard probably his closest friend, although he doubted if Ocean was as attached to the friendship as he. And why should he be? Ocean was free to go anywhere and see anyone he wanted. He probably had many close friends to choose between when he had spare time. But for Brandon, Ocean was the only game in town if he wanted friendship.

Brandon didn't even mind the fact Ocean and Arielle were also witches. They weren't the scary kind of witches like his wife was. They were quite down to earth, friendly, and fun to be around. They also seemed to keep Mara in check. In the Blanchard's company, Mara behaved as any normal wife and woman should. Of course, Brandon knew why. Arielle was her cousin, and deeply in love with her own husband, as well as expecting a child soon. This was one female who posed no threat whatsoever to Mara. And Ocean was new to her and Brandon. No preexisting stories to be discussed ad nauseum as a reminder she'd spent a lonely existence before. And though it was never said, Brandon knew because he knew his wife, Mara was a little afraid of the Blanchards. When the four of them were together, the world of witches was almost never talked about, but when it was, it had become clear to Brandon that Arielle Blanchard was a stronger witch than Mara. And Ocean's family, though dwelling in Alabama, were a force Mara never wanted against her.

Brandon grabbed himself and Ocean another beer from the kitchen and rejoined the conversation in the parlor. The recounting of the honeymoon had ended, and Arielle was now sharing with Mara the news from Alabama. Brandon was not aware his wife knew Arielle's sister, but when Arielle told her about her sister's fiancé's death Mara reacted as if she knew Salem Blanchard personally.

"She came here a couple of times," Mara informed her husband when she could see the confusion on his face. "I wouldn't call us friends exactly, but I helped her with something, and I liked her very much." She turned back to Arielle, "Please offer her my sincere condolences."

"Wait till you hear the other big news!" Ocean laughed, sipping his beer. "Turns out, for a little while the Blanchards thought I might be related to you Mara."

His remark brought surprise to his hostess' face, as well as her husband. "They think you are a D'Angelo?"

"Thought," Ocean grinned. "Past tense. It seems my cousin Demitra—excuse me, turns out she isn't my cousin. Anyway, she found out my father was not my father. When she found out I wasn't a Blanchard, she naturally thought your grandfather, Mara, planted me into the Blanchard family as a—I don't know, spy...mole. But turns out I am a Blanchard after all, just not the way we thought. Demitra isn't my second cousin; she is my great grandmother!"

Brandon crinkled his nose and asked in confusion, "She must be ancient! You are what? 30-33?"

Arielle giggled and said, "She's not old at all, she's maybe 60-61. It is a complicated lineage. But the crazy thing is Ocean's father is Howard, the man who gave me away at my wedding."

"Isn't he Echo's father?" Mara asked.

Brandon had heard the name Echo before from his wife. He was apparently a distant cousin of hers she'd grown to know a little when he visited Charleston. The thought must have brought the more common one to his eyes because Arielle quickly answered, "Yes, he is Echo and my sister Trix's father. Making Ocean, their half-brother. But no, Brandon, I can see it on your face, Ocean and I are not blood related. I did not marry my brother."

The foursome had a good laugh over the insanity of the situation, but then Arielle brought the subject matter around to more somber circumstances. "But I do have something else, something sad in some cases and not so sad in others."

"Our father is dead." It was one of the few sentences Mara's sister Ashby had contributed to the evening.

"How did you—"

"I know things," Ashby stated matter-of-factly. "Cousin Arielle wears her thoughts openly."

Brandon took hold of Mara's hand. He wasn't sure why. She did not appear upset by the news, but it seemed like the thing to do. She gave it a thankful squeeze and returned her attention to Arielle. "So, the Blanchards finally found my father after his escape during the battle at The House of Duquesne."

"No," Arielle contradicted. "I am afraid your father died at The House of Duquesne two Novembers ago. It wasn't Taub D'Angelo who escaped that night. It was Thaddeuss. He'd switched his soul with your father's body."

Brandon's eyes bulged as he tried to comprehend the conversation. Switching bodies? What all were witches capable of? Ocean gave him an assuring wink and said, "Don't try to wrap your head around it, man. You'll sleep better."

Mara stood up and walked to her sister, placing her hand upon Ashby's shoulder. "It was Father who they beheaded and Grandfather who got away. Grandfather allowed his own son to die in his place."

"You are not surprised by this," Ashby replied. "I am not."

With the settling in of this new knowledge, Mara realized what else this meant. She turned to her cousin and asked, "Where is Thaddeuss now? Do the Blanchards have any ideas?"

"He is dead." Arielle said solemnly. "Echo killed him at Blanchard House New Year's Eve when he was attempting to steal Tess' babies. Uncle Thaddeuss is finally and truly dead."

"And so it is over." Mara gripped hands with her cousin, smiling as if freed from some dreadful curse. "It is finally over. And we are free."

Arielle nodded. "We are all that is left of the D'Angelos."

CHAPTER TWENTY-EIGHT

Fable's Dilemma

The overhead fan seemed to be more on this date than she was. Nash Daihmler was almost harassed by it. It was November. Why were the fans even on in this restaurant? All he could feel was a continuous cold draft hitting the back of his neck which was made more sensitive from his fresh haircut and neck trim earlier in the day. The duct work above them had a small torn section which would have been completely unnoticeable had it not been flapping from the air of the fan. The candle on the table, with its wick way too short, kept threatening to go out with each rotation of the fan blade. Nash looked at Fable, who was slowly stirring the cherry in her drink around in circles with the slim red cocktail straw.

"Well, you are a regular chatty Cathy," he remarked finally.

His words snapped her back from wherever she had been inside her head. "I'm sorry." Fable frowned. Her next words were not words at all, only a series on stuttering stumbles as she tried to explain. Taking another sip of her drink she blurted out her distraction. "My ex is back."

Nash reared back from the table a little as if somehow feeling the need for distance. "Hey, Fable, it's okay. We have had a handful of dates. I have no holds on you, and you can pull out of this guilt free if your ex is where it's at for you."

The somber moment was suddenly broken by her startling laugh. "Oh, hell no!" she exclaimed. Reaching her hand over the table to pull his to her she stroked his fingers. "Nash, it's not like that. Believe me. There is nothing...NOTHING...inside me that wants him. This isn't a breakup conversation." Just as his face showed signs of relief, her face turned sour. "Of course, it is good to know that you don't feel like very much exists between us and you can just set me free without a second's thought."

Her pursed-up face of indignancy softened as she watched him try to backtrack his earlier statement. "No, no, no. I wasn't saying that. I was just trying to make you feel comfortable if you were ending things."

Ordinarily Fable Blanchard would have had more fun with this conversation before letting him off the hook and showing she was only playing with him. But things were far too serious right now for her to toy with the new man in her life. "Patric is a dangerous man," she explained. "His return makes me afraid. I think he is coming after—" she almost said, the boys. Catching herself, she finished her sentence, "I think he will try to take my son from me."

Nash was appropriately concerned, albeit confused. "You've been a great mother. I don't see how any court would take custody from you and give it to some man who has never been in his child's life." Then with a slight smirk of uncertainty, he added, "But didn't you say your son's father was dead?"

Fable's eyes enlarged a little uncomfortably like a soap opera vixen caught in a lie right before commercial break. "He was. He's not now."

Raising his hands with a grinning exacerbation, Nash cried, "What?!"

"We thought he died. Turns out we were mistaken. The point is he is back, and he is dangerous. I don't know what he will do."

"What can I do to help you? Anything?"

Smiling sweetly at him she took hold of his hand again, giving it a thankful squeeze. "I appreciate that. But there's nothing you can do. It will have to play out however it does."

Understanding she did not want to talk about it anymore, or perhaps she didn't know how, Nash changed the subject. "Seems like your cousin and my brother are hitting it off. They've been out a few times. What is it about Blanchards and Daihmlers?"

She smiled. His subject change helped but it also highlighted her other stressor, and that was how little he truly knew about her and how she hadn't been honest yet in the budding relationship. Echo was not her cousin. He was her grandnephew. But how could she possibly explain the connection? She could no more tell Nash that Howard, 30 years her senior, was her nephew and Echo was his son, than she could reveal her ex was a werewolf and so were her two boys. She sidestepped the guilt and simply replied, "We Blanchards are hard to resist."

Nash grinned. His light brown stubble framed his beautiful plump lips and white teeth. She wanted to kiss those lips so badly. So she did. Leaning over the small intimate table she stroked his unshaven face and kissed him deeply. "You wanna get out of here?" she asked.

"Most definitely."

Whatever plagued her mind was always sent packing whenever Fable and Nash made love. It was only their third time, but it was all encompassing. Fable had been with her share of men in her youth—way more than she was comfortable thinking about—but now as an older woman nearing her mid-thirties, she was realizing she'd never in her life felt so completely one with another person in bed. Nash Daihmler was a phenomenal lover. It wasn't anything he necessarily did that no one else never had, it was how he made her feel about herself while he was doing it. Fable had never felt more beautiful or desirable than she did when she saw herself the way Nash saw her. Every blemish, every flaw she agonized over in the mirror, he passed by without noticing or caressed with the same fervor as the parts of herself she liked best. Nash made her feel like the only woman in the world. And Fable knew she was falling in love with him, and it scared the crap out of her.

He wanted her to stay the night. She wanted to as well. She knew technically she could. If she called home and told her mother, Demitra would see to the boys for her. But as tempting as it was to stay and wake up with this gorgeous man, Patric's presence in town made her fearful to be away from her sons in the night. She said a passionate goodbye before she left, dropping hints about when she would next be free...in case, he wanted to see her then. On her drive home, she needed to bounce her troubled thoughts off someone.

"Ocean is on duty tonight," Arielle told her when she heard the ambivalence in Fable's tone. "I am just sitting in bed watching a movie I've seen a dozen times. Tell me what's on your mind."

Steering through the darkened streets of Daihmler, Fable unburdened herself to her friend. She admitted her deep fears surrounding Patric's return. She confessed her weighted guilt over being unable to be completely honest with Nash. And perhaps the most difficult for her to admit, she told Arielle how petrified she was to have such strong feelings for this new man.

"All your feelings are valid." Arielle began once Fable was finished. "It can't be easy to have to hide your true self from a person you are trying to grow closer to. You know that for this relationship to truly grow into what it could be, you must eventually tell him you are a witch. And he needs to know about the boys. I understand why you think it is too soon right now, but Fable you are quickly approaching the line of when it's been too long without the truth. You don't want him to feel as if you've been lying to him."

"Yes, but Ari, what if it scares him away? I mean, let's face it, the least of my secrets he has to accept is that I have some magical powers. Wrapping his head around the fact that I have a son who turns into a wolf and son who is a wolf that turns into a boy is kind of a lot to expect a guy to be okay with. And then there's Patric."

The sound of crunching came through the car speakers. Arielle admitted she was eating caramel popcorn clusters—her newest craving. "As far as Patric goes, we killed him once before. We can do it again. But he needs to know the rest, Fable."

"He will bolt," Fable declared. "I already know it."

"Then he bolts!" Arielle exclaimed. "Would you want to stay with a guy that would do that anyway?"

"That's easy for you to say though, Arielle. You have Ocean and he's the same as you. Neither of you feel inferior to the other or endangered by the other person's life."

Arielle's crunching was a distraction. Fable wasn't sure if the lengthy popcorn sound was because she was hungry and pregnant or just chewing while she considered Fable's point. Finally, she spoke again. "I get it. But Fable, for better or worse you are a powerful woman with some complicated baggage. A man will either rise up to the challenge or he won't. But you can never know which until you share your truth with him."

Fable was now turning onto the road leading home. She decided it was time to wrap up the call. "I will have to think about it. I know you are right. I just need to figure out when and how to have the conversation."

"Get some sleep," Arielle advised. "I'm coming back to Daihmler this weekend for the Consort. I'll be sticking around a few days after because I have a potential buyer for Blackie's house. We can talk more when I see you. Goodnight. Love you."

"I love you too."

Cold crisp twigs, dry from wind and lack of rain, snapped quickly as her body stalked through the wooded patches between the private residences lining Lake Tuscaloosa. She went alone out into the night, leaving her brother asleep in the rustic cabin they had appropriated from its once living owners. Yasmine did not want company. Patric was in human form anyway, he would not have kept up with her pace. She had a mission to follow through. Seth was still alive. She could feel him. Though she did not understand how he could still remain after having seen him blown to pieces, every dark corner of her beatless heart felt him out there, somewhere.

Light shone through large glass windows high on a cliff above where she stepped out from the trees. A long timber staircase stretched from the boat house up to a series of leveled decks until reaching the top of the cliff. Yasmine took the steps higher and higher, smashing out the mounted flood lights as she passed. At the top of the cliff the long rectangle house stood two stories with almost nothing but windows facing the still, murky waters below.

She held back behind a planter of arborvitae, observing the people inside. A man facing away from the window was watching a football game from a sofa. A woman, presumably his wife, came in carrying a bowl of something and two long neck beers in her hand. As she moved closer to the house another male, younger, came into view laying on the floor, elbows propped holding his head towards the game.

She flicked her hands, freezing like statues, the people inside before she smashed out the window with a deck chair. She went to the man on the couch first. Dark hair. Beard. He wasn't Seth. She tossed his head through the hole in the window after she had pulled it from the roots of his neck. Next, she moved to the boy, still propped on the floor. He was not Seth either. She fed upon him. As his blood coursed through her veins, she relived his day and his life. He'd been the one to dent the car that time he lied, claiming someone in the parking lot did it. He'd smoked weed that afternoon on a walk through the woods. He also hated football. He only watched with his father because football was the only interest his father ever showed. The boy's pretending had not garnered him any closer a relationship with his dad than before. Once he was drained dry, Yasmine stabbed him through the back with a fire poker. He was already dead, but she was angry he had not been the man she was searching for. She wasn't hungry anymore. She considered draining the woman anyway since she was there. But decided instead to place the ax leaning against the firewood in her hand. Police would think she killed her family. Yasmine giggled to herself on her way out imagining how the woman was going to explain this scene—even to herself. Her screams echoed through the darkness when Yasmine unfroze her halfway down the cliff.

CHAPTER TWENTY-NINE

The Whole World is Watching

It had only taken two hours to make it from the Birmingham airport to La Guardia, although it seemed longer to Salem due to fans leaving their seats in flight to snap selfies with Daphanie. Just as it had been on the flight, when Salem walked out of the terminal with Daphanie Channing, many eyes swept over them, more fans rushed them to say hello to the esteemed journalist. A car and driver waited for them outside the airport and as they ventured towards Manhattan, the weight of what they were about to do in the next few days fully hit Salem. As New York City loomed ahead, Daphanie patted Salem's knee, understanding her trepidation.

Once Salem was settled in at The Moxie Hotel in the Flower District, the two of them made their way to Times Square where they met a young woman named Jane, Daphanie's assistant. It was quickly understood Jane knew everything and was there to capture some amazing footage on film. The request from Daphanie Channing was simple, stop Times Square. Though Times Square proper encompassed many blocks, Salem centered her powers at the point where Broadway, 7th Ave and 42nd Street came together. There beneath the glowing billboard lights and standing among the taxis, Ubers, delivery trucks, and passing cars Salem released her magical time stopping power onto New York City, bringing everything in her expansive radius to a halt.

Though Daphanie had briefed her assistant on Salem's abilities, seeing it in action first-hand was astonishing to her. Jane tilted her face back away from the camera needing to allow her own eyes to take in the miracle before letting the camera lens be her eyes. It all looked as if some massive television screen had been paused. The roaring engines of traffic were not roaring. The wheels on the automotive vehicles were no longer turning. Pedestrians caught in mid-step; their stride captured in stillness. Jane's curious eyes wondered how they did not fall, balanced with one foot partially gripping the ground with the other midair ready for the next. Her logical mind knew there was no way anyone could get the thousands of people she could see in the vicinity to collectively participate in such an elaborate scheme. And even if it were possible, too many of those on the sidewalks or crossing at the intersection were so delicately balanced in mid stride it would require the entire world's Olympic gymnastics teams to pull off such a feat. But what convinced Jane more than anything else were the pigeons, mid flutter on the ground and those now paused in the air without moving a wing to know that her boss had been telling the truth. Looking at Salem with bulging eyes, Jane said softly, "You're a witch."

Without the sounds of New York traffic, the hum of footfalls, the distant rattling of jackhammers, Jane's words carried on the silent air. Salem sent her a wink and replied, "I know."

It was later in the afternoon when Daphanie, Jane, and Salem walked into Boucherie in Union Square. The French bistro was one of Daphanie favorite spots in the city, but it served another purpose as well. It was near an important location, one in which Salem hoped to kill two birds with one stone. Seth was waiting at a table when they entered.

"Did things go as you hoped in Times Square?"

"It went splendidly," Daphanie answered, quickly adding an introduction. "Jane Winslow, this is Seth Blanchard...sometimes known as Saul Buchanan here in the city. He is Salem's brother and was a vampire. He is also the owner of Nightshade down the street."

Salem reminded Jane he was no longer dangerous and reminded Seth he would not be alone. "Gideon and Alexandrea Duquesne are expected to arrive tonight. You will stay with them at Nightshade where the three of you can protect one another after the broadcast. I expect within a day or two, Yasmine will come back to New York. She knows the city and she knows your building. She will come to you there if all goes as planned."

The car picked Salem up from the hotel promptly at 6pm. It was nearing 6:30pm when they pulled up to Rockefeller Center where Jane was waiting to escort Salem inside. "You okay?" she asked Salem as they made their way to the network studio. Salem only shrugged, her eyes taking in everything around her. Most people paid little attention to her other than a couple of men who turned to get a second look at the auburn-haired beauty walking by. When Jane led her into a control room, Salem knew she was now in the company of people who had seen Daphanie's footage. An unspoken fear seemed to fill every space in the room. The staff, though polite, eyed her with suspicion and unease—perhaps even fear. Daphanie came in immediately, rescuing Salem to the sanctity of a waiting room.

"Nervous?"

"I don't know." Salem answered honestly. "We will see. I have faced down monsters. I have infiltrated frightening fortresses full of danger around every corner, but the butterflies I have right now are new to me."

"I am keeping you with me until we walk out there. Don't worry. I am not going to make you look foolish. You and I are about to educate the world, together."

The overhead lights of the studio were almost blinding until Salem adjusted. In every direction people were rushing by with freshly typed notes, or bottles of water or clipboards they read from to whoever's ears they were addressing. An intern who couldn't have been more than 25 years old, came forward and wired Salem with a tiny microphone on her collar. She was glad she wore a suit and not a strappy dress. This was her lucky navy suit and she always looked great in it. Somehow knowing that she would not look like a fool calmed her concern of sounding like one. *I can do this*, Salem told herself. *I believe in this decision.*

She sent a fast text out before the show began, *Is everything ready?*

Yes. Miranda replied. *It is all set up as you explained.*

And Trix is ready?

She's here too. Miranda explained. *We have a television on here and Titan is already placing the coins on the trays.*

All Right. Salem texted back. *Guardrails in place.*

Lost in her own anxiety, it startled Salem when the cameras began rolling and Daphanie started the broadcast.

"Hello America," Daphanie began looking straight into the camera. "You are joining us tonight for a highly anticipated three-night special." This was news to the producers and everyone in the studio. Daphanie Channing had indeed arranged a two hour special tonight, using every bit of credibility with the higher ups to be allowed such an event without divulging the true nature of the broadcast. Banking her entire career and reputation on this broadcast, Daphanie rolled the dice and went for it. If tonight was the jaw-dropping, earth shattering event she presumed it would be, the network would indeed insist on two follow ups.

Daphanie continued her intro. "I want to thank you for tuning in, especially when you consider we've been very tight-lipped about the subject matter. But as our promos have been telling you for weeks, tonight we are going to change the world. Tonight, everyone on earth will learn something only a select privileged few have ever known."

She sounds like she's about to reveal the existence of aliens, Salem thought as Daphanie went on teasing the audience.

Daphanie continued, "I am joined tonight by a remarkable woman. Her name is Salem Blanchard. She is no one you would know by name or face, but there are some of you out there who owe your lives to her and her kind. You see, Salem is a witch."

Salem watched as the technicians and staffers stopped whatever they were doing and stared straight ahead at what they perceived to be the beginning of a break from reality by their esteemed coworker on camera.

"When I say witch, I do not mean a practice of the Wiccan faith, although any of you out there who happen to belong to that population will probably not require as much convincing as the rest of us." Daphanie placed her hand upon Salem's knee as a sign of support but also to convey she was not alone in this frightening moment. "Salem and those like her, have existed alongside us for centuries. We know them well, even if we did not know what they could do, or what they have done to protect us through time.

Salem, for example, is a prominent advertising executive, a devoted mother, a tax paying American with hopes and dreams, sorrows and regrets. She is the same as you and me, with one pretty monumental exception. Salem has unusual powers. I do not want to use the term superhuman, or supernatural, or even degrade her abilities by calling them magic. She is a human being, but an amazing one. Before I talk to Salem and allow you to hear from her, watch this footage I recorded myself only yesterday in preparation for this interview."

The camera man called out that the footage was running. Salem turned to Daphanie and whispered, "Now, I am petrified."

"So am I," Daphanie admitted. "But in three minutes, all of America will have seen you stop Time Square. They still won't believe it. But we will have their attention."

The Blanchard family clustered around the television in the upstairs den of Blanchard House. Not a word was spoken—all much too riddled with knots to form words. Demitra stared ahead, unblinking, every fear she ever held for her family bubbling beneath the surface. Jerry kept his hand firmly holding hers while his other gripped Fable's knee. Sage, seated in the overstuffed chair by the couch with Sydney perched on the ottoman, was watching Vanessa sitting on the floor with the children. Everyone was gripped by the screen. Quietly, he tapped Sydney's back signaling to switch with him. He slid into her spot and placed his hand on Vanessa's shoulder. She turned to look at him, smiling in appreciation of the support. He understood her rising fear. Until a couple of years ago, she had successfully steered her life clear of the Blanchards and the drama that came with them. Now she was in the thick of it. Now she was the mother of one of them. Thanks to the newspapers, everyone in Daihmler knew the story now of how her father had kept her child from her... and that the child's father had been Seth Blanchard. Whatever was going to happen now was going to involve Theda, and Vanessa by extension. No one could predict what trouble Salem's announcement was about to cause, but one thing was certain, nothing was ever going to be the same again. When the footage of the Times Square traffic ended, Daphanie and Salem returned to the screen.

In Titan's room, Trix and Miranda sat on the bed, watching the broadcast while also watching the little boy. Titan Blanchard continued to take coins from a bucket whereupon he placed them, one by one, in a straight line atop many rectangular tin serving trays. As the broadcast aired on the TV screen, the boy's mother and cousin observed each carefully placed coin. Trix rose from the bed as Titan moved to the third tray. With a black sharpie in her hand, she made a mark beside one of the coins on the second tray. It was the coin which had been placed just moments before the segment aired. Trix returned to her seat, continuing to watch the broadcast after the world saw Salem bring Times Square to a standstill.

"You saw it for yourselves, America." Daphanie said, looking earnestly into the camera. "Salem has the power to pause time and motion when needed. It isn't permanent. The people in Times Square yesterday never even knew it happened to them. None were in danger or affected in any way, other than perhaps running three minutes late to wherever they were going." She addressed Salem now. "Salem, even with our footage I understand we still haven't convinced anyone yet. Of course, we have more to show them. But before we go further, please tell your fellow Americans, what a witch really is and why do you exist."

Salem cleared her throat nervously and began answering Daphanie's question. At first, she was staring back at Daphanie until she remembered she was supposed to speak to the camera. "Witches have been here as long as everyone else. We have lived in secrecy because mankind always fears what it does not understand. The word *witch* itself brings fear and mistrust to people's minds. Over centuries, the way we have been depicted in writing, theater, movies, and TV mostly seemed to imbue the misleading narrative that we are evil. But contrary to that misconception we are not wicked or evil. We are not products of the devil. Like with everyone else, we are simply people. Some people are nice and helpful, some people are mean and selfish. However, the witch's purpose on earth is to protect what we call The Natural Order of things. Primarily, we protect humanity."

"And give us an example of one of the ways you have helped humanity."

"Last year, my family eradicated a society of vampires who were being sheltered for centuries on Wadmalaw Island in South Carolina. Countless unsolved murders and disappearances went on for generations. We stopped it. Witches stopped it."

"Vampires?" Daphanie repeated, feigning surprise. "We are to understand vampires are also real?"

"Yes," Salem answered. "As well as werewolves, ghosts, demons, cat people, rain people, and sea spirits. Many things mythology tried desperately to describe." She did not require an audience to understand she had just lost a lot of people who may have been listening at home. The eyerolls, smirks, and looks of incredibility from the station crew was enough of a sampling to convey it.

Moving on, Daphanie asked, "Then why do most people never see these such creatures?"

Salem addressed the camera, "Some do," she answered. "But they never live long enough to report it. Once it was a rampant problem in the world, but my kind have dedicated generations to wiping them out. And most of them have been. The world is nowhere near as treacherous as it used to be, thanks to thousands of witches who devoted their lives, and sometimes sacrificed their lives for the greater good. That's what we had to do on Wadmalaw."

"Salem is referring to the mysterious House of Duquesne in Charleston." Daphanie explained, speaking directly to her viewers. "Viewers may recall how the house was famously something of an architectural anomaly. There was some question about what could have caused the explosion which crumbled it to the ground. It was dismissed as a gas leak."

"It was not a gas leak." Salem said defiantly. "I blew it up. And with it went the D'Angelo family who had been housing the vampires for hundreds of years, using them to their own wicked means."

Daphanie's follow-up question was simply, "And how did you manage to blow up such a massive building?"

Salem answered while looking directly at Daphanie, afraid if she looked into the camera while answering, might frighten people at home. "I have the power to make things explode. Normally nothing that large, but I was linking hands with my brother and sister. It always seems to amplify my power."

"A great many people died at The House of Duquesne. People who by all accounts should not have even known one another. Many members of your own family were there. Can you tell us why."

Salem swallowed, an audible gulp ringing into the mic clipped to her collar. "The D'Angelo's had an unprecedented ability to remain immortal. That wasn't a witch's power. That power derived from a demon ancestor they had. But it kept them able to live life after life for centuries. But to do it, they had to possess innocent people's bodies. Each possession basically killed the person leaving their body vacant for a D'Angelo soul. Eventually they figured out if they only jumped into the bodies of fellow witches, they could acquire their powers as well. Over many years the D'Angelo's had become more powerful than anyone ever should be. And they were attempting to do it one more time, by claiming a member of my family."

"Is that why the Blanchard family was there when The House of Duquesne came tumbling down?"

"Yes." Salem replied. "We were trying to rescue our relatives and save the world from the evil inside that house."

"And how did you accomplish this?"

"We killed all of them."

Demitra gasped out loud. "I wish she had not said it like that."

Suddenly the many cell phones in pockets and sitting on tables began to ring at once. The varying ringtones competing with one another would have been comical had it not elicited dread in everyone. As the different Blanchards answered their phones, eyes scanned everyone else as the Blanchards gestured with hands or made expressive faces to one another as they fielded their calls.

"That's right!" Jerry cried out unashamed. "Yes, sir. I am married to Demitra Blanchard...Yes, she is a witch. And a damn good woman."

Demitra wanted to check in with her husband as to whether his job was now in jeopardy, but she had her own crisis to deal with. "I know Charlie...I know...This was not my idea. I was against the whole thing...She isn't a child anymore, Charlie. I can't make Salem do anything."

As Fable tried to remind one of her clients that it is her witchcraft which allows her to know how to give proper care to the animal patients at her clinic, she saw another call coming in. NASH. "Shit."

The remainder of Daphanie's broadcast filled the time with more footage displaying Salem's powers of halting time or blowing things up—which they both now wished they'd omitted. Salem gave a complete history of The Consort of Witches and the many heroic and philanthropic things witches had done over the generations. As the final hour of the special began, Senator Jason'te Barstow came on, backing up Salem's claims and revealing many aspects of the world he had witnessed or participated in during his longer lifetime.

Daphanie's final question for her guest was hopefully enough to lure viewers back for a second broadcast the following evening. "Salem, why do you feel at this time the importance of coming forward and admitting what you are? Some people will leave this broadcast certain you and I both are delusional. Some may believe what you are telling them, and fear your kind greatly. What is the reason you have chosen to reveal yourself, and your secret world, to the public?"

Facing directly into the camera, and with all the confidence in her tone as she might address a Consort meeting, Salem told America, "Because monsters are real. They are out there. They are responsible for more deaths than we realize. I'd wager 1 out of 10 of your viewers have lost a loved one to dark forces in this world, and they do not even know it. My people fight these things. But it is becoming harder and harder to do so in a world of changing technology, video phones recording everything everywhere. Remaining secret is not possible if we are to keep this world safe. That is why I am here tonight. If the people at home will not be afraid of us, not come after us because we are different, we can promise them safer lives."

As the cameras switched over to the next anchor tasked with the impossible job to hold viewers and discuss his topics after such a sensational announcement, Daphanie was pulled aside by an official looking man in an expensive suit. Salem sat with Jason'te still on their stools until Daphanie rejoined them. "Well, I have been told my job is very definitely on the line. No one on the top floor believes *my stunt*, as they are calling it. But after the first half hour tonight, over 100 million people tuned in. We have been allowed another broadcast tomorrow night. One more chance to convince the world."

The news from New York was being played and replayed all over the country, even the world. And Charleston was taking notice, being that their city had been openly implicated in the MSNBC broadcast.

The restaurant was a buzz with whispers—whispers which began rising into audible voices. Brandon wasn't quite sure what was happening. Maybe something dramatic happened during the Gamecocks game? Maybe a senator got caught up in a breaking scandal. He could see the commotion was coming from the bar where the televisions were on. Mara looked equally perplexed. But then it all came rushing at them when several patrons stalked towards the table.

"You!" A man said, pointing his finger at Mara. "You are one of them!"

Brandon shot to his feet. "Do not point your finger at my wife."

The sneer across the man's face was menacing. An illogical hatred gleamed in his eyes as he grumbled, "Your *witch* you mean!"

Brandon was unprepared for that. He looked at Mara who returned his concerned expression. How did this guy know about Mara? Brandon became acutely aware now that this man had followers behind him, all with the same threatening faces.

"She's one of those D'Angelo's!" a woman shouted from a few feet away. "I've known who she is a long time. Used to strut around town like she owned the place. She's a D'Angelo!"

"My wife is a Rappaport." Brandon said, raring back his shoulders to where his chest stood out. He was like a bear ready to attack if necessary.

"What are you all upset about?" Mara asked. She looked almost childlike with the light fixture above glistening from her doe eyes.

Another man in back of the approaching group shouted, "The news! Some woman just went on air and claims she is a witch. Said she blew up The House of Duquesne.

173

The house you used to live in! Said D'Angelo's were evil. Said they killed folks."

"And you are one of them!" the woman added. "My daughter disappeared three years ago. Police said she ran away. But I'm not so sure. Maybe your family killed her! Did you kill my daughter?"

A dangerous mania was brewing. These people were scared and like many people do who are afraid of the unknown, they were forming a mob...and a mob validating each other's suspicions, can become violent fast. Brandon lifted his wife by the arm, pulling her around the table close to him and distancing her from them. "Let's get out of here."

"You two aren't going anywhere," the self-appointment spokesman of the group bellowed. "Not till we get some answers. Somebody call the police!"

"For what?" Brandon asked, growing angry at this outrageous ambush.

"To arrest this witch! This killer. This evil from the Devil's own kingdom."

Very few times in her life had Mara ever felt afraid. She felt afraid now. The malice in these people's eyes was something she'd never known before. They meant her harm and were not afraid to act on it. As the little mob encroached closer, Brandon swept Mara behind him, backing her up further from their reach. "All of you need to calm down. I don't know what is going on but leave my wife alone. She has done nothing to you. Whatever you've just seen or heard has nothing to do with us. We are just here to have dinner. But if we are upsetting you, we will leave."

Brandon attempted to escort Mara past them, but they only closed ranks, pinning them into the large window, unable to move. The angry man came nearer, reaching out as if to grab Mara's arm. Brandon reacted violently. He punched the man's face, knocking him back into the others whose proximity kept him from hitting the ground. Springing forward, the man lunged at Brandon. Brandon side stepped him, bringing his next punch into the man's kidney area. As the man doubled over, Brandon smashed his nose into the table. "Leave my wife alone!"

No one was listening. Brandon's defense of his wife had been viewed as an act of aggression. He had proven they were the enemy, and this mob were now even more certain in their hasty assumptions that it was their job to stop them. The crowd seized upon Brandon, grabbing at him, trying to move him out of the way so they could get to Mara behind him. There was no way out. Brandon shouted to his wife, "Do it! It's okay. Do it, Mara!"

Mara's hand crossed over Brandon's shoulder; her outstretched index finger touched the menacing man's shoulder. Instantly he engulfed into flames! Brandon watched the look of shock hit his face, followed immediately by searing agony as his clothes withered into fiery ashes exposing sizzling skin now bubbling and receding the way plastic shrivels and melts when burned. He spun in circles, igniting those close to him. They too, bursting into a raging inferno. The screams were piercing. Brandon stood shocked for a moment, then came to his senses, grabbing a chair and shattering the window. He pulled his wife to the safety of the sidewalk outside as pedestrians stopped and stared at the roaring blaze consuming the restaurant and all its patrons. Only Brandon and Mara made it out of the fire storm. He quickly got Mara down the street away from the building. Firetrucks sped by on the narrow Charleston lane. Keeping a firm grip on her hand, Brandon ducked them down a side street, sprinting towards Pirate's Courtyard. Once they were securely sheltered in the walled off passages meandering through the private residences, Brandon paused at the center fountain.

He leaned over, hands on his knees, catching his breath as his adrenaline settled. "You okay?"

"Yes," Mara smiled. "That was horrifying, Brandon."

He glanced up at her, between breaths and remarked, "When I said, 'Do it' I meant sweep them back to give us room to get out. I didn't mean set them all on fire."

Like a little girl just told she'd put on the wrong shoes, Mara shrugged and said, "Well. Either way. It doesn't matter."

He wanted to be outraged at her. But the aggressive brutality in those people's faces was stuck with him. He did not care that they were dead. He felt ashamed that he didn't care, but he didn't. And he knew Mara was not the least plagued by what she'd done. Chastising her would not teach her anything. He decided to simply be glad they were safe. There was no time to dwell on how many people he just watched his wife kill. What mattered now, was what happened to provoke them. Who outed his wife as a witch? Home was only a few blocks away. Brandon took Mara's hand again and walked her through the darkest sections of alleys, until they reached their house.

Ashby met them at the door. "There are no secrets now. The world has been told."

CHAPTER THIRTY

Outing the Monsters

Waiting for the car to pick her up outside the hotel, Salem hid herself among the sidewalk lined barricades of palms, long stem flower stalks, and greenery which ran up and down the sidewalks of the Flower District like privacy screens. Waiting in the lobby was no good, the staff and various guests coming in and out kept staring at her. Some looked fearful. Others looked starstruck. Either way she preferred the chilly February air. She called Trix to check on things at home. Trix assured her Titan had marked every moment of the broadcast with coins. Afterward, Trix used her power over metallurgy to slightly fuse each coin in place to the metal trays so that they would not budge. The trays were then locked safely away by Demitra personally. Salem knew at once where Demitra had placed them. In the secret Hecate's vault, no one except Salem and she even knew existed.

The second night in the studio, Salem did not walk unnoticed through the halls. Every head turned, every eye staring. She'd spent the day alone in her hotel room, too nervous to be seen on the streets of New York. When she got to the set of Daphanie's broadcast, she was surprised to see she was not going to be the only guest. Daphanie was across the soundstage speaking to two women Salem did not know, but in a high-top stool on stage sat someone she did know. Gideon Duquesne. Salem made a swift cross over to him.

"Hello, my dear." Gideon smiled.

"I want to thank you for doing this with me, Mr. Duquesne."

"We are past formalities, my dear. And it is I who is indebted to you. You see I have thought very much about what all of this could mean for me."

"I don't follow."

"The Duquesne family has been a dead bloodline for centuries, only tonight the world will learn it isn't. You have given me the chance to restore my name and rebuild a life out of the shadows. I have every hope my sister Bianca will take your miracle, and the Duquesne family can rise from the ashes to what we once had been before this awful curse brought us to ruin."

Daphanie appeared beside them. "I have Seth stashed in the green room until we reveal him. He is with Mrs. Duquesne." She paused, looking mighty pleased with herself. "I have another surprise for you. Two more guests are scheduled for tonight. Two who contacted our offices after your segment last night. They want to back you up. We flew them in from Nashville this afternoon."

"Who are they?" Salem asked.

"Witnesses."

The show began much as it had the previous night, with Daphanie briefly recapping the revelations of the first broadcast. Then she moved on. "We have had tens of thousands of calls and emails since last night's story aired. Many of you do not believe what we have revealed while some of you have called with stories of your own. I would like to begin tonight with the eyewitness count of two young women." Daphanie walked to the right side of the stage where the two females she'd been speaking with were on stools, wired with microphones and eager to tell their story.

"My name is Lacey Petras," one of the women said, as the camera zoomed in on their interview. "This is my friend Ellie. When we heard the lady last night talking about witches being real—"

"And vampires! Don't forget that!" Ellie cried.

"Yes, we can't forget that!" Lacey laughed, almost excitedly. Salem could see these women were eager to share a story. Probably one they had told before to other people who never believed them. Lacey continued. "Last year we were at a concert in Nashville. We live in Nashville. One of our favorite bands was playing at the Ascend Amphitheater."

"Phish!" Ellie chimed in again. "And it was awesome!"

Lacey nudged her friend playfully and added, "Well, it wasn't all that awesome. We got attacked."

Daphanie took control of the segment now. "You and your friend were at a concert, and you say someone attacked you?"

"Several someones." Ellie clarified. "Vampires were there. Like, real honest to God vampires!"

Daphanie worried if the overly eager girls would seem credible on air, but she was going to let them tell their story their way, with a little guidance. "Let's stop there and get a clear picture. You say vampires attacked the concert? Why has no one ever heard about this? I would think something like that would have made the news immediately. Explain why it didn't."

"Oh," Lacey replied, understanding now what Daphanie's meaning. "It wasn't on the news because nobody saw it happen."

Ellie broke in once more to further explain. "Lacey and I love Phish. Like, love love them. But we need space to dance. You can't get that up front. So, we always move back on the lawn behind everybody else, where we can really move."

"That's right," Lacey went on. "Everyone was into the music and looking frontward at the stage. Then suddenly these crazy people grabbed us. At first, I thought we were about to raped or robbed. I can tell you I was really scared. But then the man holding me leaned in and I swear to you, these two long sharp teeth started growing out of his mouth. It was just like Dracula or something! You watch TV and stupid horror movies where they have vampires, and you just don't care. It's not scary anymore. We are all used to it. But I'm here to tell you when it *is real* and it is *happening to you*, you are never more afraid of anything in your life."

"She's right!" Ellie exclaimed. "I remember thinking *this can't be real. This isn't really happening.* But then you realize it is and these things aren't made up. And it dawns on you all those stories and movies had to come from somewhere. Maybe it was real all along but got told so much it sounded like fairy tales."

Daphanie steered them on, "What happened when these vampires attacked you?"

"A woman came out of nowhere." Lacey answered. "She was amazing! Some kind of Wonder Woman. She swept in, pulled us free and all by herself killed those evil things. She saved our lives."

"I think she was a witch!" Ellie cried.

"She was definitely something," Lacey agreed. "She had powers and strength like nothing I've ever seen. We would be dead for sure if it weren't for her." Lacey faced the camera directly. "Whoever you are and wherever you went, thank you Lady with the purple eyes and long dark hair. We owe you everything."

"You know they are talking about Artemis!" Fable exclaimed, as the station went to commercial.

Demitra nodded. "Has to be."

Miranda held Hera tightly against her as they watched the television. But now that it was a commercial break, she turned to Demitra for answers. "Do you think this is going to be a terrible outcome? Has Salem done something wonderful or detrimental?"

"I don't know." Demitra answered honestly. "I have no idea what this is going to bring."

"I have two small children to protect." Miranda said. "I don't want to have to change our names and go into hiding. I don't want to leave you all. Or Blanchard House. But if Hera and Titan are at risk..."

Demitra reached over and grabbed Miranda's hand. "Let's not get too ahead of ourselves yet. But if it comes to having to go underground, I think we all will have to."

A commercial break gave the staff in the control room time to load some footage. It was old footage, nearly restored for clarity. When Daphanie's program came back on the air, America watched their screens as an unbelievable battle took place. At first it might have seemed like discarded Hollywood footage from a movie no one ever released. However, its "special effects" were nowhere as showy as Hollywood would have let slip by, giving the tape an air of authenticity, made even more believable with Salem narrating what they were seeing.

"These are recordings from over a decade ago, filmed in my own home. What you are witnessing is an attack by a werewolf. He is the extremely large humanoid, hairy figure, currently ripping my brother's arm off on screen. The other beings are actually natural wolves which are also attacking us, under the werewolf's control." Rather casually, Salem quickly added, "Oh this is when my cousin healed my brother's arm. See, its attached again. No worries!"

Demitra was dumbstruck by the television screen. Before all of America her family and their house were on display, mid-battle, for everyone on earth to witness.

"I forgot we recorded that night," Fable offered, her hand pressed to her mouth. She looked down at her sons, sitting on the floor. Their eyes were glued to the screen as they saw their very own father in his murderous attack on their family before they were even born.

Jerry looked over at his wife, hanging his head. "I'm sorry."

Demitra glanced at him questioningly. "What?"

"A few weeks ago, I was clearing out the 3rd floor tower room and found a bunch of old family videotape and DVD discs. Salem asked if she could have them. She wanted to have them digitally restored. I had no idea. I just thought they were Christmases and birthdays."

When the next commercial break ended and the show resumed, Daphanie was sitting with both Salem and Gideon. She had worked most of the day figuring out just how to tell this new addition to the story. She'd spent her career always attempting to remain neutral in controversial stories. She'd tried to consider the beliefs and opinions of all people. However, this time, she was going to have to take a stand and land in one decisive corner of an age-old argument. There was no other way to tell this story and no avenue to hold open the long-held beliefs of others.

"You are back with me, Daphanie Channing," she addressed the camera. "My next statement is a difficult one for me to make because it has always been my intention and this station's intention to respect all cherished beliefs when it comes to religion. I have personally struggled with religion much of my life. I considered myself an agnostic person. I cannot do this any longer because of the things which have come to light for me while investigating this story. I have learned that there is, in fact, a God. Whether it is masculine or feminine I do not know. If it is the God of The Bible and the stories told within it, I do not know. But there is one. And now I will explain to you how I know.

I am here now with the witch I introduced you to last night, Salem Blanchard. With us sits a man probably none of you know, even though he is older than anyone I, and you, have ever known. Gideon Duquesne is a vampire. Or, I should say, was a vampire until a short while ago. He has lived many centuries. He was one of the vampires we heard about last night who lived inside The House of Duquesne." Daphanie looked at Salem and said, "Salem, would you tell our viewers the story?"

For the following 15 minutes, Salem talked. She spoke from the heart, and she spoke from experience. She told America—and now the world, who was equally tuned in—about how vampires were real. She revealed that her own brother and his wife had become vampires. With tears streaming from her eyes, she gave an honest account of what pain it caused her and her family. She then switched gears, telling the story of how her cousin, a celebrated physician, became imbued with a small fraction of God's power by God Himself. As delicately as she tried to tell this portion of her story, she knew it would be a powder keg across social media the moment it left her lips.

Daphanie asked the inevitable question the evangelicals and all Christian kind would be screaming to the screen at home. "Are you claiming your cousin has become a god?"

"Basically," Salem answered. "What she actually is, is a conduit of God. A piece of Him is inside of her. I guess you could say she's God's Assistant Manager."

Her attempt at a joke did not make anyone smile in the studio as they stared in condescension or blatant offense. Daphanie did her best to move it along. "What would you say to people who accuse you of likening your cousin to Jesus Christ?"

Flippantly, Salem faced the camera and said, "Liken away. They are pretty much the same thing; except she got her power much later in life. But now that I think of it, I guess Jesus was the very first of The God Strain."

Salem told about the day Beryl presented her with God's Blood, offering salvation to the damned creatures who would accept it. And Gideon was one such creature. Gideon, with guidance from the host, told his long and involved tale. But mostly he spoke about the night he took God's second chance, and how he now feels with his soul restored.

"You see Daphanie," Salem said after Gideon's segment. "Another reason why I am coming forward now, is because for the first time in mankind's history, we have been presented with a gift. A chance to cure and restore the lost souls to the light. Forgiveness and restoration. But I cannot hope to achieve this goal unless everyone in the world knows what God has given us, so they can now open their eyes to what really exists out there, and help my kind locate and redeem them."

"Are you saying that if we as humans can shine a light on the ignorance we have up until now lived in, we can eradicate evil?"

"Something like that."

It was time for another commercial break, but before cutting away, Daphanie teased the viewers about her next guest. "One of these such creatures who has been terrorizing the shadows is here tonight. Like Mr. Duquesne, he accepted the Holy Blood Salem offered. We will hear his story after the break. We will meet, ex-vampire... and Salem's own brother...Seth Blanchard."

No one spoke for several seconds. Demitra, Fable, and Miranda stared at the television where Seth's image had long faded and was now replaced with an allergy medication commercial. Hera rose up from her seat on the floor and walked to the television, almost as if she expected Seth to be inside it. "I killed him," she said softly. Turning back to the others, she grew more animated. "I killed him! You saw it. How is he alive?"

Miranda and Demitra looked at each other and at the same time said, "Salem. Salem used Titan to bring him back."

The Blanchards at home sat glued as the broadcast resumed after the commercial break. They watched transfixed as Salem told the world about her brother's fall from grace and of his wife who had been brutally attacked and changed into the monster she had become. Seth told Daphanie a similar description as Gideon had provided as to what the elixir felt like entering his system. He explained the anguish he feels now for those innocent people he harmed during his short time as undead. And he faced the camera directly, making a plea. "Yasmine, if you are watching or if...you find out about this...I am alive. Come to me, Yaz. Come to me where we found life together. I will be waiting night after night, until you come to me."

CHAPTER THIRTY-ONE

The Chance to Show You

The third and final night of Daphanie's feature story brought higher ratings and more viewership than any broadcast in television history. More than the final episode of M.A.S.H. in the 1980's. More than the final episode of Friends in the 2000's. And even more than the falling Twin Towers in 2009. If there was a television turned on, it was tuned in to Daphanie Channing and the now most famous woman in the world, Salem Blanchard.

"Salem, last night you told us an unbelievable story about your cousin. I'll be honest, what you said has stirred a great deal of controversy since last evening. Evangelicals are in an uproar. Many Americans, and other Christians across the world, have been calling your claims about your cousin becoming God, blasphemous. This outcry is not helping advance your insistence that witches are docile and not to be feared. What do you have to say to those out there greatly offended by your statement?"

Salem could almost hear her aunt Demitra gritting her teeth back home, trying to telepathically caution her not to sound cavalier, but Salem was Salem whether she was trying to be diplomatic or not. "I can't do a whole lot about how offended people get when truth is spoken. You may not care for the truth, but the truth is unyielding despite whether or not you want to accept it. My cousin Beryl, I will repeat, is not GOD, singular. She is a vessel He works through. She is also not the only one out there. From what I understand, there have been many over the ages."

Challenging her guest a little on clarification, and for dynamic ratings, Daphanie replied, "Yes, but you did say she has God's Power."

"Yes, she does."

"Do you not see how unsettling the thought of that might be to average humans? What would stop a witch who can wield the power of God?"

"Nothing." Salem said rather frankly. "I'm not going to attempt to minimize the momentousness of the situation. If a witch possessed God's power and desired to rule over the Earth or do whatever crossed their mind to do, I don't think anyone, or anything could stop them." As her earth-shaking words filled the air, Salem faced the cameras directly with the precision of a stage actress who knows precisely when to release her show stopping line. "That is why God does not choose corruptible people to wield His power. Every man or woman who has ever carried The God Strain, has been above reproach. Only the purest heart, the sincerest soul, and the most unselfish minds are chosen. Judging from Biblical texts I'd wager those with this honor are more loyal to His will than the angels in Heaven."

"But you did say there was a family of witches, the D'Angelo family, who did try to steal the God Strain."

"Yes," Salem said. "And we stopped them. The God Strain is safe."

"You so freely admit to killing," Daphanie pointed out. "Admissions like that alone are bound to frighten people. What do you say to them?"

She gripped her hair between her hands and wringed it slightly before tossing it over her shoulder. Leaning in towards the camera crew with her hands on her knees she addressed those watching behind the screens. "This is why it is witches who are tasked with protecting mankind and this world. It isn't for the faint of heart. We make tough choices to keep you safe and we risk our lives in ways you cannot fathom, all so that you can get into your cars every morning, drive your children to school, go to work, grab groceries on your way home, eat at the table with your family, and then sit on the sofas you are on at this very minute watching this broadcast."

Salem hopped up from her stool making an impromptu move into the camera. She could see from the prompters that the screen now only showed her from shoulder to head. Staring directly into the light above the camera so that everyone watching could see her eyes, she said, "I am 38 years old. Already in my life I have lost my husband, my child, my mother, my father, my grandmother, my sister, my fiancé, and several of my cousins and many dear friends, fighting for the greater good of the world. Believe me when I tell you, I have more than *earned* the public's trust...and respect. My entire life is nothing but one long fight against darkness. And to this fight I have sacrificed nearly everything and everyone I hold dear. So, I ask you to lay down your judgments. Stop searching our words for something to take offense with. Step outside of your own self-built walls and imagine what our lives must be like. We are your sisters and your brothers. We are trying to make your lives better. Give us the chance to show you."

CHAPTER THIRTY-TWO

Daihmler Rises Up

In the days following the broadcasts, the world was turned on its head. Daphanie kept close contact with Salem and Demitra, when she wasn't appearing as a guest herself on her fellow colleagues' shows. A tidal wave of proof that the auburn-haired witch's claims were not a lie seemed to pour from every media outlet. Witches all over the world stepped out of hiding and announced their own existence. Long unsolved murder cases all over the country were now finding new life as some investigators looked at old files through supernatural eyes. It also came as quite a surprise how many church organizations hailed Salem's statements as legitimate. Though a shockwave of animosity was brewing among Evangelicals against anyone identifying as a witch, the more mainstream denominations focused more upon the admission of God being real than on whatever fears against witching kind might stir. Death threats abounded in all directions, while calmer heads argued the need to take Salem, and other witches, at their word when they claimed to want to help mankind.

At home, things were complicated. Trix had been temporarily suspended from the Academy while higher ups decided her future. The same was happening in Charleston with Ocean as his superiors weighed his merits against the worries. Fable and Miranda pulled the children out of school until things calmed down a little when a few PTA members declared their children as monsters and a danger to the other children. Vanessa too was under suspicion. Though not a witch herself, she was tied to the Blanchards, therefore her credentials as a teacher were under review. For the time being, everyone was hunkered down at Blanchard House awaiting whatever fallout to stop falling so they could assess how the pieces landed.

It was all quietly unspoken by everyone in the family that Salem was to blame for this. The hubris in her plan had uprooted the world and the general opinion by everyone at Blanchard House was she had not thought things out before acting.

Several times, Miranda pleaded with her to undo things. To use Titan's calendar to erase the broadcast from people's minds. But Salem refused, saying enough time had not passed to accurately make such a decision. At any time, Demitra could have ended the chaos herself, being she knew the whereabouts of the coins. But something inside her must have wanted to trust her niece, or perhaps it was as simple as mere curiosity. Whatever it was, Demitra was reluctant to alter the present until a little more time went by. Just in case, the world was indeed ready to accept.

Sitting on the sofa having a cup of coffee, Demitra was startled from the article about a witch in Nebraska she was reading about on her phone. The ding of her text message alert made her jump. And who it was from, was even more disturbing. He had not called Demitra, he texted. He was not a texter. For Charlie Bennet to send her a text message meant one thing, he was not alone where he could talk to her personally. Something major was happening in town and Charlie did what he could to warn her.

Get out of town NOW. NOW!!!!!! Take everyone and GO!!!! I'll call when I can.

Panicked, Demitra ran through the house flinging open every door, rousing every Blanchard to come downstairs. The Blanchards rushed down the flights of stairs to the living room where Demitra stood with Jerry, both holding the babies with Con, Hera, Titan, Rom, and Olympus with them. As everyone gathered, confused as to what the emergency was, Demitra explained.

"Charlie says we must go. I don't know why or what he means, but it is very clear we are in some kind of danger."

"Is it the town?" Fable asked. "Are our friends and neighbors turning on us too?"

"Demitra doesn't know anything more than what Charlie texted." Jerry shouted, becoming panicked. "He says we just have to go."

"Go where?" Trix exclaimed. "We don't have any other place to go."

"We aren't going anywhere," Demitra announced. "We are going into town to see what is happening. These people have been our neighbors for all our lives. Surely, we can reason with them."

"Or they'll all try to kill us." Echo remarked.

"Ya'll, I am so sorry." Salem said. "I should not have gone on television. But I felt like this was why Beryl was helping me. I thought I was meant to do this."

"Obviously, you were wrong." Trix shot back.

"We don't have time to cast blame," Fable said. "This is the time when we all stick together."

"Against a mob out to kill us?" Sydney said. "That's what this is sounding like to me."

Trix reached out, sending her power forth to melt the fire screen on the hearth, the stream of metal hit her hand, reshaping into a long double-sided ax. "Echo and I have faced hordes of deadly people before. Thought that was over, but at least we have actual working experience."

Echo winked her way, "We got this shit."

Demitra turned to her husband. With a quick smack on the cheek, she told him she loved him and that he was to take Miranda and the children to Vanessa's house. She felt sure they'd be safe there.

"I am not leaving you in the middle of all this!"

"Yes, you are." Demitra ordered. "Miranda cannot handle two babies, one toddler, and three 11-year-olds alone. The two of you need to be safe and keep our children safe."

Miranda frowned Jerry's way, "She is right."

"I know she is," he grimaced. "I hate it when she's right. And it happens all the time."

In a mad frenzy, Miranda and Jerry began rushing the kids to the car, all except Hera who remained defiantly in place in the living room.

"Hera," Salem told her. "Get going."

"No. I will stay and fight with the rest of you."

Demitra swept forward, grabbing the girl's shoulders, "No you won't Missy. Go with your mother where it is safe for you."

Rebelliously, Hera gave her aunt a wicked grin. "Aunt Demitra, do you really think I cannot handle myself? I took out that crazy woman at Thanksgiving. And I killed my father when he was trying to kill us. No one can do anything to me. I will blow them all to pieces. You need me. And you know you do."

"That girl is not lying!" Trix shouted. "If I am in battle, I would not turn down Hera as the one at my side."

"No child is entering battle!" Demitra commanded.

"I am not a child," Hera stated. "I haven't ever been a child. Not with all I have been through. I am going with you." It was not a request, and it was not a statement seeking approval. Unflinching, Hera stared at her grandmother as she clutched hands with Trix.

It was a sight unlike anything any of them had ever seen before. Demitra was not prepared for the surprises waiting for her family in town as she brought her car to a stop halfway down Main Street, unable to go further. Sage and Fable doing the same behind her. As the Blanchard family exited the three cars they'd arrived in, they all looked down the street at the swelling congregation. Perhaps as many as three hundred people filled the street and the sidewalks, forming an impassable wall blocking the road into and out of town.

"Look at them," Demitra said to Fable. "Why are they facing the other way?"

The Blanchards stared ahead at the river of people filling every possible space between the buildings lining either side of the street. Hundreds of Daihmler citizens with their backs turned on the Blanchards, crying out in unison to some unseen force at the other end of the street. Demitra started towards them, her family in lock step behind her. Approaching the back of the crowd, someone turned around and saw the advancing witches.

"They are here!" shouted a middle-aged woman brandishing a rifle.

Someone pushed through the back of the crowd, coming through the wall of people to face the Blanchards. It was Doreen McGillis, owner of the little market a few miles away near Blanchard House. "What are you doing here?" she cried. "Go back! We've got this. You all need to hide yourselves."

"Doreen, what is happening?" Demitra asked.

"Some stupid hate group has rolled into town, sayin' they are gonna wipe out the witches here! We've managed to hold them off this far, but it's beginning to get heated. Won't be long before they just bust through us and try to get to your place. You all need to get out of Daihmler till we get these thugs out of our town."

And there it was. If ever asked later in life about it, Demitra Blanchard would describe the scene as the most beautiful moment she ever experienced. She looked out among the backsides of her fellow citizens--people who held no magical powers--armed with nothing more than rifles, handguns, baseball bats and tire irons. But these people had rushed from their homes, their businesses, and their jobs to block the street. To stop a threatening mob coming to harm her family. The people of Daihmler were protecting the Blanchards.

"Look at them." Salem said, mesmerized. "They all came out to save us."

Sydney took a few steps forward, "As selfless as this is, we cannot allow them to put themselves in danger. Whatever is up there they are holding back, is our problem."

The Blanchards, led by Demitra, made their way, two by two, through the thick crowd. In all directions longtime friends and strangers who only knew them in passing, did their best to convince the witches to stay back. Demitra thanked them all sincerely as she continued her march towards the front line. Breaking through the final sentry, Demitra saw a self-formed militia of men dressed in an array of American flag paraphernalia. Some shirts had *Liberty Fighters* printed on them. Others had fiery red skull icons with the words *Sons of America* encircling them. Upon first glimpse of these heavily armed people, it was clear they were fringe hate groups. Demitra had seen them before on television, protesting gay rights organizations or specific Pride events. She'd seen them lining streets shouting the most horrible words to Women's Rights marchers and Black Lives Matter parades. And now they were in Daihmler carrying *Burn the Witch* or *God's Warriors* signs.

As she looked out at the animalistic faces of these people. She could see a line of police officers, led by Charlie Bennet holding the line at the front. Charlie was on a megaphone shouting at them to calm down and go home. He saw Demitra standing a few yards away and rushed to her. "What are you doing here? I told you to get out of town. I will handle this mess."

"I will not have you or our neighbors put yourselves at risk for us. We will handle it." Demitra took the megaphone from him and faced the vigilante group before her. "My name is Demitra Blanchard. And I can only assume you have come to our town out of fear of us. I want you to believe me when I say you have nothing to fear from my family. We are here to help people, not hurt them."

Her words, if heard by even one set of ears in the mass of hate, were quickly drowned out as the enraged group lurched forward at her. She felt a push from behind as her fellow Daihmlerians swept forward to stop the charge. Protecting hands gripped Demitra, pulling her back behind them as her neighbors arched around her placing themselves between she and danger.

Suddenly things grew significantly quieter. The roar behind Demitra softened as her fellow citizens stopped their sprint forward and stood in amazement watching the condition of their anger filled opponents. Everyone in the attacking mob was standing completely still, frozen in place. Standing atop a truck bed parked at the curb stood Salem with her outstretched arms.

The people of Daihmler were seeing for the first time her power in real time effect. "Good job Salem!" shouted Mrs. Rigsby who managed the Bakery shop.

"Wow!" cried old man Shuster who, back before retirement, had been Salem and Beryl's Algebra teacher in high school. "Those men are stuck like statues."

A man came rushing through the crowd towards the immobilized enemy. "Everybody get up here and take their guns away!"

Local attorney, Sam Meadows, stepped over to the truck, extending Salem a hand to help her down. The Blanchards watched in awe as the townspeople moved through the frozen mob, removing each of the weapons from their motionless hands whereupon they deposited them into the empty truck bed. During the weapon neutralization, Demitra caught sight of Howard and Rosamund coming towards her.

"Quite a turn of events, isn't it?" Howard said, kissing Demitra's cheek. Behind Rosamund, Fable saw Nash's face coming near. In his hands were two of the axes from his brother's Ax Tossing business.

The owner of the truck popped forward, withdrawing his keys. "Ya'll back up and let me turn my truck around. I'll drive these out to the river and throw them in."

Charlie intervened. "Don't do that Mr. Clarkeson. Two of my officers will ride along with you and you can lock it all up in a cell at the jailhouse."

As the truck turned around among the shifting crowd, Nash came up to Fable. "Well, I guess now I understand why you've kept me at an intimate distance in this relationship. Didn't think I'd be okay with who you really are."

She looked into his eyes. He did not blink or turn away despite the steely detachment emanating from her own. She was braced for rejection and Nash knew she was, even though a hint of vulnerability still broke through her façade. "Can you be okay with what I am?"

Nash raised his two axes. "I brought these, didn't I? A man doesn't come armed for a fight over a woman he isn't truly serious about."

He almost toppled over when she threw her arms around his neck. Standing with Fable's cheek pressed against his Nash knew for certain what was building between them was just as real for her. Careful not to press the ax blades into her back, he returned the embrace. She leaned back to kiss him, her teary face now shed of all its former steel.

Demitra had been watching the exchange from a few feet away and was thrilled to see her daughter so happy. She was interrupted from her eavesdropping when Trix gestured to the still frozen mass and asked, "What do we do now?"

Demitra frowned and looked around as if hoping an idea would present itself.

"I really don't know."

"Miss Blanchard," called a voice a few feet away. "Can you wipe them out while they are stuck how they are?"

Demitra located the man making the suggestion a few feet back. She went to him, touching his arm gently, and smiled, "I know we all would like to do something like that. They've come into our town and placed so many of us in danger, but they are human beings. I cannot hurt them simply because I don't agree with them. That would make us all as bad as they are."

"What do we do?" Doreen McGillis asked.

Fable removed herself from Nash's arms, giving him an apologetic smile, "I think I'm needed for a minute. But we will get back to this with us, I promise."

"Go do your thing."

Fable, tugged Salem along with her, motioning to Echo and Sydney and Hera to follow. Standing beside Demitra and Trix, Fable told Salem to unleash her hold on the crowd before them. As Salem lifted her hands to do so, Howard joined his family at the head of the line of defense while the rest of the people of Daihmler pressed directly behind them for backup.

The organized thugs, in their bastardized America garb, stumbled in place, heads turning, each looking for their weapons. Fable took the megaphone. "Your weapons are gone. As you can see, we could have done anything we wanted to you, but we only removed the things you brought to hurt us. Unlike you, we do not hurt people."

"You are whores of the Devil!" shouted an obese man wearing an American flag hat and camouflage shirt. The shirt couldn't even cover the bottom of his overhanging belly. "You ain't from God! And you ain't welcome in this country!"

Fable saw Nash grip his ax and step forward. She pressed her hand to his chest and grinned. "I got this. But thank you."

"We are protectors of this earth and we have kept you from more dangers than you can fathom. You owe us your thanks, not your hatred."

"We owe you the fiery pits of hell and we gone deliver you to it!" another man cried.

Shouts from behind the Blanchards rang out as the various Daihmlerians waged verbal threats against anyone who came one step nearer to their friends.

Trix waved the shouts down and stepped beside Fable to address the men. With her was Hera. "Let me educate you terribly stupid and, I might add, tackily dressed idiots. If we were evil or if we wanted to hurt any one of you, trust me we already would have." Trix leaned her head around until she spotted who she was looking for. "Mr. Tillman! Mr. Tillman!"

A short, balding man jumped up and down, raising his hand. "Over here!"

Trix found him and asked, "Are you still planning to tear down your old building now that you moved your wine store over to Moss Street?"

A little confused as to how this pertained, Mr. Tillman replied, "Why yes, I am. Store is just sitting empty right now. Planned on tearing it down so the grocery store can expand out onto the space."

"May we take care of that demolition for you?"

With a bewildered look on his face, the man stuttered, "Sure."

Trix looked down to Hera. "Hera, show them what you can do."

The girl tossed her hands forward, aiming 200 yards away to the empty standalone building. The building exploded into millions of pieces, falling into a neat pile between the other two storefronts, unmarred by the blast.

The vigilantes jumped back from the impact of the explosion. Their eyes wide in disbelief. The citizens of Daihmler were equally jolted by the demonstration, but glad to be on the right side of the fight. Trix directed Fable to perform next. Fable sent Nash a wink as if to brag *look at what I can do*. Her eyes closed momentarily and reopened. Folding her arms she stood patiently waiting. Voices began to murmur to each other, curious as to what was supposed to happen. Soon it became clear as neighborhood dogs, cats, squirrels, and chipmunks scurried from their homes, lining the sidewalks around the threatening men. Between the feet of the many small animals, slithered rattlesnakes, water moccasins, scorpions, and spiders. Ants began to march by the millions out of grasses and from cracks beneath the pavement. Overhead a cloud cover began to darken the street. As some people looked skyward their eyes caught sight of hundreds of feathered wingspans and sharp beaks. Crows, buzzards, blackbirds, cardinals, blue jays, robins, doves all fluttering overhead ready to strike on command. Hornets, wasps, bees, and yellow jackets filled the empty air spaces beneath the birds and above the other animals, reptiles, and insects.

Fable spoke to the now cowering men. "Your bullets would not have done you much good against my friends."

"As you can see," Demitra shouted, taking control of the situation. "If witches meant you harm, you could not stop us. But we aren't here for our own gain or dominance. We are here to do whatever small good we can to aid our fellow human beings. Please leave us in peace."

The animals, insects, reptiles, and birds parted sideways to allow an opening for, the now rushing, hate mongers as they ran to their vehicles and fled Daihmler.

The Blanchards were not able to go immediately home after the ruckus in town. The triumphant people of Daihmler, having faced down the threatening mob with the Blanchards, felt like celebrating. The entire town had jubilantly rushed to Main Street with food either prepared already or ready to be tossed on one of the many grills Tom Jenkins rolled outside from his hardware store. Demitra called Vanessa's house, letting Jerry know it was safe to come to town with the children. Soon, all Daihmler was congregated for the biggest cookout the town had ever seen.

Somehow, seeing for themselves the breadth of the Blanchards' power in action endeared people even more to them. As everyone chowed down on ribs, steaks, hamburgers, BBQ chicken and all the trimmings, Demitra and her family were regaled with countless stories of how someone in her family had helped them at one time. One of the older women told a story of how when she was a little girl a devastating tornado hit town during a 4th of July picnic. She recalled how some Blanchard women faced down the tornado, using their powers to hold it back and deflect it away from town. Demitra knew that story. Those women were her mother, her aunt Pastoria, Madam Zelda, and she strongly suspected her daughter Beryl who was visiting the past at the time, was the woman remembered as healing several people's injuries during the tornado. There were other people also sharing their tales who had been trapped inside a store last year when a violent gunman unleashed rapid fire from an assault rifle onto the store's staff and customers. Sydney and Sage saved all those people that day. Others, with less dramatic stories, told of how Dr. Beryl Blanchard once cured their cancer or healed their failing heart. More than a few wanted more details on how she had become an arm of God, though they all commented that if anyone should be, it would be her. And of course, there were those who still remembered those months decades ago when a deranged killer stalked the people of Daihmler and how they were certain, even at the time, the Blanchards had something to do with the end of the murders. Demitra, with great compassion, looked at Con's face, knowing he was aware they were speaking about his father. Someone brought up the new grisly killings which happened at the lake. Everyone felt assured the Blanchards were already on it. It was then that Doreen McGillis retold her personal story of how the Blanchard wolf, Romulus, saved her from a terrifying burglar last year. "Where is Romulus, anyway?" Doreen cried, looking around. Another voice called out, wondering the same, reminding his neighbors how Romulus had saved his family the night their house caught fire. Rom looked at his grandmother for permission. With an approving nod, Demitra gave him the go ahead.

"I'm right here, Ms. McGillis!" Rom shouted standing on top of a bench. "See!" Suddenly before all their eyes, Romulus morphed into his wolf form, his clothes tearing from his body as he grew in size.

"Oh, my Lord!" Doreen cried. "Why my Heavens! You are my Romulus! My little hero!"

Rom rushed to her on all fours while she stroked his fur and patted his side. Of course, this required Fable to make some fast explanations about her son. And as complicated and frightening as the truth was, Rom's years of helpfulness and compassion for others while in his animal form did not elicit fear. Far from it, he became even more beloved by the citizens of Daihmler. Women began approaching Fable, "You poor girl, what you must have had to go through as a mother all these years!"

"Why didn't you tell us? We loved Romulus. We'd have understood."

"And us calling him your pet all these years instead of your son. Please forgive us."

Miranda was the recipient of her own praise as throughout the course of the day several gossips put together her position in the family. "You took on those kids, raising them as your own when they needed a momma. You are an angel on earth Mrs. Blanchard."

"What those youngens must have gone through, their parents getting' turned into vampires. And you stepped in for them. I think that's beautiful."

Jerry watched the members of his family as they each received the recognition and praise they long deserved for the sacrifices they'd made and the dangers they'd often placed themselves in. He joined Demitra who was walking away from the group of women she'd been surrounded by, while they continued to jabber. "They believe you are all their heroes," Jerry whispered in his wife's ear. "This must fill you with pride. Living all these years afraid to be found out. And here they are, embracing you with their gratitude."

She patted his hand, forcing a smile. It was truly a miraculous gift for her own people to accept them so wholeheartedly. But it was the rest of the world she now worried about. Those men who swept into town earlier would not be the last like them to come after her family.

Vanessa and Miranda were chatting with a few school parents around the hot dog station. Miranda quickly set them straight that she held no magical powers, only a periphery Blanchard by marriage. But it was now clear from Hera's demonstration that Miranda's children were indeed among the Blanchard witches. When they had a few moments alone together, Miranda checked in with her friend.

"Vanessa, how are you? This must be difficult."

Vanessa nodded softly, turning to make sure no one was around to overhear them. "When you and Jerry showed up with the children today, I got scared. Really scared. I only just found my daughter. We don't even know each other yet and now her kind has been exposed. She has only known she is a witch for a couple of weeks, and now she has the world to fear."

"Maybe not," Miranda said looking around. "I was worried about it too, but this...this means there is hope."

"Here in Daihmler, maybe," Vanessa said. "But the world is larger than Daihmler. Those men today with their guns and their hatred, they came from other places."

Miranda's face turned grim. "I know. I think we are a long way from being safe. But at least now I can see a little of what Salem thought might be possible."

CHAPTER THIRTY-THREE

I Will Always Come for You

Nightshade stood as empty as a tomb. The club had ceased operations once Seth and Yasmine left New York. If Yasmine returned to him, they could reopen again if she wanted. Nightshade closed at the height of popularity; the patrons would return if the lights once again danced from the gothic dormers. Walking in the darkness, Seth remembered how beautiful Yasmine used to look coming down from their private lounge upstairs to make her presence known through the club. The vacant dance floor where the two of them had whiled away many nights seemed to carry the ghostly beat from the DJ booth. Or perhaps it was only the hum of the heating system. He poured himself a drink from the bar. The dusty bottles still sat on glass shelves, with dried splatters of alcohol now forming congealed smudges after so many weeks. Downing the glass of whiskey, Seth recalled the night he and Yaz made love on this bar top.

It had been days since Seth made his appeal to her on national television. Though it was unlikely she'd been watching, surely someone she'd eaten recently had seen it. Their memories of the broadcast, though fleeting and likely inconsequential, would still echo in her mind as she absorbed their life force and their experiences. Why had she not come to him? He'd been clear where he would be. "Come to me in the place we found life together. I will be waiting night after night, until you find your way to me."

Why had she not come home?

Suddenly he knew. How could he have been so blind? His plea had been too vague. He'd meant it to be so that only she would know what he meant. Nightshade would be safe for their reunion. Now Seth realized she wouldn't have derived Nightshade from his words. She would not be coming to New York. He knew exactly where she would go looking for him. Seth hailed a cab for the airport. On his way he made a reservation for the first flight out under the name Buchanan.

Seth arrived in Charleston the following afternoon. The remaining hours of daylight taunted him from the sky above. Each eternal minute screaming at him over his idiocy in choosing the wrong words on air, then understanding so late how she would have construed them. As darkness fell, Seth moved through the city knowing exactly where he would find Yasmine if she had learned of the broadcast and not given up on him the night before.

Church Street was quiet. The February air and the lateness of night left the streets empty of traffic and the sidewalks free from pedestrians. The quarter moon stood just behind the spire of St. Phillip's, offering a postcard-like view of the Charleston skyline. Seth knew these streets well now. His time here had given him a familiarity with the city many never know, especially at night. He reached the half wall of aging stone housing the church cemetery. The wrought iron gates topping the wall offered a clear view into the garden of headstones, trees, and draping twisted limbs. She was here. He could feel her. Obscured from sight by the monuments to the dead within the graveyard walls, he still knew she was there. He did not need his acute vampire senses, his enhanced hearing, or the smell of her jasmine perfume wafting across the winter wind. A man does not need superhuman senses to know the woman he has loved his entire life is near. Like a silvery cord no one else can see connecting their souls, he felt the pull from a block away.

The padlock on the gate was new. No doubt its predecessors had been twisted in the same broken way as this one, only just three nights before tonight when she would have come here to find him. The gate creaked with the age and unsteadiness only centuries could provide. He edged inside, hearing the rustling limbs of bare tree branches catching wind overhead. He knew where to go. As if reliving that same moment so long ago, Seth retraced the steps he'd taken that night when he followed her into this garden of death. The stone she'd broken that night during her rush back to save him was fused back in place with a sloppy mortar. He rested his hand atop it as his eyes caught sight of her beautiful white face reflecting under the minimal moonlight. Her long brown hair blew behind her in the breeze as her eyes tried to make sense of what she saw.

"I have looked for you in the face of every man I've seen, and they are never you."

Seth gave her a grin, stepping forward. "I am here."

"But you aren't," she replied, with a distance to her voice that made him afraid. It was not unlike the first time he found her here, when she could not remember him at all. Not until she killed him. "You are never him. And I will tear your heart from your chest with my bare hands for making me hope for what will never be."

He took another step closer. He saw it now, the madness in her eyes. His lovely Yasmine had lost her mind. Trembling, less from apprehension and more from heartbreak, he said, "Yaz, I am Seth. I am here."

"My Seth is gone. That little bitch child destroyed him." She looked away, looked to the ground at her feet. "He was the only thing I ever loved. We found each other again right here, on this very spot."

"I remember Yazzy," Seth said gently, easing nearer yet not at a pace which would incite a reaction. "I found you here. You were feeding. Remember? I offered you myself. You drank from me, then you remembered me. You can remember me again."

"You are lost to me now forever," she said with such an anguish in her voice he wanted to cry for her. "It is cruel for you to come here and look like him. No one is ever him."

"I am Yasmine!" he said, stepping close enough to reach her. Like one would approach a strange dog, he let his hand enter her space but not yet touching her. Little by little he drew his fingertips closer until they grazed her arm ever so slightly. She trembled. "You recognize me, Yasmine. You do. You know it's me. Hold my hand. Just hold my hand." She allowed her soft fingers to mingle into his rather slowly. In what seemed like many minutes, Yasmine edged her hand more into his until he closed his grip around hers. "Please know me, Yaz."

"No. No." She pushed her face towards his, inspecting it with flaming evil eyes. "You look like him. But you aren't him. You cannot be."

He felt afraid being this close to her. He knew her well, her every move and every intention. She could strike him dead at any minute and he knew it. But it was not death he feared, it was dying before she knew him again. "If I am not Seth," he challenged, "Then why are you here?" Slowly lifting his hand to stroke her cheek, he asked, "If you believe Seth is lost to you forever, why did you come back all this way, to this place so important to our history?"

She looked at him with a child's hope, allowing the back of her fingertips to stroke his cheek lightly in return. "Because I will always come for him," Yasmine whispered with a vacant stare. "As he always came for me."

Seth smiled. Though her eyes were hollow, still resistant to believe, her words gave him hope she might be beginning to see. "And I have come, Yaz. I have come for you. I will always come for you. We can be together again." He removed the clear vial containing the Holy Blood. It shined like phosphorus in the dim moonlight.

She looked at the liquid with suspicion. Then her eyes returned to him. Her pupils surged as if dilating then reduced as if unconvinced. "Why do you look like that?"

Seth caressed her hair and said, "Because I am your husband." He rolled up the sleeve to his shirt, presenting his exposed wrist. "Remember me."

With her gaze locked into his, she gripped his arm gently. Slowly her razor-sharp teeth protracted. Lowering her head while raising his arm to meet her mouth, she pierced his skin and drank, never removing her eyes from his. Seth saw it in her face when she relived their long life—and death—together. Then she saw his destruction at the hands of Hera. Her face contorted with anguish as those few seconds flashed again when she lost him forever. What followed after amazed her, restoring her beleaguered face back to hopefulness as she drank in the memory the auburn headed woman restoring him to life. She pulled away, not yet taking enough blood to kill him. She gripped his face in her hands, blood still trickling from the corner of her mouth, the thin red rivulet curving under her chin, starting down her neck. "Seth. Seth, you've come back." He pressed her head against his chest holding her as tightly as he could. He could feel her shaking beneath his touch. Over and over, she repeated, "My Seth. My Seth. My Seth has come back."

"I will always come for you, Yaz. Death. Time. Distance. Nothing can ever keep me from you, my only love."

"But you are not the same as me now."

"No," Seth admitted. "But I will be. Let's take a walk together, my love. Let's decide which path we will take, together. You will choose to become like me, or you will choose to make me like you. Whichever choice you make, I will follow you."

They walked the empty streets together, hand in hand, like they had before not so long ago. It felt like returning to a honeymoon after years of marriage. He explained what it felt like for him now, the regret and the horror of things he had done, but the peace and solemnity being washed clean of those sins can bring. She had questions and he answered them. She found it fascinating how he now could remember the two red headed women and tried to wrap her mind around the fact they turned out to be his sisters.

Walking along The Battery they paused to look out over the brackish water lapping up against the rocks and wall protecting the city from high tide. Nearby someone coughed. Yasmine turned to see the homeless man shivering under his ratty coat and the shield of newspapers he was attempting to use as a blanket. Without a word to Seth, she walked casually to him. The haggard man, probably much younger in years than his face portrayed, looked up at the beautiful woman, now leaning down to stroke his hair. He smiled at the kind lady. Yasmine slit his throat with the fingernail of her index finger. As he fell off the bench, gurgling and choking from the outpour of his life's blood, she clutched a handful of his hair and lifted him by it so that she could drink.

Seth watched the dreadful scene with a new perspective. Though he'd seen her do this countless times before, it now made him truly sick. He felt as if he might wretch from the sight and the sounds as she gulped from the man like a child from a milkshake. The revolting sight intrigued him a little, realizing the sight of the man's blood did not stir any yearnings within him now. Before, he would have grown hungry himself. Now he was only nauseated.

Once the man was dead and she'd thrown his body into the ocean, she withdrew a packet of wet wipes from her purse and cleaned her mouth and face. Returning to her husband as if she'd only just thrown away an emptied water bottle, she continued her walk with him. Several times she asked if he wanted to eat, but he declined. Finally, taking a seat on a different park bench beside one of the historic cannons which once protected the city from invaders, Seth made his plea.

"With this liquid," he said, showing her the vial once more, "We can be the same again. It is an important choice you must make my darling Yaz." She listened intently while staring into his eyes. Her own still dancing with madness, a madness he hoped would not impact the moment. He continued his plea, "Yasmine, will you suffer the torments you've inflicted so you might accept forgiveness for them? Will you accept the Holy Blood and restore your soul?"

She stared into his face for several silent moments, gingerly caressing his strong jaw and chin line with her soft fingers. Then she spoke. "No. None of that means anything to me." His heart shuddered. He felt himself die again inside. But as his sister had resurrected him, so now did Yasmine with the rest of her declaration. "I do not care about salvation. I only care about you, my beautiful Seth. I will drink the Holy Blood, if it means we may be together."

It was what he wanted to hear. She had accepted the terms. He could have left it at that, but their love was deeper, stronger than redemption or faith. Though he wanted her to take the vial, he felt compelled to be forthright with her so that the choice was one of purity and not of loneliness. "Yasmine, I want you to take the liquid," he told her as he kissed her soft red lips. "But as I said, no matter what you do, we will remain together. You are free to stay as you are without fear of losing me. If you choose Hell, I will walk into it with you. You, Yazzy, are my salvation. Whatever choice you make, I will join you in that life."

Though the house was enormous, Oleander was old and its grand design with its high ceilings lent itself to amplifying sound. Even from their room on the second-floor side wing, Arielle heard the pounding at the door in the entrance hall. For a cop who was supposed to have honed attention and lightning-fast reflexes, Ocean's snoring drowned out the noise to his ears, causing his wife to jab him in the ribs to wake him. "Honey, someone's at the door."

Grabbing his phone from the nightstand he saw the time, "At this hour?"

"What if it's some kind of trouble?" Arielle asked. "There are a lot of crazy people out there who are scared to death of us now."

"I don't think attackers would be polite enough to knock," Ocean said, getting out of bed. Dressed only in his pale blue pajama bottoms, he started down the hall in his bare feet. Arielle followed, wrapping her robe around her as they went.

The light in the entrance hall clicked on, shining through the sidelight window panels of the front door. The sound of shuffling feet could be heard from inside. Ocean opened the door, astounded to see who was on his porch. Peeking over his shoulder, Arielle's eyes caught sight of their visitors.

"Arielle," Seth said. "May Yasmine and I stay here for a few days?"

As Seth attempted to enter, Ocean thrust his arm against the frame, blocking them. Arielle gripped his shoulder, "It's alright, Ocean. Seth isn't dangerous."

Ocean raised his right eyebrow, locking eyes with his cousin, "Maybe. But what about her?"

"She has taken the Holy Blood," Seth explained. "She has relived every kill, and she is rather distraught. My wife needs rest. So, we came here. It was the only place I could think to go."

Arielle pushed Ocean aside gently and extended her hand. "Of course it was. This is your home, Seth. You are an Obreiggon just as much as I am. Welcome home big brother."

CHAPTER THIRTY-FOUR

Solomon's Choice

Both Fable and Demitra sat at complete attention as Salem told them the events of the previous night in Charleston. They had many questions, but Salem had few answers. "All Ari told me was that Seth and Yaz showed up on her doorstep around 4am. Seth says Yaz drank the elixir and got her soul back. They went upstairs to bed and that is all I know. Arielle hasn't seen them since. She'll have more details later, I'm sure."

"So, we have them back!" Fable cried. "This is fantastic! Seth and Yasmine are human again!" The memories they had all shared in this house together came rushing back to Fable now. They were thoughts she never allowed herself to remember because the pain of having lost them was too great. Yet now everything could be set right again. Life could go back to the way it used to be. "Seth and Yazzy will be coming home soon," she smiled. "They will be back with their children, and everything will be the way it should have been."

Salem grimaced, "I wouldn't count on it yet, Fable. They aren't the same. There is no way they could be. I don't think we can be certain what they will do."

Demitra wasn't saying much. Though thrilled her niece and nephew would no longer be monsters roaming the earth, her attention was focused on the half shadow casting onto the wall of the kitchen stairs landing. As Salem and Fable left the room, Demitra called out, "Miranda. I know you're there."

Miranda stepped down the remaining stairs, her face white with apprehension, her eyes reflecting defeat, or perhaps loss. "That is good news about Seth and Yasmine. If they are in fact no longer dangerous."

"Sit with me," Demitra directed. "This news must invoke many emotions for you. Let's talk it out."

The woman who had come to live with the Blanchards a few years ago had been timid, unsure of her place, grateful for whatever fragile threads tied her to the family. Time can change people. Miranda Perkins had been a docile, anxious, pitiable figure. Miranda Blanchard, however, was a self-possessed and confident woman. She had found her footing, and she knew her value. "I am glad about Seth and Yasmine," she repeated. "And I understand this is their home. But I want it understood, those children, are my children. I will not let them go without a fight. I have been here for them…they haven't. Titan is too young to remember them at all, and Hera remembers all too well. No one is taking my children from me unless I hear from Hera's mouth it is what she wants."

Demitra had not expected the directness but was glad to have it on the table rather than having to dance around it. "We have been through this before," she offered Miranda. "When Seth's mother returned there was friction between her and Artemis. You see, Artemis raised Salem and Seth, and when Nacaria came home it was like her role had been usurped. It was not her fault she hadn't been here to raise her children, but she hadn't. She and Artemis had some terrain to navigate, but it worked itself out."

"Yes, but Salem and Seth were adults by then." Miranda pointed out. "Hera and Titan are not. I will not stand in the way of Seth and Yasmine if Hera wants to rebuild a relationship with them. But it will be understood, they are my children."

"Yes, Ma'am," Demitra smiled, hoping to break the tension. She patted Miranda's hand and said, "If it eases your mind in any way, I am on your side. Now that doesn't mean a hell of a lot. I cannot decide who those children belong to. That will have to be worked out and will largely be whatever Hera wants. But if it means anything, in my mind, you are their mother, Miranda."

Relaxing a little, though still ridden with anxiety, Miranda nodded, replying, "It means a lot, Demitra. Thank you."

As the hours passed, everyone living in Blanchard House seemed to have heard about Seth and Yasmine. What was the most disturbing to Miranda was the fact no one was talking about it, driving the point further that the ramifications could be devastating. Pretending nothing had changed was easier than thinking about what might change and the outcome it would bring. Miranda found herself unable to be around people and their loyal avoidance of discussing the new development. She hid herself in Hera's room, folding her daughter's clean laundry on the bed. Hera had been away with Vanessa, having bonding time with Theda. Judging by the empty laundry basket and folded clothes not yet put away on the bed, Miranda had lost all track of time when Hera returned home and found her in her room. Miranda did not at first notice Hera come in, until the child removed something from her dressing table and joined her on the bed. Raising up on her knees behind Miranda, Hera began brushing her hair. The soft bristles felt good, relaxing Miranda's tension a bit. "What are you doing?" Miranda asked, attempting a lighthearted tone.

"Whenever I feel bad, you brush my hair."

"Oh," Miranda nodded, understanding the gesture.

Hera was only eleven years old, but she had the wisdom of someone decades more seasoned. Though Miranda never knew Olympia Blanchard, she imagined she must have been like Hera as a child whenever she heard stories told about her. Hera stroked Miranda's hair slowly, allowing its shoulder length waves to frizz slightly at the edges. "I don't know how many times you have sat here brushing my hair," Hera reflected. "It is just something mothers do, I guess."

She couldn't see it, being behind her, but her words lifted a smile from Miranda's lips. "They do."

"I do not remember Yasmine ever brushing my hair."

"Don't." Miranda said, momentarily covering Hera's hand with her own mid brush. "It isn't necessary." She could see what Hera was trying to do, and it meant a great deal.

"It is something mothers do." Hera repeated. "I know that no one around here ever thinks about how I have thoughts and opinions about stuff too."

"That isn't true, baby."

"Yes, it is. Grandma, Aunt Fable, Echo, Sage, and Sydney. Nobody around here except you, Grandpa, and maybe Trix ever ask me what I think."

Turning around to face her, Miranda asked, "What is it you think, Hera? I'd like to know."

Hera turned Miranda's head back so that she could begin brushing the other side. "I have a mother. A real mother. I do not need another one and I do not need a father. If they come here, Momma, I'd like for you and me and Titan to leave."

Whirling back around, Miranda placed her hands on her daughter's shoulders. "Darling, this is your family. We cannot pack up and leave."

"I do not want them here. We do not need them around. Let them live with their choices."

It was the way she said it which struck Miranda as to how adamant and how wise her daughter had truly become with age. Miranda wrapped her arms around the girl, squeezing her tight. "I love you so much, Hera."

"I know you do," Hera whispered into Miranda's ear. "You and me and Titan are all we need. If those people come back here, we will go away."

It was midafternoon at Oleander, when Seth and Yasmine came downstairs to find Arielle and Ocean in the parlor with two strangers. Arielle stood up with excitement dancing behind her eyes. Yasmine held her head down as if not desiring eye contact with anyone. As Arielle started towards her, she heard Seth whisper into Yasmine's ear, "It's okay, honey. I promise."

Arielle stood before Yasmine now, reaching to grasp her dangling hands. Yasmine shivered at the touch, but it didn't deter her sister-in-law. Arielle gave her arms a mild shake to engage Yasmine to look up at her. Arielle could see the pain Yasmine was carrying. Her sins forever marking the woman who had once been the innocent, caring, heart of the family.

"Yazzy," Arielle smiled. "It is all over. That was not you." Behind Yasmine, Seth winked gratefully to his sister. Arielle continued, "Any one of us would have done the same dreadful things if we'd been attacked and changed the way you were. It is not your fault. And it's over. You're home. Home with the people who love you."

Tears dripped across Yasmine's twitching cheek. "Really?"

"Really." Arielle pulled her into a warm embrace, "And my God how we've missed you. I have missed you so much, Yaz." She dragged an arm around Seth's neck, pulling him in with them, "Both of you."

Arielle busted up the tender reunion to make introductions with her cousin Mara and Brandon, before they all settled down to catch up. Mara addressed Yasmine right away, "You and I never met, but we both lived in The House of Duquesne together. I am Thaddeuss' granddaughter or...was."

"I liked Thaddeuss," Yasmine replied. "He was kind to me. And Bianca saved my life not long ago."

Mara sat back and gave out a small gasp, "Bianca Duquesne. I haven't thought about her in a long time." She turned to her husband and explained, "She is a distant cousin of mine, Brandon. A vampire. But in truth rather friendly, at least she was to me the few times I encountered her. Of course, that was probably only because the D'Angelo's were off limits to the vampires because without us, they couldn't survive."

Shaking his head, Brandon sighed. "I cannot believe this is my life now. Hell, I guess it's everybody's life now that everyone knows everything."

Ocean tapped his friend's knee with his knuckle. "It is a lot, man. It's okay to be overwhelmed." Ocean filled Seth in on the current situation. "Ever since Salem outed us to the world, Mara, Brandon, and Ashby have been staying here with us. Oleander has a large wall, gate, and right now is magically protected with charms to keep us safe."

"I guess we are all refugees right now," Seth sighed apologetically. "I'm sorry, Arielle. We will try to get out of your way as soon as we figure out our next step."

Looking affronted by the statement, Arielle sat up straight, "What are you talking about? You have a home already."

Waving his hand in disagreement, Seth replied, "No, I don't think we can assume we are wanted back at Blanchard House yet. Yaz and I are going down to see the family...and hopefully the kids. But it's too soon to make assumptions."

"What assumptions?" Arielle scoffed. "I'm not talking about Blanchard House; I'm talking about Oleander."

Yasmine was confused. "Oleander?"

"Yes," Arielle replied. "I have restarted the tea plantation. By next year our crop will be ready and the tea company will be back in business. My manager already has several contracts with local restaurants and plans to expand through the state and eventually the country."

"What does that have to do with us?" Seth asked.

"Oleander built the Obreiggon fortune on tea. And Seth, you are Xander Obreiggon's son. This house and this business belong to you, me, and Salem. One third of all of this is yours."

"Tea?" Seth exclaimed. "Arielle, Oleander and the Obreiggon money are your heritage, not mine."

"No," Arielle argued. "They have always been your heritage too, only you and Salem were locked out of it. But you aren't anymore."

Ocean spoke up, "Surely, Seth and Yasmine plan to return to Daihmler. To their children."

"Their children are Obreiggon's too," Arielle pointed out. "Hera and Titan could live here with their parents."

"And Miranda?" Ocean remarked.

Arielle shrunk back in her chair, realizing she had temporarily forgotten about Miranda. Seth hadn't. "I don't know what Yaz and I are going to do. We haven't made it that far yet. For now, we are just happy to be together again. And grateful to be here. That's all we can process right now."

Yasmine inadvertently fell back into her old routine of smoothing the rough patches and chipperly attempting to keep things light and breezy. She ignored the intensity of the room and pushed the conversation forward into what else they might have missed in their absence. Thankful to be reminded of what the old Yaz had been like, Arielle joined in on her diversion, steering the topic to Ocean's recent development. Her story had its intended outcome as Seth snapped from his melancholy once hearing the news. He was so confused as to how Ocean had changed from being Pastoria's grandson to Demitra's, that Arielle had to tell the story twice. "Howard is your father?" Yasmine gasped, turning to Ocean. "This blows my mind."

"It was a kick in the head to me, as well." Ocean chuckled, then without thinking first, asked Seth, "Speaking of crazy situations, have you met Theda yet?"

"Theda?" Yasmine repeated. "Who is that?"

Ocean shot his wife a panicked look, understanding he had said something he shouldn't. Seth gave him a look as well, shaking his head. Ocean quickly corrected his faux pas, "Um...she is a friend we know. Well, you don't. But you will. Or maybe you won't. I don't know! But she's a person who exists and we know her."

Rolling her eyes at her husband, Arielle, simplified things, "Theda is the daughter of a friend of ours. You will meet her later I am sure, but for now it isn't important."

Brandon was even more quiet than usual during the group conversation. When pressed by Ocean if he was all right, he answered honestly, "Never in my life would I have ever dreamed I would have the weird people in my life that I have now. No offense. My wife's a witch. Her cousin's a witch. My friend is a witch. And now two vampires."

"Ex-vampires," Mara corrected.

"Well," Yasmine smiled. "I am not a witch, normally. I am really more like you Brandon than the rest of them. The only time I have ever had powers has been when I was pregnant."

Arielle, Ocean, and Seth suddenly stared at Yasmine, then each other, then at

Yasmine again. "Yaz, as a vampire you were able to freeze people, like Salem can."

"Yes, but that was only because when I got turned, I was pregnant. But that's all over now."

Blank-faced and still staring at her, Ocean was the only one of the trio daring enough to ask. "Are you still?"

"Still pregnant?" Yasmine repeated, as if the question itself were ridiculous. "How can I be? I was a vampire for almost three years. That would be the longest pregnancy in the universe! Surely, the baby miscarried when I turned. Afterall, I technically died."

"But if the baby had died when your human-self did, you wouldn't have had witchcraft powers as a vampire." Ocean pointed out.

Breaking the growing tension of the room, and trying any tactic to be relevant or even participate in this conversation, Brandon tapped Seth's arm and said, "Ocean is a cop. He questions everything."

"It is rather a curious situation though," Mara remarked. "Could it be possible for your baby's life to be reinstated when your own was?"

Arielle stood up with her hands on her own baby bump, "There is a way to find out! The same way I found out that I was having a baby."

Arielle went out into the entry hall and called up the stairs for Ashby. Within a couple of minutes, Mara's younger sister joined everyone in the parlor. "Ashby knows everything about a person anytime she is in their presence." Arielle explained to Yasmine and Seth. "You can't hide anything from her, and she only speaks the truth."

Mara directed Ashby to take stock of Yasmine Blanchard. Staring without any expression, to the point where Yasmine was not even sure if Ashby was trying, Ashby gathered her information. "What are you wanting me to tell you?" Ashby asked. "She was a vampire until yesterday. Is that it?"

"No, we knew that." Mara told her sister. "Is she pregnant?"

"With a living baby," Arielle clarified, "Not a dead one."

"Yes," Ashby answered flatly. "I am confused by it all. Her baby is in the first trimester, although it has been there for a very long time."

"I don't believe it!" Seth cried with excitement, kissing his wife exuberantly. "We are having a baby! The baby still exists!"

Yasmine was beyond words. Dazed and bewildered by all which had happened in the last 24 hours, she gave in to the initial pangs of joy and smiled back at her husband. "The baby is still here. Seth! Our third child!"

And in her typical, dry, unintentional way of shaking a moment to its core, Ashby replied robotically, "Well...for you three. For him this will be number four."

It was early evening back at Blanchard House when Fable ended a phone call and went into the kitchen where Miranda and Salem were finishing the dinner dishes. Demitra was wiping down the counter when she noticed Fable's uneasy expression. "What now?"

"Seth and Yaz want to drive down," Fable informed them. "Sort of a test visit."

"I see." Miranda replied, busying herself with the remaining dishes.

Demitra went to her, placing a compassionate hand on her arm. "Miranda, I know this is a complicated situation..."

Pulling her hand away, not in aggression, but determination, Miranda said, "Don't be gentle with me, Demitra. I have no intention of being gentle with them. And I do not intend on walking away from my responsibilities as easily as they both chose to."

Rarely one at a loss for words, Demitra looked back to Fable for guidance. Fable shook her head, signaling she should leave it alone for now. Salem merely watched Miranda quietly put the dishes away. Demitra and Fable made excuses to exit the room while she remained, observing Miranda's untheatrical resilience. Clueless as to what the tension was in the air, Echo came in carrying a hamper of his laundry. Miranda, still silent, took it from him as she put the last few forks in the utensil drawer. "I can do it," Echo declared. "It's my dirty clothes."

"It's fine," Miranda replied. "I am about to get Sydney's load from the dryer anyway. I'll wash yours after I switch Sage's out of the wash." She disappeared down the hallway with Echo's laundry in hand.

"Is she okay?"

"No," Salem informed him. "Seth and Yasmine are coming home."

"Home for good? Or home to make amends?"

"Your guess is as good as mine." Salem told him. "I think Miranda is afraid they will want to step back in with the children as though nothing happened."

Echo admitted he couldn't blame her for being afraid of that happening.. He also reminded Salem that if Seth and Yasmine managed to ease back into life at Blanchard House, where would that leave Miranda? She was finally feeling equal and like she belonged. This might change everything. Salem pushed her fingers through her hair, sighing in frustration. "I did not think this through," she admitted. "Saving Seth was so important to me; I did not consider the ramifications on everyone else."

"Meaning you regret saving him?"

"No," she scoffed. "He is my brother! I had to try. But I also must be honest, Seth and Yaz aren't integral to the family anymore. Most of you have lived here without them longer than with them. Them returning home means something to us it doesn't to the rest of you. The rest of you either barely knew them, or knew them for a very short time."

"That's not exactly fair to say," Echo argued. "I liked Seth! "He was very good to me."

"Yes," Salem acknowledged, "But Seth and Yaz aren't *Blanchard House* to you. Seth and Yaz, Fable and Beryl, they are my childhood. All my life's milestones. For us, when we think of home...we are all here with Olympia, and Artemis, and Demitra. And Arielle and Howard fold into that picture as well."

Echo fell silent a moment. Lost in his thoughts. She hoped she hadn't hurt his feelings. "I suppose it is the same you must feel about Trix and Tess," she added for clarification. "And how Ocean, Syd, and Sage feel when they think of Forest and Pastoria."

"I understand," Echo said. "But if all this is true, Salem, why do you seem unhappy about them coming home? It can't just be Miranda's feelings."

Smearing a tear across her face with the palm of her hand, Salem nodded her head. "I am unhappy because I am Queen. If a fight breaks out over the children, with Seth and Miranda on opposite sides, Witch Law dictates I decide the matter."

Pulling a chair around, straddling it backwards, Echo sighed in understanding. "Oh. And you don't want to be the one who must hurt Miranda."

"No," Salem explained. "It will not be Miranda I hurt."

CHAPTER THIRTY-FIVE

The Price of Humanity

Out in the deep wooded forest around Lake Tuscaloosa, Patric had been resting when his sister fled in the night without his awareness. He roamed the woods for miles the following days, but she was nowhere to be found. There was only one place she might go and if not there, they might know where she was.

Patric rapped at the door of Blanchard House in broad daylight, knowing his human form would not immediately intimidate whoever answered. "Yes?" Sydney asked the stranger when she opened the door. "We have had enough reporters banging on our doors these last weeks. What do you want?"

Con appeared behind her in the hall. Sydney did not notice, keeping her eyes on the pesky visitor who had knocked too rudely. Con placed a finger to his lips, signaling to Patric to not reveal him. Then he motioned behind himself. Patric understood. "My apologies, Miss," he offered the woman staring daggers into him. "I should not have bothered you."

She closed the door and went back to her phone where she continued to enjoy reels of funny pet sea lions. Patric made his way around the side of the house to the backyard. Con was stepping out of the back door. Con motioned for him to follow, leading him to the chicken houses down the foot trodden path. "No one can see us from the house out here." Con explained.

"Hello, my son."

"You are him, aren't you? The only time I saw you I was a wolf. I see things differently then. But now I can see you better. You're my father."

"Yes, boy. I am your father." Patric grinned. "Would you like to shake hands? Or hug? Though I am not generally a hugger. It in no way reflects my pleasure in seeing you, my son."

"My mother said you used to hurt people."

"I still hurt people," Patric replied boldly. "Just as you hurt people in your wolf form."

Con fidgeted on his feet and revealed, "But I don't hurt people. They lock me in a concrete house, so I won't."

He was noticeably exacerbated, "They lock you up? My son? They lock you up and deny you your natural born instincts? Your very internal nature? You are a beast of the night! How dare anyone rob you of the honor."

"They do it to protect me from hurting someone."

"There is much I must teach you, my son. But there will be time for that later. For now, I must ask you if you know the whereabouts of your Aunt Yasmine."

Con appeared surprised by the question. "Why would you care?"

"Don't you know, Con? Yasmine is my sister."

It seemed strange to the boy how he had never put that together before. His family was full of aunts and uncles and cousins who were not at all related to each other in regular ways like other families. It fascinated him to realize now his father had a sister. "My cousin Hera was talking about it last night. Her real parents are coming back here. They've been in Charleston."

"I don't understand," Patric replied. "Your cousin is mistaken. Her father is dead."

Con shrugged. "He's not anymore. I don't know how. But they are coming back. They aren't vampires anymore. Uncle Seth was on TV!"

It was something Patric never expected to hear. How could the witches manage such a feat? To restore vampires to human form again was unprecedented. But if it were possible, and Yasmine was in fact human again, Patric could turn her to wolf rather easily. She, he, and his sons could start over somewhere else together. Their own little pack.

Patric bid his son goodbye for now. He momentarily considered taking him but waited. There would be time for that later. For now, nothing should disrupt the Blanchard family until Yasmine comes home.

Howard was sitting in the Lazyboy recliner in his apartment when a knock came at the door. At first, he wasn't going to answer it until the knocks turned into banging and Demitra's voice shouted out from behind the shaking door.

"I want to know what's going on with you." Demitra declared as he twisted the knob open. "You have not been yourself for weeks. You keep avoiding the house when you used to be over all the time. Rosamund says you are even distant with her and drinking more than usual."

She pushed past him and sat down on his couch, tossing two magazines, a business file, and a pair of dirty socks onto the coffee table. Howard sat down beside her and opened his mouth to issue denials that anything was wrong. But her eyes. Those violet eyes of hers. He couldn't lie to them. He shrank down onto his knees and began sobbing. It was so unlike him to display this kind of emotion, yet it flooded from within him, and he could not stop.

Demitra leaned over his back, holding him by the sides, she rested her cheek onto his upper back. She let him cry it out before pulling him upright and turning his face towards her own. "Tell me."

"I can't," he whispered. "I can't tell anyone. Especially you."

"Why especially me?"

Howard's eyes locked in place as he answered, "Because you will hate me. And I cannot bear it if you hate me."

Demitra slid off the couch and placed herself at his knees. Clasping his two hands with her own she lifted his chin to look at her. "Nothing, and I mean nothing can make me hate you, Howard."

"You don't know that."

"Oh, but I do," she vowed. "We've been the best of friends my whole life. More than that, you are a part of me. A part of my daughter. I promised you once I would always be here for you. Trust in that now. Tell me what you have done."

Howard began shaking. His eyes began to well up and he began to have a shortness of breath. "I killed Miles."

Demitra leaned back against the coffee table. As her back pressed against it the magazines and file toppled off the back onto the floor. "Miles had a heart attack. How could you be responsible for that? You weren't even there."

"Because I traded his life to restore Yasmine. But Beryl is responsible for that, not me. I was tricked and because of me Miles is dead."

Her eyes blazed with a mix of curiosity and outrage. She demanded he explain. He did. After he finished speaking, she continued her recline against the coffee table until she'd pushed it forward with her back to where she was completely seated on the floor.

"Howard."

"I know."

She shook her head in disbelief as the information set in. "I don't know where to begin," she said. "I cannot believe you have that kind of power. But how could we have known? There has been no way to test it. I have never heard of such a power." She paused as her mind registered something, "The Power of God."

"Dee, I thought we'd get Yasmine back! I had no idea Beryl had given Salem Holy Blood."

Demitra rose from the floor angrily, "Because you didn't grow up a Blanchard! If you had, then maybe you might have known to trust the Natural Order!"

"I was only thinking of making Yaz human again."

Demitra paced the room, filled with a mixture of anger and sympathy. "What you did, Howard, was resurrect Patric! He was who Thaddeuss was manipulating you into bringing back to life."

Howard raised his hands in aggravation, "I didn't know!"

"Of course, you didn't!" she screamed. "That's why you should have come to me the moment you thought Taub had come to you. I could have figured out it was Thaddeuss. And I could have explained to you he had nothing to gain in restoring Yasmine to humanity. Hell, Fable could have told you that! You aren't knowledgeable enough to act on your own. Especially with things so devastatingly important! It was stupid Howard! Stupid!"

He began sobbing again. "I know. I know. I just thought...Yaz. We'd get our Yaz back. Hera and Titan would have their mother. Maybe if it worked, I could bring Seth back too. I thought..."

"No," she roared. "You didn't think! You didn't think at all! You cannot cheat The Natural Order! No matter how many people you think would benefit from it. You were tricked Howard! Tricked by a man you already knew to be evil. How could you do something so idiotic? If you'd only come to me."

"I'm sorry Demitra!" he cried. "I'm so damn sorry! Look at what I've done. Look at what I've done to Salem! I just want to die!"

As he huddled over his legs crying, Demitra could only stare at him. She was so angry with Howard she didn't know what to do. Never had she felt so disappointed in someone. Still, as he sobbed uncontrollably, she knew she could not hate him. She felt almost sorry for him. Yes, he'd caused a man's death—but hadn't she practically almost done the same thing once? Had her family not discovered it was Larry's soul possessing Jerry's body, Jerry would have eventually ceased to exist. Had that happened, she would have killed someone as well, and for practically the same reasons. Because at the time she felt Larry's presence in the world was more important than Jerry's. If Howard was guilty of a heinous offense, so had she been.

And it was Howard. Looking at him crumpled in despair she could not hold onto her rage. Howard was Beryl's son. Her grandson. Even had that never turned out to be the case, Howard had been in her life since she was born. The Blanchard family's most loyal friend. Demitra crawled to him and held him in her arms.

"I love you, Howard Caldwell. We will figure this out together. I will not turn my back on you. Nothing can make me do that. Not even this."

They sat together on the floor a while in silence until Howard regained his composure. He pulled himself back up to the sofa and then lifted Demitra to sit by him. They looked at each other through their messy, watery faces and simply sighed holding hands.

"What do I do now?"

Demitra squeezed his hand and answered, "We do nothing."

He looked at her in disbelief. "Nothing?" Howard repeated. "Shouldn't I confess to Salem? Shouldn't I try to make this right?"

Demitra grabbed his cheeks in her hands, forcing him to look into her lavender eyes. "Salem is never to know this! Never. No one will. Not Rosamund, not even Jerry. This dies with you and me Howard. It would destroy Salem, split the family apart, and you would be tried by the Consort for murder. I will not lose you for one inexperienced mistake."

"I am just like Nacaria..." the realization made him shudder.

Caressing his brow, Demitra pulled him close into her arms, "No, you will not be like Nacaria. Because no one is ever going to know."

Howard felt wobbly, slightly dizzy. He closed his eyes then suddenly jerked awake, the symptoms subsiding. "What happened?"

Demitra made a short laugh and answered, "I think I squeezed you too hard. You okay?"

"Yeah," he said, still feeling slightly disoriented. "All I remember is you coming in and hugging me."

Smiling back at him, Demitra lied. "Well, that's basically all that happened. I was so stressed over Seth and Yasmine returning home tomorrow and what mess that will turn into, I just needed a hug from my rock of support."

"Well, I will always be that for you, Dee. Always."

"I know you will."

Demitra left Howard's place and drove back home. Maybe twice in her life she'd used her psychic ability to erase someone's memory. It was always such a dangerous risk to try. But it was necessary tonight. No one, not even Howard, needed to know what he had done to Salem or to Fable, with his trade of Miles for Patric.

CHAPTER THIRTY-SIX

Knox's Past

He did not enjoy these feelings of jealousy which had begun to creep into his mind but one too many times Echo and Knox had run into Knox's ex, and now Dillon Asher was haunting him. The first time had been a complete surprise and one Echo had not been prepared for. It happened in the grocery store of all places, while Echo was picking up a few household items someone else at home had forgotten to grab. When you live in a house with 15 people, no one can remember to get everything. He was pushing his shopping cart to the next aisle when someone spoke out to him. Echo looked up to see a gorgeous rugged blonde man with broad shoulders and a chiseled chin line. "Are you Knox Daihmler's boyfriend?"

"Yeah," Echo said with confusion.

The nearly perfect specimen of a man thrust his hand out to shake. Echo obliged with a questioning look on his face. The man replied, "I am Dillon. Knox and I used to go out."

*Shit, the ex...*Echo thought. *And he would be hot as fuck too.* "Nice to meet you," Echo lied.

"You too," Dillon grinned. "I've seen you in a couple of his Instagram pics. When I saw you, I recognized you. What's your name?"

"Echo. Echo Blanchard."

Dillon appeared to be the one surprised now, "Blanchard? Like in *those Blanchards*?"

"Yeah. That's us. The whole world knows who we are now."

"That's crazy. And Knox is okay with it all?"

Not quite understanding how to take the implication, Echo replied how Knox seemed to be. It was at that time when Echo looked down to his cart and noticed among its many items were two boxes of tampons, two packs of diapers, several boxes of Little Debbie snack cakes, and foot fungus crème. "Well, it was nice to meet you," Echo said again, hoping to move the cart along before Dillon looked down. Dillon's cart only had a bag of charcoal, a pack of steaks, and two packs of sparkling water.

"Say hey to Knox for me."

"I will!" Echo said far too cheerily to be believable.

After they parted, Echo headed towards the dairy section to grab three more jugs of milk for the house. Passing by the store bathrooms, Echo parked the buggy out of the way and went into the Men's room. He wasn't completely sure if he did actually have to pee or not, or was the creeping jealousy setting in. Closing himself behind a stall door, Echo took advantage of one of his powers and shapeshifted his body into the image of Knox's ex. Pulling himself free to pee, Echo got the chance to size up the competition. "Goddammit!"

The second time Dillion Asher showed up, Knox and Echo were having dinner in town. Dillon, who was also on a date, dropped by the table to say hello while on his way out. Knox stood politely and hugged him, then made the introduction for Echo. He was very surprised to hear Echo had previously met Dillon a few days before. Dillon reciprocated and introduced his companion before they left. Echo searched Knox's face for any glimmer of emotion as he shook his ex-boyfriend's date's hand. In the few seconds of small talk among them, Echo was on the lookout for whatever might show up in Knox's eyes while in the company of Dillon again. Once they were alone at their table again, neither said a word for a moment. Echo took the silence as a sign of Knox being lost in memories, perhaps even regret.

"Dillon seems nice," Echo stated casually.

"He does seem that way, doesn't he." Knox answered.

"Meaning he isn't?"

Knox put his fork down and asked, "What are you trying to find out?"

"I'm not trying to find anything out," Echo replied. "You made a comment implying he isn't really as nice as he pretends, leading me to wonder what kind of awful things he did to you or put you through."

Returning to his pork chop, Knox remarked, "You pack a lot of insinuation into a simple statement." He gave Echo a wink and moved the subject to other things. Echo only half listened to the rest, his mind racing with worries as to why Knox avoided the subject. Was he still in love with him? Did he hate him but missed the way they were in bed together? Did he compare Echo to Dillon when they were in bed together?

"Echo!" Knox said in a raised voice. "Are you hearing anything I am saying?"

"Sure.... what did you say?"

Knox wanted to know what was going on with him. He asked him outright if seeing Dillon bothered him. Echo stammered around the subject answering both yes it did and no, of course it didn't, making neither point believable. Knox sighed and tried to ease the tension, "Dillon and I are over. You don't have to worry about him. We all have exes."

"I don't." Echo said. "Not any living ones."

As if he were not anxious enough after two run-ins with Dillon, it was only a few nights later when they ran into him again at the local gay bar. Dillon had friends with him, but not his date from earlier in the week. Echo saw Knox's face brighten when he saw the group of men together. Pulling Echo along, Knox went over to them, hugging each one. He introduced his friends to Echo. Two of the guys were brought up right, shaking Echo's hand and expressing the pleasure to meet him. The third man, obviously pithier, snarled his upper lip and with an exaggerated effeminate manner and lilty voice, pronounced, "Well, this must be terribly awkward for you."

Taken aback by his remark, Echo shook his head and asked, "Why would it be awkward?"

The little flouncy man, who held his hand upright as if waiting for a prince to kiss it, gestured between Dillon and Knox, "These two were quite the pair. We all lived through it. Drama, drama, drama, I can tell you."

"Well, don't Bart." Knoxville said. "Nobody cares for yesterday's news." Conversation steered away from Bart's intended subject as Knox began asking one of the other men about his family. Echo pretended to be interested in the man's family update for Knox, but mostly he was listening for clues. As he stood silently listening to what was now strictly a dialogue between the two of them, Echo realized the guy and Knox must have grown up together. Knox asked all about the man's parents and sister. Likewise, the guy (whose name Echo never heard) wanted to know how Nash was and their sister who lived out of state now."

For an uncomfortably long time Echo stood by as little more than an observer, listening to this once tight group of friends catch up. Eventually, the chat was over as the flouncy little Bart wanted a drink and the others accompanied him, leaving Knox and Echo alone again.

"Your friends are nice," Echo said. "Except that short fat one."

"Bart has always been a shit starter. When they are all together, it typically devolves to that. But it was nice to see them again."

"I take it Dillon won the friends in the breakup?"

Knox gave a short laugh and replied, "I guess. Never thought about it. I never was the type to go paint the town red bar hopping all night. So, I rarely hear from anybody in that social group."

Knox left Echo to grab a couple of drinks from the bar. Echo watched as he walked to the alternate bar across the dance floor. Pleased Knox avoided another encounter with his ex, Echo simultaneously wondered why he did. Was it because he'd had enough of Dillon's presence, or was he afraid being too close to him again might hurt? Sometimes the emotional pull to someone causes a self-placed distance between them and you. Echo wondered which this was.

While Knox was across the bar in line, Bart pranced up once again, the drink in his hand already more than half consumed. "You are kinda cute," Bart admired. "When it doesn't work out with Knoxville maybe you and I can get together."

Echo never understood how people with the least appeal are never aware how repelling they are. He let the comment slide without reply. But Bart went further. "He's going to run back to Dillon eventually. They had it too bad for each other. But you know how it is."

"And how is it exactly?" Echo asked, giving the drama-maker what he wanted.

Bart snarled his upper lip in a way he probably assumed was cute. It wasn't. "You know, it's hard getting over your ex when you were so crazy hot for them for so long?"

Understanding Bart's remark was meant to make Echo feel even more vulnerable, Echo decided to not allow him the satisfaction. "I wouldn't know. Men don't leave me."

Bart giggled. Not chuckled. Not laughed. Giggled, then asked, "Are you telling me nobody has ever dumped you before?"

"Never."

"So, it's always you who does the breaking up, then?"

"I don't know if it could quite be called breaking up. My last relationship ended with his stomach slashed open while his entrails spilled out all over the ground. He tried and tried to stuff them back in, but it didn't really work out all that well."

He left Bart's stunned face under the flashing blue and yellow lights streaming from the edge of the dance floor as Echo joined Knoxville on his way back with cocktails.

CHAPTER THIRTY-SEVEN

Choices and their Consequences

Uncomfortable moments are never made less uncomfortable with delay. While the Blanchards did their best to pass the endless minutes waiting for the arrival of Seth and Yasmine, no one quite knew what to do with themselves, and no one was talking. Outside, the cloud cover was blocking out the sun as heavy rain fell making tapping noises on the eaves and the porch roof. Ironic for the sun to hide himself now when the expected guests could no longer be killed by him. It was also noteworthy, albeit unmentioned, that while Demitra sat in her chair periodically checking her phone for the time, she could have easily used her psychic powers to sense how close they were to arriving. Perhaps she didn't want to know. Knowing meant having to snap into mode, when she wasn't quite sure what that mode should be. This was not a joyous occasion, nor was it one of sadness. *There should be a word for something positive, yet you dread,* she thought to herself. She tried to think of one, but her thoughts were interrupted as she heard Fable remark, "I forgot about that. I guess that means they are here."

Demitra knew at once her meaning. The rain had stopped. A faint light was beginning to cast through the living room windows. Seth could control the weather. She could not remember a single time he had ever come home in the rain. It slipped her mind on this dreary day that the best indicator of their arrival would be clearing skies. Though a hush had long fallen over the house while waiting, it seemed even quieter now as everyone waited for the footsteps to sound from the porch. Demitra made her way to the foyer, inhaling a deep breath of courage before pulling open the door.

Her immediate thought upon seeing their timid faces was how they looked like guilty teenagers caught breaking curfew. In some ways perhaps it was exactly like that. They'd been out on a reckless night of overindulgence—except this night lasted a few years and caused countless deaths. Seth and Yasmine once again stood in the foyer of Blanchard House. However, unlike the last time, they were not there to kill anyone. With the rest of the family lingering either on the stairs, in the hall, or standing in the living room, Demitra presented a welcoming smile and outstretched her arms to welcome the prodigal Blanchards home. She thought it would be easy to resurrect her deep love for the adults she helped raise—but it wasn't. She could feel herself bristle slightly as they nervously stepped into her embrace. Her mind racing back to the last time they stood in this spot when they tried to kill her daughter, grandchildren, and steal the babies. *They are not those same monsters now.* Yasmine and Seth felt their own anxiety, heavy with remorse over what they put Demitra, and everyone else, through these last three years.

Echo, Sage, and Sydney gave hugs, smiles, and told them how good it was to see them, then graciously excused themselves upstairs, understanding the momentous event concerned them the least. Trix was not present, opting to skip this little reunion. She had not been as close to Seth as her brother, and she had never known Yasmine well, or for very long. But the truth in her absence was she still harbored ill feelings at their attempt to steal Jinx and Lucky. For this reason, Trix left home before their arrival, taking the twins with her to Rosamund's house. Howard, despite his daughter's misgivings, could not bring himself to miss Yasmine's return. The moment she removed herself from Demitra's arms, he encased her in his.

"Howard," she wept. "I'm so so sorry."

"Hush," he whispered to her. "We have all done things we wish we could take back. What matters is you are yourself again. And I have missed you."

Fable came next, pulling her cousins close, unexpectedly bursting into tears of her own. "God, I have missed the hell out of the two of you!"

Jerry took his turn, welcoming them home genuinely. He took his place behind Demitra, knowing his role only needed to be backing her up if necessary. "Glancing around the foyer," Yasmine asked. "Where is Salem? She's the only reason we have our souls again."

Demitra, almost too casually, explained Salem was on her way back from a meeting with the state governor. Yasmine gave Fable a confused look, to which Fable replied, "A lot has changed."

It only took a few seconds more for Yasmine and Seth to see what else had changed. Moving into the living room, they saw Miranda standing by the window.

Yasmine had little frame of reference regarding this woman. She only knew her as someone who'd looked after her children in her absence. She was also theoretically, Seth's second (and probably *legal*) wife. However, knowing her better than Yasmine, as Seth saw Miranda standing by the window it was as if meeting a stranger. The mousy, timid person he entrusted his children with by means of marriage, resembled little of the woman he remembered. Miranda had not changed much physically. She was still attractive, though not an overwhelming beauty, yet something in her demeanor made him think of a butterfly. She was not yet a butterfly, but she was certainly no longer the caterpillar he'd wed. Miranda was on the verge of shedding a cocoon, from which she would come into her own. Seth went to her, stammering out a clumsy compliment about how well she looked. From over his shoulder, Yasmine stared, her hands fidgeting behind Seth's back. Miranda had her eyes locked onto Yasmine, tension filling the room. Yasmine yearned to say something, but Miranda was practically a stranger to her. She could not even recall a single conversation they may have had before Yasmine changed. What could she say to a woman who had been raising her children for three years. Her only tangible memory of this woman was when she tried to kill her weeks ago.

"Miranda," Yasmine smiled gently. "I want you to know how horribly sorry—"

"I understand." Miranda nodded. "You were not...yourself."

Demitra, Jerry, Howard, and Fable took seats in the living room, all three brimming over with anxiety. Unsure what they should do, Seth escorted Yasmine to a side table flanked with two chairs. Sitting down, Yasmine broke the awkward silence with a much too optimistic, "Are the kids here?"

"Hera wants to speak to you," Miranda told them, pushing away whatever ambivalence she may be feeling about it. "I have agreed, but Titan is too young. He is also a self-insulated child. Strangers upset him. Change upsets him."

Pushing back somewhat on her statement, Seth said, "We still want to see our—"

"Hera, you may talk to." Miranda repeated sternly. "Only because she asked to see you. Titan, I will not allow. Later, maybe. But not today."

Demitra decided to step in, taking charge of the meeting now that Miranda had been allowed to assert her authority over the children. Demitra let Seth and Yasmine know how happy it made her to hear they took the cure and came back to their former selves again. Like any mother, however, her forgiveness was accompanied with the reminder that a great deal of damage was done to all parties concerned and they should not expect everything to fall quickly back into place without a period of adjustment as well as atonement.

Feeling as if her lifelong best friends were being admonished enough, Fable tried to ease the mood with a voice of support, "It'll take some time, guys. But before you know it, things will get back to normal. Or something resembling it."

Quiet until now, Jerry felt the urge to speak up. He recognized he probably carried little authority with Seth and Yasmine. He'd merely been Demitra's new husband of just a few years when they'd left. Jerry was more now. He was the accepted, and respected, patriarch of the Blanchard clan. "Fable is more optimistic than I think either of you should be." Jerry warned. "Not that I want to make either of you feel more uncomfortable than you already feel, but a lot has happened. A lot has changed. This is not going to be an easy transition for anyone. But we are all willing to go through the growing pangs to see if we can all become a family together again."

Silence cloaked the room as another presence entered. Hera was in the doorway, peering directly at Seth and Yasmine. At first, Yasmine's instinct was to rush to her daughter, sweeping Hera into her arms and tearfully kissing her sweet face. She almost succumbed to the urge, but stopped herself when she saw Hera's sweet face was not as she remembered it. An iciness emanated from the child. A stoney reserve typically found in someone much older, but Hera had acquired hers early and it was undeniably strong. "Hello, my sweet girl." As the words fell from Yasmine's lips she regretted them. She started to rise from the chair so as to lower herself on her knees to speak to the child, much the way she had when Hera was little. Seth reached out, gently grabbing her elbow, stopping her from the gesture. He knew this was no longer a child before them. Hera had grown up fast and hard. Though she followed Seth's caution, Yasmine could not help, as a mother, to plead for her daughter's forgiveness. "My sweet girl, can't you remember me? Remember how we used to read together. We used to laugh. We used to sit on the floor and work those puzzles with the large thick board pieces."

"I remember you smashing my face into the clock." Hera answered with an icy chill. "And how the glass felt cutting into my eyes. And when you pounded my head against the wall until my skull began to break. Yes, I remember you."

Yasmine's horrified face stared at her daughter. Hearing what she'd done to her own child, from the very lips of her child, was so painful she almost wished she still had no soul. Seth placed his loving hands upon Yasmine's shoulders, bracing her from collapsing, or rushing forward to beg forgiveness. He remembered what Hera is capable of doing when crossed. The intensity was reaching the pinnacle of what Miranda could tolerate. She moved to Hera, placing a reassuring hand on her back. "Hera, just tell them what you told me you want to say. Then you can go back upstairs, and I'll come up shortly."

Yasmine attempted again to say something, but again Seth stopped her. "Go ahead, Hera," he said.

Everyone listened to the child's curt words as she conveyed her feelings. "I have a mother. The one you gave me before you left, Seth. She's been to me what you two never were." Hera broke her arctic stare, looking only into Yasmine's eyes now, where there seemed to be a touch of sympathy—but only a touch. "They tell me you were sick. It wasn't your fault what happened to you. I do believe that." Yasmine's face released some of its tension as Hera's generosity set in. But it was the extent of the child's generosity, as she addressed them collectively again. "They tell me you are both normal now. But I don't care." Her honesty was a jarring thing to hear, not only by her parents, but by those in the room who once loved them, "Every person you killed," she went on. "I saw die. I felt their fear. Every night. Then you came here and almost killed me. It doesn't matter if you were sick, and I don't care that you are better. Parents don't leave." Hera looked up at Miranda, who now was not very much taller than she. Yasmine and Seth saw the change in her expression looking into Miranda's teary eyes. They loved each other. It wasn't spite on Hera's part. And it wasn't anger causing Hera to say these things. She was a girl arguing the case of why she wanted to remain with her mother. Hera ended her speech simply, "I am going to try to stop hating you. I really am. But this is my mother. I don't want the two of you living here with us. Titan and I are happy. Leave us alone."

Hera left the room, going upstairs. Jerry looked apologetically to his wife, who gave him a nod of understanding, as he followed after Hera to make sure she was all right. Demitra turned to the speechless couple. "I am sorry. I know that cut deeply. Some mistakes can't be undone, no matter how much we wish they could."

Yasmine was nearly inconsolable, "My daughter hates me. She was my baby, and she hates my guts!" Seth took her in his arms as she wept, "Seth, remember the day she was born? You came running up the stairs and I was holding her. Our baby, Seth. Our baby hates us so much."

"It'll change." Fable assured them, rushing to Yasmine's side, rubbing her arms gently. "Yazzy, she will come around."

"She won't." Salem said standing in the doorway. She had returned in time to hear some of what Hera had said. "Seth, Yaz, can I talk to the two of you alone?"

The others were happy to oblige, wishing to remove themselves from the awkwardness of the situation. Fable gave both Seth and Yasmine a kiss to the cheek before she left, also adding a sympathetic pat to Salem's arm as she went by her. This was now Salem's predicament to settle, even Demitra recognized the fact, mouthing *good luck* to her niece before joining Jerry upstairs. Howard left the house without a word, regretting he would have no more time with Yasmine for the moment, but knew that might come later. Miranda disappeared through the swinging door to the dining room on her way to the kitchen stairs. Conflicted as to whether she should have stayed since whatever would be said affected her as well, she chose to trust Salem.

Salem directed her brother and sister-in-law to join her on the couch. Sitting sideways against the cushions to face them both earnestly, Salem took them each by the hand. "I say this with a heavy heart, but also with love for you both. You cannot stay here. It isn't good for anyone, not even yourselves."

"We hadn't decided to stay," Seth told his sister. "Arielle wants us with her. She wants me to help with the tea plantation. I haven't decided. We only came here to see if maybe the kids—"

"The kids aren't leaving Blanchard House." Salem informed them with authority. "I have thought about little else since you found Yaz." She pulled Yasmine's hand to her lips, kissing it affectionately, "I love you so much, Yazzy. I love the both of you so much. And this isn't goodbye. Not to me. Not to anyone living here."

Cutting her off, fearing where she might go with this, Seth asserted, "The children will get used to us again. You'll see. They just need time with us."

Shaking her head in disagreement, Salem told them bluntly, "You are not Hera and Titan's mom and dad anymore. Titan doesn't remember life with you at all. And Hera chooses Miranda."

"What about us?" Yasmine wept.

"I think if you go back to Charleston, the two of you can build a life there without the constant pain of living in what you caused here."

"But the family? Our children?" Yasmine shouted.

As sincere as she could be, but without backing down from her statement, Salem told them, "Your family is still your family. We do not have to live together for that to be true. But your children belong *here* with Miranda. You may have created them, but she has nurtured them. Seth, it's not that different from our mother and Aunt Artemis."

Seth's head hung heavy with shame. He knew she was right.

"But your mother was cursed, and your father knew where you were, he chose to stay away" Yasmine argued, attempting to paint a different picture, despite the similarities. "Seth and I wanted our children! I was attacked by vampires! I didn't ask for any of this to happen!"

"But you did, Yaz," frowned Salem. "That day when Seth, Arielle, and I left to rescue Howard from that parallel dimension, you were told to stay here. But you didn't. You clamped onto Seth and sailed off through time with us. You made a choice then. You were supposed to stay here with your children, but you chose Seth."

Hanging his head, Seth stroked Yasmine's arm with trembling fingers. "I did it too. I chose to leave those kids to find you Yasmine. We both abandoned our children."

"For each other!" Yasmine cried. She did not understand why no one could see the larger picture. "We left to find each other."

"But we left, Yaz. It was still a choice." Seth whispered. Though the feeling of shame ran rampant throughout him, he still couldn't denounce his actions. "I don't regret it, Yaz. I love our kids, but I would make the same choice again. Both of us chose the one we loved most, and it was more than we loved our children."

Salem patted their hands, nodding. "You see it now. Not everyone has a love like you two. If faced with a choice, Miranda would choose Hera and Titan. Every time. The way Artemis gave up whatever life she might have had, for us."

Yasmine still wanted to argue the parallel, "But you loved your mother. When Nacaria came back you welcomed her. Your father too!"

Looking into his wife's eyes, Seth explained the difference. "Yeah, but it never changed who Artemis was to us. Artemis was our mother."

Salem enclosed Yasmine in her arms, resting her chin on her shoulder. Pushing Yaz's hair back away from her ear, Salem whispered into it, "The children will care about you one day. They may even love you one day. But the only way for that to happen..."

Yasmine finished the sentence, "Is to let them go."

Blanchard House was very still. Not a sound was made from anywhere within its walls. Salem removed herself from the couch where she had pretended to be frozen beside Seth. Yasmine must not know, or didn't remember, that a witch with the power to stop time, is also immune to any witch with the same power. Salem allowed Yasmine a few advance steps before she followed. Initially, it ran through her mind that Yasmine might be sneaking upstairs to steal her children since she was not successful winning them back. But Salem reminded herself Yazzy was not such a person. Even Salem needed time to separate evil Yasmine from good Yasmine.

She could hear Yaz talking as she tiptoed around the corner. Salem did not look into the room. It wasn't that she feared Yasmine seeing her, it was only her desire to allow Yaz this private moment with her children. Salem was sure Miranda, and possibly Jerry was in the room caught by Yasmine's immobilizing spell. And Hera must have had Titan with her, because Yaz addressed them both. Salem listened unsuspectingly in the hall.

"You were my everything, Hera." Yasmine said, choking a little on her tears. "I'd never been so happy as when you came along. And Titan, my baby boy...I had so little time with you. But whatever I thought was full in my heart after Hera was born, must have stretched my heart bigger when you came because I love you just as much."

Nothing was said for a moment. Salem assumed Yasmine was stroking their hair or caressing their faces—all the things Salem spent years daydreaming about if she had been awarded a final moment with Michael. "I know you hate me now," Yasmine said after a few minutes. "And I know you love Miranda." She must have addressed Miranda's unknowing mind next as she said, "Miranda, thank you for loving my babies. Thank you for...being...their mom." Salem was in full tears now behind the wall, overhearing the heartbreaking scene. "Hera, Titan, I love you more than you know. Because I love you, Daddy and I are leaving you here, where you are happy. Please give us a chance one day. If I can't be your mom, then please try one day to be my friend."

A little while later, standing on the front porch of Blanchard House, Yasmine and Seth looked out across the windblown field. "Where do we go now, Seth?"

"Anywhere, as long as we are together," he told his wife as he gently rubbed her tummy. "And this time, we won't make mistakes."

CHAPTER THIRTY-EIGHT

Sinclair Industries

In the three months since Salem outed all supernatural kind to the public, the world had not loosened up very much on its divisiveness over witches, vampires, and the like. Numbers were growing in support of Salem and all she represented, primarily due to Daphanie Channing and journalists such as she who now were telling the stories of others coming forward to be heard. The talking heads of news and media had settled into a *wait and see* stance on the subject, harkening on the merits of such powerful beings now becoming actively involved in solving world problems.

More conservative minds remained reluctant to take chances. Their tolerance for witches dwindling day by day thanks to sensationalized stories being posted with regularity across the internet. Evangelical groups took great offense at the audacity of the witches claiming they were imbued with special powers from God himself. Even more blasphemous to them were the claims that a member of the Blanchard family was being hailed as The Almighty God. Despite numerous attempts to explain Beryl Blanchard was not God, only a vessel through which He moved, nothing dissuaded them. Relations between opposing opinions were reaching unparalleled levels of divisiveness in America.

The one saving grace was that the American Government was pledging it's support to working with the witches, lending much needed credibility to the new Council Salem Blanchard had organized. Declassified documents regarding the FBI and CIA's pre-existing knowledge of vampires leaked to the press, substantiating Salem's televised claims. Calls for the witches to vaccinate the vampire population with Beryl's blood supply were growing day by day.

Wall Street was going through its own variety of adjustments and fluctuations centering on new knowledge. Already brokerage houses were scrambling to hire psychics.

Pharmaceutical companies directed their laboratories to hire witches skilled with potions. And municipal offices urged fire stations and police departments to recruit witches with usable abilities to join their ranks. Even several Fortune 500 corporations were entering bidding wars to employee witches into their ranks, flimsily disguising their intention to capitalize upon whatever magical skillset or manipulations their new discoveries could add to their company before Congress figured out a way to legislate and regulate such things. But with all the giants of industry vying for magical on boarding, one company was doing their best to shed their mystical ties.

Sinclair Industries, upon learning the heirs of their chief shareholders, Olympia and Yasmine Blanchard, were the same Blanchards causing such controversy across the world, decided to distance themselves from their founder's extended family. The Board of Directors had not enjoyed answering to Randolph Sinclair's widow, Olympia Blanchard, all the years after his death when she was the majority stockholder. They offered slightly less aversion after her death to Yasmine owning controlling interest. She was, at least, a true descendent of Randolph Sinclair. It was also an easier pill to swallow that Yasmine had nothing to do with the decisions involving the company. Her solicitor, Howard Caldwell had been the man to deal with for some time. However, now other shareholders were skittish, and a few right-leaning company CEOs had terminated contracts based on the publicity connecting Sinclair Industries to the Blanchard family. Because of this, the Board of Directors unanimously voted to remove Howard from the Board and wanted to distance the entire family from the company and its financial ventures.

As the Board convened for their next meeting, the eight present members, and the Chief Financial Officer, had only just begun to convene, when muffled commotion could be heard not far away. As the sound came closer, it was audibly clear a woman was shouting. Alongside her voice were the voices of security guards calling out demands for her to stop. Suddenly the double doors to the conference room flung open as a strange young woman burst inside. She was rather plainly dressed in an off-the-rack ladies-pant suit of pale blue. It was the kind of suit a woman would buy to give the appearance of professionalism when in truth she was out of her depth. The guards had caught up to her, grasping her by the arms as they looked embarrassedly on to the table of important people before them. The woman wrenched herself free, declaring, "I have already told you, if you do not leave me alone, I will have all of you fired."

Rising from his chair at the head of the elongated pristinely clear glass table, Faulkner Lloyd demanded, "What is going on here?"

Taking the opportunity to shove one of the guards in the chest to clear the way, she marched forward, announcing, "I am Miranda Blanchard. I believe there is a seat for me at this table."

"Young lady," a man in an overpriced gray suit said, rising. "What is the meaning of this? This is a private chamber, and you are not a part of this Board of Directors." He motioned to the security guards to remove her immediately.

Miranda raised her hand towards them to pause their approach. "Unless you guys want to lose your jobs, I would stand down. I am your boss." She turned back to the Board and the man who had stood up. "I said my name is Blanchard. Miranda Blanchard. Mrs. Seth Blanchard to be precise."

Several Directors reacted in surprise, each turning to look at the CFO. Faulkner Lloyd walked to Miranda, offering an insincere smile along with a condescending shake of the head. "I do not quite comprehend your meaning, eh, Mrs. Blanchard. This is Sinclair Industries. As we understand it, Yasmine Sinclair is still legally deceased. This company's ties to the Blanchard family are over, except for whatever stock they draw income from. And in light of the current temperature of public opinion, Sinclair Industries no longer welcomes the counsel of Howard Caldwell, nor do we any longer extend the courtesies which were long over-provided to our Founder's distant relatives."

Miranda noticed an unoccupied leather rolling chair against the wall. She rolled it to the end of the table nearest the door, opposite Mr. Lloyd, and sat down. "The stock," she smiled, edging closer to the table. The pinch faced woman who had been seated there was staring at Miranda incredulously. With a frustrated smile, Miranda told her, "You know, you *can* scoot over a little." The woman reluctantly did so although she didn't know why she complied. Miranda returned to her original point. "The stock is the reason for my visit."

"The Sinclair shares are now divided among Yasmine Sinclair's minor children. The Board of Directors will be voting their proxy in compliance with the terms of Miss Sinclair's last will and testament."

Miranda could feel the surge of courage inside her, even if she also could not overlook the nervousness or the complete inexperience she had in such a setting. She rested her folded arms on the table. The glass was cold. She quickly removed them, then noticing the smudge she'd made on the otherwise transparent top, made two circular wipes on the glass with the sleeve of her suit. Suddenly aware she was not at home wiping toothpaste splatter from her children's bathroom mirror, she smiled again, and pretended she'd done nothing weird. Placing her folded arms down once more—smudge be damned—she revealed, "I will be voting their shares from now on."

Laughing at her audacity, the CEO sneered, "Well miss, I am afraid things do not quite work that way. The Blanchard family was not listed as proxy for Yasmine Sinclair in the event of her death. Out of respect, we did continue to keep Mr. Caldwell informed on Board decisions, however now things have changed."

"I realize things have changed," Miranda said defiantly. "As a matter of fact, that is why I have flown all this way to be here today. So that I can tell you just exactly how things have changed."

"You are going to tell us?" The woman who did not appreciate sharing her spot at the table smirked.

"Yes."

Lloyd placed his pithy hand onto Miranda's shoulder, gripping it in a way to display his authority. "It is obvious you do not understand the fundamentals of a corporation our size. As I have said, everything is in accordance with Yasmine Sinclair's will."

Removing his hand from her shoulder by two fingers, Miranda made a playful sigh before declaring, "Yes, I am sure. But you see, gentlemen," she looked at her table neighbor, "And lady. Yasmine Sinclair was married at the time of her death. Her husband, Seth Blanchard became sole heir of her Sinclair stock."

"Her children became heirs." One of the Board members pointed out. "Seth Blanchard was declared dead—whatever else he became after does not change the legal status. Therefore, his children are heirs to their mother's shares. And we shall be overseeing their interest in the company."

"Not now," Miranda smiled. "The children did not technically inherit those shares. You see, Gentleman...and lady, I am the widow of Yasmine Sinclair's husband. I am Mrs. Seth Blanchard. My husband died intestate. His financial matters have been settled and probate has been closed. Not only am I the legal mother of Yasmine Blanchard's children, I am also the legal inheritor of Seth Blanchard's stock."

"What are you saying?"

Feeling the same inner burst of satisfaction she imagined Sydney must get when she knocks down a wall, Miranda answered, "I am Sinclair Industries. And I, and I alone, will look after my children's interests. You will reinstate Howard Caldwell to this Board to vote my proxy. And if any one of you attempts to block his participation in this company again, I will short sell every share at the lowest possible price and drive this conglomerate into financial ruin." Rising to make her exit before she had to bluff her way through any understanding of the matters they had on the agenda to discuss, Miranda walked to the door. Turning around for one final last word, she told them, "Don't fuck with the Blanchards. No one who has ever tried, has ever won."

CHAPTER THIRTY-NINE

A New Day Has Come

The last three weeks of Salem Blanchard's life had been a whirlwind of covert meetings, investigations into her background, and what almost felt like governmental interrogations. Salem had met with the President of the United States, several Congressional committee heads, and been flown in an unmarked helicopter to an unidentified army base where she spent an entire day proving the validity of her powers to military leaders. Once the skeptics were satisfied that she was not a charlatan, officials began to take her seriously and offer her the respect she deserved. Congress was now working on funding for its new governmental agency— The American Betterment Council. Salem wasn't sold on the name, but lately she'd had to pick her battles. The President felt the name would strike less fear with the public, so despite the Queen of the witches' objections, her new organization was to be forever known as the ABC. Compromise was now a daily part of her life. However, after speaking with a few other kings and queens of Consorts in other nations, Salem learned she was experiencing a much smoother time with this agenda in America.

A plan was in place at some future time, for the construction of a permanent and highly secured facility in Virginia for these future assemblies. In the meantime, secrecy being paramount, Salem arranged with her sister to use the, still unsold, Quinlan Castle for the inaugural meeting of The American Betterment Council. The public had not been informed of the ABC's inaugural meeting in order to keep protestors and zealots away. The four block radius around Quinlan Castle was currently blocked off by police citing a gas leak in the area. Unseen by Birmingham residents were the dozens of secret service and federal agents guarding the perimeter.

Salem was the first to arrive, feeling it her duty to personally welcome each new Council member upon arrival. Among the chosen members of Salem's roundtable, were several beings hand-picked by Salem for the experience or the magical asset they would offer the organization. Ashby D'Angelo would be Salem's lie detector and guard rail. A witch from Nebraska named Jacinda was chosen for her ability to psychically weigh various outcomes of a decision based upon choices made. Gideon Duquesne was awarded a chair at the table for his expertise on vampire culture and habits, as well as his experience being the first person ever cured by the Holy Blood. The council members without supernatural powers, were chosen to represent the interests of varying sectors of the American population. Among these officials were well respected champions of race equality, perspectives of elderly citizens, LGBTQ+ viewpoints, several various religious representatives, a chief health administrator from the Center for Disease Control and Prevention, and a renowned scientist from the National Oceanic and Atmospheric Administration. Council members would hold their seat until retirement, death, or being voted out by a majority of other members on the ABC committee.

Of all the delegates of this new agency's board of directors, only three would hold their seats in perpetuity. The current King or Queen of the Witches Consort, Salem at present, would retain their position as Chief Council member until a time when they either retired, died, or a new Consort leader was chosen.

The second chair ineligible of being removed, would belong to whoever held the office of the Vice President of the United States. This was Salem's suggestion when meeting with Congress. Her argument being that the Commander in Chief had far too much on his plate, but her real reason, which she kept to herself, was she rather liked the female VP and hoped one day Jocelyn Franks might be elected the first female President.

The third perpetually assigned seat at the round table belonged to an official exclusively chosen by The Pentagon. This was a non-negotiable on the government's part, but their insistence did allow for Salem's demand on the Vice President choice.

The final seat at the table went unquestionably to Artemis Blanchard. Perhaps, at present, the most vital member of the assembly. The trifecta of witch, wolf, and vampire yet still possessing her soul made her crucial for the eradication of supernatural monsters who refused to take the cure.

Vice President Jocelyn Franks arrived soon after Salem, accompanied by the Pentagon's delegate, General Malcolm Gillis. Salem never found out just what he was the General of, but it really didn't matter. He was simply a concession she made to Washington. Half expecting her arrivals to marvel at the beauty and uniqueness of

Blackie D'Angelo's former home, Salem was a little disappointed to discover no one really gave much thought to Quinlan or its design. The guards walking the turrets up top thought it was cool, so that would have to be enough.

Within an hour, Salem's round table of advisors were all seated except for one. Salem, centered in the middle, assured the General and Vice President that her aunt would be there before the meeting began. Artemis just wasn't someone you could pinpoint very well. Gideon Duquesne smiled proudly from his seat on the council, happily representing ex vampires, but feeling especially triumphant to have the name Duquesne once again associated with a station of prominence. Ashby D'Angelo sat quietly in her seat, making no discernable gestures or reactions as she waited to begin.

Everyone was rather impressed with themselves for being chosen for this new assembly, but all shed some of their bravado once Artemis entered the room. With her long glistening raven hair, piercing white eyes, and methodical movements, she commanded full attention. Salem noticed even the brave General shuddered in his seat. As Salem introduced her, she explained Artemis represented the darker creatures, both known and unknown.

Everyone assembled had their own personal agenda, or at least the regular human members did. Salem listened as each laid out what they believed the new Council and the powerful beings behind it, might do for their causes. As any good leader should, Salem allowed them all to speak before steering the agenda where it needed to be.

"This is new to all of us, myself included," Salem cautioned. "I think we should keep in mind that none of us here have been chosen to advance the causes of those they represent, but to act as guardian to their interests in matters we decide here."

The spokesperson for Jewish Americans, Rabbi Kellerman, spoke up, saying, "I am not following you, Miss Blanchard."

Salem stood, removing individual folders from a case she had before her on the table. Asking those next to her to pass a copy down to everyone, she explained. "Our first primary act should be assigning a member to act as Treasurer, administering the funding Congress provides us this week."

"I am confused, Miss Blanchard." General Gillis said. "Are you suggesting Congress will be paying you, or us, to oversee this council?"

Shaking her head, Salem smiled. "Not specifically or exclusively this council, but this organization will be dispersing funding to its operatives and directives."

"For what use exactly?" asked the evangelist minister.

Salem faced him directly, "For much the same reason your churches require donations. You use your funding for mission trips, or fighting hunger, possibly building roads or water sources in underdeveloped nations. This council will require assistance from people with enormously powerful abilities. We will have to compensate them."

"It was my understanding witches hoped to make the world a better place," the leader of the NAACP replied. "I understood them to be altruistic in their devotion to the cause."

Salem began walking around the table, feeling the need to clarify the realities of the world they all shared. "Witches have jobs and responsibilities. Children in school. Electricity bills to pay. Medical bills, gasoline, car payments, homeowners' insurance. We are not without the same life constraints as the rest of our neighbors. If there is a hurricane on the Gulf Coast and I have a witch with the power to slow it down or evaporate it completely, wouldn't I need money to buy their flight passage to get them there? An Uber ride to bring them from the airport? A hotel room for them to stay in? And the dangers involved in standing in the center of a deadly storm while projectiles are shooting by you constantly, doesn't that act of bravery and time away from their jobs and families, deserve compensation? You must be realistic ladies and gentlemen. Just as the Department of Homeland security pays its employees, so must this agency."

"Do you have folks who can control the weather?"

Smiling Salem nodded, "Absolutely. And since we are currently on this subject, our first order of business should be addressing our changing climate." She turned to the NOAA representative. "I would like a comprehensive list of areas in current crisis from drought, flood, famine, and wildfires." Addressing the entire committee now, she added, "In this file are the names of five witches who possess powers we can use to combat these events. The sooner we know where to send them, the sooner we can put a dent in the devastation being caused."

"Remarkable," Vice President Jocelyn Banks replied, scanning through the file. "These people can reverse these conditions all across the U.S.?"

"Not all at once, no." Ashby spoke up. "She just told you to provide her a list of the most critical areas affecting the most people. It should not be expected for the conditions besetting any of these regions to be immediately solved."

"Are we talking years?" the man from NOAA asked. "For example, the Mississippi Delta is experiencing devastating flooding as well as the river rerouting itself into areas that were not tributaries before the storms that recently struck there."

Salem addressed the question, hoping to provide insight as to how things would work. "Had we been alerted to the storm's trajectory by the weather service beforehand," Salem explained, waving her file. "These witches could have dispersed the storm over many miles, greatly reducing flood probabilities. However, that toothpaste is out of the tube. What we would need are witches, like my brother-in-law actually, who are capable to directing water manually. A few people like him on the job, with a few others who possess earth moving abilities, or massive telekinesis, or my cousin for example who can meld metals together, even those in the ground, and the flood plain can be dammed up and the water placed back on its original course."

General Gillis looked astounded. Rubbing his chin, and slightly stuttering, he asked, "Is this truly possible?"

Smiling brightly at her committee, Salem clapped her hands together softly and said, "That is why we are here ladies and gentlemen."

Flipping through the file Salem provided, General Gillis seemed puzzled. He voiced his concern at the reports making no mention of the Council offering the military assistance in critical and strategic strikes against hostile foreign attacks.

Salem responded firmly, "For now, witches will leave military matters to the government. This Council operates under a different set of goals and directives."

Proving Salem's faith in her, Vice President Franks voiced agreement. "Our mission with the establishment of this new agency, is to solve our problems at home. Starvation. Homelessness. Environmental emergencies. Our healthcare. We aren't here to wage war."

"This is an American agency," the General argued. "If your country needs you…"

Salem interrupted, "Then our country must prove the absolute life-threatening necessity. We are not here to empower America militarily nor are we here to use our resources to dominate other lands. For us to consider entering such conflict, it would require undeniable evidence that our intervention serves the greater good of humanity, not just American interests. The Natural Order applies to the entire world, not one nation."

Artemis stood suddenly from the table, as her hands pressed onto the wooden top, everyone in contact with it felt the quake quiver down the line. "None of this concerns me at present." She turned to address the General. "I require from you on a monthly basis, a report on the locations of vampire and werewolf nests which the government has collected."

"Those are often classified," General Gillis scoffed.

Artemis, without any person registering the movement until it happened, was now standing atop the table directly over the General. Staring commandingly down at him, Artemis stated, "Nothing is classified from me. Get me the locations, I will rid the problem."

"After..." Salem urged her aunt, "After the offer of redemption is made. If they take the cure, they will be allowed to live. If not, then do as you will."

"Yes, the cure." Artemis smiled. "I need to get accustomed to that. I usually just take their heads without question. I will need to remind myself; things have changed."

"I will get you some Post-it notes, Artemis." Salem teased.

CHAPTER FORTY

A Wolf by Any Other Name

Never in the history of Daihmler Elementary had a student been more eager to spend his evening on homework than Romulus Blanchard. Everything was a struggle for him, but he was very excited with every bit of new knowledge he acquired from his lessons. It should have pleased his mother, but it was having the opposite effect. Finally, Fable had to insist he put the books away and go to bed. The others had long gone to sleep while he was still hard at work. While Rom was on his knees gathering up his notebooks and textbooks from the floor, Fable offered what she thought might be a fun idea he'd agree to, she asked, "Hey Rom, do you want to morph back into your normal body and sleep with me tonight? I can lay there stroke your fur the way I used to."

Twisting his head up to give her a sarcastic look, he scoffed, "Why would I do that?"

The lump in her throat did little to mask the cracking of her heart. "Well, I just thought...that's how you and I used to go to sleep."

"I'm not a pet, Mom! I am a boy."

Trying to not feel so stupid for the question, Fable faked a smile and said, "I know you are a boy now, Romulus. But you are a wolf too. That's what you have been your whole life. Why do you want to forget all that? We had great times, me and my wolf."

Slinging his fully loaded backpack over his shoulder to exit the den, he balked, "Get over it Mom! This is me now. And I like this being me."

As he left her alone in the den, Fable slowly lowered herself to the sofa staring blankly onto the floor. She remembered how that little cub used to jump and bark and scramble all over the carpet, tearing magazine paper he'd pulled from the lower coffee table shelf. The pillows he chewed up so thoroughly. How he'd yap and bark trying to get up onto the couch before his tiny legs perfected their springiness. Her wolf was gone. And in his place was this smart mouthed kid she wasn't even sure yet if she liked it or not. Laying back against the pale blue cushions she sighed, recalling another era when it had been she, Yasmine, Seth, Salem, and Beryl sprawled around the den doing their homework at night together. Unable to stop the thought, Fable said to herself, *then we all went and grew up and ruined our lives with children.*

It was never something she expected to affect her this way. Not to the degree it was. Fable was surprised at herself and welling inside with shame for the way she was feeling. It wasn't a problem there was any kind of support group for. Moms could go online and chat with others about their child's illness or drug use, or disability. There were even support systems out there for mothers dealing with violent children. But no one had ever written a blog for moms whose sons used to be wolves. It was a rainy afternoon, torrential in fact. So much so that the schools declared an inclement weather day in case the roads washed out. Likewise, most of Fable's appointments at the clinic were cancelled, so she rescheduled the rest for another day. When the schools close, the town closes for the most part. The children were in the upstairs den playing Twister. Hera found the decades old box in a closet and thought it to be a great way to pass a rainy day. She harangued her cousins to play, as well as Theda who was over for the day as part of the family and Vanessa's plan to acclimate her into the fold. Fable tried to sit in the den and watch the children play. Some of her favorite memories of her own childhood were when she, Beryl, Salem, Seth, and Yasmine played that very same Twister set. But she could not do it. Rom had switched into his human form to play the game. He seemed to be taking human form more and more lately, even when not necessary. Though Fable knew his new ability to shapeshift at will was to be celebrated, she hated that he could.

Finding solace in the window seat on the second-floor tower room, she looked out at the heavy downpour behind the glass. The sky knew how she felt, if no one else could understand. She was startled from her thoughts by a tap on the open door. It was Vanessa. "Hi there," she said gently. "I came over to pick up Theda and saw you sitting there as I went by. Are you okay?"

"No." Fable said sharply. "You know what Vanessa? I am not okay and I'm tired of pretending I am."

Vanessa eased into the small square room, closing the door behind her. "Unload on me. I've certainly been through the emotional wringer lately myself. I can't promise solutions, but I can promise empathy."

She sat on the floral padded cushion of the window seat beside her friend. Fable Blanchard was typically a bastion of confidence, but Vanessa could tell that wasn't the case right now when Fable pushed a stray tear from her cheek and clasped Vanessa's hands with intensity. Squeezing as she spoke, Fable admitted, "I want my son back. The way he was. I don't know this Rom boy running around here with the others. His voice, his laugh, his fidgety hands. I want my wolf! My soft, cuddly, growly Romulus back. I want to watch him chasing rabbits through the field and racing with the deer in the back meadow. I want to see Titan latching on to his fur while Romulus rides him around the yard."

"I see."

"And it's like he doesn't even care that he's forgotten himself!" Fable exclaimed, purging even more pent-up resentment. "He has come downstairs in that human body every single day this week! I don't think I've seen him as a wolf at all."

Vanessa almost smiled, but quickly stopped herself. Of all the things she was guessing might be upsetting Fable, this was not it. Still, it was a problem for her. Vanessa needed to respect that. Then suddenly, she understood. "Fable, it is alright for you to mourn the Rom you think you've lost."

"Please don't say, you haven't lost him. That's all I get from my mother."

Vanessa sighed and replied, "I think you have lost him. Oh, sure, he will change into his wolf side here and there I'm guessing. But all his life he's felt separate from everyone else, and now he doesn't have to. He can be exactly like the other children. It's doubtful he will reject that in favor of who he used to be."

"That's why I feel like I am in mourning or something."

"Because you are, Fable. Romulus Blanchard as you loved him is shrinking away, and Rom Blanchard is in his place. But I promise you will grow to love Rom every bit as much as Romulus, just in a different way."

Fable let out a silly chuckle. "I sound crazy, I know."

"No, Fable. No, you don't." Vanessa offered. "What you sound like is a mother adjusting to a change in her child's identity. Have you considered reading some books by women who have had children change their gender identity?"

"Do you mean trans kids?" Fable replied. "But he's not—"

"Trans? No," Vanessa agreed. "But aren't the emotions you are feeling basically the same as if you were mourning a son who internally feels like he's your daughter?"

Fable said nothing for a moment, she only looked at her friend with a newfound peace in her expression. Suddenly she gripped Vanessa by the shoulders, crying, "It's so simple. Why has that not occurred to me?" Fable pulled her into a thankful hug. "Vanessa, you are right. Here I have been feeling sorry for myself while believing no other mother can ever understand what I am going through, because even I can't comprehend it. But I am not the first person to go through something like this. My kid is shedding the identity I have known and loved all his life. It's not just a me thing. Other parents are coping with these very emotions all around the world. Except in my case, it's a species thing rather than gender. But the feelings are still the same."

"I think so," Vanessa grinned, happy she had been helpful. "You need to read up about how other families cope with their loss of one person, and their journey of acceptance of the new person. You aren't crazy and you aren't selfish. You just loved your kid, that's all. Now you must learn to love the new one."

CHAPTER FORTY-ONE

Sins of the Father

The long shadows stretched over the lawn from the powerful oak stretching its leafless February limbs across the brown grass of Blanchard House. A distinct chill was in the air and not only from the winter wind. Fable stood on the front porch as Patric walked towards her. Behind Fable, saying nothing, yet postured in their most intimidating sentry stance stood Echo, Trix, Jerry, Nash, Knox, and Skillet.

"It appears you have valiant protectors, my dearest." Patric sneered. "Not that any of them could stop me if I wished to harm you."

"Oh, I bet they could." Fable smirked. "Why did you ask for this meeting, Patric?"

"You know my reasons. I am back to reclaim my pack. My family. Those boys are mine. And so is their mother."

Nash started to step forward, but Jerry nudged him back with a shake of the head. Fable had this under control. "You are not a part of this family. We are the people you tried to kill over a decade ago! Do you remember that at all? There is nothing here for you Patric."

No one had noticed the children standing at the corner of the house. Undoubtedly, they came out of the back door and sneaked around the side. Only when Con's voice spoke out did anyone see them. "That is not true, Mama. He is our father. Rom and I want to know him."

With a look of revulsion and fear upon her face, Fable looked at her two sons. "You two have no idea what he's like. You don't know what he has done. What he is still capable of doing."

Stepping away from her cousins, Hera came closer to the porch steps. She had something in her hand. "Aunt Fable, what about this?" Holding the vial of Beryl's blood up for Patric to see, she approached him fearlessly, ignoring the adults' orders for her to stop. "Sir, if you drink a drop from this, you won't be evil anymore."

He laughed. Such childish notions of good and evil were simply feeble man's constructs to delineate between how they lived and how they secretly wished they could. He stopped laughing suddenly, sniffing the air in her direction. His face changed somewhat, he appeared almost sentimental. "You, girl. Come closer."

Jerry and Fable both shouted to Hera not to do as he said, but she did it anyway, unafraid because she knew her capabilities if needed. She eyed the man strangely as he whiffed the air around her even more noticeably now. It made Hera think of how Rom used to do when he was on the scent of something, back when he was more fun...when he was a wolf. "I know you." Patric said to her. "We are the same. Your mother...you have the essence of your mother all over you."

Hera understood at once his meaning. Tersely, she replied, "I am not discussing that woman."

Patric admired her passion. Even her hate. She had spunk. She was a fighter. She was...a part of him. He snatched the liquid from her hand more quickly than even Hera had time to register. He popped the cork top from it and turned to Fable, "Whatever this is, will this please you? Will this make me worthy in your eyes?" He turned to look at the boys. "My sons, is this the path to reenter your lives?"

"Drink it...Dad." Con said softly, pleadingly. Patric could see in his eyes a hopeful light dance just behind the pupil. His boy wanted this. Wanted it for himself because he wanted his father. Patric looked at the other one, the one they called Romulus. He was much more skeptical yet the same light which had flashed in his brother sparked for a moment in his as well. Patric lifted the vial to his lips and allowed a drop to fall onto his tongue. It burned. Burned the way he now began to remember cinnamon could burn when drinking hot cocoa. Why such a memory came to him, he hadn't a clue. He never recalled any times from before he became what he is. It was a strange thing to enter his mind. Soon more such strange remembrances overcame him, as if reliving his life again in quick succession. And then came the horror. The kills. The hundreds of kills he'd left in his wake these last decades. He could hear their screams as if they were pouring from his very own lungs. He could feel the excruciating agony they felt from the unspeakable things he'd done to them. An arm ripped away. A shoulder with a chunk bitten off. Necks gushing with blood as the sharpest teeth imaginable sliced through. He felt it all, even their deaths. Their pitiful, silent, convulsing deaths as life leaked from their bodies and their eyes weighed down into blackness.

He wasn't sure how long he'd been on the ground writhing and shrieking. Everyone from the house was standing around him when his mind returned to his present time. Beside him, holding his hand, was Hera, with Con just beside her. Behind them both stood Teague, whether he was there to guard the children from him or looking on out of sheer curiosity he didn't know.

"Patric," Fable said softly standing a few feet away. "Patric, what do you feel?"

His tear-stained face stared up into the eyes of a woman he now realized he had never done anything but terrorize. "What happened to me?"

"You just had your soul jammed back into you," Fable grinned. "From the looks of it, it was quite a judgment day."

He sat with Fable, Demitra, and Jerry at the kitchen table, sipping on a cup of hot coffee. He barely raised his eyes from the cup, his brow heavy with shame and his eyes too embarrassed to allow anyone access to them. He couldn't help but notice the firm grip on Fable's shoulder from a man standing behind her watching. "I don't know who you are," Patric told him, raising his eyes slightly from the cup in his hands, he addressed Nash. "But you've made it clear you're with Fable. I am not going to hurt her." He turned his head back down to his cup, trying to find his reflection on the quivering surface of the coffee, hoping he might recognize himself again. "I think I have put her through quite enough already."

Fable wanted to feel sorry for this man, after all she had once believed she loved him, but that was so long ago. Right now, Patric was giving every appearance of penitence. Still, she didn't trust him. She'd never known him to be anything but cunning and deadly. Although she understood the whole purpose of Beryl's gift was to give salvation to lost souls, to make them compassionate humans again, she did not know Patric when he was a compassionate human. That part of him died as a little boy. Patric had been a monster for far more years than he hadn't been. Too many for her to trust him. "I'm glad you say you understand the hell you have put me through, both now and 12 years ago. But you'll forgive me if I need a minute to believe this."

He didn't reply. Heavier with even more shame and regret from the remark. "What do I do now?" he asked. "I don't know how to be anything else."

"Surely, you've worked?" Jerry asked curiously. "You must have had a place where you lived. Skillet here works for Demitra. He only had to hunker down a few days a month. The rest of the time he lived a normal life."

The humor of the question, and the answer, came out with a mild chuckle as he raised his head for the first time to look earnestly into Jerry's eyes. "I was a kid. And we hunted." He made a nod towards his maker, "Teague...or Skillet, I guess now... taught me to hunt wild game. We lived to ourselves in the mountains. Then, well, as I grew up I wanted more. My urges rose above animals. I ventured out on my own, stalking my way across the country, till I got here...to find my sister."

Demitra and Fable remembered that time all too well. For a short time after discovering the werewolf in town was Patric, they believed Fable was his target. It was quite a shock when his endgame turned out to be Yasmine.

He went on with his story. "After I found Yasmine, I thought I would turn her, and we'd start a new life somewhere. Then I got killed." Giving Demitra and Fable a congratulatory salute, he grinned again and said, "Then I was just alive again. Don't know how or why. I was just alive back in the exact place I died, a few miles from here." His eyes went to Jerry, wrapping up his point, "So you see, I don't know about work, or jobs, or apartments. I don't think I can mark *was dead* on a job application under previous experience."

Slapping him on the back, Jerry said, "Well, we will figure something out."

Fable leaned back in her chair, folding her arms across her chest before she asserted herself so as to be clearly understood. "You are not staying here Patric."

Demitra did not disagree with the statement but was a little appalled at the callousness in the tone stating it. "Okay, Fable. Let's not be totally unsympathetic."

Fable stood from her chair, nearly knocking Nash down, as she walked to the fridge to grab a canned cola. "I don't care about sympathy, or empathy, or whatever you all think I should feel right now. I'm very glad Patric isn't trying to kill us now but pardon me if I am not very concerned with what he does now. That'll happen when somebody tries to kill you over and over."

"I don't expect to stay here," he said. "I'll figure it out on my own. But could you all not call me Patric anymore."

The request surprised them. "I don't understand," Nash said. "Isn't that your name?"

"No, it isn't." Fable answered him.

Patric the werewolf had shown up earlier that night for a confrontation or a battle, the Blanchards would never be sure, but it was Oliver Sinclair who walked out of the kitchen, through the living room, and out of the front door hours later.

As he stepped onto the crunchy grass of the front yard, he paused. He was at a loss for what he was doing. Considering the matter a moment, he almost started forward on foot, but then turned around to go back up to the porch to knock. He didn't have to. Jerry was standing at the railing with a smile. "Figured you would figure it out in a minute. I guess a man who is used to being able to run like a wolf anywhere he needs to go, doesn't think about how to get anywhere without a car."

Jerry clicked his key fob, unlocking his car and motioning for *Oliver* to get in. "Thank you for the ride, but where are we going?"

"I'll take you into town and get you a hotel room. You can begin figuring out your plans in a few days. Right now, you have enough to work out."

They drove several miles. The streetlights casting a blinding beam into the passenger seat at regular intervals as they went by. Oliver had said nothing else until now, but he felt he needed to know something. "Why are you helping me?"

Jerry shook his head, shrugging. "Hell, if I know. Except I keep thinking that my grandsons seem to want you around. Maybe they only think they do. Maybe they truly do want to get to know their father. You may not turn out to be a man I approve of in their lives. Then again, maybe you will. But until we have more time to make informed decisions, I owe those boys a chance to get to know you. You just stay away from Fable, and you contact me if you need anything."

"And I can see my sons?"

"That is up to their mother," Jerry admitted. "I will talk to her. But the choice is hers and hers alone."

Jerry found Fable a few hours later sitting alone on the foyer stairs. Sliding in beside her against the wall he placed his arm across her shoulder, pulling her close. "It is a mess."

"It is."

"Talk to me, Fable. Does Patric, now that he is human, still frighten you?"

She looked behind them to check if anyone was coming their way from upstairs, she peered through the side rail, checking down below. With their privacy assured, she confided to Jerry, "I don't believe anyone else but myself has thought about this, but I am terrified about Con."

"Meaning?" Jerry asked. "Do you think you will lose his love now that his father is here?"

Pressing her hands onto Jerry's knees for emphasis, Fable shook her head, "No, I'm not talking about parental jealousies. Jerry, Patric took the cure and is human again. But Con...none of us have considered that Con is still a werewolf. The cure won't work on him. He was not bitten. He wasn't changed by an attack. Con was born the way he is. Born with a soul. I don't think he is curable."

CHAPTER FORTY-TWO

The Blanchard Family
of Daihmler County

Had the Blanchard family not had a witch among them who possessed the power of blinking, the generations old tradition may have been broken. In her ninth month of pregnancy, there was no way Arielle Blanchard was up for a long car ride from Charleston to Daihmler. However, adamant her baby be born at Blanchard House the same as its cousins had been, Salem accompanied Theda, guiding her in her power as she zapped to Charleston to bring Arielle and Ocean to the family homestead. Arielle now lay in bed, breathing deeply with Salem, Fable, and her husband at her side. Demitra, having delivered nearly all the births of this generation, positioned herself at the foot of the bed.

"You are doing so great, honey." Ocean said kissing his wife's sweaty forehead.

"Thank you, baby," she smiled up at him. "You know this isn't as bad as I thought it would be. I mean...it's uncomfortable, but not very painful."

Salem rolled her eyes toward Fable. "Wouldn't you know, it *would be* Arielle who has the easy birth!"

"Yeah," Fable remarked with a huff. "You almost died having Olympus. Echo and Trix were hysterical when they delivered, and my kids literally ripped themselves out of me. And here Ari is all daffodils and lavender."

Shouting up at them, Arielle quipped, "Well, excuse me for not having a horrible delivery. Would you rather I be screaming in agony?"

"No, of course not." Salem smiled.

"I kind of would," chided Fable. "Your next child better hurt like hell."

It didn't take long for the baby to be delivered. In fact, it came so quickly and so easily, Salem and Fable grew more miffed. "She barely even whimpered!" Fable shouted at her mother as Demitra pulled the baby free. "I mean come on!"

Ocean stroked his wife's cheek, beaded with mild perspiration. They stared proudly ahead while Demitra held their daughter up to show them. "I present the next Blanchard." She carried the baby to the dresser where she washed her off with a soft cloth, before wrapping her in a yellow blanket. Demitra moved to the bed, handing the baby to her father, but pausing momentarily as if it only then flashing back to her mind, "This is my great-great granddaughter."

Taking his daughter from Demitra, Ocean smiled to the woman he now knew was his great grandmother. He displayed the baby in his arms where everyone could see her properly. "I introduce to you, Atlantis Blanchard."

"Atlantis?" Trix repeated, when Ocean brought the baby downstairs to show the others. She moved to take her niece from Ocean only to have Howard elbow her out of the way.

"As grandfather, I get first hold." He looked down into his newly born granddaughter's eyes feeling overcome with gratitude. It had not been too many years ago when Howard Caldwell lived a singular life. Things had certainly changed since then. He had children, including this little angel's father. And he now had three beautiful grandchildren. Life had provided him with a bounty of love and family. "Hello little Atlantis. I am your Pop Pop."

"Can we go back to this name?" Trix asked. "Ocean, you've only been my brother for about five minutes, but as your sister I have to tell you it's a terrible name."

"Says the woman who named her baby Jinx," Echo grinned, peering over his father's shoulder to see his niece. "I like it."

"You would," Trix remarked. "She is named after a city that drowned."

Ocean laughed it off. "Arielle came up with it and I think it's fine. She said it is tradition, just like our seeing to it Atlantis was born here."

"Tradition?" Trix repeated. "Stupid names?"

Ocean clasped his hands over her shoulders, "I'm with our brother on this one. Anyone with a daughter named Jinx probably shouldn't be casting stones at baby names." Ocean sent Echo a wink, then continued his reasoning. "The name fits. I am Ocean. Atlantis *is in* the ocean. Plus, look at her cousins on her mother's side. Hera, Titan, and Olympus. Atlantis works."

Howard declared he didn't care what her name was, that she was as beautiful as all her cousins and carried her to the playpen in the living room where Lucky and Jinx were sitting up playing with toys. He showed them the newest addition, reminding them it was their job to look out for her.

Salem came downstairs to tell Ocean he could go back up to Arielle now that she'd been cleaned up. As he took the baby to return upstairs, Salem gave her new niece another kiss on the cheek. Propping against the doorframe to the living room, Salem grinned, as she considered an interesting point. "It never ceases to amaze me about Arielle. When I first met her, she was so alone and hungry for a family to love her. Now she is probably *the most related to everyone* member of the Blanchard family and now so is Atlantis."

Upstairs, Vanessa and Miranda brought the older children in to meet their new cousin. Hera was delighted, throwing a clinched fist in the air and pulling it down, "Yes! Another girl!" Arielle, ever the empath, understood how all of this was still so very new to Theda, reached her hand out pulling Seth's eldest child closer. "Would you like to hold your cousin, sweetheart?"

"Can I?" Theda asked, looking to Vanessa for permission. Vanessa nodded, instructing her to keep the baby's head held securely.

Theda investigated the cooing baby's face and smiled. "I will look out for her."

Smiling from the bed, Arielle replied. "I'm counting on it. She's going to need her sister cousins to show her how things are in this world and this family."

"Can I blink over and see her whenever I want?"

Hera didn't like that idea without a caveat. "Only if you take me with you."

"You are both welcome to pop over anytime and see Atlantis," Ocean agreed. "But only if your mothers say you can."

Demitra soon ushered everyone out, leaving the new little family alone for some time together. She made her way downstairs and out onto the porch. The air felt a little warmer than it had lately. Spring might be coming sooner than expected. She placed her hands upon the porch rail and breathed in the air. There was not yet a scent of honeysuckle or jasmine, but it would come soon enough. The morning glory vines across the front porch were already starting to green out their leaves. She heard the front door open and close behind her, then felt Jerry's arms placing around her waist, pulling her into him.

"We have quite a family."

Demitra sighed against him, "That we do."

Resting his chin against his wife's shoulder, Jerry looked out across Blanchard land, his mind racing through a thousand memories and a thousand futures. He could barely recall his life before Demitra. It was a lonely existence. And though his current life had never been short on problems, the triumphs always outweighed them. He kissed her head, snuggling her closer.

"The whole world knows now," he whispered into her ear. "No more secrets. No more fear of discovery. Atlantis and her cousins will never have to live under the burdens you did."

Demitra turned to lean her forehead onto his cheek. She closed her eyes and whispered, "I am afraid the new generation will face things we haven't prepared them for. In a world where everything is out in the open, I don't know how to lead my witches through this strange new terrain."

Jerry took her face gently in his hands, staring into her mesmerizing purple eyes. "Maybe you won't have to. Seems like that is Salem's job now. Maybe you can finally just sit back and enjoy our big, amazing family."

"It does appear as if everyone is settled," she smiled. "For the time being."

"Yep," he replied. "Salem and Artemis are running the world. Fable is in love. Arielle has a family of her own...with lots of brothers and sisters. Seth and Yaz are starting over somewhere. I suspect Howard and Roz will get married soon. Echo—"

"Echo will mess his relationship up," Demitra snickered. "And I don't need my psychic powers to see that. And Trix..."

"Trix will do as she always does," Jerry smiled. "And none of us will ever be able to predict what that will be." Jerry grinned, enjoying their forward-thinking predictions. "And the children..."

Demitra playfully sighed, shaking her head. "So many children," she laughed. "Lord, Jerry. We have a plethora of grandkids, don't we?"

"It's nice," he answered. "Look at how this family has flowered."

Demitra moved back to the railing. Grasping the top under her hands, she inhaled the sweet Spring air, then touched the arm of the rocking chair as it tilted gently in the breeze. "Olympia would be very proud of her family."

"No," Jerry corrected. "She would be proud of her daughter. You, Demitra, are the reason this family continues and thrives. The Blanchards have never been in better hands."

It began long ago, when a gypsy witch named Nancy Norwood married an unremarkable man named Blanchard. A legacy began, passing through many generations, and several forward thinking Hecates. Blaze, Victor, Constantinople, Olympia, Artemis, and Demitra. There would be more of course, many more. Their job would be the same as those who came before them. To navigate their family coven through the upheavals and dangers that would come their way. There was a world to protect and a natural order to maintain. They would have big shoes to fill if they hoped to live up to the legends of the past...perhaps Demitra Blanchard being the most challenging of them all to measure up to.

ABOUT THE AUTHOR

Micah House is the author of *The Blanchard Witches* series which has won several awards since its debut, including the NYC Big Book Award, The Indie Excellence Award, and The BookFest Award. His southern style of storytelling weaves drama, humor, emotional connection to characters, and plenty of page-turning suspense. He currently resides in Birmingham, Alabama with his husband and son and their five dogs.